"Macomber's work is as comforting as ever." —*Booklist*

Cottage by the Sea

"Romantic, warm, and a breeze to read—one of Macomber's best." —*Kirkus Reviews*

"Macomber never disappoints. Tears and laughter abound in this story of loss and healing that will wrap you up and pull you in; readers will finish it in one sitting."
—*Library Journal* (starred review)

"Macomber's story of tragedy and triumph is emotionally engaging from the outset and ends with a satisfying conclusion. Readers will be most taken by the characters, particularly Annie, a heartwarming lead who bolsters the novel."
—*Publishers Weekly*

Any Dream Will Do

"*Any Dream Will Do* is . . . so realistic, it's hard to believe it's fiction through the end. Even then, it's hard to say goodbye to these characters. This standalone novel will make you hope it becomes a Hallmark movie, or gets a sequel. It's an inspiring, hard-to-put-down tale. . . . You need to read it."
—*The Free Lance–Star*

"*Any Dream Will Do* by Debbie Macomber is a study in human tolerance and friendship. Macomber masterfully shows how all people have value." —*Fresh Fiction*

If Not for You

"A heartwarming story of forgiveness and unexpected love."
—*Harlequin Junkie*

"A fun, sweet read." —*Publishers Weekly*

A Girl's Guide to Moving On

"Beloved author Debbie Macomber reaches new heights in this wise and beautiful novel. It's the kind of reading experience that comes along only rarely, bearing the hallmarks of a classic. The timeless wisdom in these pages will stay with you long after the book is closed."
—SUSAN WIGGS, #1 *New York Times* bestselling author of *Starlight on Willow Lake*

"Debbie dazzles! A wonderful story of friendship, forgiveness, and the power of love. I devoured every page!"
—SUSAN MALLERY, #1 *New York Times* bestselling author of *The Friends We Keep*

Last One Home

"Fans of bestselling author Macomber will not be disappointed by this compelling stand-alone novel."
—*Library Journal*

ROSE HARBOR

Sweet Tomorrows

"Macomber fans will leave the Rose Harbor Inn with warm memories of healing, hope, and enduring love."
—*Kirkus Reviews*

Praise for Debbie Macomber's bestselling novels from Ballantine Books

Must Love Flowers

"A testament to the power of new beginnings . . . Wise, warm, witty, and charmingly full of hope, this story celebrates the surprising and unexpected ways that family, friendship, and love can lift us up."

—KRISTIN HANNAH,
bestselling author of *The Nightingale*

"Uplifting, warm, and hopeful . . . With her signature charm and wit, Debbie Macomber proves that the best relationships, like the perfect blooms, are always worth the wait. This can't-miss novel is Macomber at the height of her storytelling prowess. I absolutely adored it!"

—KRISTY WOODSON HARVEY, *New York Times*
bestselling author of *The Summer of Songbirds*

"Debbie Macomber never fails to deliver an uplifting, heartwarming story. Whether you're just starting out, just starting over, or anything in between, *Must Love Flowers* should be at the top of your summer reading list!"

—BRENDA NOVAK, *New York Times*
bestselling author of *Before We Were Strangers*

The Best Is Yet to Come

"Macomber's latest is a wonderful inspirational read that has just enough romance as the characters heal their painful emotional wounds." —*Library Journal*

"This tale of redemption and kindness is a gift to Macomber's many readers and all who love tales of sweet and healing romance." —*Booklist*

It's Better This Way

"Macomber has a firm grasp on issues that will resonate with readers of domestic fiction. Well-drawn characters and plotting—coupled with strong romantic subplots and striking coincidences—will keep readers rooting for forgiveness, hope and true love to conquer all."

—Kathleen Gerard,
blogger at *Reading Between the Lines*

"Macomber keeps her well-shaded, believable characters at the heart of this seamlessly plotted novel as she probes the nuances of familial relationships and the agelessness of romance. This deeply emotional tale proves it's never too late for love." —*Publishers Weekly* (starred review)

A Walk Along the Beach

"Macomber scores another home run with this surprisingly heavy but uplifting contemporary romance between a café owner and a photographer. Eloquent prose . . . along with [a] charming supporting cast adds a welcome dose of light and hope. With this stirring romance, Macomber demonstrates her mastery of the genre."

—*Publishers Weekly* (starred review)

"Highly emotional . . . a hard-to-put-down page-turner, yet, throughout all the heartache, the strength and love of family shines through." —*New York Journal of Books*

Window on the Bay

"This heartwarming story sweetly balances friendship and mother-child bonding with romantic love."

—*Kirkus Reviews*

"Overflowing with the poignancy, sweetness, conflicts and romance for which Debbie Macomber is famous, *Sweet Tomorrows* captivates from beginning to end."

—*Bookreporter*

"Fans will enjoy this final installment of the Rose Harbor series as they see Jo Marie's story finally come to an end."

—*Library Journal*

Silver Linings

"Macomber's homespun storytelling style makes reading an easy venture. . . . She also tosses in some hidden twists and turns that will delight her many longtime fans."

—*Bookreporter*

"Reading Macomber's novels is like being with good friends, talking and sharing joys and sorrows."

—*New York Journal of Books*

Love Letters

"Macomber's mastery of women's fiction is evident in her latest. . . . [She] breathes life into each plotline, carefully intertwining her characters' stories to ensure that none of them overshadow the others. Yet it is her ability to capture different facets of emotion which will entrance fans and newcomers alike." —*Publishers Weekly*

"Romance and a little mystery abound in this third installment of Macomber's series set at Cedar Cove's Rose Harbor Inn. . . . Readers of Robyn Carr and Sherryl Woods will enjoy Macomber's latest, which will have them flipping pages until the end and eagerly anticipating the next installment." —*Library Journal* (starred review)

"Uplifting . . . a cliffhanger ending for Jo Marie begs for a swift resolution in the next book." —*Kirkus Reviews*

Rose Harbor in Bloom

"[Debbie Macomber] draws in threads of her earlier book in this series, *The Inn at Rose Harbor,* in what is likely to be just as comfortable a place for Macomber fans as for Jo Marie's guests at the inn." —*The Seattle Times*

"Macomber's legions of fans will embrace this cozy, heartwarming read." —*Booklist*

"Readers will find the emotionally impactful storylines and sweet, redemptive character arcs for which the author is famous. Classic Macomber, which will please fans and keep them coming back for more." —*Kirkus Reviews*

"The storybook scenery of lighthouses, cozy bed and breakfast inns dotting the coastline, and seagulls flying above takes readers on personal journeys of first love, lost love and recaptured love [presenting] love in its purest and most personal forms." —*Bookreporter*

The Inn at Rose Harbor

"Debbie Macomber's Cedar Cove romance novels have a warm, comfy feel to them. Perhaps that's why they've sold millions." —*USA Today*

"Debbie Macomber has written a charming, cathartic romance full of tasteful passion and good sense. Reading it is a lot like enjoying comfort food, as you know the book will end well and leave you feeling pleasant and content. The tone is warm and serene, and the characters are likeable yet realistic. . . . *The Inn at Rose Harbor* is a wonderful novel that will keep the reader's undivided attention."

—*Bookreporter*

"The prolific Macomber introduces a spin-off of sorts from her popular Cedar Cove series, still set in that fictional small town but centered on Jo Marie Rose, a youngish widow who buys and operates the bed and breakfast of the title. This clever premise allows Macomber to craft stories around the B&B's guests, Abby and Josh in this inaugural effort, while using Jo Marie and her ongoing recovery from the death of her husband Paul in Afghanistan as the series' anchor. . . . With her characteristic optimism, Macomber provides fresh starts for both." —*Booklist*

"Emotionally charged romance." —*Kirkus Reviews*

Blossom Street

Blossom Street Brides

"A wonderful, love-affirming novel . . . an engaging, emotionally fulfilling story that clearly shows why [Macomber] is a peerless storyteller." —*Examiner.com*

"Rewarding . . . Macomber amply delivers her signature engrossing relationship tales, wrapping her readers in warmth as fuzzy and soft as a hand-knitted creation from everyone's favorite yarn shop." —*Bookreporter*

"Fans will happily return to the warm, welcoming sanctuary of Macomber's Blossom Street, catching up with old friends from past Blossom Street books and meeting new ones being welcomed into the fold." —*Kirkus Reviews*

"Macomber's nondenominational-inspirational women's novel, with its large cast of characters, will resonate with fans of the popular series." —*Booklist*

Starting Now

"Macomber understands the often complex nature of a woman's friendships, as well as the emotional language women use with their friends."
—*New York Journal of Books*

"There is a reason that legions of Macomber fans ask for more Blossom Street books. They fully engage her readers as her characters discover happiness, purpose, and meaning in life. . . . Macomber's feel-good novel, emphasizing interpersonal relationships and putting people above status and objects, is truly satisfying." —*Booklist* (starred review)

"Macomber's writing and storytelling deliver what she's famous for—a smooth, satisfying tale with characters her fans will cheer for and an arc that is cozy, heartwarming and ends with the expected happily-ever-after."
—*Kirkus Reviews*

CHRISTMAS NOVELS

The Christmas Spirit

"Exactly what readers want from a Macomber holiday outing." —*Publishers Weekly*

"With almost all of Debbie Macomber's novels, the reader is not only given a captivating story, but also a lesson in life."
—*New York Journal of Books*

Dear Santa

"[*Dear Santa*] is a quick and fun tale offering surprises and blessings and an all-around feel-good read."
—*New York Journal of Books*

Jingle All the Way

"[*Jingle All the Way*] will leave readers feeling merry and bright." —*Publishers Weekly*

"This delightful Christmas story can be enjoyed any time of the year." —*New York Journal of Books*

A Mrs. Miracle Christmas

"This sweet, inspirational story . . . had enough dramatic surprises to keep pages turning."
—*Library Journal* (starred review)

"Anyone who enjoys Christmas will appreciate this sparkling snow globe of a story." —*Publishers Weekly*

Alaskan Holiday

"Picture-perfect . . . this charmer will please Macomber fans and newcomers alike." —*Publishers Weekly*

"[A] tender romance lightly brushed with holiday magic."
—*Library Journal*

Merry and Bright

"Heartfelt, cheerful . . . Readers looking for a light and sweet holiday treat will find it here." —*Publishers Weekly*

Twelve Days of Christmas

"Another heartwarming seasonal Macomber tale, which fans will find as bright and cozy as a blazing fire on Christmas Eve." —*Kirkus Reviews*

"*Twelve Days of Christmas* is a charming, heartwarming holiday tale. With poignant characters and an enchanting plot, Macomber again burrows into the fragility of human emotions to arrive at a delightful conclusion."
—*New York Journal of Books*

Dashing Through the Snow

"This Christmas romance from Macomber is both sweet and sincere." —*Library Journal*

Mr. Miracle

"Macomber spins another sweet, warmhearted holiday tale that will be as comforting to her fans as hot chocolate on Christmas morning." —*Kirkus Reviews*

"This gentle, inspiring romance will be a sought-after read."
—*Library Journal*

Starry Night

"Contemporary romance queen Macomber hits the sweet spot with this tender tale of impractical love. . . . A delicious Christmas miracle well worth waiting for."
—*Publishers Weekly* (starred review)

"[A] holiday confection . . . as much a part of the season for some readers as cookies and candy canes."
—*Kirkus Reviews*

Angels at the Table

"Rings in Christmas in tried-and-true Macomber style, with romance and a touch of heavenly magic."
—*Kirkus Reviews*

"[A] sweetly charming holiday romance." —*Library Journal*

BALLANTINE BOOKS FROM DEBBIE MACOMBER

Must Love Flowers
The Best Is Yet to Come
It's Better This Way
A Walk Along the Beach
Window on the Bay
Cottage by the Sea
Any Dream Will Do
If Not for You
A Girl's Guide to Moving On
Last One Home

ROSE HARBOR INN

Sweet Tomorrows
Silver Linings
Love Letters
Rose Harbor in Bloom
The Inn at Rose Harbor

BLOSSOM STREET

Blossom Street Brides
Starting Now

CHRISTMAS NOVELS

The Christmas Spirit
Dear Santa
Jingle All the Way
A Mrs. Miracle Christmas
Alaskan Holiday
Merry and Bright
Twelve Days of Christmas
Dashing Through the Snow
Mr. Miracle
Starry Night
Angels at the Table

2-IN-1 COLLECTIONS

A Bright New Day:
Borrowed Dreams and
The Trouble with Caasi

All Roads Lead Home:
A Friend or Two and
Reflections of Yesterday

The Perfect Holiday:
That Wintry Feeling and
Thanksgiving Prayer

What Matters Most:
Shadow Chasing and
Laughter in the Rain

Tying the Knot:
Yesterday's Hero and
White Lace and Promises

DEBBIE MACOMBER

Tying the Knot

Yesterday's Hero and

White Lace and Promises

BALLANTINE BOOKS

NEW YORK

Tying the Knot is a work of fiction. Names, characters, places, and incidents are the products of the author's imagination or are used fictitiously. Any resemblance to actual events, locales, or persons, living or dead, is entirely coincidental.

2024 Ballantine Books Mass Market Edition

Published in the United States by Ballantine Books,
an imprint of Random House, a division of
Penguin Random House LLC, New York.

Ballantine is a registered trademark and the colophon is a
trademark of Penguin Random House LLC.

Yesterday's Hero and *White Lace and Promises*
were originally published separately in the United States
by Silhouette Romance, New York, in 1986.

ISBN 978-0-593-35984-6
Ebook ISBN 978-0-593-59953-2

Cover design: Derek Walls
Front-cover images: © Andrei Zveaghintev/Shutterstock (chairs),
© BK foto/Shutterstock (bushes), © RUNGSAN
NANTAPHUM/Shutterstock (flowers in bushes),
© Amir Kaljikovic/Stocksy (bouquet)
Back-cover image: © boonyarak voranimmanont/Shutterstock

Printed in the United States of America

randomhousebooks.com

2 4 6 8 9 7 5 3 1

Ballantine Books mass market edition: July 2024

Summer 2024

Dear Friends,

It's such fun for me to see these stories have a new life. *Tying the Knot* is two novels I wrote early in my career. Both stories are bookmarked as favorites. Even now, all these years later, I remember what prompted the ideas for each story. I thought you might enjoy learning about what inspired me to write these books.

The idea for *Yesterday's Hero* came from a short newspaper article about migrating whales. I was fascinated and came up with the idea for a story of a photographer and scientist working together, only the small island where they were headed insisted if the two lived together, they must be a married couple. Leah and Cain agree to marry even though Leah is already engaged. You may well guess what happens.

The idea for *White Lace and Promises* came from real life. Karen, a teacher friend of mine, had been a bridesmaid for several of her friends. She yearned to marry and have a family of her own but all the guys she met turned out to be zeros. At her ten-year class reunion, she met up with a guy she'd known since junior high and everything clicked into place. They were married within only a few weeks.

The title came directly from a Carpenters song. I've used lyrics for several of my book titles.

And racehorse names. I'm not making that up. Some horses have the coolest names.

Now you have the inside scoop.

Enjoy,

Debbie Macomber

P.S. You can always reach me at my Debbie Macomber website and leave me a message or write me at:

P.O. Box 1458, Port Orchard, WA 98366.

And all the other social medias.

Yesterday's Hero

Chapter 1

"You must understand that the government of the Diamantina Islands is understandably circumspect. The people are the direct descendants of Puritan missionaries." Dr. David Brewster took a clean handkerchief from his pocket and wiped his perspiring face.

He's flustered, Leah Talmadge mused. Dr. Brewster, California's most renowned marine biologist, man of steel at seventy-five, the solid department head, was obviously nervous. Something had gone wrong. Disconcerted, Leah stiffened in the high-backed leather chair. A cold sweat broke out across her upper lip, and she nervously ran her finger over it. Dear heavens, this expedition was the chance of a lifetime.

"Just what are you saying, Dr. Brewster?" Cain Hawkins interrupted abruptly.

Leah's gaze skidded to the world-famous photographer who would be accompanying her on this whale watch. Cain's work had appeared several times in *National Geographic* and other nationally known magazines. The talented photographer had made his name taking spectacular shots of wildlife, landscapes, and people; his skill wasn't limited to any one subject. His work hung in some of the best art galleries in the world. The entire department was elated that he'd been assigned to accompany Leah on this expedition to the islands.

His pictures might be fantastic, Leah reflected, but the man was a disappointment. He didn't look anything like what she'd expected. In some ways he resembled a hippie left over from the nineteen-sixties. His chestnut hair was unfashionably long, and he wore it brushed away from his face. It curled out just below his collar, and an unruly patch defiantly brushed his brow. His face was weathered from exposure to the elements, and he looked closer to forty than the thirty-five she knew him to be. Of course, she'd heard the rumors. Her colleagues had delighted in feeding her tidbits of information about the unorthodox Cain Hawkins. A rebel. A nonconformist. Tough as leather. Hard as nails. Leah had heard it all and secretly hadn't believed a word. His pictures told a different story.

David Brewster paused and cleared his throat. Again he wiped his face with the wrinkled linen cloth. "I was in communication with the governor of the Diamantinas this afternoon."

Apprehensively, Leah scooted to the edge of her seat. "And?" she urged.

"In light of the fact that you two unmarried adults would be spending considerable time in the uninhabited archipelago together, the request has been denied."

Leah felt her heart drop. "Denied," she repeated in shocked disbelief. The opportunity of a lifetime washed away by the moral righteousness of a government official. "Good grief, man. We live in the twenty-first century."

Cain Hawkins's dark eyes sparked with disbelief and irritation.

"Indeed," David Brewster agreed, "but no one bothered to inform the islanders of this. The people in these islands are deeply religious."

"But, Doctor," Leah said, struggling to disguise her exasperation, "surely you explained that Mr. Hawkins and I are professional people. Our purpose isn't to . . ." She left the rest unsaid as hot color invaded her pale face. The worst part of being a blonde was the way her complexion signaled her thoughts.

"I fear we must either find a female photographer or make the—"

"Oh no you don't." Cain shot to his feet and glared intimidatingly at Leah, expelling an angry breath. The dark eyes narrowed to points of steel that looked capable of slashing through any barrier, any defense. "You can just as easily find a male marine biologist. I'm not giving up this opportunity because of her." An accusing finger was pointed at Leah.

"How . . . how dare you," Leah stuttered. "I've waited years for this and I won't be denied my chance because—"

"Children, children." Dr. Brewster waved his hand authoritatively.

So angry she could barely speak, Leah defiantly crossed her arms. Whom did Cain Hawkins think he was dealing with, anyway? She hadn't worked this hard and come this far to let a boorish chauvinist walk over her because she was a woman.

"If you two would consider marriage . . ."

"What?" Leah spat. "Surely you don't mean to each

other." Slowly, deliberately, she gave Cain Hawkins a practiced look of distaste.

The corner of his upper lip curled into what she assumed was humorous disdain. He was telling her without words what he thought of that idea.

Leah forced herself to think through this sudden obstacle. Finally she suggested, "Surely, if I were a married woman and Mr. Hawkins a married man—not to each other—then this expedition would be sanctioned by the governor."

David Brewster loosened his tie and ran a finger along the inside of his collar in an agitated movement. "That's a possibility, of course—and, frankly, one I haven't considered."

"I'm sure that once I talk to Siggy he would be willing to move up our wedding plans."

"Siggy?" Cain repeated, and his voice dripped with sarcasm. "You look like the type of woman who would marry a man named Siggy."

Despite her attempt at disciplined self-control, Leah bit off an angry retort. "Siegfried Harcharik is an honors graduate of MIT and is currently employed as a biochemist for the largest drug company in the United States." Siggy's credentials, she thought, would quickly put Cain Hawkins in his place. "I consider myself fortunate to be his fiancée."

Cain's low snicker filled the room. "Honey, if I were you, I'd consider myself lucky to be any man's future wife."

The words came at Leah like the cutting edge of a sword, and with as much power to inflict pain. She hated herself for wincing. No one needed to remind her that though she was blonde she wasn't beautiful. Too tall. Too thin. Too . . . no need fencing around the word . . . ugly. From the time she was in junior high she'd known her uneven features weren't likely to attract a man. All brains, no beauty, was what the boys in high school used to say.

Standing, Leah clenched her hands together in a show of determination. "I can see that Mr. Hawkins and I are only capable of hurling insults at each other. I suggest we schedule a meeting for a later date. Tomorrow, perhaps, when we've both had the opportunity to cool our tempers."

"I couldn't agree more." David Brewster's pained, wrinkled face relaxed. "Shall we say Thursday at the same time?"

"Fine." The clipped response was followed by the scraping of a chair as Cain left the room.

Leah avoided looking in his direction and lingered in the office an extra moment.

"My dear," Dr. Brewster said, and cupped Leah's elbow. "I know this announcement has come as a surprise to us all. But I personally chose you for this whale expedition, and I won't easily be dissuaded. So rest assured, things will work out."

Leah's returning smile was feeble at best. "Thank you, Doctor." She didn't know that she should be all that reassured. Dr. Brewster had also handpicked Cain Hawkins.

"I'll talk to Siggy tonight."

"You do that," he returned, patting her back. "I'm confident we'll find a way around this."

Leah was skeptical, but she gave him a polite nod on her way out the door.

The long drive down the San Diego Freeway was accomplished by rote. Traffic, smog, faceless people were all part of life in Southern California. Leah learned early that she must either accept it, or be defeated by the congestion that met her morning and night. But this afternoon, California had never seemed farther from the rolling hills of wheat in her home state of South Dakota. It had been a long time since she'd visited her family. When she returned from the Indian Ocean she'd make a point of doing that.

The first thing Leah did when she entered her condominium was pull Cain Hawkins's book of photographs from the shelf beside the fireplace. With a sense of incredulity, she ran her fingertips over the bottom of each page. The photos were beautiful. Each one looked as if the man who took it was revealing his soul.

But Cain Hawkins wasn't anything like these pictures. The ruthless quality in him had astonished her. In her mind, she had formed an image of what he would be like. Not so much his looks, but his personality. Any man who could reveal so much with his camera must be capable of deep insight. Today she had learned that he was ordinary. Hurtful. Arrogant. And, indeed, insightful. Within fifteen minutes of their meeting, he had found her weakest point and attacked.

Angry with herself for letting his cutting words disturb her so much, Leah reached for her cell to connect with Siggy.

The phone rang only once. "Harcharik here."

"Siggy, it's Leah." A short silence followed her announcement.

"Hello, darling."

Leah knew Siggy didn't like it when she phoned him at

the office, but she couldn't help it. This was important. "Can you stop by for a few minutes after work?"

Again he hesitated. Siggy had never been one to move quickly on anything. The trait was part of the scientist in him. "Yes, I suppose I could."

In her mind Leah could see him pushing up the bifocals from the bridge of his nose, and she smiled softly, appreciating him.

"Good, I'll see you then. Goodbye, darling." The word stuck in her throat. So far in their relationship, they'd never done anything more intimate than call each other darling, and that had troubled her from the beginning. But the time was fast approaching when she'd be far more intimate with him. She liked Siggy. No, she corrected herself mentally, she loved Siggy. She wanted to be his wife. They shared so many of the same interests. They were perfect for each other. Everyone said so. And Leah was the first woman Siggy had introduced to his family that his mother approved of. That said a lot.

After tucking Cain's book back onto the shelf, Leah delivered her briefcase to her small office in the back of the condominium. For the hundredth time in as many days, she read over the Australian government's report of the sighting of an ancient whale. The report had been received with a high amount of skepticism since ancient whales were assumed to be extinct.

But when the corpse of an ancient whale had been found washed up on one of the Diamantina Islands, the world had taken serious note. Scientists from all over the globe had converged on the tiny cluster of islands a thousand miles southwest by south of Australia and found nothing. Now, a year later, Leah was going during migration time, when she could study the pods and keep meticulous records. This was more than a golden opportunity; it was one that wasn't likely to be repeated.

By the time Siggy arrived Leah had released her tightly coiled hair so that it cascaded down the middle of her back. Siggy had always loved her hair down. She prayed now that it would be all the inducement she needed for him to agree to her plans.

"Hello, darling." He brushed his lips across her cheek.

"Come in." Nervously, Leah gestured toward the fashionably furnished living room. "Would you like something to drink? Coffee's on."

"That'll be fine."

With Siggy, Leah was forced to wear flat-heeled shoes. He exactly equaled her five-foot-eight stature and disapproved when she wore anything that made her taller. And although he claimed to like her hair worn down, Leah sometimes wondered if it wasn't that, with the blond length piled on her head, it gave an illusion of height. Not that any of this mattered; she was happy to do anything to please Siggy.

"I had a meeting with Dr. Brewster and Cain Hawkins today," she said, forcing a casual note into her voice as she delivered his coffee.

"Yes, I remember your saying something about that. How did it go?"

Sitting across from him on the white leather couch, Leah expelled a shaky breath. "Not so well."

"Why not? Isn't this Hawkins fellow what you expected?"

"Not at all." She pushed the hair away from her face. "Siggy, has it ever bothered you . . . I mean, have you ever been concerned about the fact that I'll be spending several weeks alone with an unmarried man?"

Straightening the corner of his bow tie, Siggy stiffened slightly. "Of course not. You're going to be my wife, Leah. I trust you implicitly."

Leah's heart softened, and she gave him a loving look. "Oh, Siggy, you're so good for me."

His returning smile was brief. "You are for me, too, darling." Fidgeting, he glanced at his wristwatch, then cleared his throat. "Mother's holding dinner."

"Oh . . . well, the reason I asked you over tonight was . . ." she began, and her hands were so tightly clenched she felt the blood supply must be cut off. Suddenly Leah felt unsure that she was doing the right thing. Marriage, after all, was forever. "I've been thinking that I'd like us to be married before I leave for the Diamantina Islands." Leah watched him closely, but no emotion showed in his blue eyes.

"Leah, I'm afraid that's quite impossible. Mother doesn't know yet that I've asked you to be my wife."

"Then don't you think it's time Mother did?" she said crossly. "You told me yourself that your mother approved of me. I can't see the necessity of putting my life on hold because you're afraid of your mother."

His coffee cup made a clanking sound as he set it roughly on the coffee table. As far as Leah could remember, this was the most emotion she had ever seen from Siggy. "I find that comment unforgivable."

The flaxen length of Leah's hair fell forward as she bowed her head. "Maybe you should leave then. I wouldn't want you to be late for dinner with Mother."

Standing, Siggy straightened his pant legs. "I don't

know what's come over you, Leah. You're hardly the girl I fell in love with anymore."

"Woman," she corrected brittlely. "I'm not a little girl who can live on promises. I'm a woman."

Her back was ramrod straight as Siggy walked across the carpet and paused at the door. "I'll phone you tomorrow. You'll have come to your senses by then."

Refusing to answer. Leah pinched her mouth tightly closed until her teeth hurt. Her lashes fluttered closed when the front door clicked, telling her that Siggy had left. Frustration came in waves, lapping at her from all sides, until she wanted to lash out at anyone or anything. Naturally, she didn't.

An hour later, disheartened and miserable, Leah tossed a TV dinner into the oven and set the timer. The local evening news was blaring from the TV when the doorbell chimed. Leah's heartbeat quickened. Siggy had reconsidered.

She fairly flew to the door, but her welcoming smile died an instant death when she saw it was Cain Hawkins and not Siggy.

"Can I come in?" he asked brusquely, and paraded past her, not waiting for a response.

"Feel free," she returned mockingly. "Make yourself at home while you're at it." She stepped aside and closed the door with her back, suddenly needing its support. "What can I do for you?"

"You and I have to reach an understanding."

"I'm going, Mr. Hawkins. There is nothing on God's green earth that's going to keep me from the Diamantinas."

Cain jerked a hand from his pants pocket and ran it

through the dark hair along the side of his head. "Me, either, lady."

Lady! Well, at least that was an improvement over Siggy, who apparently viewed her as a disobedient child.

"Did you talk to this Sidney fellow?" he demanded, pacing in front of the sofa.

"Siggy," Leah corrected calmly, still standing at the front door.

"Whoever." Impatiently, his hand sliced the air.

"Yes, as a matter of fact I did discuss the situation with Siggy." Primly, Leah folded her hands. She wasn't about to announce to this arrogant male that Siggy hadn't asked his mother's permission yet.

His hand returned to the corduroy pocket. "I don't suppose you've got a beer?"

"You're right. I don't."

He gave a look that said he'd guessed as much. "Well, what did ol' Sidney say?"

Leah lowered her gaze. "He's . . . he's thinking about it. And it's Siggy," she returned with marked patience.

"Whoever," they said together in perfect unison.

For the first time, Leah saw Cain smile. Despite everything she felt about this man, she had to admit she liked his smile. His rugged face was affected by the movement of his mouth. His eyes grew a richer shade of brown until they looked almost black, and she saw a glimpse of the man she'd always thought him to be.

"Did I hear something ding?" Cain turned his ear toward the kitchen.

Leah nodded. "Yes. Please excuse me a minute."

He followed her into the compact kitchen and idly

leaned against the counter as she opened the microwave and took out the packaged meal.

"You don't honestly eat that garbage, do you?" he asked, his voice rising with astonishment. "Good grief, no wonder you're so thin. Come on, I'll take you to dinner and feed you properly. You need some meat on those bones."

Leah bristled. "How could I possibly turn down such a flowery invitation?" she asked with more than a trace of sarcasm.

"Right." A reckless grin slashed his mouth. "How could you?"

The next thing Leah knew, she was being ushered out the front door and into the lot where a red Porsche speedster was parked.

Stopping, Leah ran her hand along the polished surface of the car and shook her head knowingly. "Honestly, Hawkins, you're so predictable."

He mumbled something under his breath and left her to open her own door and climb inside.

Leah had barely snapped the seat belt into place when Cain revved the engine and shoved the gear into place. They left the parking lot with a spray of gravel kicking up in their wake. The tires screeched as they came to the first red light.

"Do you have to . . . Is it necessary to drive quite so fast?" Leah asked, holding on to the seat with both hands.

"Just wait. This baby does one eighty-five."

"Not with me, it doesn't." Leah reached for the door handle to climb out, but the light changed and Cain shot across the intersection like a bullet out of a gun. Leah's head was jerked back with such force that it bounced against the headrest.

"Isn't this great?"

"No." Leah screamed, instinctively reaching for the dashboard. Her heart was pounding so fiercely she didn't know which was louder, her pulse or the roar of the engine.

Suddenly, Cain slowed down to a crawl and laughed. That mocking, taunting laugh Leah hated. She was so angry, she couldn't breathe.

"Now." He pulled over to the curb and parked. "Isn't that what you expected? You took one look at my car and immediately assumed that I was a crazy man at the wheel."

Unable to answer, Leah placed her hand over her heart and shook her head.

Cain's fingers tightened around the steering wheel. "We'll get along a lot easier if you learn something right now, lady. I'm never predictable. I do what I want, where I want and when I want. Got it?"

The grip on her anger was so fragile that Leah's voice shook dangerously. "Don't ever do that to me again. And . . . and you get one thing straight. I have a name, and it isn't lady or honey or princess. It's Leah." Her shoulders were heaving, her breasts rising with every panting breath.

Their eyes locked, hers filled with determination and pride, his with an unreadable quality she couldn't quite define. She hoped it was grudging respect. When his hands loosened their grip on the steering wheel, she relaxed.

"Hello, Leah, my name is Cain Hawkins." He extended his hand to her, and with a trembling smile she placed her much smaller one in his.

"Hello, Cain."

A smile briefly touched his eyes before he checked the side mirror and pulled back onto the street. "I hope you're hungry," he said with a laugh.

"I don't know." Leah's returning laugh was shaky. "I think you might have to go back the way we came. My stomach is about a mile behind us."

He didn't laugh; his concentration was fixed on the road. Trying not to be obvious, Leah studied him from beneath long lashes. He was a complicated man, and she doubted that anyone could truly understand him. A genius. Few would deny that. For the first time she noticed a small dimple in his cheek. It wasn't apparent except when his face was relaxed, Leah concluded. His hair was unkempt and his beard showed a five o'clock shadow. She wondered if he often forgot to shave, then smiled because she knew intuitively that he did.

They arrived at an Italian restaurant that emitted the aroma of pungent spices and tomatoes. It seemed like weeks since Leah had eaten a decent meal.

Cain was recognized immediately, and there were shouts from the kitchen as a short, stout man came through the swinging doors, wiping his hands on a white apron. A flurry of Italian flew over Leah's head.

The man from the kitchen, whom Cain called Vinnie, directed his attention to Leah and nodded approvingly. He shook his head dramatically, his white teeth gleaming.

Never had Leah felt more as if she was standing on an auction block. Nervously she tucked a strand of hair around her ear and shifted her weight from one foot to the other.

A woman with a lovely olive complexion appeared, her dark hair filled with strands of silver. She, too, joined in the conversation, then slapped her hands with apparent delight.

Leah recognized only a few words of Italian, but *bambino* was one of them. Leah surmised that the restaurant couple were expecting their first grandchild and offered them a smile of congratulations.

Smiling happily, the woman took Leah by the shoulders and nodded her head several times. Again a flurry of Italian was followed by laughter.

When Cain put his arm around her shoulder, bringing her close to his side, Leah was all the more confused.

The couple led Cain and Leah into a secluded corner of the restaurant and smiled broadly as they held out the chairs. Almost immediately, a flurry of activity commenced. A large loaf of freshly baked bread and a thick slab of cheese were delivered to the table.

"You speak Italian," Leah said to break the silence between them. It wasn't one of her more brilliant deductions.

"I picked it up as a kid in Europe," Cain explained, pulling apart a hunk of bread and cutting off a slice of cheese.

Leah followed his example, taking a smaller piece of both the bread and the cheese. "You were born in Europe?" She wouldn't have guessed it.

"No, I was an Army brat. My dad was stationed all over the world. My mother and I were with him much of the time."

"How interesting." Leah realized her comment sounded trite, and she regretted having said anything.

"Actually, I was born in California, but soon afterward we were stationed in Formosa." He paused and took a sip of wine. "That's Taiwan now."

She knew that much from Trivial Pursuit.

"What about you?"

Her fingers worked the stem of the wineglass. "I'm originally from South Dakota. My father's a farmer. Wheat, barley, soybeans." She didn't mention how much she loved Cain's photos of America's farmlands and how she'd given that book to her father for Christmas last year.

If Cain was surprised by her homey, Midwest background, he didn't show it. But Leah was quickly learning that Cain didn't divulge anything unless it suited him. Something told her that he usually didn't talk about himself. Even in his books there was little information given about him. Most of what she knew she'd heard through gossip.

The bread and cheese disappeared, to be replaced with a relish plate filled with crisp, fresh vegetables and dark olives. Their wineglasses were replenished.

"You must come here often." Leah felt as if she had to carry the conversation. The looks Cain was giving her were unsettling. His thick brows were drawn together as if he were seeking something beyond her obvious lack of beauty. Either that, or something was troubling him. Lowering her eyes, she cursed their color for the thousandth time. They weren't quite green, nor dark enough to be brown, but some murky shade between.

She reached for a celery stick, then laid it against the

side of her plate. Opening her mouth would only have drawn attention to how full her lips were.

"Your eyes are the most unusual color," Cain commented thoughtfully.

Leah's hand gripped the linen napkin in her lap. "Yes, I know." It looked for a minute as if Cain would say something else, but the waiter interrupted to deliver a small salad covered with a creamy herb dressing.

"You obviously know these people," Leah tried again.

"We go way back."

That absent, thoughtful look returned, and if Leah didn't know better she'd have said he was nervous about something. "I thought you must. They were saying something about a baby. Are they expecting a grandchild?"

Cain regarded her blankly. "No."

Leah's fork played with a lettuce leaf. "Oh, I thought I heard her say *bambino,* but then I'm not exactly fluent in Italian."

"You did," he said, but he didn't elaborate.

The salad was taken away and quickly followed by a plateful of spaghetti with a thick, rich meat sauce.

"I don't know if I can eat all this," Leah said with a wistful sigh.

A half smile deepened the grooves on one side of his face. "Be sure and save room for the main course."

"The main course," Leah repeated, her round eyes giving him a shocked look.

"I guess I should have warned you." His smile was replaced with a frown of concentration as he wove the long strands of spaghetti around his fork, using his spoon as a guide.

Leah watched him for a minute and shook her head,

unwilling even to attempt his method. Setting her fork aside, she studied Cain. There was something bothering him. She could sense it in the way his brow knitted as he manipulated the spaghetti.

Cain looked up and their eyes clashed. "What's wrong?" she asked softly.

Cain heaved a sigh and set his fork aside. "I'm no good at this."

Leah blinked uncertainly. *Good at what?* she wondered.

"I thought if I created a romantic mood it would help. But, I don't go in for this romance garbage."

Leah was stunned into speechlessness. She'd never thought of herself as stupid, but at the moment she felt incredibly so. Cain looked as if he wanted to punch a hole in the wall, and she hadn't an inkling why.

"You know what's going to happen Thursday, don't you?"

She shook her head, more confused than ever.

"Brewster's going to come up with a compromise team."

Forcefully, Leah shook her head. "He wouldn't do that." He couldn't. David Brewster knew how much this trip meant to her.

"Of course he would. It's the only answer. If he doesn't he takes the risk of offending us both. And whether he feels like admitting it or not, we're both valuable to the university."

It didn't take much thought for Leah to recognize that what Cain was saying was true.

"And—" he tossed his napkin onto the table "—you

may have this Sidney fellow to solve your problems, but there isn't anyone I can marry at the drop of a hat."

Leah couldn't believe that. "What . . . what are you suggesting?"

"There's only one thing to do." Cain looked thoroughly miserable. He reached for his wine and took a gulp. "Leah . . . ?" He hesitated.

"Yes."

"Damn it anyway. Will you marry me?"

Chapter 2

"Marry . . . you," Leah repeated, dumbfounded.

"It isn't like this is any love match," Cain inserted, clearly angry. "We're adults. How old are you, anyway?"

"Twenty-eight." That, at least, was easily enough answered.

Cain looked surprised. "You look younger. I checked with a judge friend of mine this afternoon and found out all we need are blood tests. We can have those done tonight, get the license and be married before your first class in the morning."

"I . . . I suppose we could." A cauldron of doubts bubbled in her mind, but Leah could marshal no argument. Cain was right. They were adults, they were professional people and they both desperately wanted to be a part of this expedition. The choice was clear.

"Does that mean yes?" Cain demanded.

Leah chose to ignore the warning lights blinking in her brain. "Yes," she murmured.

"Thank you," Cain said with an exaggerated sigh. He called out something in Italian, and the entire kitchen staff appeared. Someone brought out an accordion, and the man Cain had called Vinnie pumped Cain's hand and kissed him on both cheeks.

Music filled the restaurant. Violins, accordions, guitars. Champagne flowed freely, and Leah quickly lost count of the number of people who congratulated her with kisses on both cheeks. It seemed she waltzed with more men in that one night than she had in her entire life.

The next thing she remembered was Cain delivering her to her apartment and asking her if she was going to be sick. The whole world was singing and dancing, spinning and weaving, and it was all she could do to wave him aside. Leah didn't know if she was going to be sick or not. But if she was, she didn't want Cain around.

The next morning Leah awoke in the clothes she'd worn to dinner the night before. She was suffering from the worst headache of her life. The base of her skull was throbbing as if an avenging demon were hammering on it.

Leah staggered into the bathroom and brushed her teeth but the sound of running water only intensified the ache in her head, and she turned off the faucet. Pressing a hand against her forehead, she took in deep breaths and winced when the doorbell chimed. With her hand still to her head, she moved to the living room and, as quietly as possible, undid the dead bolt lock and opened the front door.

"Morning," Cain greeted her stiffly. "How do you feel?"

"About the same as I look," she whispered.

Idly he stuck his hands in his pockets and cocked his head to one side. "That bad, huh?"

Leah gave him a frosty glare. "I just woke up. I'd like to shower and change first."

"Sure. Do you mind if I make myself a cup of coffee?"

In her worst nightmares she had never dreamed that her wedding day would be anything like this. Cain wasn't even wearing a suit. He was dressed casually in dark cords and a sport shirt. She watched as he removed his leather coat and draped it over the kitchen chair, then paused to look at her expectantly. "The coffee?"

"Go ahead."

She left him to his own devices while she surveyed the contents of her closet. She didn't have a thing to wear. And the urge to use that as an excuse to back out of the wedding was almost overwhelming. Finally she chose an olive-green dress. The color matched her mood.

The shower took some of the ache from her bones, but the whine of the hair dryer nearly drove her insane. Before twisting the blond strands into her usual chignon, Leah stepped into the kitchen. Cain was at the table reading the morning newspaper.

"Would you prefer my hair up or down?" she asked as she poured herself a cup of coffee.

Cain glanced up and blinked. "Would I what?"

"My hair," she returned with marked patience. "Should I wear it up or down? Siggy prefers it down."

Cain's blank stare continued. "Good grief, why should I care? You could be bald and it wouldn't make any difference."

Leah successfully resisted the urge to shout at him that this whole thing was ludicrous and she wouldn't have anything to do with it. "I'll leave my hair down then."

"Fine." Already his attention had reverted to the newspaper.

Leah had hardly taken more than a few sips of her coffee when Cain straightened and checked his watch. "The courthouse is open. Let's get this over with."

"Before we do anything with legal ramifications, I think we should make certain aspects of this relationship clear," Leah asserted.

"Of course." Cain gave her a strange look. "I've already thought of that." He lifted his coat from the chair and took out a folded piece of paper. "Read this over and see if I've left out anything."

Scanning the list, Leah was impressed with his thoroughness. Everything she'd thought to mention was there. She didn't want him to have any legal claim to her assets, and she wanted to keep her surname. "I'd like the divorce proceedings to start the first week after our return instead of a month later."

Cain hesitated. "Fine. Write that in if you want, but I can't have my time tied up in court. I'll be working day and night developing the film."

"I'm sure it will be a relatively painless process." Leah spoke with more confidence than she was feeling. "If it would make things simpler, we could make a quick trip into Nevada."

Again Cain glanced at his watch. "Let's decide that later."

"Fine," was Leah's clipped response. He didn't care how she styled her hair, and she didn't care how they went about the divorce as long as there was one.

"You'll notice that I've left a space for each of us to sign. You can keep a copy and I'll take the other."

"Good." Leah penned her name in flowing, even strokes and handed the ballpoint to Cain, who scribbled his signature below hers.

"You ready now?" he asked.

Leah answered him by reaching for the short olive jacket that matched her dress.

Obtaining the license was a simple matter of handing the clerk the results from the blood tests, penning their signatures and paying the fee. Leah watched the money change hands and felt they were selling themselves cheap.

Recognizing how strange it would sound, Leah resisted questioning the clerk about where they could file for the divorce. That would be easy enough to find out when they returned from the Diamantinas.

Judge Preston's quarters were in the same building, only a matter of a short ride in the elevator.

Leah paused outside the door, staring at the evenly printed letters on the glass door. Nervously, her fingers toyed with the strap of her purse as she bit into her quivering bottom lip.

Cain opened the door and pressed a hand in the small of her back, urging her forward. "Come on," he said impatiently, "we're running on a tight schedule."

Squaring her shoulders, Leah stepped into the office. Her throat was desert dry with apprehension.

"Judge Preston is expecting us," Cain announced to the receptionist.

The attractive young woman flashed them an easy smile. "You must be the young couple the judge mentioned this morning. He asked me to be your witness. That is, if you don't mind?" She directed her question to Leah.

Both the receptionist and Cain seemed to be waiting for Leah to respond. "That's very kind . . . thank you."

They were ushered into the judge's quarters, and the gray-haired, fatherly-looking man stood immediately. "Welcome, my boy. It's good to see you." Enthusiastically, he shook Cain's hand and turned to Leah. "You've chosen well, Cain. Your father would be proud." He centered his attention on Leah and smiled at her with blue eyes that had faded with age but retained their sparkle. Taking her cold, clammy hand in his, he said, "There's no need to be nervous. Cain Hawkins took his time in choosing a bride. He'll make you a good husband."

Obviously Cain hadn't explained the situation to anyone, and Leah was supposed to fall in with this happy-bride act.

Leah saw Cain glance at his watch, and she seethed silently. If he announced once more that they were on a tight schedule, she swore she was going to turn around and walk out that door.

The judge leaned forward and flipped a switch on the intercom. "We're ready now, Joyce. Would you ask Mr. Graham to step into my office?"

At Cain's look of surprise, the judge explained, "Your other witness."

Cain looked uncomfortable as he took the license from his coat pocket and gave it to his friend.

As soon as everyone was in their place, the judge reached for his little black book and flipped through the pages.

"We are gathered here today. . . ."

The words droned in Leah's ear as she struggled to pay attention. This wasn't right. Marriage was forever, a commitment meant to last a lifetime. Her parents had recently celebrated their thirtieth wedding anniversary. *Divorce* was such an ugly word. No one in her family had ever been divorced. Panic grew within Leah until she wanted to turn and bolt from the room and Cain Hawkins's craziness. Nothing was worth compromising everything that she believed was right.

"Do you take this man to be your lawfully wedded husband, in sickness and in health . . . ?"

"I don't know," Leah cried, desperately close to tears.

Four stunned faces turned to her. Cain looked as if he wanted to wring her neck, and she couldn't blame him. Leah swallowed and fought back the rising hysteria. "It just doesn't seem right to talk about divorce on the way to the wedding. I . . . I was raised to believe in the sanctity of marriage."

"Leah," Cain's low voice threatened, "we agreed."

"I know." Her newly discovered resolve was faltering.

"Think of the whales," he whispered enticingly.

Oh how she loved those marvelous creatures. Her hazel eyes pleaded with Cain to understand.

"Miss Talmadge," the judge spoke gently. "If you have any questions about this ceremony . . ."

Cain's eyes sharpened with determination. "There's no problem. Carry on."

"Miss Talmadge?"

Leah could feel Cain stiffen at her side. His hand at the back of her waist pressed into her painfully. She couldn't believe he was hurting her consciously.

"Leah," Cain urged.

"I do," she screamed. "All right, all right, I'll go through with it."

A minute later a recognizably flustered judge asked for the ring. Cain and Leah looked at each other with growing frustration. They'd completely forgotten the wedding bands.

In an apparent move to stall for time while he thought of something, Cain pretended to search through his pockets.

"I think we may have left those at Leah's apartment," Cain murmured, and gave Leah a panicked look.

"You can borrow mine," the receptionist offered generously, slipping the small diamond ring from her finger.

"No . . . I wouldn't want to do that." Marrying under these circumstances was difficult enough; Leah refused to borrow a ring. "Molly Brown wore a cigar band," she offered, hoping to lighten the mood.

"Who?" The same four faces glared at her.

She swallowed uncomfortably. "*The Unsinkable Molly Brown* . . . it was a movie with Debbie Reynolds, one of my mother's favorites."

"Will this do?" The young attorney who was standing next to Cain withdrew a pull tab from a soda can out of his pocket. "As I understand the law, a ring isn't actually required. This will do until you replace it later."

"Good idea." Cain brightened. "Thanks."

Fifteen minutes later, Cain and Leah were on the freeway, heading toward Leah's apartment.

"Well, that wasn't so bad, was it?" Cain broke into the oppressive silence that filled the car.

"Not bad?" Leah returned, shocked. "It had to be the most horrible experience of my life."

"You're letting your emotions get in the way. The little

girl in you is waiting for orange blossoms and the flowing white gown and veil. You can have that the next time."

Leah wanted to hate him for being so analytical. None of this had troubled Cain.

"I . . . I don't care what you say, I don't feel right about this."

"Honestly, Leah, it isn't like we did anything wrong."

"Then why am I filled with regrets? Why is there a lump in my throat and I feel I could cry?"

"Oh, good grief, here it comes."

Leah ignored him as best she could. If she couldn't disregard Cain's sarcasm, she'd end up looking for some painful way to lash out at him. "We were wrong to have married like this. And whether you admit it or not, we've lost something we'll never be able to recapture."

Cain stopped at the light at the bottom of the exit ramp and thumped his fingers against the steering wheel. "You've been a good sport until now. Don't go all melodramatic on me."

Staring straight ahead, Leah murmured caustically, "Right."

Cain came to a halt beside her car in the parking lot. She slipped the ridiculous soda can ring from her finger and left it on the console.

"I'll stop by tonight," Cain said as he leaned across the car seat when she climbed out. "We've got lots to discuss."

Leah couldn't think of a thing she had to say to him.

"About the trip," he said, apparently having read her thoughts. "I'll see you about seven. Okay?"

She never wanted to see Cain Hawkins again. "All right," she found herself agreeing.

Leah's classes that day were a disaster. It would have been better to have phoned in sick, for all the good she did. Her mind refused to function properly, and she made several embarrassing mistakes. All she seemed able to think about was that this morning she had married a man she didn't know, who was probably the coldest, least demonstrative, most analytical being on earth. Cain Hawkins's pictures may have been wonderful, but they were nothing like the man.

As promised, Cain was at her apartment at seven, bringing a six-pack of beer with him. He delivered it promptly to the refrigerator.

"Feel any better?" he asked on his way out of the kitchen.

"No," she answered stiffly. She was about to tell him what he could do with his beer, when he spoke.

"This should improve your mood." He took a plain gold wedding band from his pocket. When she ignored it, he reached for her hand and pressed it into her palm. "It was my mother's."

The ring warmed her hand, and Leah realized he must have been holding it for quite some time before giving it to her. Leah stared at it, unable to believe Cain would do something like this. "I . . . I appreciate the thought, but I don't want your mother's ring."

"What am I going to do with it, anyway?"

Leah gave him a look of disbelief. "Someday there'll be a woman you love that you'll want to give this ring to." Someone beautiful, no doubt, she added silently.

Cain removed his jacket and tossed it over the leather love seat. "If I can go thirty-five years avoiding the marriage trap, then . . ."

Leah started to giggle. She couldn't help it. Laughter consumed her, and she covered her mouth. Giant tears welled in her eyes and rolled down her pale cheeks.

"What's so all-fired funny?"

"You . . . us," she managed between peals of laughter. "Avoiding the marriage trap, indeed. You *are* married. *We're* married."

His mouth was pinched as he went back into the kitchen and returned with a can of beer. "Wear the ring. You'll need to have one or there'll be questions."

"But not your mother's ring." Leah watched him with mounting incredulity. Maybe he didn't care. Apparently there was little in life that did concern him.

"Yes," he insisted tightly. "My mother's ring. What do I want with it?"

His face tightened with anger. Or perhaps it was pain; Leah couldn't tell.

"It's obvious this sort of thing means something to you," he continued. "So keep it."

"Don't you care about anything?" Leah asked, perplexed by this complicated man. True, the ring wasn't worth much, but it must have had some sentimental value if he'd kept it all these years.

"I care about a lot of things," he countered swiftly. "Good beer." He saluted her mockingly by raising the aluminum can. "And gourmet food, which reminds me, have you eaten yet?"

"Stop it," she shouted unreasonably. For the first time since they'd met, Leah felt she was close to understanding this man. So this was how he'd remained single all these years. He allowed people to get only so close before shutting them out. Cain Hawkins was running from life, from commitment, from everything that his photographs revealed. Only when he was behind a camera was he comfortable.

"I take it you ate," he prompted.

She hadn't been able to down anything all day. "No."

"Good. Why don't you throw two of those frozen dinners in the microwave? I could eat a cow."

Ignoring him, Leah fingered the plain gold band. Cain hadn't fooled her. The ring meant a great deal to him, and he was giving it to her to prove to himself in some perverse way that it meant nothing.

"I can't accept this," she said, holding out the ring.

Cain looked stunned. "Why not? It isn't like it was all that important to my mother." He laughed mirthlessly. "She left it on the kitchen counter when she ran off."

Just by the way his voice dipped to a low, husky tone, Leah realized how painful that episode must have been for Cain. "But you kept it?" she prompted softly.

"No." He took a long drink from his beer. "My father did. I found it recently when I was going through Dad's things." A glazed look flitted across his face as he explained softly, "He died six months ago."

"I'm sorry."

"Why? Was it your fault?" The sarcasm laced through his words said she was getting too close and it was time to push her away. He took another swig of his beer and took a small pad from his coat pocket.

Leah moved into the kitchen, took out two frozen dinners and set them in the microwave. The ring sat on the white countertop and magnetically drew her attention. No matter where she was in the kitchen, her gaze was attracted to it. Finally, she picked it up and slipped it on her finger. The fit was perfect.

In a way she couldn't explain, Leah *felt* married. And although they'd only met a day ago, there was a bond between them. A spiritual bond. Cain didn't go around telling people about his mother, she was convinced of that. Nor would he mention to a mere acquaintance that his father had recently passed away.

When they'd agreed to get married, neither of them had expected it to have any effect on their lives. Not really. This marriage was for one purpose—so they could both be included in the ancient whale expedition to the Diamantina Islands. Yet it was only hours after the wedding and Leah felt indelibly marked. An invisible link existed between them, and Leah doubted that either one of them would ever be the same again.

Carrying a cup of coffee with her, Leah moved into the living room. She sat opposite him and crossed her long legs. "I thought we might talk about the goals of the expedition."

"First tell me something about the ancient whale."

"All right," Leah agreed. "There are about a hundred known species of whales divided into two suborders. The scientific names are *Mysticeti* and *Odontoceti*. Or to say it another way, whalebone whales and toothed whales."

Cain nodded, his eyes lowered. Leah realized that she was probably giving him more information than he wanted. But it was important that he understood the significance of the discovery of this whale last year.

"Ancient whales," she continued, "are in a third separate category. The reason they're called ancient whales is because it's been presumed for years that they were extinct."

"What are our chances of photographing one?"

Leah wouldn't be anything but truthful. "Slim, at best."

"But there will be ample opportunity to view the other species."

"Definitely. Probably closer than you've ever thought you would get to a whale. There's been a boat supplied and—"

"You're wearing the ring."

His statement caught her off guard, and her gaze fell to her left hand. "Yes." She didn't elaborate, not sure why she'd relented and slipped it on her finger. "As I was saying about the boat—" she swallowed, suddenly ill at ease "—I'm hoping that we can get—"

"Why?"

"For the photos, of course."

"I'm asking about the ring. What made you decide to wear it?"

Leah didn't know how to explain something she wasn't sure of herself. "I only hope there's enough time to gather all the material I'll need."

The room became quiet. "That wasn't what I asked."

Deliberately, she uncrossed her legs and stood. "I think I'll check the microwave, I think I heard it ding."

"I'll only follow you."

"I don't know why," she shouted, unreasonably angry that he would demand an answer when she obviously didn't have one. "It was there, and you're right, I'm going to need one. And this will save us the trouble of going out and buying one. Now, are you satisfied?"

The doorbell chimed before Cain had the opportunity to answer.

Leah glared accusingly at the door, marched across the room and turned the handle. "Yes," she said heatedly.

"Darling." Siggy stood on the other side. Shock moved across his eyes. "Is something wrong?" he said gently, reaching for her limp shoulders and bringing her into his embrace. "Of course you're upset. It's about yesterday, isn't it?"

"Siggy."

"No, no. It's my turn. You're right, so right, my love. I was cheating us both by not telling Mother about us. I talked to her this evening and—"

"Siggy, please, let me explain," Leah pleaded as she stepped back out of his arms.

"Mother approves, darling. Do you understand what that means?"

The urge to laugh was almost overwhelming. "Mother approves," Leah echoed.

Cain stood and moved behind Leah, placing a possessive hand on her neck. "Is there a problem?"

Siggy stiffened, then straightened the corner of his bow tie. "Who is this man?" He directed his question to Leah.

"Is there something I can do for you?" Cain answered stiffly. "I'm Leah's husband."

Chapter 3

"Leah?" Siggy couldn't have looked more stunned. His eyes rounded and his cheeks puffed out like someone who had come under sudden attack. Slowly he regained his composure enough to continue speaking. "Is this true?"

Frustrated and impatient, Leah glared angrily at Cain. He had no right to adopt this high-handed attitude. From the smug smile that played across his mouth, he was obviously enjoying her fiancé's discomfort. "Siggy, let me explain," Leah pleaded, a thread of despair weaving its way through her voice.

The hand at the base of her neck tightened as Cain drew her possessively closer. "Just answer the question, darling."

"Leah?" Again Siggy's shocked, hurt gaze sought hers. "Is it true?"

"Yes, but there are . . . extenuating circumstances."

The smile Siggy gave her was decidedly dispirited. "There'd have to be. Only yesterday you wanted to be *my* wife."

Her heart leaped with pity at the hurt-little-boy look in his pale-blue eyes.

Siggy took a step in retreat, his shoulders hunching. "Everything would have been all right now that Mother knows. Couldn't you have waited?"

"No, we couldn't." Again Cain had answered for her.

Siggy's gaze skidded from Leah to Cain and then back to her again. Confusion and pain marked his expression. "Then there's nothing left to say. Goodbye, Leah."

"Siggy." The aching sigh of his name must have caused him to hesitate.

"Yes?"

"I'll give you a call in the morning." She ignored the way Cain's fingers were digging into the nape of her neck. "All this can be explained quite simply."

"You won't have time, darling," Cain insisted, his eyes narrowing. "We're both going to be extremely busy from now on."

If possible, Siggy went all the more waxen. A figure of rejection, he turned and walked away, closing the door.

Anger washed over Leah in turbulent waves. The first swells rose quickly to storm intensity, so that she had difficulty forming her thoughts.

"How . . . how dare you!" With a sweep of her hand she slammed the front door closed and turned on Cain like an avenging archangel. Quivers of rage sharpened her voice. The sound of her anger vibrated through the room like a violent ocean storm attacking the shore. This was no squall, but a full-blown tempest.

Even Cain looked shocked at the extent of her wrath. "You can't honestly love that pompous, bureaucratic windbag."

"Why should you care one way or the other? Siggy is part of my life. He had nothing to do with you." To her horror, stinging tears pooled in her eyes, so that Cain swam in and out of focus.

"But he doesn't love you," Cain argued. "Can't you see what he—"

"And you do love me, is that what you're saying? Are you such an expert in love that you know instantly who does and doesn't?" Pride was the only thing that carried her voice now as it quivered and trembled with every word.

His gaze narrowed as he plowed a hand through his hair. "You're misinterpreting everything."

"I am?" She gave a weak, hysterical laugh. "Weren't you the one who said I'd be lucky to be any man's wife? Look at me. Do you think I don't know I'm no raving beauty?"

Clearly flustered now, Cain stalked to the other side of the room. "You're not that bad."

"Oh, come now. Be honest. If it hadn't been for this assignment, you wouldn't have given me more than a passing glance."

He gestured indecisively with his hand. "How am I supposed to know that? If it weren't for this assignment we wouldn't have met."

"I'm too tall, too thin, and blatantly unattractive. Do you have any idea what that means to someone like me? Siggy cares. For the first time in my life there was a man who looked beyond my face and loved me enough to want to share his life with me. And . . ." She paused as her voice cracked. "And now, you've done your best to ruin that."

"Leah." He clenched his hands into tight fists. "I apologize. I have no excuse. My behavior was stupid and irrational."

She sniffled and reached for a tissue to blow her nose. "An apology isn't going to reverse what just happened. You may very well have ruined my life."

"All right, all right. Call . . . Sidney, and we'll get together and explain everything."

"When?" she demanded.

"Whenever you like."

She reached for her phone and left Siggy a message in voice mail. "He'll return the call," she murmured confidently. Siggy would be willing to clear away any misunderstandings. It didn't matter what Cain Hawkins thought, Leah reminded herself. Siggy loved her and that was the most important thing. When she returned from the Diamantinas her routine could return to normal. Cain would want her out of his life as quickly as possible.

While she was phoning, Cain had gone into the kitchen, and he returned now with a strong cup of coffee. "Here." He set it on the glass coffee table. "Drink this."

The gesture surprised Leah. Cain had already apologized and had promised to make things right between her and Siggy. Now he was thoughtfully taking care of her. "Thank you."

"Do you feel like going over the list of supplies?" He sat across from her and leaned forward as he pulled the tab from his beer can.

Leah waited until he'd taken his first long drink before she answered. "I hope you're not planning to bring that stuff along."

"What?" His gaze followed hers, and a low, husky chuckle escaped. "This, lady, is as essential as film for my camera. Don't worry, I seldom drink more than one or two at a time. Think of it as my brand of cola."

Leah wasn't convinced. If they were going to be spending a lot of time together, alcohol could be a dangerous thing. But the dark gleam in his eye discouraged argument. This was one area where Cain wouldn't compromise. His look confirmed as much.

"Here, take a look at this." He withdrew a pad from his jacket and handed it to Leah.

She glanced over the itemized list of food supplies Cain had typed. The list was extensive and seemed far beyond what they could possibly eat during the course of their trip.

"You've got that look in your eye again," Cain grumbled.

"What look?"

"The one that says you disapprove."

A smile danced across her face, her first since Siggy had come . . . and gone. "It's just that it seems like so much."

"Perhaps it is, but I'd like to fatten you up a little while we're there."

A small laugh escaped. "My dear Mr. Hawkins, better men than you have tried."

At ease now, Cain chuckled, but the amusement slowly drained from him as his gaze captured hers and the room went still. An expression she couldn't read filtered over his features, an odd mixture of surprise and incredulity. Silence fell between them.

"Is something wrong?" Concerned, Leah wondered what had happened to alter his mood so quickly.

"You're not ugly—or even plain. In fact, you're lovely."

His announcement came out of nowhere. Self-conscious, Leah dropped her gaze to her hands. With the movement, her long hair fell forward, wreathing the delicate features of her oval face. "Don't, please," she whispered entreatingly.

"No, I'm serious. You were laughing just now, and your eyes sparkled, and it struck me—Leah Talmadge is really pretty."

Involuntarily, she flushed. "Cain, I know what I am." In many ways, she knew, she was like the Leah from Scripture, the plain, weak-eyed first wife of Jacob. The unloved one.

"And you think I'm making it up?"

No, she knew exactly what he was doing. In his own way, Cain was trying to make up to her for what had happened with Siggy.

"Believe what you want, then. But I didn't imagine what I just saw."

Where only minutes before they had been fiercely arguing, now there was kindness in his words. For a time, it had seemed impossible that they would ever manage to work together. Now Leah had no doubts that they could and would.

"Everything's going to work out fine," Cain said with a confidence that was irrefutable. "Tomorrow we'll meet with Dr. Brewster and your . . . Sidney. I'm hoping that we'll be ready to leave by the end of the week."

Leah was stunned. "So soon?"

"The faster we're out of here, the better. If we stick around California another week, something else might crop up that could cause a change in plans. Can you be ready?"

"If I can meet a man one day and marry him the next, I can do anything. Lead the way, partner."

"Now you're talking. We're a team. We can't forget that."

The microwave dinged again, reminding Leah their dinner was ready. Cain followed her into the kitchen, and while she took them out of the microwave he set the table. Wordlessly, they worked together. What Cain had said was true—they were a team. In the coming weeks they'd be spending a lot of time together. Yesterday the thought had terrified her, but tonight she felt at ease with Cain Hawkins. Their peace would hold because they both wanted this expedition to succeed.

With all that needed to be discussed and planned, Cain didn't leave her apartment until the early-morning hours. She turned the dead bolt lock after he'd gone and leaned wearily against the door. Releasing a soft yawn, she brushed the hair off her face with her hands. Surprisingly, Cain was a meticulous organizer; his expertise was undeniable. The opportunity of a lifetime was opening up for them and her heart swelled with excitement.

Not until Leah had undressed and climbed into bed did the realization come. A chill raced up her spine, and her fingers went cold as they gripped the sheets. Her chest ached with the unexpected pain of it, and she pressed her palm over her heart.

Tonight was her wedding night!

A heavy frown formed deep creases in her brow as Leah's gaze slid to the simple gold band on her ring finger. This so-called marriage was wrong. Her heart had known that from the beginning. The uncertainty she'd experienced as she stood in front of Judge Preston was only a foreshadowing of what was sure to follow.

Slowly Leah lay back and stared at the ceiling. A flip of

the lamp switch and the room was cast into instant blackness. The night seemed to press down on Leah. As a teenager, she had often dreamed of her wedding, seeing it as the one day in her life when she was sure to be beautiful. Wearing a long white gown and flowing veil, she would stand before friends and family and give testament to her love. A love that was meant to span a lifetime. Her wedding night would be one of discovery and joy. Not in her crudest nightmares had she suspected that she would be spending it alone.

Moon shadows flickered across the walls as Leah rolled over, pulled the blankets over her shoulders and took in a shuddering sigh. Even ugly women should be allowed their fantasies. But not Leah. So much for dreams. So much for romance. So much for love.

The relief on Dr. Brewster's wrinkled face was evident in every craggy line. "My children, I couldn't be more pleased." He slapped Cain across the back and shyly kissed Leah's cheek. "I realize that marriage must have sounded a bit drastic, but I can't imagine sending a better team to the islands. Everything will work out splendidly. Just you wait."

"I think it will," Cain agreed.

Perhaps the project would work out well, but as to carelessly linking their lives, Leah wasn't nearly as confident. Their marriage was supposed to be a two-month business arrangement, but the gold band around her finger felt as if it weighed a hundred pounds. Leah knew that when she slipped it from her hand to return to Cain after the expedition, her finger would be indelibly marked by its presence for all her life.

They left Dr. Brewster's office with their travel documents, airline tickets, and a list of contacts in Australia and New Zealand.

"Where to from here?" Cain questioned once they'd reached the university parking lot.

With a false smile of courage, Leah lowered her chin fractionally. "I'm having lunch with Siggy."

"You, not us." Cain's voice was clipped and direct. "In that case, I'll drop you off at your apartment." He held the car door open for her, and she gracefully swung her long legs inside.

"It's not that I don't want you to come." She felt obliged to explain, and her soft voice thinned to a quivering note. "But I think it will be a lot better if I see Siggy alone."

"Sure." His gaze seemed to lock on the pulsing vein in her neck, and it was all Leah could do not to turn up her collar. While she stared ahead, unnerved by his sudden interest in her heart rate, Cain started the car and pulled into the heavy traffic in the street.

"Without getting too personal, maybe you can tell me what you find so intriguing about Sidney."

Leah had difficulty disguising her grimace. If Cain called Siggy Sidney one more time, she'd scream. From the first, she'd known his game. He did it on purpose, just to get a rise out of her, and she refused to give him one.

"Well?" Cain prompted. "You were going to marry the guy. Certainly you saw something in him."

"Of course I did . . . do," she corrected hastily. "Siggy's intelligent, sensitive, hard-working."

"From what he said about *Mother,* I'd say he's tied to the apron strings, wouldn't you?"

Leah had despaired over that herself, but there wasn't anything that she and Siggy couldn't settle once they were married. "Siggy has a strong sense of family."

Cain's attention shifted from the slow-paced traffic to her. "Are you always this loyal?" The lines etched about his eyes crinkled as he studied her. But it wasn't a smile he was giving her.

"When you care deeply about someone, then it's only natural to want to defend him."

"Care deeply or love?" Cain demanded.

His question struck a raw nerve. Leah had trouble herself distinguishing between the two when it came to Siggy. She cared about him. She was planning on being his wife. Of course she loved him.

"You can't answer me, can you?"

"I love him." Leah tore the admission through the constricted muscles of her throat. "No woman agrees to be a man's wife if she doesn't love him."

Cain's thick brow arched mockingly. "Oh?" Pointedly, his gaze fell to her ring finger as a mocking reminder that only yesterday she had married him without love or commitment.

For a mutinous moment, Leah wanted to shout at him for being unfair. Instead, she pressed her lips tightly closed and stared out the side window.

They didn't speak again until Cain dropped her off in her parking lot. Leah started to let herself out.

"What time will you be back?" Cain wanted to know.

Leah shrugged noncommittally. "I haven't any idea."

At the scowl he was giving her, she added, "Did you need me for something?"

"No." His gaze refused to meet hers. "Enjoy yourself."

The instant Leah closed the car door, Cain sped away, his tires screeching as he pulled out of the parking lot.

Bewildered, Leah watched him go. Cain was acting like a jealous husband. Not that he cared for her himself; he just didn't like the idea of her seeing Siggy. Why, she didn't know. But Cain Hawkins wasn't an easy man to decipher.

Siggy was already seated at their favorite restaurant when Leah arrived. As a vegetarian, Siggy would dine at only a handful of restaurants, even though Leah had often argued that he could order a meatless meal almost anywhere.

"Leah." As she approached the table, he stood and held out a chair for her.

"Hello, Siggy," she murmured self-consciously. "I'm so pleased that you agreed to see me."

"Well, yes, that was rather considerate of me under the circumstances."

Unfolding the napkin gave her something to do with her hands as Leah struggled with her explanation. "Marrying Cain isn't what it seems," she began haltingly. "Cain and I were forced to marry or give up the expedition."

A smile relaxed Siggy's tense features. "I thought as much. I knew you'd never do something like this without good reason. It's not a real marriage, is it? I can't imagine you making love with that unpleasant fellow."

Leah could feel the color flowering in her face. Two bright rosebuds appeared on each cheek and flashed like neon lights for all to witness her embarrassment. "Of course we haven't."

Siggy's chuckle was decidedly relieved. "This is strictly a business arrangement then."

"Yes, strictly business." This entire discussion was humiliating.

"And . . ." Siggy hesitated, obviously disconcerted. "How shall I put this?"

"I don't plan to ever sleep with him, if that's what you want to know."

Clearing his throat, Siggy flashed her a warm smile. "I had to be sure you weren't going to mix business with pleasure." Finding himself highly amusing, Siggy snorted loudly.

"Siggy," she flashed. "I'm a scientist with a mission. Just because Cain and I will be alone on the island together doesn't mean I'll find him attractive."

"You may be a scientist, my dear, but you're also a woman. A man like Cain Hawkins herds women in unconsciously."

Cain wasn't a ladies' man, Leah knew that much. If anything, he avoided relationships. His camera and his pictures were his life; he didn't need anything else and made a point of saying so.

"Now you're being unfair. Cain's not like that," she said, fighting back the urge to defend him even further.

Siggy's response was a loud cough as he lifted the menu and studied it carefully. Leah wondered why he bothered to read it. He never ordered anything but the zucchini quiche anyway.

The waitress arrived and took their order. True to

form, Siggy ordered the quiche; Leah asked for the spinach salad.

Their meals arrived a few minutes later. As Leah dipped her fork into the bowl of greens, an unexpected smile quivered at the corners of her mouth. She knew exactly what Cain would say about this meal. He'd insist that she have pasta on the side and cheesecake for dessert.

Obviously troubled again, Siggy toyed with his meal. "You do plan to divorce the man."

"Of course," Leah returned instantly. "We've agreed to take care of that the first week after we return."

Siggy seemed to breathe easier. "Mother must never know. You understand that, don't you, Leah?"

"I won't say a word," she promised. "It isn't as if it's a real marriage," she went on, "but one of convenience strictly for professional reasons." She couldn't understand why she felt compelled to repeat that. The thought flashed through her mind that she was saying it more for her benefit than Siggy's.

"I understand why you've done this," Siggy continued. "But I can't say I'm pleased. However, trust is vital in any relationship, and I want you to know I trust you implicitly." Having said his piece, Siggy nodded curtly.

"Thank you," Leah murmured, and bowed her head. A ray of light hit the gold band on her finger, causing her to catch her breath softly. This marriage was one of pretense. Deep down in her heart, she doubted Cain Hawkins had it in him to love someone of flesh and blood. His wife was a camera, his children his pictures. Then why, oh why, did she feel so married?

The Los Angeles airport was crammed with people, all of them in a hurry. A blaring voice over the loudspeaker announced a flight's departure gate, and Leah paused to be sure it wasn't hers. Nerves caused her stomach to knot painfully. Excitement seared through her blood. It had been a test of endurance, but together she and Cain had managed to meet the deadline they'd set for themselves. Barely. Leah was convinced that the first week she was on the island, all she'd be able to do was sleep.

Showing his concern for her well-being, Dr. Brewster had kindly arranged hotel accommodations in Sydney, Australia. From Sydney they would fly directly to Perth and meet with the contact, Hugh Kimo.

"Excited?" Cain's eyes smiled into hers.

"I don't think I can stand it." Her gaze scanned the milling crowd. They'd be heading for security any minute, and Siggy had said he'd be there to see her off. That was one thing she could count on: if Siggy said he was going to be someplace, he'd be there. Of all the people Leah had known in her life, Siggy was the most dependable—and predictable.

"Looking for someone?" Cain's mouth was pulled up in a mirthless smile.

He knew exactly whom she was expecting. "I don't understand it—Siggy's never late."

"I hope I didn't inadvertently give him the wrong flight time."

"Cain!" She expelled his name with the cutting edge of anger. Neither man had made any pretense of liking the other, but to have Cain stoop to lying was unfair.

"Leah, Leah, there you are." Breathlessly, Siggy arrived, flustered and obviously relieved to have found her in time. "I've had the most horrible afternoon. This place is a madhouse."

Cain's gaze was hard and disapproving as he made no attempt to disguise his dislike of Siggy.

Apparently not wishing to cause a scene, Siggy ignored Cain and reached inside his jacket pocket for a jeweler's box. He handed it to Leah.

"Siggy," she breathed in surprise.

"Go ahead," he urged, "open it."

Lifting the black lid, Leah discovered a small gold heart and a delicate chain, nestled in a bed of velvet. "Siggy, it's beautiful." Tears stung the back of her eyes. The gesture was so unexpected and so thoughtful that she gently brushed her lips over his cheek, finding no better way to express her appreciation.

Her genuine pleasure caused Siggy to flush with satisfaction. "I want you to wear it while you're away so you won't forget me." He fixed his gaze pointedly on Cain.

"I'd never forget you." She hardly knew what to say. Siggy wasn't much for gifts. "I don't know how to thank you."

The grim set of Cain's mouth told her that he didn't care for this sentimental exchange. His attitude was difficult to understand. She supposed that in some mysterious way his male pride had been challenged by Siggy, although she couldn't understand why.

Lifting the delicate necklace from its plush bed, Siggy held it up, prepared to help Leah put it on. She turned and lifted her hair as he placed the heart in the hollow of her throat and closed the clasp. Never one to display his affection publicly, Siggy was somewhat clumsy as he turned Leah around and kissed her soundly. The unexpected force of his mouth grinding over hers shocked Leah; his violent embrace knocked the wind from her lungs. Instinctively her hands sought his shoulders to maintain her balance.

Releasing her, Siggy gave Cain a self-satisfied glare. "Don't you so much as touch her," he warned smugly. "Leah's mine."

With a savagely impatient movement, Cain turned and stalked away.

Looking pleased with himself, Siggy stood in front of Leah and placed his hands on her shoulders. "Remember that I'll be waiting for you. Be true, my love, be true."

"You know I will." Lowering her gaze, Leah fought the urge to wipe his kiss from her mouth and was relieved to see it was time to get to her gate. Their flight would be boarding soon. She had wanted Siggy to come to the airport, but his selfish, brutal kiss had ruined her enjoyment of his unexpected gift. Siggy had come to stake his claim on her so that Cain would know in unconditional terms that she was his. Maybe, after all these months, she should be glad that Siggy was finally showing some signs of possessiveness. But she wasn't.

A quick survey of the area confirmed that Cain had already gone to the gate and had entered the line for security without her. Securing the strap of her carry-on bag over her shoulder, Leah offered Siggy a feeble smile.

"I'll call you in two months," she said, eager to be on her way.

Hands in his pants pockets, Siggy gave her his practiced hurt-little-boy look. "Hurry back."

Not goodbye, not good luck, just a reminder that he

wanted her to hurry through the most important assignment of her career.

"Goodbye, Siggy." Turning, she handed the TSA agent her passport and proceeded to the gate. Their flight had already started boarding the 747.

Cain was in his assigned seat when Leah joined him. His attention was focused on a magazine taken from the pocket in front of him. After she'd stored her carry-on bag in the compartment above their seats, she joined him.

Their eyes met, and his gaze raked her face, pausing on her swollen lips. The look he gave her made her feel unclean.

The silence stretched between them oppressively. Within minutes the huge aircraft was taxiing down the runway. The roar of the engine was deafening as a surge of magnificent power thrust them into the welcoming blue sky.

Still Cain didn't speak, and in agitated reaction, Leah fingered the gold heart at her throat. The movement attracted Cain's attention.

"You must be pleased with yourself," he declared cruelly. "There aren't many unattractive women who can be married to one man and engaged to another."

Leah struggled not to react to his taunt. "Not many," she agreed, her voice sarcastically low and controlled to disguise her anger. It cost Leah everything to meet his gaze with a look of haughty indifference. That accomplished, she swiveled her head and closed her eyes. Cain had attacked her where he knew he would inflict the most discomfort, and he had succeeded beyond anything he would ever realize.

"Leah," he murmured her name with what sounded like regret. "I didn't mean that."

"Why hedge now? It's true. A girl like me is lucky to have any man want to marry her."

Cain's features hardened. "I didn't mean it." His hand reached for hers and squeezed so hard it almost hurt.

Her eyes blazed for an angry second. "Whether you meant it or not is immaterial. What you said is true." Jerking her hand free from his grasp, she continued to stare out the window, blind to anything but the ache that throbbed in her heart.

The next thing Leah knew, she was being gently shaken awake. "Leah," Cain whispered beside her ear. "Lunch is arriving."

To her acute embarrassment, Leah realized that in her sleep she had used Cain's shoulder as a pillow.

"I would have let you sleep, but I don't want you missing any meals." Her fiery gaze produced a soft chuckle from him. "Now, now, my dear, we're going to spend two months together. There's no call to be testy at the start of our adventure."

Their flight between Los Angeles International Airport and Sydney, Australia, was fourteen hours and spanned two calendar days because they crossed the international date line.

Although Leah slept—or made a pretense of sleeping—almost the entire time, she was exhausted when they touched down in Sydney.

Like a puppet with no will of its own, she followed

Cain out of the plane, through customs, and into the taxi that delivered them to the hotel.

Not until they were in the lobby, with people bustling around them in a flurry of activity, did Leah acknowledge how drowsy she was. Sitting on the edge of her suitcase, Leah waited while Cain signed the register and murmured something that caused the man at the counter to smile.

"Welcome to Sydney, Mr. and Mrs. Hawkins," the bellhop said in greeting as he held up the key to one room.

Chapter 4

"Just what do you think you're doing?" Leah whispered fiercely while they waited for the elevator. "I insist on having my own room."

"Leah, darling," Cain murmured, smiling beguilingly behind clenched teeth. "Let's not air our dirty laundry in the hotel lobby."

"I refuse to sleep in the same room with you. Isn't that clear enough, or do I need to shout it?" She ground out the words angrily, unconcerned if anyone was listening or not. She was tired and crabby, and she didn't want to stand outside an elevator arguing with the infuriating Cain Hawkins.

Whistling, his hands clasped behind his back, the bellhop gave no indication he heard any of her angry tirade, although Leah noticed that he avoided looking directly at her.

The heavy metal doors of the elevator swished open, and pressing a firm hand at the small of her back, Cain escorted Leah inside. "We'll talk about it later," he returned just as insistently. "Not here and not now. Understand?"

With cool haughtiness, Leah stood with her back ramrod straight, counting the orange lights that indicated the floors they were passing. Chancing a glance at Cain as they left the elevator, Leah found that his gaze was opaque, his face schooled to show none of his thoughts. Not so much as a twitch of a nerve or a flicker of an eyelash disclosed his feelings. And yet, she could feel the frustration and anger that exuded from him with every breath.

The bellhop opened the door to the suite and delivered their baggage with an economy of movement, seemingly eager to be on his way as quickly as possible.

Leah offered him an apologetic smile as he hurried past her. With her arms crossed, Leah was determined to stand in the outside hall until Cain acquiesced to her demand to sleep in a room of her own.

"Are you coming in or not?" Cain's eyes sliced into her from the other side of the doorway.

"Not."

"For for the love of heaven, be reasonable, will you?" Cain's weary frown revealed the extent of his fatigue and the fragile thread that held back his anger. "If you think I'm going to attack you, then rest assured, I'm too tired to do anything, and that includes arguing with you."

"It's not unreasonable to want some privacy."

"I requested two beds. That, at least, should please you." A hint of amusement touched his dusky, dark eyes. "I told the hotel clerk that my wife snores."

"There's no way I'm going to spend the night in that room with you," she replied in a taut voice. "And, for your information, I don't snore."

Rubbing a hand over his tired eyes, Cain released an

irritated breath and slowly shook his head. "All right, come in and I'll phone the front desk and arrange for another room. You can have this one. I'll move."

"Thank you." But there was no sense of triumph as Leah crossed the threshold into the hotel room.

The suite was surprisingly large, with huge picture windows that granted a spectacular view of Sydney and the harbor below. Leah's eye caught a fleeting glimpse of the renowned Sydney Opera House, and her first impression was that the huge white structure resembled oversized sails billowing with wind.

The two beds dominated the room and shared a common nightstand where the telephone rested. Cain sat on the edge of the mattress and reached for the phone.

"Leah, won't you kindly reconsider? What if the government official for the Diamantinas hears that we insisted on separate rooms? He may wonder if we're really married."

"I brought a copy of the wedding certificate." She had already anticipated a problem there. "We were married in a civil ceremony and I have the paper that proves it."

"Barely civil, as I recall."

Cain's sarcasm was lost on her. He could throw all the barbs he wished and nothing would affect her. She was simply too tired to care.

The silence became oppressive as Leah lifted her overnight bag onto the top of the mattress and removed the things she needed. Her fingers shook slightly, and she could feel Cain's gaze following her movements, his mouth ominously taut.

Without another word, he called the front desk. She waited until he'd finished before she spoke. "If you'll excuse me, I'd like to freshen up before going to bed." With her nightgown and bathrobe draped over her arm, she paused. "You will be gone before I'm finished?"

His look was filled with angry resentment. "Would it be too much to ask to let me stay here until there's another room available?"

"Of course not. I didn't mean . . ." Everything was going wrong. She hadn't meant to sound like such a prude, but if he were to see her in the revealing nightgown, he'd know how thin she was, and how flat-chested. She might be exhausted, but this was a matter of pride.

"Take your bath," he demanded tightly. "I'll do my best to be out of here."

"Thank you." An odd breathlessness came over her. The door to the bathroom clicked closed, and she prayed the soothing water would dispel the black mood that wrapped itself around her like a cloak of gloom. His heartless words on the plane returned to taunt her. Cain believed she was ugly. She knew that herself, so it shouldn't bother her. But for a minute, just one moment, he had made her believe that she could be beautiful. His cruelty had ruined that and set the record straight.

The water lapping against the edge of the tub had cooled before Leah could summon the energy to climb out of the comforting water. She took longer than usual drying off in the hopes that Cain would have gone and he wouldn't see her. But if he did, that couldn't be helped, and she was determined to hold her head high and ignore any sarcastic comment. Loosely tying the sash around her narrow waist, she squared her shoulders, mentally preparing herself for the coming assault. She'd known from the beginning how intuitive Cain Hawkins was, but she had only suspected his ruthlessness. Within minutes he had recognized her vulnerability, and he had no compunction against using it to his advantage.

The sun had set, casting the room in hues of pink. As she opened the bathroom door, Leah's gaze was drawn magnetically to the scene outside her window. It reminded her of some of the magnificent sunsets she'd seen in Cain's books—the brilliant golden orb low on the horizon; the silhouettes of a hundred skyscrapers reflected in shades of red. From the scene outside her window, Leah's gaze sought the man who dominated her thoughts. A soft smile touched her eyes as she found him sprawled across the top of the mattress sound asleep. Slumber relaxed the lines of his face and made him seem younger. Unexpectedly, a surge of something akin to tenderness brushed her heart. She admired and respected Cain the photographer, but Cain the man was a dangerous puzzle.

An extra blanket was folded on the shelf in the closet across from the bathroom. Standing on tiptoe, Leah brought it down, then gently laid it over his shoulders.

Standing above him gave her the opportunity to study his face. Relaxed, it had a childlike vulnerability. The deeply etched lines about his eyes showed faded areas where the sun hadn't tanned his skin. His hair needed trimming; it curled upward slightly at the base of his neck. Leah had thought he would cut it before they left California, but clearly she couldn't second-guess Cain. He was his own man and would wear his hair down the middle of his back if he wanted. A lazy smile curved the corners of her mouth. The urge to reach out and touch him was almost irresistible. What she was experiencing, she decided, was a latent maternal instinct.

Leah had just peeled back the sheets to her bed when the phone rang urgently. She grabbed it and whispered into the receiver, not wanting to wake Cain. "Hello?"

"Mrs. Hawkins?"

"Yes . . ." It was on the tip of her tongue to correct him and explain that her name was Talmadge.

"Your husband requested another room. We have that suite available for him." The clerk sounded friendly and helpful.

"I apologize for any inconvenience, but we won't be needing the extra room."

"That's no problem," the man assured her. "Gudday."

"Gudday," Leah answered with a tired smile, and replaced the receiver.

A glance at Cain assured her that the phone hadn't awakened him. With the alarm set on her cell, Leah slipped her long legs between clean, fresh sheets. Her forearm was tucked under her pillow as she stared across the narrow space that separated her from Cain. Her eyes drifted closed, but she forced them open again, desiring one last look at Cain before she slept. Her last thought before she slid into peaceful surrender was that she was glad he was there.

A sharp clicking noise found its way into her warm dream and Leah winced, irritated to have her fantasy interrupted. She was on the rubber raft off Kahu, the island where they'd be staying, when forty tons of whale broke the surface amid a storm of spray. Excitement caused her heart rate to soar. These marvelous giants of the sea were her greatest love.

The clicking sound returned and was soon followed by

another. Grumbling at the intrusion, Leah rolled over, bringing the sheets with her.

"Good morning, lady."

Cain. Her eyes flew open. He was in the room with her, and that awful sound was his camera.

"It's a beautiful morning," he continued, undaunted by her irritated grumble.

She struggled to a sitting position, keeping the blanket under her neck. "What time is it?" she asked, rubbing the weariness from eyes that refused to focus.

"Six." Cain was balanced on the arm of the chair and leaned against the window, snapping pictures of the city below. "Breakfast is on the way," he announced without turning around. "And you're right, you don't snore." He paused and turned to her, his gaze gently examining her face, lingering for a heart-stopping second on her lips. "But you do gurgle."

"I don't, either," she snapped.

"Oh." He jumped down from the chair and smiled broadly. "And when was the last time you slept with someone who'd know?"

The quick flow of color into her face caused Leah to cover her hot cheeks with her hands.

Cain's laugh was low and sensuous. "Just as I suspected."

"I should have had you carted out of here." She wasn't up to trading insults with him. Not this early in the morning, when she hadn't had her first cup of coffee.

"You probably should have," he agreed. "But I'm glad you didn't."

"How could I? You were sound asleep by the time I got out of the bath."

"Was I?" Cain teased softly, sitting on the edge of his unmade bed and fiddling with his camera lens.

Leah went cold, then hot. "You mean . . ." Flashing hazel eyes darted him a fiery glare. So he'd been playing a game with her last night as she stood above him and felt that surge of tenderness. Siggy was right, Cain Hawkins wasn't to be trusted. Not even for a minute.

A suggestion of controlled amusement was in the slight curl of Cain's upper lip, and her palm itched to slap that awful grin from his face.

"That was a rotten thing to do," she stormed, reaching for her robe at the end of the bed. "You really are unscrupulous. Siggy warned me about you. He said—"

Cain's sword-sharp gaze silenced her immediately and pinned her against the bed. "Listen and listen good, Leah. I won't have lover boy's name tossed at me for the next two months. Yearn for him all you want, but don't mention his name again. Understand?"

The violence with which he spoke shocked her, and she blinked back in surprise. She didn't know why Cain disliked Siggy so much, but it put her in an uncomfortable position. If he didn't want her to mention Siggy, then she wouldn't. But it didn't make sense. Cain stood and crossed the room, his hands stuffed into his pockets. He stood with his back to her, granting her the privacy to climb out of bed. "Breakfast will be here any minute. Maybe you should dress now."

Heeding his advice, Leah fairly flew into the bathroom, dragging her overnight case with her.

The flight between Sydney and Perth took the better part of the day. As a seasoned traveler, Cain didn't seem to be troubled with jet lag, but Leah felt as if she'd been turned inside out. Not only were they eighteen hours ahead of California time, but the seasons were reversed, and what had been lingering autumn days in San Diego had turned into early spring "down under." Dr. Brewster had warned her that it would take several days for her body to adjust, and Leah acknowledged wryly that he was more than right. It didn't seem to matter that she'd had a good night's sleep in Sydney and had slept extensively on the flight from California. She felt a weariness that reached all the way to her bones.

They were met at the airport in Perth by a government official from the Diamantinas. Dressed in a dark business suit, he was tall, with intensely dark eyes.

"Welcome to Perth," he said, shaking Cain's outstretched hand, then doing the same to Leah's. "My name is Hugh Kimo."

Dr. Brewster had mentioned that Hugh would be contacting them in Perth, and would later escort them to Ruaehu, the Diamantinas' capital city.

"My government is most anxious to have your stay in the Diamantinas be profitable to science and to man's understanding of our friends the whales." The formal speech was followed by a warm smile of welcome.

"Thank you," Cain said for them both. "And we're most eager to arrive and begin our study."

Their luggage was beginning to appear on the carousel, and Cain reached for a heavy suitcase.

"First," Hugh continued, "I want to assure you that the supplies you requested have been delivered."

"The parabolic microphone?" Leah questioned eagerly. The device would be invaluable for recording whale location, especially at night when she would be unable to view their progress from the lookout post hewed out of the rock cliff. In addition to studying migration routes, Leah hoped to investigate the sounds of the whales and their correlation to behavior. But that goal was secondary.

"Yes, the antenna has been installed according to your instructions." Hugh's smile was filled with pride. Leah's happy eyes met Cain's. They were so close now, that she regretted they wouldn't be leaving immediately for the islands. An extra day in Perth would only delay their study. Cain's look revealed that he, too, was eager.

"How soon can arrangements be made to leave for Ruaehu?" Cain asked. "As you can understand, both Mrs. Hawkins and I are eager to begin our research."

Research! Leah nearly laughed out loud. Cain's camera finger had been itching since before they left the airport. Already he'd taken scores of pictures of Sydney. And they'd only been there overnight.

Hugh Kimo laughed outright. "Dr. Brewster said that he doubted you two would remain in Perth for long. I'll make arrangements for you to fly to Ruaehu in the morning."

Leah was so excited that she had to restrain herself from throwing her arms around Cain's neck. Her goal was only hours away, and a deep sense of unreality remained. This adventure had been a dream for so many months that even now, when she was preparing to arrive, she couldn't believe it was all going to happen. Early tomorrow morning they would fly to the island's capital and leave the same afternoon for the cliff hut.

Cain's arm came around her shoulders and tightened in a brief hug.

"I'll be dropping you off at the hotel. Perhaps we could meet for dinner later?" Hugh Kimo continued. "There remain only a few details we need to discuss."

"We'll look forward to that," Cain assured the tall man.

The hotel was close to the airport, so that the drive was accomplished in only a few minutes. Hugh Kimo didn't come inside, but asked that they meet him in the lobby later that evening.

As the bellhop loaded their luggage onto the cart, Cain smiled down at Leah. Their delicate truce was holding, and she was convinced that maintaining peace between them was as important to Cain as it was to her.

A hand at her elbow, Cain directed her through the large double glass doors and into the hotel lobby. "I'll see about getting connecting rooms this time," he said somewhat dryly.

"I'd appreciate that," she murmured, feeling ridiculous.

Leah's room was connected to Cain's by a common door. With less than two hours before their dinner date with Hugh, Leah spent the time taking a long, luxurious bath and doing her hair. Rarely did Leah spend so much time on her appearance. But she reasoned that it would be a long time before she could pamper herself this way again.

Leah's spirits soared at the look Cain gave her when he joined her in her half of the suite. Automatically, he reached for his camera and was snapping pictures before she had a chance to protest. Long ago, Leah had learned to hate the camera. Her mother had claimed that Leah wasn't photogenic and that that was the reason her photos turned out as they did but Leah knew differently. A camera might distort a likeness to some extent, but mirrors didn't lie.

"Don't, please," she begged, casting her gaze down to the carpet.

"What's wrong?" Cain's look was bewildered as he lowered the sophisticated camera.

Turning, Leah made the pretense of checking inside her purse. "I just don't like having my picture taken, that's all."

"Why not?" he asked curtly.

"Because." She hated him for dragging this out.

"That's no reason." He was as determined to find out as she was not to tell him.

"Leah?" A hand at her shoulder turned her around. "Answer me." His enticing, velvet-smooth tone added to her confusion. She kept her eyes centered on the pattern of the carpet, unwilling to meet his gaze.

"Shouldn't we be in the lobby?" Her heart was doing a maddening drumroll that affected her voice so that it trembled softly from her lips.

"Hugh won't be there for another fifteen minutes."

"Please," she begged, hating the crazy weakness that was attacking her knees. His hand that cupped her shoulder seemed to burn through the navy-blue wool dress and sear her sensitive skin. It was unfair that his touch should affect her this way. Her fingers were clenched in front of her, her knuckles white.

"All right, I won't force the issue." He dropped his hand and returned briefly to his room to store the camera.

When he returned, Leah noted that his mouth was curved cynically, adding harshness to his uneven features.

"Are you angry?"

He looked up, surprised. "No, should I be?"

Gently, she shook her head and reached for her room key, which lay on top of the dresser. Forcing her chin up, she offered him a weak smile. "Shall we go?"

Hugh Kimo was waiting for them in the lobby as arranged. His car was just outside the hotel. The restaurant on the beach where he took them specialized in lobster, one of Leah's favorite foods.

Although she joined in the conversation, her gaze drifted constantly to the ocean and the pure white beach. Cain's eyes followed hers, and when their gazes met once, briefly, he smiled, letting her know he thought the scene just as beautiful as she did.

The meal was fantastic, and just when Leah was convinced she couldn't eat another thing, Cain ordered dessert for her.

"Cain," she whispered nervously as she smoothed her hand over the white linen napkin on her lap. "Really, I couldn't eat anything more."

"I'm fattening her up," Cain explained with a chuckle to Hugh Kimo.

His laugh infuriated her all the more, and her heart beat with frustration. When the chocolate torte was delivered, Leah tilted her chin a fraction of an inch in a gesture of pride. Her murky brown eyes flashed with avenging sparks that told Cain exactly what he could do with his high-handed methods.

Shaking his head in mock disgust, Cain reached over and took the dessert and ate it himself.

Leah was surprised when Cain suggested that he and Leah would return to the hotel by taxi. Outside the restaurant, they shook hands with their host and agreed upon a time to meet in the morning, then watched as Hugh drove away.

"You don't mind, do you?" Cain asked, casually draping his arm across her shoulders. "A walk along the beach will do us both good."

"I'd like that." She forgot about being angry over the dessert. Having lived in Southern California all these years, Leah was ashamed to admit that the only time she had been to the beach was for her work.

She didn't protest when Cain's arm moved to her waist. As he'd mentioned several times, they were a team. And if she was honest, she'd admit that she enjoyed being linked with Cain.

A crescent moon lit their way down the flawless beach. Sand sank deep into her pumps, and Leah paused to slip her shoes from her feet, loving the feel of the cool, damp sand.

"Tomorrow night we'll be on the island," Cain said, his voice coated with eagerness.

"I've waited so long for this." She recalled how excited she'd been when Dr. Brewster first considered her for this assignment. And later, how thrilled she'd felt when she learned that the world-famous photographer Cain Hawkins would be coming with her. Little had she dreamed that she would be accompanying him as his wife.

They walked so far that the lights of the restaurant behind them looked like fireflies on a summer's eve.

"Cold?" Cain's deep voice was disturbingly close to her ear.

"No," Leah breathed with difficulty. Cain was pressed much closer to her side than necessary. His hand at her waist had slid up so that it rested just beneath her breast. Unbidden, unwanted, the thought came to her, and she wondered insanely what it would be like if Cain were to caress her breasts. Would their smallness disappoint him? A shudder of longing shook her.

"You are cold." Cain sounded almost angry as he released her and yanked his jacket from his arms to place it over her shoulders.

Humiliating color flowed into her face, and she lowered her gaze, afraid he would read the desire in her eyes.

"Are you warmer now?" he asked. His hands remained at her neck.

"Yes . . . yes." Her voice was low and throbbing.

"Leah." His finger under her chin raised her eyes to his. "What's wrong?"

Desperately she shook her head. A bubble of apprehension was lodged in her throat; she doubted she could have spoken if her life depended on it.

"Leah." Her name was a whispered caress. In the dim light of the moon, he lowered his mouth to hers in a feather-light kiss that lasted but an instant.

Closing her eyes to the delicious sensations that wrapped themselves around her, she swayed toward him slightly.

Hands at her shoulders, Cain paused and waited as if he expected her to reject him. But she couldn't. Not when for days she'd really been wanting him to kiss her. Not when she yearned for the feel of his body close to hers. Not when the man holding her was her husband.

His hands eased up from her shoulders to the smooth line of her jaw, directing her face upward to meet the hungry descent of his mouth. With a small sigh of surrender, she parted her lips, eager to experience the depth and passion of his kiss.

Cain's mouth was on hers, hard and compelling, kissing her with a fierceness that stole her breath and rocked her to the core of her being. Again and again his mouth sought hers until her arms slid convulsively around his neck and she clung to him. Her fingers ruffled through the thick growth of his dark hair, loving the feel of it.

"Leah?" He was asking so much with just the sound of her name. He wanted her. Now. Here. On the sand. And she hadn't the will to refuse him.

"I need you," he whispered urgently against her lips. He seemed to want her to tell him how much she needed him. But she couldn't. The only sounds that passed from her lips were small, weak cries of longing. She had never felt anything this strong and overpowering.

"Tell me you want me." His voice was a hoarse whisper as he ordered her to answer him. His hands were driving her to the limit of her endurance as they roamed her back and buttocks, arching her against his hard body. Still she couldn't; words were impossible as she struggled to speak. Cain buried his face in the gentle curve of her neck, kissing her hungrily.

Suddenly, abruptly, he stopped, and with a tortured sigh, he pushed himself away.

Bereft, Leah was left to face the cold, her shoulders heaving with shock. Cain was taking in deep breaths of air, fighting for control.

"Cain?" She blinked, still not comprehending what had happened.

Without a word, Cain reached out a hand and lifted

the small gold heart that was nestled in the hollow of her throat. The heart Siggy had given to her.

"I promised that I'd send you back pure as the driven snow to that bastard. And I intend to keep my word." He let the heart drop back against her skin.

Instinctively her hand reached for the heart, her fingers nervously toying with it.

"As long as you continue to wear that necklace, I won't touch you. Understand?"

Wordlessly Leah nodded, telling him that she did.

"Then let's get back to the hotel. We have a big day tomorrow. We'll need a good night's sleep."

But neither of them got one, Leah was convinced. Back at her suite she lay awake, thinking of Cain.

The fierce wind bobbed the motorboat like a toy upon the rough waves.

"There's a storm coming," Hugh Kimo shouted, trying to be heard above the roar of the wind and sea. "I'm afraid I won't be able to stay on the island long."

"Don't worry. Once our things have been unloaded, there isn't any reason for you to stay."

Hugh looked relieved and nodded appreciatively.

The spray from a large wave splashed against Leah's face, and she wiped the moisture aside. No longer was she able to keep watch ahead as the wind and sea tossed their craft at will.

Everything had been going smoothly as they crossed the five miles of water that separated the main island from the smaller one of Kahu. The squall had come on quickly and without warning.

Suddenly a cloud burst overhead and thick drops of rain began pounding at them from every side. Someone handed Leah a slicker to protect her from the downpour. She slipped her arms into sleeves that were miles too long.

The motorboat hit the sandy beach with a heavy thud, and Leah was jerked forward unexpectedly. Cain's arm prevented her from slamming into the side of the boat. She tried to thank him, but the wind carried her voice in the opposite direction.

Once they were beached, there was a flurry of activity as the boat was unloaded and the luggage carried up the rickety stairs that led to the cliff house. Leah stayed at the boat to make sure nothing was left behind.

"The radio . . ." Hugh began haltingly.

"Yes . . . yes." Cain nodded sharply. "I've worked one before. Don't worry, I'll take care of everything. Go while you've got the chance." He waited until Hugh and his men were back inside the boat before pushing against the side of it, guiding it back into the water.

Leah returned Hugh's hand signal. They had arrived and were safe.

Cain didn't try to speak as he helped her up the wooden steps built into the steep cliff. Leah was panting when they reached the top, and she paused for a moment to catch her breath.

The heavy wooden door to the hut was open, their luggage set just inside. Leah and Cain stumbled into the large room. The area to her left would serve as their kitchen. An old black stove and a small table were set against one wall. To the right was a much larger table stacked high with the equipment they had requested. Two doors led off from the main room.

Stripping the wet coat from her arms, Leah moved into the place she would call home for two long months.

Cain closed the door, blocking out the fierce sound of the wind. "That was quite a welcome," he murmured, removing his drenched jacket.

"I'm hoping this storm moves out as fast as it came."

"It should." But Cain didn't sound overly confident.

Now that they had arrived, their work was only beginning. Lifting a suitcase, Leah moved to carry it toward the bedroom.

Cain stopped her, his large frame blocking the door. "Before you go in there, I think I should tell you there's a small problem."

Her searching gaze sought his. "What?"

As Cain swung open the door, Leah felt a sinking feeling attack her stomach. The room—indeed, the entire hut—contained only one bed. A double one.

Chapter 5

"I assumed . . . I thought . . ." Leah stuttered, feeling the blood drain from her face, leaving her waxen and unnaturally pale. In the past week they'd nearly worked themselves to exhaustion to meet their self-imposed schedule. The sleeping arrangements hadn't crossed Leah's mind. Not once. How incredibly stupid she'd been.

"I take it you don't want to share the bed?" Cain mocked lightly.

"Absolutely not. I don't even want you in the same room." Crossing her arms to ward off a sudden chill, Leah paced the compact area that comprised their living quarters.

Doing a quick survey of their stark quarters, her eyes gleamed with satisfaction. "That table would work." She pointed to the one stacked with boxes at the other end of the room.

"As a bed?" Cain looked shocked. "Leah, that table is meant to be used as a desk. We're going to need it. Be reasonable, will you?"

"So what's to say we can't clear it off every night? You

don't have to do it, I will," she volunteered, her voice sharp and vigorous. "It'll be my responsibility."

"Are you offering to sleep there as well?" Cain cut in sarcastically. "Because I have no intention of doing so. I have work to do, and there's no way I'm sleeping on a narrow table to satisfy your perverted sense of modesty."

"All right, I don't blame you. I'll sleep there." Her fingers closed tightly over the back of the chair until she feared her nails would snap. "I don't mind. Really."

The scowl darkening Cain's features revealed what he thought of the idea. But the shrug he gave her was indifferent. "If that's what you want, feel free."

The storm grew in intensity; a demon wind howled outside until Leah was sure the small dwelling would be torn from its foundation. The storm in her heart raged with the same intensity. This situation was quickly going from bad to worse and she didn't need it. Of course Cain wanted to share the bed—and probably whatever else he could take. He didn't have anything to lose. But Leah wasn't fool enough to believe that once they returned to California it would make a difference. Without a care, without a thought, Cain would be on his way to the next adventure, to another assignment. After all, that was their agreement.

Her mind buzzing, Leah inspected the supplies she'd requested. Cain lit a fire in the cast-iron stove that would serve as a means of cooking and as their only source of heat.

"Where's the bathroom?" she asked shyly after a while. "I like to freshen up before dinner."

"Bathroom?" He cocked his brow in sarcastic amusement. "If you mean the outhouse, it's outside and fifty yards to your left."

Leah spun around. "You've got to be joking."

"Leah, this isn't exactly the Hilton. Didn't you stop to think about the living arrangements?"

Perhaps it was stupid not to have considered the more mundane aspects of this expedition, but this cliff house hadn't entered her thoughts once. She wasn't here to vacation. "No," she admitted somewhat defensively. "There was so much else to consider that the living arrangements didn't enter . . ." Flustered now, she wiped her hand across her face. "I came to study the whales."

"And I came to take their pictures." His words were a subtle reminder that he wasn't on Kahu to steal her virginity. When she didn't respond, he turned his back to her. "I'll cook tonight and you can do the honors tomorrow."

"Fine."

Determined to make her plan work, Leah stepped to the table. She'd sleep there and make the best of it. Several boxes were stacked on top of each other, and Leah realized it would be a monumental task to unpack and assemble them tonight. Already she was tired, the effects of jet lag having hit her with as much impact as the storm.

While Cain worked silently in the kitchen area, Leah feverishly took down the boxes, examined their contents and set them aside. Most of the equipment, the telescopes and recorders, would be used exclusively by Leah. Since many of the tools she'd requested had to be run with batteries, she would need to conserve power.

The dim light cast from the two lanterns was barely

enough to work by, and before she was halfway finished, it became necessary to move one closer.

"Dinner's ready," Cain announced.

"I'm too busy right now."

A disgusted sound of exasperation came from him. "I don't care if you're busy or not, you're eating now."

If he made so much as one wisecrack about how she couldn't afford to skip meals, Leah was determined to dump his dinner over the top of Cain's arrogant head.

"In a minute."

"Now, Leah!" Cain repeated his demand. A muscle twitched warningly along the side of his jaw.

"Oh, all right," she conceded ungraciously, knowing it would be useless to argue. There would be far more serious matters to expend her energies on later. Like the matter of the bed.

They ate in silence, and afterward Leah washed the dishes, using water heated by the stove. Not until she'd finished did she realize that the storm outside had abated. Unfortunately, the one in her heart continued to rage.

"It's late," Cain announced without preamble.

He didn't need to remind her; she felt bone weary. "You go to bed. . . . I'll make do out here."

The deep-grooved lines beside his mouth went white. "Have it your way. There's a soft mattress in there or a hard, cold tabletop out here."

"I know," she replied miserably. The crazy part was that if she were shapely and beautiful, she wouldn't have minded nearly so much. Logic had nothing to do with it. Cain felt no constraint when commenting on her looks and figure. Long ago she had come to terms with her plainness, but at the same time Cain's remarks had the power to sting. Every thoughtless word he uttered cut her to the bone. With Cain out of the room, Leah examined the gold band on her ring finger. This single piece of gold Cain had placed on her finger had somehow allotted him the power to inflict pain. Leah could toss aside thoughtless, cruel words from other men. But not from Cain.

Carrying an armload of blankets, Cain returned to set them on top of the table. He hesitated. "Leah," he breathed slowly, carefully choosing words. "I swore I wouldn't touch you as long as you continued to wear . . . what's his name's . . . heart."

Unconsciously she reached for the necklace, rubbing the gold trinket between two fingers.

Her actions produced a heavy scowl from Cain. "We're here alone. Trust is essential. I promised not to touch you, and I'll keep my word."

Holding a thick wool blanket against her stomach, Leah cast her gaze to the plain wood floor. "I . . . prefer to stay out here." In some ways Leah was more afraid of her response to Cain than any fear that he would take her against her will.

Cain threw up his hands. "Have it your way, then." He returned to the bedroom and left the door ajar.

Mumbling under her breath, admitting she was a fool, Leah spread out a couple of blankets for padding on the table's hard surface. With the pillow in place, she climbed on top and spread the warm wool blanket over her. The first thing she readily acknowledged was how incredibly unyielding a table was. And dressed in jeans and a sweater wasn't exactly conducive to a good night's sleep, either. Lying on her side with her forearm tucked under the feather pillow, she leaned over and turned off the lantern.

The hut became pitch-black, so dark that a shiver of nervous apprehension raced up her spine.

"Good night," Cain called out, and she cursed him silently for sounding so comfortable.

"Good night," Leah returned, forcing a cheerful, happy note into her voice. After everything else she'd gone through to come to this island, a tabletop for a bed was something she could do without.

Ten minutes later, her own bones causing her the most discomfort, Leah rolled over. The wool blanket fell to the floor. "Damn," she muttered impatiently, and reached for it. To her horror her whole body slid off the table, and with a frightened cry she landed with a loud thump on the cold, hard floor.

"What happened?" Cain shouted.

Although she couldn't see him in the dark, she knew from the direction of his voice that he was standing in the doorway of the bedroom.

"Nothing, I . . . I fell off the table, that's all."

"Are you okay?"

He didn't need to sound so smug, she fumed. "Fine," she answered, doing her best to sound just as amused.

Situated atop her makeshift bed once again, Leah forced her eyes closed and did her utmost to fall asleep. An hour later, cuddled in a tight ball to keep warm, she rolled over and, to her horror, tumbled off the side of the table again. Landing with a jarring thud, she was too stunned to move. Her breath came in uneven gasps.

"That does it." The unrestrained fury in Cain's voice tightened the muscles of her stomach. "I've had it."

"I'm fine . . . I just fell . . . again, that's all." Her voice thinned to a quivering note as she heard Cain storm into the room.

"Where's the lantern?" he shouted at her. Before she could answer, he crashed into a cardboard box, knocking it over. His cry of pain filled the room as the contents of the crate spilled onto the floor.

Struggling to a standing position, Leah blindly reached out for him. Her groping arm came in contact with the solid wall of his chest. "You okay?"

"No, and I'm damn mad. You're coming into that bed before your stubbornness kills us both."

"I won't."

Cain snorted.

"I won't," she repeated.

Cain said nothing, but an arm looped around her waist and lifted her off the floor. Against his superior strength, her weak struggles were a futile effort.

The next thing Leah knew she was falling through space to land on a soft cushion of comfort and warmth. A hand on each shoulder held her in place. "Now listen, and listen good." Cain spoke with infuriating calm. "You're sleeping here tonight and so am I. To soothe the outraged virgin in you, I'll remain outside the covers. Understand?"

"Yes." Her soft voice was pitifully weak.

He released her and pulled back the thick layer of blankets. "Get in."

Wordlessly she did as he demanded, feeling incredibly small and stupid.

Once she was in place, he lowered his weight beside her and rolled over so that she was presented with a clear view of his back. Within minutes his even breathing assured Leah he was asleep. Soon after that she fell into an uneasy slumber.

And so their adventure began. The first week was spent unloading and setting up the monitoring equipment. In this area, Cain was an invaluable aid. At night, exhausted, they fell into bed, Leah under the covers, Cain curled up with a wool blanket on top of them. And every morning, to her utter embarrassment, Leah woke with her arms wrapped around Cain's lean ribs, her head pillowed by his broad chest. Drawn by his warmth and comforted by his arms, she came to him naturally in her sleep.

Waking first, Leah would slip from his loose hold, praying that he would never be the wiser. If he was aware of the way she unconsciously reached for him, he never spoke of it. For that, Leah would be eternally grateful. She found the situation embarrassing in the extreme.

The sixth day after their landing, Leah spotted her first whales. She'd discovered that, although the telescopes allowed her to view miles of water, it was easier to stand and look over the rolling waves of the Indian Ocean using her field glasses.

The vast, dark shapes resembled huge black submarines. As the massive forty-ton creatures came closer to shore and into her view, Leah realized that these were the first in the large family of right whales, southern right whales, a once-abundant species that was now among the rarest.

"Cain," she screamed, pointing toward the lolling creatures. "They're here."

Standing on the beach far below, Cain shielded his eyes

from the sun to study the swelling seas. Turning, he signaled that he'd be right up. In record time he was at her side.

"Holy Moses, look at those babies." Crouched down behind his camera, Cain began working at a furious speed. The clicking noise was repeated so fast that the sound blended to a low hum. "Humpbacks, right?"

"No." Laughing, Leah shook her head. "Southern rights."

"Right? That's not any kind of name for a whale."

"The sailors of old named them that because they were the right ones to hunt," Leah explained. "They float after death and can easily be towed to shore or butchered at sea." She winced as she explained, hating the thought of any of these lovely, graceful creatures dying such a brutal death at the hands of man.

The entire afternoon was spent watching the herds frolic close to shore. Cain was in photographer's heaven, carrying cameras and equipment between the beach and Leah's perch on the cliff top.

Now that the first pods were arriving, Leah wanted to secure the sonar equipment in place. In the morning they would take out the motorized rubber raft and anchor three transmitters. The underwater microphones suspended from them would catch the whales' sounds.

In the evening, when Cain radioed his report to Hugh Kimo in Ruaehu, he asked Hugh to send up a spotter plane in the morning to report the whales' course.

"What's all this sonar equipment going to tell you?" Cain asked as she finished with the evening dishes.

Leaning a hip against the sink, Leah wiped the last plate clean with a dishcloth, her hands continuing to rub in a circular motion long after the plate was dry. "Several things. First, I don't need to keep my eyes peeled on the ocean or count on the Cessna to know when they're coming. And second, I'm hoping to monitor and record the whale sounds. Later, when I'm back at the university, I'll study the sound waves to see if I can further decipher their meaning."

"Like breaking a code?"

"Exactly." She smiled, pleased at his interest. "Oh, Cain, this is so exciting I can hardly stand it." Her heart swelled with joy.

Gingerly, she put the plate aside and set the kettle back on the stove to heat. "Coffee?"

"Please." Cain delivered his cup to her, coming to stand at her side. His eyes studied her, narrowing slightly. The last time he'd looked at her that way had been in California, when he'd told her she was lovely. Her cheeks warmed with rising color, and she glanced away.

"It's been quite a day," she murmured as a means of breaking the uneasy silence. When she did look up, it was a mistake; she recognized it immediately. The warmth and nearness of his body were distractions she couldn't ignore.

Those wonderful, intense eyes were fixed on her moist lips. Leah couldn't stop staring at him. Nervously, her fingers tightened around the empty mug. His gaze was bright and glittering, his desire evident with every breath he drew. A mere inch separated them, and Leah could see every line in his sun-bronzed face, every pore, every lash. His mouth, hard and straight, was silently beckoning her to come taste the pleasure of his kiss.

A surge of longing raged through her, and Leah shuddered slightly. Cain saw it and his nostrils flared. Their eyes were locked in a silent battle of wills. He wanted her to come to him, to make the first move. She couldn't. How much better it would be if Cain had never kissed her, had never shown her the marvels of his touch. For today, this minute, he filled her senses. But reality was only weeks away, and she couldn't allow the beauty of this island, of this time, to sway her.

Every beat of her heart was demanding that she step into his arms, but somehow, somewhere deep inside a strength she didn't know she possessed came to her rescue and she resisted.

"You said you wanted coffee?"

"Yes, I did."

Her hand shook as she poured him a cup. Cain took it and returned to the desk, sitting with his back to her.

Several hours later, Leah pretended she was asleep when Cain came to bed. Her back was to him as he eased his weight onto the soft mattress and stretched out beside her. Leah didn't know how any two people could be so close and yet have the whole universe stretch between them.

The wind whipped Leah's long blond hair about her face as the rubber raft skipped across the top of the waves. A feeling of exhilaration caused her heart to soar. Behind her, in the rear of the raft, Cain sat beside the motor.

Leah planned to place the sonar equipment in a huge triangle, each underwater microphone separated by half a mile. Earlier, Hugh had radioed the location of approaching whale pods, and it was now their job to get the equipment in place before the whales arrived.

They had just finished placing the third and final orange buoy in the swelling water when Cain pointed to a huge shape in the distance. Leah turned just in time to see the great right whale hurl itself out of the water. The huge mammal was as black as a raven's wing and as sleek as silk. It hit the ocean surface with a boom that sounded like a cannon blast. Water sprayed in every direction, and although they were a safe distance, a few drops managed to wet them.

Cain, with his ever-ready camera, took a series of shots and beamed her a brilliant smile, giving her the thumbs-up signal. The triumph, however, soon drained from Cain's eyes to be replaced with a wary light. "He's coming our way. Should I try to outrun him?"

"We can't." Leah's heart moved to her throat as the creature, fifty feet long and weighing at least a ton for every foot, approached and circled their rubber raft. "Cut the engine," Leah cried.

Cain did as she asked, but his look was skeptical.

"She may have a calf in the area and just wants to check us out to be sure we mean her no harm." Although Leah wouldn't admit it, she was frightened. Their rubber raft could be easily overturned, and with all the equipment Cain insisted on keeping around his neck, he'd sink straight to the bottom. Mentally, Leah chided herself for her crazy thoughts. They were about to become whale fodder, and she was worried that Cain wouldn't be able to stay afloat.

"Would it help if I promise to touch up her photo—you know, hide a few of those extra pounds?"

Before Leah could respond, the whale turned its tail flukes and swished the raft strongly from side to side, with Leah and Cain clinging for their lives. Leah held on to the edges in a death grip, closing her eyes to the terror that strangled her throat muscles. Their small raft was tossed about like a trembling leaf caught in an autumn windstorm.

A cry of pure terror froze in her lungs as the mammoth creature, tired of its game, backed up and, with its giant flukes, lifted the rubber raft, Cain and Leah inside, about six inches off the water's surface.

Tense, every cell, every muscle alert, Leah began to shake violently. Panic wouldn't allow her to breathe, and when she did, the air rasped painfully in her throat. Finally a noise penetrated her dulled senses: a clicking sound, followed by another and another, with whispered phrases of "Wow, fantastic, unbelievable."

Their lives were balancing precariously on the whim of a fifty-ton whale and Cain was taking pictures.

The rubber raft hung in the air for the longest minute of Leah's life; then the whale slowly, with the utmost control, lowered its flukes and deliberately set them back on the water unscathed.

Leah released a sigh of relief and tasted the blood in her mouth, unaware that all the while she'd been viciously biting her own lip.

For the first time Leah spotted two young calves who loafed nearby. Cain saw them at precisely the same moment as Leah, and again she heard a long series of clicks. More pictures.

The gargantuan creature circled the raft twice more before rejoining her young and swimming away.

"That had to be the most fantastic adventure of my life," Cain called, his voice heavy with excitement. "You won't believe the shots I got."

Leah couldn't believe that he could be that unaffected. She had faced a watery grave with Cain at her side and worried about his safety. All he'd thought about were his precious pictures.

Leah was silent until they reached the shore. Doing her best to restrain the growing dismay, she wordlessly helped him secure the raft. His eyes burned over her questioningly, but Leah paid no attention. Her only desire was to be away from him as soon as possible.

"Leah," Cain called to her as she raced up the wooden stairs, but again she ignored him.

When he arrived at the hut, Leah was pacing the floor, her arms crossed, her knuckles clenched. She stopped and glared at him with all the fury of her pounding heart.

Standing just inside the door, Cain regarded her grimly. "All right, let's have it. What's wrong?"

Her arm swung out as she pointed toward the ocean. "We could have been killed out there." Even speaking was difficult as the words crowded on her tongue and escaped on a giant rush of anger.

"Come on, Leah, that mama was just protecting her young. She gave us a warning, that's all."

His calm only served to fuel her fury. "And you loved it."

"You're this angry because I wasn't scared?"

"Are you so incredibly stupid that you don't know the destruction those whales are capable of? Our lives were in jeopardy."

"I wasn't unconcerned," he flared.

"You could have fooled me."

What really angered Leah was that her thoughts had been on Cain. Her fears had been more for him than for herself. Whirling, she stormed into the kitchen area and made herself lunch. Taking the sandwich with her, Leah picked up her gear and headed toward her observation point on the cliff top.

Cain looked stunned for a minute. "Where's my lunch?"

"Take a picture of mine and eat that," she shouted.

Leah didn't make it out the door. Cain's hand snaked out and gripped her arm, hauling her against him. "Leah, for the love of heaven, you're not making any sense."

Her shoulders heaved as she forcefully pushed herself free. "I should have known that you'd be more concerned about your stomach. That fits right in with your character."

"Would you be serious!"

"It's difficult to talk to a man whose hair is practically as long as my own."

Cain regarded her sharply, his eyes narrowed and confused. "My hair? We're arguing about my hair? For heaven's sake, woman, be real."

"You know what your problem is, Cain Hawkins? You don't care. Nothing in this world or the next is more important than those pictures you take. Not relationships. Not family. Nothing." Her sarcastic gaze blazed across his face. "The irony of it all is that you hide behind a lens and reveal your soul."

Cain clamped his mouth shut, but his eyes glinted dangerously.

"But once the camera is gone, there's only this . . .

this . . . immature idiot. A man who takes pride at shouting to the world that he doesn't care."

"Who gave you the right to dictate how I should live?"

"No one," Leah admitted dryly. Cain was incapable of understanding what had upset her. Care and consideration were beyond a man like Cain Hawkins. Everything today had been her fault. She'd allowed herself to get too close to Cain emotionally, allowed herself to care. Well, no more. He could rot and she wouldn't lift a finger to aid him.

He smiled, but his expression was decidedly unpleasant. "Go sit on your perch, Queen Leah, and when you've worked everything out in that twisted, irrational mind of yours, then maybe we can talk."

She scooted past him, but not before she was gifted with a hard, taunting smile and a verbal jab of his own. "If you want to bring up the subject of hair, then maybe you should consider cutting your own."

Leah usually wore her long blond hair tied back at the base of her neck. But today, her hair had somehow worked itself free during their ordeal with the whale. The long stringy strands hung limp and lifeless across her cheek.

"You're right," she muttered, dumping her lunch and binoculars in his arms. "You're absolutely right." Charging across the room, she flung open a drawer and took out a large pair of scissors.

"Leah?" Cain gasped. "I didn't mean—"

"Maybe not, but I did." Tilting her head to the side, she grabbed a handful of her hair and chopped away. Six inches fell to the floor. She quirked her head in the opposite direction and lopped off another handful, letting it fall heedlessly away. Her bangs followed next.

"Leah, stop," Cain shouted, and the horror in his voice made her look at the cold, hard floor now covered with a thick layer of golden hair. Shaken, Leah cupped her mouth as tears burned her eyes. The first drops scalded her cheeks as she recognized what she had done.

"Cain, oh, Cain." She raised stricken eyes to him and lifted a tentative hand to the side of her head. The clump her fingers investigated prompted a sob.

At her side, Cain removed the scissors from her numb fingers.

In her anger, she'd lashed out at him and ended up hurting herself even more. Her hair, her lovely golden hair, was the only beautiful asset she possessed. And now that, too, was ruined. Gently, Cain put his arms around her and held her as if he would never let her go. At first she shrugged, resisting his touch, but he would have none of it, holding her fast in his strong arms.

She cried then in earnest for caring so much and for hurting just as much because he didn't.

His kiss was at her temple, offering her the comfort she craved. Of their own volition, her arms slid around his waist, molding her slight frame to him, seeking his warmth.

Cain's healing lips found her eyes as he kissed aside each fresh tear. Unable to bear another moment of this torture, Leah tilted back her head so that her lips sought his first. Trembling, her mouth stroked his in a caress so light that it was tantalizing torment.

With a muted groan, Cain ravaged her lips as if he were starving for the taste of them. Leah met his urgent hunger with her own, winding her arms around his neck, her head thrown back under the force of his kiss.

Again and again he kissed her until he shuddered and left her lips to slide his mouth across one cheek. "Leah . . ."

"I was so scared," she wept. "I thought the whale would kill us, and all you cared about were your pictures."

"I'm sorry, love," he breathed into her ear. "So sorry."

"Hold me," she pleaded. "Just hold me." Her whole body trembled.

"Always," he promised. "Always."

Chapter 6

Taking a step backward, Cain cocked his head to study his handiwork. A pair of scissors dangled from his index finger as he positioned Leah's head first one way and then another before nodding slowly and smiling. "It doesn't look half bad, even if I do say so myself."

Tentatively, her fingers investigated the blunt cut, expecting to find gouges and nicks. Instead, her fingertips brushed against her exposed ear. With a rising sense of dread, she let her hand fall lifelessly to her lap. "It's horrible."

"The least you can do is look," Cain chastised, and gave her a small hand mirror.

Her reflection revealed incredibly sad eyes, red and glistening from recently shed tears. Her full lips were slightly swollen and tender from the heat of Cain's kisses. And her hair, her once-lovely long hair, was gone, replaced with short choppy curls. The sides were styled above her ears and then neatly tapered to the base of her neck. Leah couldn't remember the last time her hair had been this short—probably grade school. To his credit,

Cain had done an admirable job of softening the butchered effect resulting from her craziness.

He was right; her hair didn't look bad, but it wasn't her. The stranger whose face flashed back from the mirror was someone else. Siggy wouldn't know this woman, and upon her return she'd be forced to deal with his disapproval. Siggy had always loved her long hair.

"Well?" Cain waited for her approval.

"You did the best you could."

"Leah, you look fine. I mean it."

Standing, she brushed the blond hair from her shoulders and lap. The ache in her heart was heavy as she reached for the broom and swept up the remnants of what once had been her greatest asset. Never had she done anything so foolhardy. She'd behaved like a crazy woman, lashing out at Cain, and then destroying the one part of herself that was lovely.

Replacing the broom, she gave him a feeble smile. "I'd better get back outside." She retrieved the equipment, then paused in the doorway. "Thank you, Cain."

"Anytime." He let her go without an argument, for which she was grateful.

To Leah's surprise, the afternoon passed quickly as she charted her finds and recorded the various sounds of the whales on the battery-powered recorder. The sun was settling from an azure sky into a pink horizon when Cain reappeared. Usually he spent part of the afternoon with her, but today he'd granted her some badly needed privacy and she was grateful.

"How'd it go?" He stood at her side on the cliff top, gazing over the long stretch of rolling waves that crashed onto the virgin shore below. Silently he slipped his arm around her shoulders.

"I saw my first southern blue." Despite the despair that had wrapped itself around her only hours earlier, Leah's voice rose with enthusiasm. "It was magnificent."

"You say that every time," he teased.

"This time it's different. Blue whales are the largest creatures ever to inhabit the earth."

Cain's gaze was skeptical. "Larger than the dinosaurs?"

"Yup."

"You're kidding?" He looked genuinely surprised.

Laughing, she shook her head and slipped her arm around his waist. "I'm not. The largest whale ever recorded was a female blue that measured over a hundred and thirteen feet and weighed about a hundred and seventy tons."

"Wow." The hand that cupped her shoulder tightened, bringing her even closer to his side.

"To put that into perspective, that one blue whale weighed the equivalent of thirty-five elephants or more than two thousand humans." Having him hold her like this, linking herself to him, was flirting with danger, and Leah knew it. But his arm helped ease the ache in her heart, and she couldn't resist this small comfort.

"If you're trying to impress me, you just did."

"Good." Their eyes met, and by unspoken agreement they turned and sauntered lazily toward the hut.

"Now it's my turn to impress you," Cain murmured, his voice an intimate caress against the sensitive skin of her neck.

"Oh?" Quivers of awareness raced down her arms. It

cost her the earth to remain stoic. "And just how do you plan to do that?"

"Wait and see."

Leah didn't have to wonder long. When they reached the hut, Cain swung open the door, allowing Leah to step inside first. A flash of unexpected color captured her attention, and Leah gave a small cry of pleasure. In the center of the small wooden table was a handful of wildflowers. White, blue, and yellow blossoms stood proudly in an empty beer bottle that served as a vase.

"Oh, Cain, they're lovely." No man had ever given her flowers before, and happiness surged through her. These simple wildflowers were more precious to her than exotic orchids.

His eyes crinkled with a smile at her obvious pleasure. "I read somewhere once that flowers are supposed to lift a woman's spirits."

"Thank you." Impulsively her lips brushed his cheek. "They're beautiful."

"There's a method to my madness." He straightened and held out the chair for her. A half smile touched his hard mouth. "After dinner I want you to cut my hair. And when you do, I want to make sure you're in a happy mood."

Leah raised stricken eyes to him. "I can't cut your hair. Good grief, look what I did to my own."

"I took that into consideration."

Shock receded into astonishment. "You're serious, aren't you?"

"As far as I'm concerned, we have a deal. I cut your hair—now it's my turn."

"But—"

"It should have been trimmed weeks ago."

Leah opened her mouth to argue, but his look discouraged further discussion. She wasn't sure she could do as he asked, but clearly Cain wasn't going to let her out of it.

The meal, succulent white fish sautéed in a delicate wine sauce, was another surprise. Cain had spent the entire afternoon doing little things to lift her spirits. Not only had he hiked across the island in search of wildflowers, but he'd gone fishing. Leah loved him for it because she knew he'd much rather have been out with his camera.

When the table was cleared, Leah dried her damp palms on her thighs as Cain held out the scissors.

"You're sure?" she questioned for the tenth time in as many minutes.

"Leah!"

"All right, all right." He sat in the chair, and Leah draped a towel over his shoulders, using a clothespin to hold it together. Stepping back, she tilted her head to one side and bit into her bottom lip, unsure where she should begin. She chose the back of his head so he wouldn't see how badly her hands were shaking.

The comb brought the disobedient locks to order, and she ran her hand over his crown and down to his nape. The first snip would be the worst. His dark, silky hair curled over her finger. Holding her breath, she cut. She didn't take much, just enough to keep the length above his shirt collar. The dark strands fell to his shoulders and littered the floor. More confident now, Leah moved from his left side to his right, trying to keep the lengths evenly matched.

Content with her progress, Leah moved to stand in

front of him as she considered the best way to trim the crown of his head and the loose hair that fell haphazardly across his forehead. Cain seemed constantly to be brushing it aside.

"Well?" he teased. "You're looking at me as if you've seen my picture in the post office. Let me assure you, I'm not on the FBI's most-wanted list."

Not the FBI's list, but certainly on hers. The thought struck her dumb. She did want Cain. Siggy seemed a million miles away, and the necklace she wore felt like an albatross around her neck.

"Leah?" His hand reached for her waist. "Are you okay?"

"I'm fine." She forced a smile and ran her fingers through the hair at the top of his head, pretending she knew what she was doing. The gesture gave her time to align her wandering thoughts. Cain had made his position clear; giving him her heart would only complicate an already complex situation.

"Are you going to finish this or not?" he demanded irritably, beginning to squirm like a five-year-old. "I hate sitting still."

"All right, all right." She used the comb to lift the first locks and snipped carefully, fearful of cutting too much. As she worked, she inched closer and closer. Not until Cain's labored breathing disturbed her concentration did she realize that her breasts were directly in his line of vision. Abruptly, she stopped cutting as the color blossomed in her cheeks. She tried to ignore the obvious and concentrate on cutting his hair, but every move made her all the more aware of how intimate it was to stand so close to him. When she lifted her arms higher, her breasts brushed Cain's cheek, and he breathed in harshly and shifted to pull back from her.

Leah felt her face go ten shades of pink, but as hard as she tried she couldn't tame her body's response to him. Leah closed her eyes to the onslaught of foreign sensations that rushed over her with an intensity that made her knees go weak.

"That's enough." Abruptly Cain gripped her waist and pushed her back so he could stand. They faced one another, Cain unnaturally pale, the grooves bracketing his mouth white with barely restrained frustration.

Leah knew that her reddened cheeks were as bright as a lighthouse lamp. Surely Cain didn't think she'd purposely tried to seduce him.

Impatiently, he jerked the towel from his shoulders and tossed it on the table. "I'm going out for a while," he mumbled gruffly, and was gone before Leah could reorient herself.

She was reading when Cain returned an hour later. Or at least she made a pretense of being caught up in the book, hiding her face behind the large volume to disguise her uneasiness. Cain apparently didn't feel all that comfortable either, and ten minutes after his return he made an excuse and went to bed.

Leah waited until she was certain he was asleep before joining him. His body was turned away from hers, his back rigid. The mattress dipped as she slid under the blankets. Feeling more self-conscious than ever about their sleeping arrangements, Leah rolled onto her side and forced her eyes closed. It was a long time before she slid into peaceful slumber.

The early-morning light stirred her awake, and unconsciously she turned over, automatically seeking the comforting warmth of Cain's back. When she realized what she was doing, she jerked back. With a small gasp, she sat upright, surprised to find Cain's side of the bed empty.

The coffeepot on the stove was full, and a note propped up on the wooden table told her that he was going to the other side of the island and not to expect him back before late afternoon.

She crumpled up his brief message and tossed it inside the wrought-iron stove to burn. The coward! What did he think she was going to do, play Salome and entice him to her bed? In case he hadn't figured it out, he already was in her bed.

Dressing in washed-out jeans and an old sweatshirt, Leah was determined to make herself as unattractive as possible. To her deepest regret, that didn't take much doing.

By the time she'd positioned herself at the lookout perch, her temper had cooled. Within minutes, she was once again content with her world. Placing the earphones over her head, Leah recorded what she was sure was the courting ritual between two whales. The squeaky, high-pitched vibrations grew fainter and fainter as the whales headed south, but the simple message stirred a breath of excitement. A brief smile touched her eyes as she imagined Cain's look if she were to sing such a blatant song for him.

Later, she decided with a chuckle, she'd play back the tape for Cain and see what he thought. No! If she suggested that these sounds were a courting ritual, he could misinterpret her motives.

At noon, Leah spotted the largest pod she'd seen since

the first whales arrived. She was so busy documenting their numbers and route that she didn't break for lunch. When she glanced at her watch again it was past four. It didn't make sense to break for lunch now when dinner was only a few hours away.

Cain reappeared sometime after six. Not wanting to appear overanxious for his company, Leah did little more than acknowledge his wave. Mud caked his shoes and pants, and she wondered what adventures he'd gotten himself into today.

"I'm going in to wash up," he shouted as he threw open the door of the hut.

In other words, she was to give him a few minutes of privacy. Not that she minded. There were several things she wanted to do yet this afternoon. It went without saying that she'd missed him! As much as she hated admitting it, Cain's active involvement with her work had cemented a bond between them. The hours they had spent together in the sun were her most pleasant times on the island.

Leah was kneeling down, collecting her equipment, when the gentle breeze carried the sharp sound of the hut door slamming closed. She tossed a look over her shoulder and was shocked to see Cain's angry strides devouring the distance separating them. His fists were knotted at his sides, his hard features twisted with disdain. Leah couldn't imagine what she'd done to displease him.

Not allowing his anger to intimidate her, she rolled to her feet and brushed the sand and grit from her jeans. Squaring her shoulders, she met his fiery gaze with an outward calm.

"When was the last time you ate?" he demanded.

Leah cringed inwardly. Not that again! From the moment they'd arrived on the island, Cain had appointed himself her nutritionist. He cooked breakfast every morning and sat at the table with her until she'd finished eating. Although they divided the lunch duties, Cain insisted that she eat whether she was hungry or not. Rather than argue, Leah complied.

Her shrug of indifference only flamed his fury. "I am sick to death of having to babysit you."

The facade of indifference evaporated, and Leah flashed him a look as cold and brittle as an Arctic wind. Anger swelled up inside her. From the moment they'd stepped foot on this island, Leah had more than carried her share. "Babysit me!"

"What else do you call it when I'm forced to spoon-feed you three times a day?"

"I don't need a guardian," she snapped.

His face turned to hard, cold stone and filled with such intense anger that it frightened her. There was no reasoning with him, she told herself, and she wouldn't try again. He'd twist her words to suit his anger. It wouldn't do any good to provoke him. And, admittedly, part of her couldn't help cowering from the savage fury in his eyes.

He stormed away, descending the stairs to the beach far below, leaving Leah stunned and shaking. Her legs felt like rubber, and she sank to her knees in the sand. Although she made an effort to refocus her attention on her duties, she discovered she couldn't. Her hands shook, and she pressed her cool palms against her hot cheeks.

Cain didn't reappear until dinner was on the table. Without a word, he pulled out his chair and started eating, attacking his meat with a savagery that really was directed at her.

"The beef's already dead. There's no need to rekill it," Leah chided him.

Cain's jaw tightened ominously, and he shoved his plate aside and stalked into the bedroom. It struck Leah how ludicrous this whole situation was. If Cain weren't so serious, she'd have laughed.

Days stretched into weeks, and Cain acted as if he were on the island alone. It was as though he couldn't tolerate being around her. Leah didn't know what she'd done that was so terrible, but after a while she gave up trying to guess. When she spoke to him, he snapped one-word replies. What he did with his time, she could only guess. He disappeared in the morning and returned late in the afternoon.

At night they would lie side by side, not speaking, barely moving, the sound of their breathing filling the strained silence. She was convinced that if Cain edged any closer to the side of the bed, he'd fall off.

Leah felt trapped in a maze with no exit. She was thoroughly confused and bewildered by his actions. The afternoon she'd cut his hair, Cain had seemed profoundly affected by what had happened. He'd wanted her. She wasn't so naïve and inexperienced that she didn't recognize that. Yet, he had rejected her and hadn't treated her the same since. Whatever it was that was troubling Cain had destroyed their friendship.

Leah's fingers toyed idly with the gold heart hanging from her neck. She missed Cain's friendship, missed sharing her findings about the whales. She'd been lonely and hurt these past weeks. Part of her longed to reach out and touch him, yet she couldn't, and a sadness seemed to press heavily on her chest.

Her dreams that night were heavy and dark. She was on the rubber raft alone, pulling up the sonar equipment while Cain stood watching from the beach. Out of nowhere came the blue whale. Its huge flukes rose out of the sea and slammed into the ocean surface, flooding the small raft. Leah clung for her life. Frantically she cried out for Cain to help her, but he was intent on taking her picture and ignored her pleas. Trapped on the surging waves, Leah was tossed into the dark depths of the ocean. Water closed over her, but she clawed her way to the surface. Salt water filled her mouth and eyes, and she gagged as she fought for every breath. She was drowning while Cain emotionlessly documented her demise.

"Leah . . . Leah." Cain's voice was a soothing purr in her ear.

He'd come! He wasn't going to let her drown.

"Leah." A hand on each shoulder shook her gently. "Wake up."

Her heart pounded as her chest rose and fell dramatically with every hoarse breath. Panic-stricken, Leah clenched his shirt, still trying to save herself from the terrifying depths.

"Leah," Cain's voice rasped close to her ear. "It's only a dream."

A dream. Dazed, she stared at him with eyes that refused to focus. She was going to live. The raft, the whale, the frantic fight for her life had all been a figment of some horrible nightmare. Relief coursed through her as she sagged against the bed and relaxed her death grip on Cain's shirt.

"Are you all right?" he asked in a rough whisper.

She lifted her gaze to his and nodded. The constricting muscles in her throat made speech impossible. Tears shimmered in her eyes and spilled down the side of her face.

Gently, Cain wiped them aside, his calloused thumb slightly abrasive against the softness of her cheek. "None of it was real," he murmured.

She nodded, still unable to formulate words. Cain parted his lips as though he wanted to say more, then reconsidered. His mouth hovered above hers, their breaths merging, and she knew he was going to kiss her. His hands roved from her cheeks to cup her ears, tilting her head to receive his kiss. But neither moved. A soft, choppy breath shuddered through her as she flattened her palms against his chest, feeling the wild hammering of his heart. Cain groaned and rolled onto his back.

Together they lay side by side, not speaking, not moving, hardly breathing.

"Would it help if I apologized?" she whispered, not chancing a glance at him.

"For a dream?" he scoffed, and some of the old anger crept into his voice.

"No," she murmured, and her lashes fluttered closed as she swallowed her pride. "I want to apologize for whatever I did that made you so angry."

"Leah," he groaned, and rolled onto his side, propping his head up with the palm of one hand. Tenderly, he brushed the short blond curls from her temple. "You didn't do anything."

"Then why?" She turned her head so that she could read the answer in his eyes.

In response, Cain lifted the delicate gold chain from the hollow of her throat, winding it around his index finger until Leah feared it would snap. His brow knit as his grip relaxed. "I made a promise to you in Perth, and with God as my witness, I mean to keep it."

"But?"

"But being with you twenty-four hours a day is making it more than difficult."

Using her elbow as leverage, Leah raised herself, wishing she wasn't so affected by his nearness. "I didn't mean . . . for that to happen . . . when I was cutting your hair." Embarrassment caused her voice to quiver, and she lowered her gaze, not wanting him to see how much the incident had stirred her as well.

Cain chuckled lightly and her heart melted. "Do you think I don't know that?"

Leah lowered her head to the feather pillow and released a deep sigh. "I've missed you."

"Me, too, lady."

He seldom called her that anymore. In the beginning it had been a minor source of irritation to Leah. But tonight, in the distant light of the moon, it sounded very much like a lover's caress.

"Friends?" she whispered.

For a moment, a furrow of concentration darkened his brow. "Friends," he finally agreed.

The reluctance in his voice dimmed the brilliant light of joy that had shone so brightly just seconds before. "Good night," Leah mumbled, rolling onto her side so that her back was to him.

"Good night," he repeated a moment later, drawing his words out slowly.

The tense silence was back, and Leah forced her eyes closed, wondering if things could ever be the same between them again.

Leah felt the weight on the bed shift as Cain turned toward her, slipping his arm around her middle. His hold was firm but gentle.

"We'll talk in the morning," he promised.

"Yes," she breathed, and a tremulous smile touched her mouth.

Again Cain was gone when Leah woke in the morning, and she wanted to cry with frustration. Hadn't last night meant anything to him? He'd promised they'd talk this morning, and instead he'd run like a rabbit bent on escape. Well, he couldn't avoid her forever.

She quickly donned her mauve cords and a thick cable-knit sweater. The leaden gray skies promised a storm, and the room was cold. She was further surprised that the stove hadn't been lit and the coffee wasn't made.

After tucking her feet into tennis shoes, Leah moved outside to investigate.

"Cain."

Her call went unanswered.

Wandering to the edge of the cliff, she buried her hands in her pockets and looked out over the crashing surf. The sight below made her knees go weak and trapped the breath in her lungs.

Cain was in the rubber raft, the angry seas tossing it about like a toy boat. Without warning, a humpback hurled itself from the water and slammed back onto the surface with a thunderous roar.

Leah gave a cry of alarm and covered her mouth in horror. The tiny raft rocked with the impact.

Soon Leah realized it wasn't just one humpback, but a pod of eight feeding from a rich underwater pasture of krill. Like graceful dolphins, they leaped from the ocean bed, their cavernous maws open and spanning thirteen feet.

Amid the humpbacks, oblivious to any danger, was Cain, snapping pictures as fast as his fingers would allow.

Chapter 7

Leah was pacing the beach when Cain landed the craft. His face was flushed with exhilaration as he pulled the raft onto the shore and hurried toward her, his feet kicking up sand.

"You idiot," she stormed, her eyes burning with a smoldering light. "You unmitigated idiot. What did you think you were doing?"

"Did you see them? Eight humpbacks feeding cooperatively. It was like a riotous pack of school kids." Oblivious to her fear and anger, he continued to describe what he'd managed to document with his camera. "They launched themselves out of the water like they were bouncing off trampolines. Those pictures were the opportunity of a lifetime."

"Is your life worth so little? Are your pictures that important?" Leah was so frustrated that her voice throbbed. She was shaken to the core of her being, frightened out of her mind for him. And he hadn't even acknowledged the danger.

"Leah," he pleaded, gripping her by the shoulders.

"Don't be angry. These pictures are going to impress the world."

"But you could have been killed." She stuffed her trembling hands into her pants pockets and hung her head, reluctant to reveal the tears that clouded her vision. "But I wasn't," he cried exultantly. "Don't you understand? I can't wait to show these shots to my editor."

Once again he had taken his life in his hands with nary a thought. What would she do if anything happened to Cain? Her life wouldn't be worth living.

Draping an arm over her shoulders, Cain led her to the rickety weatherworn stairs built against the cliff wall. "Let's have coffee and I'll tell you all about it."

Leah raised the angle of her chin several degrees, not wanting him to know how much his adventure had terrified her, nor the reasons for her deep-seated fear. With a wry twist of her mouth, she decided that it would serve no useful purpose for Cain to know she loved him.

Back at the hut, hugging a steaming cup of coffee in her hands, Leah listened to Cain talk nonstop for an hour. He'd awakened early, before first light and wandered outside. The thunderous commotion coming from the ocean was what had drawn him to the cliff. The sight of the humpbacks had caused him to run for his camera, and there hadn't been time to wake her. Or at least that was what he said. Leah knew better. Cain must have realized an argument would have ensued had he told her his plans, so he'd left her behind to discover his absence later.

As if he wanted to make it up to her, Cain spent the day at her side, using the telescope while she documented migration patterns and routes.

They chatted about inconsequential details, afraid to speak of the matters that were prominent in their minds.

"Once we're back, how long will it take you to develop the film?" Leah wanted to know, sitting beside him in the grassy brush at the cliff's edge. What she was really asking was how long he'd stay in California before moving on.

"Not long."

Leah blanched. That answered it: Cain wouldn't stay a moment longer than necessary. "I suppose you'll be anxious to get these pictures to your editor."

He hesitated for a moment. "He'll be anxious to see them."

"Of course."

He didn't mention the divorce, although it was paramount in both their minds. Three weeks was all the time that they had left together. A sad smile touched her troubled eyes. Three weeks. It seemed decades too long and a lifetime too short.

The morning air was cool and scented by the fresh breeze coming off the ocean. A shiver danced up her arm, and Leah didn't know if the chill came from without, or within. She'd never forget this moment: Cain was at her side, his look tender, his smile so warm it seemed capable of melting her heart. Her spirit soared like a kite racing toward the heavens. Yet as free as she felt this moment, she knew the reality, the string that controlled her flight.

To distract herself from bewildered thoughts, she plugged in the recorder and slipped the earphones over her head. The faint sounds being transmitted were ones she didn't recognize: deep, mournful sounds unlike the high-pitched squeaks she normally cataloged. Leah thought they sounded like a funeral dirge.

Lifting her binoculars, Leah studied the ocean to see if she could identify the source of the distress signal she'd overheard.

Two humpbacks, possibly from the same pod that Cain had seen in the morning, were lagging behind the rest of the pod. A mother and her young calf swam side by side. Although it was difficult to determine its age, the calf didn't look more than a few months old.

"Cain," she murmured, slipping off the headphones, "listen to this and tell me what you think."

He eyed her curiously, and then did as she'd requested. His brow creased into thick folds of concentration. Slowly he shook his head. "A mother and her calf?" He arched his brows in question.

Leah nodded, handing him the binoculars as well.

"I don't know," Cain admitted soberly a few moments later. "What do you think's wrong?"

"I'm not exactly sure." All her textbook knowledge wasn't a help to her now. "I'd say it has something to do with that calf of hers." A dark glow of uncertainty entered her hazel eyes.

Turning off the recorder, Leah stood, preparing to deliver her equipment to the hut and pick up what she'd need from inside. "I'm going to take the raft out and investigate."

"Oh no, you're not." Cain bounded to his feet like a rocket, his eyes shooting hot sparks. "You can't go out there. The humpback's first instinct will be to protect her calf."

"But I want to help her," Leah argued.

"You get within ten feet of that calf and the mother will come right for you. You wouldn't have a chance."

"I'm not going near the calf."

"The calf's by the mother." His piercing gaze and sarcastic tone shredded her faulty reasoning.

Leah's fingers tightened into a fist. "In other words, it's perfectly fine for you to take a risk, but not me."

"You're exactly right. I'm the man."

Seething, Leah closed her eyes to the rising surge of anger. How any man could be so unreasonable, she didn't know. "I'm going out there to help that whale," she stated flatly, brooking no argument.

Cain mockingly inclined his head toward the beach. "And I'd like to see you try." An unnatural smile curved his mouth, and his dark eyes glittered with challenge.

Undeterred, Leah squared her shoulders and with long, purpose-filled strides headed back to the hut.

Cain was blocking the doorway when she reappeared, her rain gear draped over her forearm. "If you think I'm letting you out of here, then you can think again." There were overtones of mocking laughter in his voice that provoked her all the more.

Crossing her arms over her chest, Leah unflinchingly met his gaze. "I'm the scientist here."

"And I'm the one with common sense."

"Ha!" Leah scoffed. "This morning your life was hanging by a thread because you wanted a fistful of snapshots. So don't think you can dictate to me." Not two inches separated them as she came to the doorway of the hut. His outstretched arms prevented her from proceeding.

"Cain, please." Leah's words were filled with anxiety and urgency. Her fists were clenched at her sides. "I'm losing precious time."

A muscle leaped along the line of his jaw and captured her attention. Her gaze strayed down the tanned column of his throat to the unbuttoned front of his shirt. The smooth muscles of his chest gleamed like those of a statue. Leah scolded herself for being affected by his virility. This wasn't the time to notice these things about Cain. Not when she had a mission to accomplish.

Cain hesitated, seeming to measure his words. "I'm asking you as your husband not to go."

Leah's jaw sagged with surprise. The fact that they were married had never been mentioned, never discussed. Yes, they were bound to each other, but not in the normal sense. That he would use that form of persuasion with her now was unscrupulous and unfair.

The flash of resentment from her narrowed eyes must have convinced him of that.

"Leah," he whispered enticingly. His hands gripped her shoulders, keeping her at arm's length. "If you're so concerned. I'll contact Hugh by radio and have him send someone out."

"Whoever came wouldn't be able to do anything more than I could."

Cain held her gaze for a long moment, looking deep into her hazel eyes. What he saw there, she didn't know.

"I'm sorry," he muttered, tightening his grip on her shoulders, his gaze narrow and menacing. "I won't let you go."

"Cain." The breathless tremor in her voice betrayed her frustration. "Please." Her eyes were shimmering with the powerful desire to aid the distressed whale.

Leah felt Cain's resolve weaken as he slowly shook his head. "Can't you see what you're sailing into?" His face turned grim, and white lines formed around his tight mouth. "If you're going out, then I'm going with you."

Leah's pulse leaped wildly. He was conceding even when he felt she was wrong, but he wasn't letting her go alone. Her lips curved into a faint smile. "Thank you," she whispered, knowing what it had cost him to bow to her wishes.

He dropped his arms and moved across the room to where his rain gear was stored in the corner of the hut.

"Hurry," she pleaded, "they may have already moved on."

Together they ran to the edge of the cliff to descend the wobbly stairs. The rubber raft was high on the beach, where Cain had left it earlier that morning.

Abruptly, Cain stopped running. His hand gripped Leah's elbow as he pointed toward the spot where the two humpbacks had been sighted.

"What's wrong?"

"They're swimming closer to the shore."

Leah's heart sank, and she felt an oppressive weight settle onto her chest. The humpbacks' direction meant only one thing. "She's dying," Leah whispered.

The fifty-foot humpback came within a stone's throw of the beach. The calf remained close by his mother's side, swimming around her in tight circles. It was apparent that whatever had caused the mother's illness was not afflicting the child. Leah and Cain stood by helplessly; all they could do was watch.

By evening the mother was dead and the mewling sound of her son could be heard up and down the beach. Two days later, the calf was so weak that he didn't protest when Leah got into the water with him. Swimming at his side, using a snorkel and goggles, she could do little more than let him become accustomed to her presence.

With Hugh Kimo's assistance, Leah attempted to feed the young calf enriched milk using a hot water bottle, rubber tubing, and a five-gallon drum. Hugh made the trip to the island daily, bringing in large quantities of the formula, but it all ended up in the sea. Leah spent hours coaxing the calf to eat. Cain did what he could to help, holding her makeshift device.

"Leah," he groaned, standing in the surf. "It's not going to work. Give it up before you collapse."

"No," she refused stubbornly. "Come on, Jonah, eat. Please eat."

A half hour later, shaking with cold, miserable in body and spirit, Leah abandoned the effort and walked out of the ocean.

Cain draped a thick towel over her shoulders and set her down in front of a warm fire he'd built on the sand. He sat behind her so that she could lean her back against him and be comforted by his warmth. With his arms wrapped around her, he brushed the wet strands of hair from her face. Numb with cold, and utterly discouraged, she battled back tears of exhaustion.

"I want him to live so much," she whispered.

"I know, love."

The affectionate term barely registered. "He's just a baby. He needs his mother."

"I know."

Completely drained of energy, Leah closed her eyes and fell into a deep, dreamless sleep. Lying side by side in front of the fire, Cain and Leah slept on the beach. Leah woke at dawn, her arms and legs entwined with Cain's. Her first thought was of Jonah, and she rushed to the water's edge. Jonah was alive, but for how much longer she couldn't know.

That morning, using the rubber raft, Cain hauled the decaying mother out to another part of the island. On close inspection, Leah was amazed at how heavily encrusted with seaweed, worms, and crustaceans, especially barnacles, the humpback was, but she doubted that any of this had contributed to her demise.

When Hugh arrived later that same morning, he brought another specialist with him from the Diamantinas to aid Leah with the autopsy. The postmortem revealed that a liver ailment had caused the mother's death. Antibiotics were administered to the three-month-old Jonah, although the calf showed no signs of the mother's sickness. After an hour's struggle, the four managed to get the young whale to accept the rich, creamy formula, but the young calf was nervous and objected strenuously to all these humans fussing over him. Only Leah would the young mammal accept at his side.

Five days later, Jonah gave up eating, and Leah realized it would only be a few days before he joined his mother.

Death was just a matter of time, but Leah refused to allow her friend to die without her at his side. She spent several hours every day in the water, swimming at the calf's side, stroking the top and sides of his head, doing what little she could to encourage him.

Other humpbacks passed, and Leah came to enjoy their sporty nature. She smiled at their antics and was amazed to see that they sometimes scratched themselves against the rocks. When Cain asked her about two whales that he saw smacking each other with their flippers, she explained that this was part of their mating ritual. The sounds could be heard up to a mile away.

In the evenings, Cain built a fire on the beach so that Leah could warm herself when she came out of the water. The flames flickered invitingly as he stood ready with a towel to dry her.

Miserably cold and defeated in spirit, Leah welcomed the iron band of his arms as he draped a thick towel over her shoulders.

"How much longer can he hold on?" Cain whispered, leading her to a blanket spread out in front of the warm fire that crackled with dry wood.

"Soon. Not more than a couple of days," she answered, holding back the tears.

No one would have guessed that Jonah would hold on to life as long as he had. For two weeks, Leah had expected him to die, and for two weeks he had held on, growing weaker, less and less responsive.

Leah was at Jonah's side the following morning when he died. She shed tears, grateful that she had been there with him, and continued patting his head long after he'd stopped breathing. Only when all her tears of sadness had been shed did she come out from the water. Cain met her on the shore and held her tight in his arms. Willingly Leah accepted his comfort.

Once she was warm and dry and sitting at the kitchen table with a hot cup of soup in front of her, Cain radioed the news to Hugh, who promised to return the following day.

For the second time in as many weeks, Cain hauled the corpse of a humpback whale out to sea.

An incredible sadness filled Leah as she watched Jonah being towed away. She stood on the beach, holding back the tears until Hugh, Cain, and Jonah were out of sight. Her arms cuddled her stomach as she tried to beat down the emotion. Staring sightlessly ahead, she closed her eyes and fought back a sob, but still tears flowed from the corners of her eyes and down the sides of her face.

By the time Cain returned, Leah had composed herself and was busy at the duties she had neglected while working with Jonah. Cain had kept a log of the passing whales, and she spent the afternoon reviewing his brief notes.

When dusk arrived to purple the sky, Leah paused from her position at the lookout over the Indian Ocean and sighed sadly. In a few days, less than a week now, they would be leaving the island, and this magical adventure would be at an end. Once in California, she and Cain would separate and there would be only her memories to remind her of this enchanted time.

Even Cain noted her mood that evening as they readied for bed. The entire time Leah was working with the young calf, she had slept on the beach, Cain at her side. He had cuddled her close, spoon fashion, his arm draped protectively over her waist. He'd warmed her with his body and comforted her with his quiet concern. He'd brought her meals, but didn't force her to eat. He'd spoken soothingly to her when she was too cold and weak to answer. He'd held her, encouraged her, and cared for her. Leah never stopped to question Cain's gentleness during that time. He was there. She needed him and she didn't analyze his motives. If the situation had been reversed, she would have done the same for him. There wasn't any reason to read something more into his actions.

"You've been quiet tonight," he murmured as they lay side by side in the darkened room.

Leah's fingers gripped the sheet. "I haven't been good company lately. I apologize for that."

His hand reached for hers and squeezed it gently. "There's no need to feel sorry. You were busy." His thumb made lazy, circling motions at the inside of her wrist. A warm, tingling sensation was creeping up her arm. He was so close, she could smell the fresh scent of the sea mingled with the faint smell of hard work and the spicy aftershave he'd used that morning.

"After the past two weeks, I'm willing to promise never to take the raft out in a pod of humpbacks if you promise not to risk your health by nursing a sick whale."

Leah bit into her lower lip and nodded. She'd so desperately wanted Jonah to live. She'd have done anything to help him. Fresh tears burned for release, and she inhaled a shuddering breath. "Okay," was all she could manage.

Cain rolled to face her and wiped the tear that had started down her cheek. "Don't cry." The words were filled with a warm tenderness that she'd never thought to hear from this man who cared only for his work.

"I'm sorry," she sniffled, rolling away from him. It was bad enough that he was witness to this display of weakness and emotion. She couldn't stand to face him.

"Leah." He moaned her name, and tugged gently at her shoulder, easing her onto her back. "Don't block me out. Let me hold you."

With a weak cry, she did as he asked, reaching for him

in the dark. Her arms went around his neck as she buried her tear-streaked face in his throat.

Half sitting, half lying, Cain tightened his arms around her. One arm was draped across the small of her back while the other hand stroked her head.

"I wanted him to live," she moaned.

"I know. I wanted him to live, too." The words were so soft, so tender that Leah lifted her red, blotchy face to him and smiled tentatively. She didn't speak, although her heart was bursting with a thousand things she realized she could never say. Her eyes filled again, but these tears weren't for the loss of the young whale. They were the tears of a virgin wife who would never know her husband's love.

Cain shifted their positions so that she was lying flat on the mattress and he was bending over her. His finger wiped the moisture from her face and paused to skim her tear-moistened lips. His gaze locked with hers in the golden rays of a disinterested moon.

Leah felt the small shudder that went all the way through him. She knew before he dipped his head that he was going to kiss her. This was a time predestined, a kiss ordained, and her heart pounded erratically in eager anticipation.

At first his mouth merely touched hers, as if he expected her to push him away. Leah didn't move. He retreated, bringing his head back so that he could gaze into her eyes. Willingly she met his look and gave him a weak, trembling smile of encouragement.

He groaned her name, and his mouth moved closer to hers until their breaths mingled. He was a scant half inch from her when he paused. Her mind reeled crazily, demanding that he give her what she craved. How could he come so close and deny her? Deny them both? A weak cry of protest slipped from her parted lips. Cain ignored her pleas. Her hands tightened their grasp at the nape of his neck to force his head down. He resisted. Timidly she arched her back and he groaned as she pressed herself intimately closer. Yet he wouldn't yield and grant her the kiss.

No longer demure, no longer shy, Leah brought her mouth to his and outlined his bottom lip with the tip of her tongue.

Cain went rigid. Every hard muscle in his body grew taut, and reaction rippled over him as if his world had exploded. Yet he didn't move to gather her more fully into his arms. Nor did he kiss her with the passion she knew was simmering just below the surface.

Dazed with these strange, unrelenting waves of longing, Leah kissed him with a lifetime of suppressed womanhood stored in her heart.

His mouth played over hers, tasting and nibbling, taking and giving. Giving so much that Leah's world spiraled crazily.

Her arms moved possessively over the hard muscles of his back, glorying as his bronze muscles rippled under her fingers. Pressed together as they were, Cain pushed the covers down from her waist so that his hard thighs molded her against him.

After what seemed like forever, he lifted his mouth from hers and took in deep, shuddering breaths as he cradled her face between his hands. Leah covered his hands with her own, turning her head so that she could kiss the inside of his palm. Cain's reaction was immediate as he slowly, languorously buried his mouth in hers until a need, a desire she had never known, sent flames shooting through her. Straining to be closer to him, her hips rocked, seeking more.

His hand lowered to her flat stomach, and it was Cain who groaned. The sound throbbed in Leah's ears, and she tightened her grip on him, teasing him with her tongue, giving him biting little kisses over his face and ears until his mouth branded hers in burning, searing possession.

Without warning, Cain tore his mouth from hers and raised himself. He took in deep, measured breaths as if he were holding on to the last vestige of his control.

"Cain," she whispered, not knowing what had stopped him.

"Leah," he murmured, and gathered her in his arms. "Dear, sweet Leah, shall I go on?"

The air felt trapped in her lungs.

"You know what I want?" he asked slowly.

"Yes." Her whispered voice trembled. "Oh, yes. I want you."

He hesitated for only a moment. His hand reached for her neck, locating the delicate chain that held the gold heart. With a vicious jerk, he broke the chain and tossed it aside. The sound of it hitting the wall barely registered in Leah's passion.

When dawn came to lighten the room, Leah gave a soft sigh of satisfaction. Cain was cuddling her, his hand around her middle. He had made love to her last night until she thought she would die from the pure joy of it.

"Morning," he whispered near her ear.

"Morning." Maybe she should feel shy and awkward, but she didn't. Rolling onto her back, she looped her arms around his neck. "I had the most wonderful dream last night."

He nuzzled her throat, fiercely holding her to him. "That wasn't a dream."

"It had to have been," she teased lovingly. "Nothing in my life has ever been that good."

"Maybe we should have a repeat performance so you'll know," he said, his voice hoarse with tenderness.

"I think we should," she breathed. "Oh, Cain, I think we should."

The island became their personal paradise. With less than a week left of the expedition, they spent long hours with each other, never speaking of the morrow or life back in San Diego. At night, Cain would reach for her, loving her with a tenderness that managed to steal her breath.

During the day he was often at her side, taking her picture. Leah was uncomfortable with that, but didn't want anything to ruin this idyllic happiness.

With a deep sense of regret, Leah packed for their return trip to San Diego. They had found this complete sharing of themselves so late, Leah feared it would all be ruined once they returned to civilization.

On their last morning together, Leah lay in Cain's arms, dreading the time Hugh would arrive. Their luggage was packed, their gear lined up in the outer room ready to be delivered to the boat.

Almost shyly, Leah dressed, pulling the jeans over her slim, narrow hips. Not until she was finished did she realize that Cain had been watching her. There seemed little need for modesty now, and yet she blushed when she discovered he'd been studying her so intently.

"Hugh will be here anytime now," she murmured, glancing away.

"Yes," Cain answered awkwardly.

She was headed for the door when Cain stopped her. "Leah."

She turned, uncertain.

"I thought you might want this." The gold necklace Siggy had given her was dangling from his hand.

Leah couldn't have been more shocked if he'd slapped her face. She stared at it, and the color drained from her motionless features.

Then she understood as clearly as if he were shouting it at her. Their time together was over. When they arrived back in San Diego, he would go about his life, and she should do the same.

Her chin trembled, and she bit into her bottom lip as she reached across the short distance and snapped the gold heart from his grasp.

Chapter 8

"Leah!" Surprise and delight lit up the aged face as Dr. Brewster stood and moved to the front of his desk. "My dear, you look absolutely radiant." He gave her a brief hug and, shaking his round face with wonder, took a step back. "How tan you are. You remind me more of a golden goddess than a capable scientist."

Leah's thick lashes lowered with the praise, not knowing how to deal with such wholehearted approval. "Thank you."

"Where's Cain?"

Leah's heart constricted painfully. She didn't know where he was. Not exactly. Somewhere in San Diego, she assumed. He'd dropped her off at her apartment, his face a tight mask, wiped clean of expression. His last words were that he'd contact her when the film had been developed. With her heart crying out to stop him, Leah had given a perfunctory nod and told him that would be fine. Neither one mentioned the divorce, although according to their written agreement it was to take place within a week of their return.

"Leah?" Dr. Brewster prompted. "I was asking you about Cain."

"He'll be contacting you soon." Her answering smile was weak and a little wobbly. Being without Cain was still so new. She had tried to sound reassuring and happy but knew that she had failed miserably.

"Sit down," he ordered, his voice laced with concern. "You look like you're dead on your feet. I'm so anxious to hear of your findings. Tell me everything."

Leah did as he bid, sitting on the chair opposite her mentor's huge desk. She didn't know where to begin. "Cain was a wonderful help," she murmured, lacing her fingers together tightly in her lap. "He helped me in every aspect of the expedition and still managed to obtain some fantastic photographs."

"I knew he would." Walking to the other side of the small office, Dr. Brewster poured Leah a cup of tea, adding two lumps of sugar to the steaming liquid.

Dr. Brewster was well aware that Leah drank her tea straight, and the action brought a sad smile to her face. Like Cain, Dr. Brewster seemed intent on fattening her up.

"I personally chose Cain Hawkins," he explained, and handed Leah the cup and saucer. "Of all the people I know in this world, Cain seemed the best man for the job."

"Yes, of course." Leah's gaze refused to meet his.

"I can't tell you how pleased I am that you two resolved your differences."

A bubble of laughter nearly escaped from her throat. She wondered what Dr. Brewster would think if he knew to what extent they had settled their "differences."

Facing such eager enthusiasm, Leah began to tell him

about her adventures on the island. They talked nonstop for an hour, until Dr. Brewster was reluctantly forced to leave for class. He hugged her again as she rose, a gesture Leah found strangely comforting.

"I'll be bringing the documents in to you at the end of the week," she assured him as they stepped out of his office. Together they headed across the lush rolling hills of lawn that comprised the university campus.

Two young men dressed in tattered cutoffs, probably freshmen, were throwing a Frisbee. With a gentle smile, Leah watched the red disk float through space. Once she would have found this sight disconcerting. The university was an institution of higher learning, not a playground.

When Leah returned her attention to Dr. Brewster, his brow was knit in thick lines of concentration. "Bring Cain with you the next time you come."

Leah dropped her gaze and nodded miserably. "I'll do that."

Back at her apartment, Leah examined the luxury that surrounded her. She would gladly have traded it all for another day with Cain in the stark island hut that had been their home. She hadn't thought she'd miss him so terribly, but this ache was far worse than anything she'd ever known. The pain in her heart was a thousand times heavier than any hurt she'd ever suffered.

They'd only been back three days, and it felt more like three years. The nights were the worst. A hundred times she'd rolled over, unconsciously searching for the warm, loving body beside her. Her thoughts were shameless. It wasn't only his warmth she missed, but his touch, slow and infinitely gentle. His lovemaking had never been hurried or urgent. He'd loved her as if they'd had all the time in the world.

Without thinking, she moved her fingers to her throat as she recalled in vivid detail the way Cain would slide his hand over her throat and body as if every inch of her was a treasure. Leah had shivered with delight, teasing him with her own fingers. She had thrilled with unexpected pleasure at how responsive his body was to the mere brush of her fingertips as they lightly grazed his chest. In the darkened room, Leah could refuse him nothing, completely entrusting herself into his gentle, skilled hands. He'd whispered the most wonderful things to her, his voice hoarse and tender, and not once had she doubted him. For those few, all-too-short days, the world had been theirs. Little had she realized their utopian happiness was to be so short-lived. From the moment Hugh arrived to deliver them to Ruaehu, Cain had been like a polite stranger.

Leah drew in a long steady breath as her gaze fixed on the telephone. He'd promised to call; with everything that was in her, Leah demanded that the phone ring. She was dying to hear from him, though she had no idea what she'd say once he did. Nonetheless, her whole concentration was focused on the telephone that stood tauntingly silent.

When the doorbell rang later that afternoon, Leah's heart raced until she was forced to stretch out a hand and grip the kitchen counter to steady herself. If it was Cain, she was determined to meet his gaze with the same lack of emotion that he had shown toward her. With her head held high, she would greet him coolly and invite him inside. Then, with complete indifference, she would ask him to sit down. She was determined to do nothing to ease his discomfort when he told her that the past three days had taught him he couldn't live without her. Only when he'd revealed the depth of his love and humbly come to her would she disclose that she, too, had come to love him. Against her will, of course.

The doorbell chimed impatiently a second time before Leah moved. She forced a plastic smile on her tight lips and opened the door.

The disappointment that surged through her was so strong that she was forced to swallow back a cry. Siggy, dressed impeccably in a pale-blue suit and navy-blue bow tie, stood on the opposite side of the threshold.

"Leah . . . darling." He took her by the shoulders and kissed her lightly on the forehead. "My heavens, what have you done to yourself?"

"Hello, Siggy." The happiness she should have felt at seeing her fiancé simply wasn't there. Only an aching heart for the man she loved, the man who hadn't come. Cain.

Siggy slid an arm around her narrow waist and impetuously closed the door with his foot. Thinking himself devilishly suave, he chuckled and swung her around to embrace her tightly. Leah gave him all the response of a rag doll. She purposely hadn't contacted Siggy. She didn't want him to know she was in town until she knew what was going to happen between her and Cain.

"Let me look at you," Siggy said, stepping back and frowning. "Your hair," he moaned, shaking his head. "Is that hippie photographer responsible for destroying your lovely golden tresses?" His mouth tightened, and with a display of anger he smashed his clenched fist into the open palm of his other hand. "That Hawkins man did this to you, didn't he? Now don't bother to defend him, Leah. It's just the kind of stupid stunt I'd expect of someone like Hawkins."

She managed to contain the laughter that welled in her throat. "I'm the one responsible," she explained.

"One can only wonder what else he forced you to submit to."

"Siggy," Leah groaned with a decided lack of patience. "Cain didn't force me to submit to anything."

Stroking his chin, Siggy nodded thoughtfully. "That's what he said."

"*He* said?" Desperately, Leah's gaze cornered Siggy's. "He's talked to you?" Her mind whirled in fury. Cain had no right to contact Siggy. Heaven only knew what he'd said to him.

With a snort, Siggy crossed the room, sat on the leather sofa and crossed his legs. Leah sat across from him, studying his tight features.

"Threatened me is more like it," Siggy continued indignantly. "He said if I didn't make you happy then I'd be answering to him personally." A finger edged the shirt collar from his neck as he cleared his throat. "I do care for you, Leah." As he spoke, a flushed color crept up from his neck. "Deeply. Enough to remember that your hair will grow back and that eventually . . . you'll be my same lovely Leah once again."

"Oh. Siggy." How could she explain that she would never be the same again? Never wanted to be. Now that she was back from Kahu, she realized that what she'd shared with him was only a pale imitation of what love was supposed to be between a man and a woman.

"Yes . . . darling?" He leaned forward, bracing his elbows on his knees as he looked adoringly into Leah's deep, hazel eyes.

Straightening, Leah offered him a tight smile. "I . . . I think that I should be completely honest with you."

"Yes?" He stiffened, his action mirroring Leah's.

"While we . . . Cain and I . . . were on the island . . ." Leah paused and sucked in a troubled breath. This was a thousand times more difficult than she'd ever dreamed. She didn't feel ashamed over what had happened. Never ashamed.

"What are you trying to say?" Siggy prompted, moving closer to the edge of the cushion.

"There was only one bed on the island."

"And so you slept together?" His words were low and shocked.

"We had to," she returned forcefully. "There was only the one bed."

"And . . ." Siggy paused and cleared his throat. "And did you do . . . anything else?"

Closing her eyes, Leah nodded.

"I . . . see," Siggy said with infinite sadness as he pushed himself upright. "I guess it's only to be expected. The two of you alone on the island like that." The hurt-little-boy look was back again. Squaring his shoulders, Siggy met her gaze. "I think you should know that I forgive you, Leah."

It was on the tip of her tongue to scream at him that she didn't want his forgiveness. She had no regrets. Instead, she nodded and smiled, knowing what it must have cost him to say that. "Thank you," she murmured gently.

He wiped a hand across his face and dramatically pinched the bridge of his nose. "I need time to think."

"Of course you do."

"I love you, don't misunderstand me, but in the light of what happened between you and this Hawkins fellow, maybe we shouldn't see each other for a few days. We both need time to think things through."

"I understand." She stood and clasped her hands in front of her.

"There isn't a possibility . . . ?" he mumbled, and gave a small cough. "You wouldn't be pregnant, would you?"

Pregnant? The word hit Leah's mind with the impact of a hand grenade. Of course there was that possibility, but crazily it hadn't occurred to her.

"Leah?"

"I don't know," she answered honestly.

"I see." Siggy edged his way toward the front door. "Let's say the first of next week?"

Leah looked at him blankly. "Pardon?"

"I'll call you the first of the week. We can have dinner."

The offer flabbergasted her even more than the possibility she could be bearing the fruit of those last days on the island with Cain. "Fine."

"I'll call you." His hand was on the doorknob. "I do care for you, Leah."

"Thank you, Siggy."

The door closed after him, and Leah leaned against it and placed a hand on her flat abdomen. A smile touched her features and grew and grew until she was on the verge of breaking into great, gulping laughter. A baby. Emotion welled in her heart as she raised her head, lifting her eyes to the heavens, and offered a silent prayer.

Heaven answered her three days later. A visit to a local gynecologist confirmed that she was indeed in the early stages of pregnancy. Happiness flowed through her until she wanted to dance and sing and laugh. Maybe she should be experiencing bitter regrets. Instead she felt like stopping strangers on the street to announce her wonderful news.

The gold band around her finger that had once felt awkward and heavy now seemed right, almost a part of her. Once home, she opened the refrigerator and poured herself a glass of milk. With a baby to consider, she wouldn't be skipping any more meals. Cain had finally gotten his wish and was responsible for fattening her up. The thought produced a happy laugh.

Cain. She'd have to tell him. That was when the niggling apprehensions started to mount. How would her news alter their relationship? Would Cain insist on delaying the divorce? With his lifestyle, Leah was confident he wouldn't try to take the baby from her. A child would only complicate his life, and he wouldn't want complications. That was fine, because she wanted this baby very much.

Ironically, the first person she thought to call was Siggy. Her heart was burning to contact her mother, but her family didn't even know she was married. There would be plenty of time later to talk to her mother. In fact, she would probably have to move back to the farm later in the pregnancy. She'd want to be with people who loved her.

Her finger shook as she punched out Siggy's office number.

The line rang three times, and when he answered, Siggy sounded slightly flustered. "Harcharik here."

"Siggy, it's Leah."

"Leah." His voice filled with pleasure and surprise. "How are you?"

"Wonderful." Curtailing her happiness was impossible; even with Siggy. "I went to the doctor today."

A stark silence followed her announcement. "And?"

"And I'm going to be a mother."

Another shocked silence followed. "I see."

"Listen, Siggy," Leah murmured gravely. "I can understand if you decide you don't ever want to see me again. I realize that this is a shock to you."

"How are you feeling?" he interrupted her sharply. "You aren't ill or anything?"

"No, no, I've never felt better." Her spirits were soaring to the highest heavens because her love for Cain was bearing a precious fruit. How could she have believed for even a moment that what they shared wouldn't produce a child? It had been so beautiful, so right.

"You sound happy about it," he whispered accusingly.

"Oh, I am. Very, very happy."

"I see."

Leah wondered if he really understood any of this. "I apologize for hurting you, Siggy," she whispered contritely. "That was never my intention."

"Yes, well, the best intentions aren't going to change the facts, are they?"

"Not in this case."

"Goodbye, Leah," he said, his soft voice cracking, and almost immediately the line was disconnected.

For the first time since hearing the test results, Leah

experienced regret. She hadn't meant to hurt Siggy, but clearly she had.

Replacing the telephone receiver, Leah curled up on the couch and reached for a book the doctor had given her. She read it straight through, so engrossed that Siggy was soon driven from her mind.

When the doorbell chimed, Leah glanced up with surprise. If it was Cain, she wouldn't know how to tell him about the baby. Maybe it would be best not to say anything.

But when she opened the door, it wasn't Cain who stared back at her. Siggy, white-faced and obviously flustered, met her gaze.

"I've been thinking," he said as he strolled into the room. "The baby doesn't matter."

"What?" Leah looked at him with openmouthed disbelief.

"You heard me. We can raise it as our own."

Her jaw remained open and refused to close.

"Of course, we couldn't tell Mother that the baby isn't mine. That would shock her into an early grave."

"Siggy." His name was all she could manage.

"I love you, Leah. I've always wanted you to be my wife. I refuse to allow this unfortunate experience with Hawkins to ruin our lives."

Chapter 9

Cain phoned Leah the first part of the next week. She'd been awaiting his call for so long, but she made herself answer calmly.

"Hello, Leah."

"Cain." Her hand tightened around the receiver as she forced her voice to remain level and devoid of emotion. He sounded tired, and his voice dipped with a trace of impatience.

"How have you been?"

Miserable. Lonely. Afraid. Excited. "Fine," she murmured finally.

"Would it be inconvenient for me to stop by for a few minutes?" he inquired with starched politeness.

How could they talk to each other like this? Leah's heart cried. It was as if he had never held her in his arms or whispered that he ached all the way to his bones with wanting her. Apparently, he'd blocked out the love they'd shared on Kahu as effectively as if he were changing rolls of film in his camera. Leah wanted to cry out at the injustice of it. Instead, she found her voice and assured him he was welcome anytime.

"I'll be there in fifteen minutes."

"Good," she said, her voice as flat as his had been.

Pacing the living room carpet, Leah tried desperately to decide what she should tell him. She found the irony of the situation highly amusing. She had been the least attractive girl in her high school. The brain. The girl most likely to succeed outside the bedroom. And here she was pregnant by one man, with another eagerly waiting for her to divorce Cain so they could be married. Leah didn't doubt Siggy's sincerity. He would be a good father to her child. And he certainly must love her to be willing to accept these unusual circumstances.

With the minutes ticking away, Leah made her decision. If Cain sauntered in and asked that they make the arrangements for the divorce, then she wouldn't let him know she was going to have a baby. It was important that they not stay married simply because of the new life they had created. She didn't want to trap him.

On the other hand, if he came and told her he was miserable and had missed her dreadfully, that would change everything. Then Leah would tell him she was pregnant. From there a reconciliation would come naturally. Leah yearned with all her heart to tell Cain how much she loved him, but after the way he'd so heartlessly handed her Siggy's necklace, pride wouldn't allow her to speak first.

The doorbell chimed, and inhaling a steadying breath, Leah strode across the apartment and opened the door.

"Hello, Cain," she greeted, even before looking to see who it was.

"Leah." He marched into the apartment, carrying a briefcase. His hair was mussed as if he'd raked his hand through it several times. Finely etched lines fanned out from his eyes, giving the impression he hadn't slept well in several nights. Yet when her gaze met his, she saw the sparks of anger igniting. He looked as if he couldn't decide whether to haul her into his arms and kiss her senseless or berate her.

She smiled uncertainly, hesitated, and then gestured toward the sofa. "Would you care to sit down? I've got a beer, if you want one."

His hot gaze shot to her. "When did you start drinking beer?"

"I . . . I didn't."

"You bought it for me?"

It had been an insane thing to do. From the morning Cain had dropped her off at the apartment, Leah had known he was coming back. Ever since that day, she'd been doing little things to prepare for their meeting. Buying a six-pack of his favorite beer had seemed the natural thing to do.

"Yes, I picked up a six-pack at the store this week," she answered thoughtfully, lowering her gaze so he couldn't read her eyes.

"Why?"

Because I've thought of you every minute since we left the island. Because doing a wifely thing like buying you beer made the ache inside me lessen just a little. Because your child is growing in my womb and I'm so happy I want to shout it from the hilltops. "I . . . I knew you'd probably want one," she supplied lamely, still centering her gaze on the carpet. "Do you want one or not?" she asked with a trace of defiance, more angry with herself for buying it than with him for making an issue of it.

"Have you got anything stronger?"

"No."

"Then a beer is fine."

At least getting it for him gave her a few moments to compose herself. Cain was sitting on the edge of the sofa when she reappeared, his face hard and unreadable. He accepted the open bottle mechanically and, without looking, set it aside.

Stiffly, Leah sat opposite him, waiting.

Slowly, gently, his gaze moved over her, and in his eyes Leah witnessed uncertainty, indecision, and a multitude of doubts. She longed to reach out and reassure him, but they both remained as they were—silent, intimate strangers. A lump of desolation swelled in her throat, and Leah swallowed back the tears that threatened to spill at the least provocation.

She spoke first, needing to break the horrible silence. "Have you developed the film?"

Cain shook himself lightly and nodded. "Some of my best work is in those photographs."

"I knew it would be," she said.

He set the briefcase on the coffee table and pushed back the lock. The clicking sound vibrated across the room. Without a word, he removed the first one and handed it to her. It was one of her, taken when she hadn't expected it that night in Perth when they were meeting Hugh for dinner. Leah recalled how upset she'd been at the time and how she had attempted to look away. It was that night that they'd walked on the beach and Cain had kissed her for the first time.

"Well?"

Speechless, Leah stared at it and shook her head. He'd

caught her with the element of surprise lighting up her face. Her eyes glowed, and a soft smile turned up the edges of her mouth appealingly. "It's very nice." Probably the most flattering photo ever taken of her.

"Now look at this." He handed her the second photo.

This time Leah gave a small gasp of surprise. This one had been taken while she was sitting at the cliff's edge. She was wearing white shorts and a red pin-striped cotton top that accentuated her deep tan. Her hair had been cut, the short style wind-tossed and ruffled about her face. She was laughing into the lens, waving her hand, yelling at Cain to take his camera away. She didn't want her picture taken. Again, Leah was shocked at how attractive the photo made her look. Cain had captured her image in such a way that she looked stunningly attractive. No, beautiful.

Speechless, Leah stared at him, shaking her head. Numbly, she accepted the third and last photo from his outstretched hand. This one had been taken the day before they left. She was walking along the beach, her arms reaching to him, imploring Cain to put the camera down and come to her so she could kiss him. Her eyes were sparkling with warmth and laughter and so full of love that she wondered how Cain could ever look at it and not realize her feelings for him.

"Well," Cain demanded harshly. "Do you see it?"

Leah set the photo aside. Unwanted, embarrassing tears brimmed in her eyes, threatening to spill. "How'd you make me so beautiful?" she whispered.

Cain cocked his head and gave her a fiery glare. "Are you fishing for compliments?"

Leah stood and walked to the other end of the room;

her arms hugged her waist. "Of course not," she answered softly. "But in each one of those pictures, you made me something I will never be."

Cain rose to his feet and tiredly wiped his eyes. "What do you mean?"

"My eyes." She walked back to the coffee table and picked up the first picture. "Look. You made my murky brown-green eyes look radiant."

"Murky eyes?" Cain repeated, and slowly shook his head. "They've never been that. You have an unusual eye color that reminds me of aged brandy."

"Me?" Leah flattened her hand across her breast.

"Come on, Leah, I didn't bring these photos to discuss the color of your eyes."

"But . . . but you made me look so pretty," she argued. "How did you do it?"

Cain jerked his hands inside his pants pockets, then angrily pulled them out again as if he weren't sure if he could refrain from shaking her. "Do you or do you not see anything different in these photos?"

So he was back to that again. "Yes," she barked, "you made me . . . pretty."

"And that's all you see?"

"Yes." What else could he possibly mean? Magnetically Leah's gaze was drawn back to the three pictures. Once, a long time ago, Cain had told her that he took pictures exactly the way he viewed the subject. She couldn't keep her gaze from the three images. Cain saw her like this? Beautiful, warm, full of life? Her heart swelled with appreciation. No one had ever thought she was beautiful. Not even Siggy. But if Cain could see all the love in her eyes that shone only for him, then why had he given her back Siggy's necklace?

"Leah." Cain murmured her name, pacing the floor. "Look at me." He stopped and turned to her, his face twisted with anguish and some unspeakable torment. "Are you pregnant?"

Automatically her hand flew to her flat stomach. Cain knew, but how?

"Are you?" he demanded with a wealth of emotion, his fists clenched at his side.

Words refused to come. Nodding seemed a monumental feat.

"You've seen a doctor?"

Again all she could do was answer him with a brief nod of her head. "How did you know?"

A crooked smile slashed across his face. "The picture," he said cryptically. "It's in your eyes in the last photo, the one taken on the beach."

Sinking into the chair, Leah picked up the one he'd mentioned and studied it again. Heavens, she'd only been a few days along. As far as she could see there wasn't anything different about that picture.

Silence reigned in the confined quarters as Cain continued pacing. He stopped and regarded her with narrow eyes. "Are you going to marry lover boy?" Cain demanded next, revealing none of his thoughts.

"I . . . I don't know yet," she answered honestly.

"Does he know you're pregnant?"

"Yes."

Cain looked furious enough to shake her senseless. "You told him, but not me."

"I was going to let you know."

"When? After the baby was born?"

"No," she answered weakly. "I've been waiting for you to get in touch with me."

"Don't give me that," he tore out angrily. "You could have found me if you really wanted to tell me the news. Were you waiting until after we were divorced and you were married to Sidney? Which brings me to another point." He paused and leaned forward, his hands gripping the back of the sofa. "Is that spineless idiot prepared to marry you while you're carrying my child?"

"Don't call Siggy that," she protested.

"Just answer the question," he barked.

"Yes . . . Siggy said it didn't matter to him. He wants children. He'll be a good father."

"And I won't?"

Leah didn't know it was possible for anyone to look so angry. "I didn't mean to imply that."

"Then just exactly what did you mean to imply?" His question held blazing animosity.

Leah dropped her gaze, suddenly feeling weak and a little shaky. "Nothing," she mumbled, her weakness reflected in her voice.

Instantly, Cain was kneeling at her side, his look contrite. "Are you feeling sick?"

"Just a little," she murmured, fighting to keep her voice level. All this anger and bitterness was taking its toll. "I'm sorry," she gulped miserably. "I didn't mean for any of this to happen. The consequences never occurred to me. I suppose it was stupid of me."

His eyes cut into hers as if he were penetrating her soul. "Are you sorry?"

"No." She wanted to tell him so much more but found

she couldn't. If he couldn't tell that she loved him by looking at those pictures, then explaining the joy she felt at discovering she was pregnant wouldn't help.

"You're going to keep the baby?"

Her eyes flew to him in horror. How could he imagine anything else? "Of course."

"And you and . . . Sidney are going to go ahead with your wedding plans?"

"I told you I don't know yet," she cried.

"When will you know?"

Forcing herself to her feet, Leah lifted one shoulder in a shrug. "In a few days, I imagine." She longed to scream at Cain that everything depended on him. But it wouldn't do any good.

"You'll let me know right away?"

"Yes, yes, of course." The muscles of her throat were constricting painfully, and Leah knew she was just seconds away from bursting into tears. As it was, her legs felt like rubber and her heart was pounding so loud it was a miracle Cain didn't hear it. Sick with defeat and failure, she walked to the door and held it open for him. "I'll call you by the end of the week."

Carelessly, Cain stuffed the photos inside the briefcase. Leah knew by the furious way he was handling the pictures that he wished his hands were around her neck. Straightening, he stalked to the front door. "I'll be waiting."

The apartment was as silent as death after Cain left. Feeling exhausted, Leah lay down and was shocked to wake up two and a half hours later. She felt she could sleep her life away. Whether that was because of the baby or a desire to escape the dilemma that faced her, Leah didn't know.

At dinnertime her appetite was nonexistent, but she forced down scrambled eggs, toast, and a tall glass of milk. Cain would be pleased to know she was at least eating properly.

After her extended afternoon nap, Leah had trouble sleeping that night. With her hands tucked under her head, she stared at the ceiling of the darkened room. Her mind whirled with ideas. The spare room she now used as her office could easily be transformed into a nursery. And although her skill was limited, she was capable of sewing what clothes the baby would need. As for the blankets and such, she'd always wanted to know how to knit. There was no better time to learn than the present.

Someone pounding against the front door startled her, and she bolted upright. Had she imagined the commotion? A repeat of the pounding assured her she hadn't. Dragging the robe from the bottom of the bed with her, Leah turned on the hallway light and moved into the living room.

"Who is it?" she called without opening the door.

"Cain," he answered, and continued beating on the door. "Let me in. I want to talk to you. I demand to talk to you." His voice was slurred and angry.

Concerned more that he'd do himself harm than with any fear for herself, Leah unlatched the lock and opened the front door.

Cain staggered into the room and made a three-hundred-sixty-degree turn attempting to find her. With his index finger pointing to the ceiling, he laughed loudly. "There you are."

"You're drunk," she announced accusingly, smelling the offensive odor of whiskey. In all the time they'd worked together, Leah had never known Cain to overindulge. Not in alcohol.

"So you noticed."

"For heaven's sake, sit down before you hurt yourself." Convinced he'd never make it to the sofa without help, Leah slipped an arm around his muscular waist.

As if he found her touch painful, Cain froze and gave a small cry. He pulled her into his arms, crushing her against his chest until Leah was unable to move. He buried his face in the silken curve of her neck and breathed in a deep, shuddering sigh. "Oh, Leah, my sweet Leah," he muttered unevenly; then, stiffening, he pushed her away. "Before you tell me your decision, I want you to know I've made one of my own."

Leah's blood was pounding in her ears. "Yes?" she murmured meekly. Even if he admitted that he loved her in a drunken stupor, it wouldn't matter.

"You can have your stupid divorce," he shouted with a harsh edge, cutting through her meager defenses. "But you aren't marrying your Sidney creep while you're carrying my child. Understand?"

Tears stung the back of her eyes, and Leah boldly met his fierce gaze. She held herself stiff, her whole body tensing into a rigid line. So he was going to give her a divorce. What difference did it make if it was before or after the baby arrived?

"I see," she said quietly.

"I don't want that stuffed shirt raising my child," he declared, collapsing onto the sofa as if his legs would no longer support him.

So that was his reasoning. Not that he loved her. Not that he cared about the baby. Not that he couldn't bear to live his life without her. No, he didn't want Siggy raising his son. "You're drunk," she said, her eyes limpid pools of misery.

"That I am. Does it please you to know you have the power to drive me to the bottle?"

Hands on her hips, Leah glared down at him and shook her head. "At this moment," she confessed, "it thrills me."

Suddenly she stormed into the other room, then returned with a blanket and pillow. "Look, right now I don't want to hear a thing from you. But I can't let you drive home like this. You're staying here."

"Good," he said, groping for the sofa arm to help him stand upright. His face fell when he saw the blanket and pillow in her arms. "You don't honestly expect me to sleep in here? This sofa is as hard as a rock. I'll toss and turn the entire night." His gaze slid longingly down the hall to her bedroom.

"Good. A miserable night on a hard, cold surface is exactly what you need to sober you up." She tossed the pillow at his face, then whirled around. "And don't you think of leaving. The minute you walk out that door, I'm phoning the police. You have no business endangering your life or anyone else's by driving."

"Yes, Your Honor." He saluted her mockingly. The action caused him to lose his balance, and he teetered awkwardly before falling onto the sofa, his head hitting the arm. He let out a muffled curse.

A smile curved Leah's soft mouth as she left him alone, Cain rubbing the side of his head.

The smell of fresh coffee woke her the following morning. After donning her clothes as quickly as possible, Leah hurried into the kitchen. Cain was sitting at the table, his head cushioned between his palms, his elbows propped on the tabletop.

"Morning."

His response was little more than a grumble.

Leah took a mug down from the cupboard and poured herself some coffee. The aspirin was tucked in the back of a drawer; she slid it out and set the plastic bottle in front of Cain. The slight sound made him grimace.

Without speaking, he flipped off the lid and shook two tablets into the palm of his hand, then downed them without water.

"Thanks," he mumbled, still not glancing her way.

"You're welcome."

"Do you have to sound so cheerful?" Again he scowled at the pain his own voice caused him.

"No." Carefully she slid out the chair and sat across from him.

"Good. Now . . ." He paused and sucked in a breath. "Quietly, please, tell me what I said last night."

Her palms cupped the mug, seeking its warmth. "Not much." Her voice was barely above a whisper. "You said you'd give me the divorce after the baby was born."

He lowered his hands for the first time. "Well?" His gaze sought hers. "Do you agree?"

"No." She gave an uncompromising shake of her head. What difference did it make when they were divorced?

The only thing Cain wanted to do was ruin any chance of happiness she'd have with Siggy.

"Why not?" he barked, and widened his eyes at the pain that shot through his head.

"Because our agreement states that you're to give me the divorce one week after our departure from Kahu. That time limit is long past."

"That was before—"

"We didn't list any extenuating circumstances that would prolong our affiliation."

"You call our marriage an affiliation?" Cain emitted a harsh laugh.

"Why?" Leah ventured timidly.

"Why what?"

"Why do you want to wait . . . you know . . . for the divorce?"

His mouth went rigid. "I told you I didn't want that pompous stuffed shirt delivering my kid."

What he'd said was that he didn't want Siggy *raising* their child. Cain didn't expect her to notice the difference, but she had.

Lowering her gaze, Leah traced her finger in lazy circles around the rim of the coffee mug. "Is . . . is that the only reason?"

"Should there be another one?" he challenged.

"No," she whispered soberly. "No reason that I know."

"And?"

"And I say no. The divorce will proceed according to the agreement."

Abruptly he stood up, knocking the kitchen chair to the floor with a horrible crash. "Fine. Have it your way. Can you be ready by ten tomorrow morning?"

"Ready?" So soon? her heart cried in anguish.

"Yes, we'll fly to Reno and be done with it. You can have your freedom and your precious Sidney."

It took a full minute for her to compose herself enough to raise her head and meet his rigid gaze. "I'll be ready."

Chapter 10

The front door clicked shut behind Cain. Slowly, with excruciating effort, Leah lowered her lashes to accept the pain that she'd gambled and lost. Cain would grant her the divorce and be done with her.

Her fingers tightened around the ceramic handle of the mug, and she forced down her first sip. The hot coffee burned her throat, but Leah welcomed the pain. She marveled at her composure. How could she sit and drink coffee when her whole world had just shattered into a thousand pieces? Tears burned for release, and her throat grew thick with the effort to suppress their flow.

Her gaze dropped to her hand and the gold band that adorned her ring finger. This plain gold band had been Cain's mother's, and she had given it up freely. Tomorrow Leah would be forced to relinquish it, too. But Leah knew she would face a lifetime of doubts without this gold ring. It seemed so much a part of her now that she couldn't imagine life without it.

Her melancholy persisted for the remainder of the day. Siggy arrived for their dinner date at precisely six o'clock and studied her covertly as she opened the door.

Leah let him in and nervously clasped her hands in front of her. She didn't feel up to an evening in Siggy's favorite restaurant, watching him down another plate of zucchini quiche.

Briefly, he placed his hands on her shoulders and kissed her cheek. Not for the first time, Leah noted that he treated her as if he were an affectionate older brother rather than a fiancé.

"Sit down." She motioned toward the sofa. For a half second she toyed with telling Siggy that Cain had spent the night. She couldn't; it would be too cruel. But something in her wanted to know if he'd forgive her for that, too. Somehow she suspected he would.

"How are you feeling . . . darling?" The endearment almost stuck on his tongue, and Leah hid a sad smile. Siggy didn't love her any more than Cain did. She was the prize in a battle of fierce male pride. Cain couldn't tolerate the bespectacled, nonathletic Siggy, and Siggy was determined to prove that what he lacked in the he-man department he could overcome with brains and persistence. He was the preferable of the two, and Leah would prove it to the egotistical Cain Hawkins. Though by this time, she was thoroughly disgusted with them both.

Sinking into the deep, cushioned chair opposite Siggy, Leah guiltily lowered her gaze. "I'm not feeling all that well tonight," she murmured tightly. The ache in her heart had made this the worst day of her life. Putting on a cheerful facade for Siggy tonight was beyond her.

"I can order something and bring it back here," Siggy offered eagerly.

Even that was more than she could bear. All she

wanted was a few hours alone to prepare herself for the ordeal in the morning.

"Cain and I are flying to Reno tomorrow," she supplied reluctantly.

Siggy slid closer to the edge of the leather sofa. "For the divorce?"

Her fingernails cut unmercifully into her palms as she nodded her head.

"But, darling, that's wonderful. Now you'll be free for us to marry." He sounded so eager, so pleased. "I'll make you a good husband, Leah," he said almost reverently. "Making you my wife will be one of my life's greatest accomplishments."

"Siggy . . ." Leah swallowed, profoundly touched that this man was willing to overlook so much to marry her, no matter what his reasons.

"Yes?" He gave her a nervous glance.

"I can't marry you."

"Leah." His hurt response was immediate. "But you must for . . . for the baby's sake. I've already explained that as long as Mother doesn't know, I'm perfectly happy to be its surrogate father."

Standing, Leah walked around the coffee table and sat beside a flustered and unhappy Siggy. Taking his hand in her own, Leah offered him a genuine smile and tentatively touched the side of his face, wanting to ease some of the hurt and disappointment.

Siggy's cheeks flowered with color. Clearing his throat, he pushed up his glasses from the bridge of his nose. "I'm hoping you'll reconsider, Leah."

"I want you to know I'll always treasure you as one of my closest and dearest friends."

"But . . . but I want to be so much more," he entreated on a faint pleading note.

"Don't you understand that I'm a married woman? I'm going to have a child by my husband."

"But . . . but you said it wasn't a real marriage. You said that you and this Hawkins fellow were getting a divorce in the morning. You said that everything was going to work out fine and that nothing was going to happen between you on the island."

"But it did," she countered softly. "I'll have my baby by myself, and someday, God willing, Cain and I will be together again. I love him, Siggy." It was the first time Leah had openly admitted her feelings. Ironically, it was Siggy who heard her admission, and not Cain.

For a full minute Siggy didn't speak. Hoping to reassure him, Leah squeezed his hand. She was convinced he was about to burst into tears, and she couldn't bear that.

"Nothing I can say will change your mind, will it?" he asked again stiffly, and tugged his hand free from her light grasp.

"I'm afraid not," she answered honestly.

"Just as I thought." Proudly he rose to his feet, holding his back rigid. His mouth was compressed so tight that his lips were an unnatural shade of white. "In that case, I must ask for the necklace I gave you. I can't see wasting good money on a . . . on a vixen like you."

Leah managed to restrain a gasp. She forgave Siggy without his ever asking her pardon. He was hurt and angry, and in his pain he was lashing back at her. Leah understood and granted him that much pride.

She did as he asked, retreating into her bedroom and returning a few moments later with the necklace.

Siggy gave her a long, penetrating look, and his mouth twisted with open disdain.

Awash with regrets, Leah held her trembling chin high and watched him go. No matter why they'd parted, or Siggy's feelings toward her, Leah would always have a special place in her heart for him. Before Cain arrived in her life, Siggy had been the only man to care about her, genuinely care.

The next morning Leah packed an overnight case. Cain hadn't mentioned spending the night, but Leah assumed it would be necessary. A heaviness pressed against her heart as she folded her nightgown and placed it inside the small suitcase. Twice she stopped and took in deep, calming breaths in a desperate effort not to cry. Only heaven knew how she would manage to stand before a judge and not make an idiot of herself by bursting into tears.

Ten minutes before Cain was due to arrive, the doorbell chimed. A sad smile touched Leah's tired expression. Cain was eager to get this over and be done with her. Emotions were warring so fiercely inside her that for one crazy moment she considered throwing herself into his arms, admitting her love and pleading with Cain that they stay married. The insanity passed as quickly as it came.

But it wasn't Cain who was at her door.

"Siggy!" Taken unaware, Leah hadn't time to disguise her surprise. Although he was impeccably dressed in a suit and his ever-present bow tie, Leah could see that he was distressed.

"I didn't mean it, darling. Not a word." He moved

past her into the apartment, turned and fiercely hauled her into his arms.

Totally taken by surprise, Leah let out a small cry. "Siggy." Her breath came in a giant gulp. "It's all right. Don't worry about last night." Not knowing exactly what to do with her arms, Leah patted him gently on the back. Siggy buried his face in her neck, his words muffled and incoherent.

A movement behind Leah shocked her into utter stillness.

"I suggest you take your hands off my wife, Harcharik."

Never had Leah heard anything so chilling. Her breath was stopped in her lungs, and she felt the accusing eyes that bored into her shoulder blades.

Immediately Siggy dropped his arms, freeing her, and Leah turned to face the icy rage that contorted Cain's features.

He said nothing, his face as hard as granite and his eyes as cold as ice chips. Speechless, he stood, feet braced, waiting for the slightest opportunity to crush Siggy.

Knowing he had lost, knowing his health was in imminent danger if he proceeded, Siggy cleared his throat and straightened his glasses. "Goodbye, Leah." His voice was low and wavering as he stepped around her, taking short, sliding steps.

"Goodbye, Siggy," she whispered.

Still Cain didn't move. Even after Siggy had left the apartment and closed the door, Cain didn't budge. The controlled fury exuded from him at every pore. His fists clenched and unclenched at his sides as if he remained eager for a fight.

She stepped into her bedroom and returned with the suitcase. Slipping her arms into a light jacket, she met him at the front door. "I'm . . . I'm ready now," she whispered, her eyes downcast.

"I'll just bet you are," he said with a snarl.

When Leah locked the front door, Cain took the overnight case from her hand and headed to his car, leaving her to follow. It was as if he couldn't get away from her fast enough.

They drove for an hour, and Leah was tempted to demand just where they were headed. The airport, any airport, was miles in the opposite direction. But she was too angry to speak up. When Cain pulled into a huge parking lot, Leah understood. They were at a lake, the name of which she missed. Several floatplanes were moored along the dock. Neither of them uttered a word as Cain helped her out of the car and carried her suitcase. Perilously close to tears, Leah followed him down the long, narrow dock to the plane moored at the end.

Two men were waiting for them, and Cain paused to talk for a few minutes. Leah stood back, not wanting to be forced into light conversation with people she didn't know and would never see again. Like Cain, all she wanted was to get this divorce over with, she decided miserably.

Cain returned and helped her into the passenger side of the two-seat Cessna. It became immediately obvious that he was to be their pilot. Leah didn't know he could fly; but then, she doubted that she really knew this man at all.

Like a robot programmed for servitude, she did everything he instructed. Even when he handed her a cup of light decaffeinated tea, she drank it. Why argue? What good would it do now?

Leah kept her face averted as they sped over the glassy surface of the lake.

"Don't . . . don't you have to contact an air traffic controller?"

"No," he answered crisply, not glancing her way. "Visual flight rules apply here." His words were clear and precise. The way their relationship should have been. Where did they go wrong? Leah wondered wretchedly. In her mind's eye, she tried to pinpoint the exact minute that they had made their first mistake. An unbearably sad smile touched her eyes. The turning point for them had been the last time they stood before a judge. Now it was just as much of a mistake, and she was helpless to prevent it.

Without a glance in her direction, Cain accelerated the little plane. Leah emitted a soundless gasp as they left the glass-surfaced lake and were cast into the blue heavens. Her tense fingers bit into one another, then gradually relaxed.

Her gaze fell to her clasped hands in her lap. The ring felt heavy and awkward again. Briefly, desperately, she toyed with the idea of telling him that because of her pregnancy her fingers had swollen and she couldn't take the ring off. The thought produced a silent sob that heaved her shoulders.

"You sick?"

"No." She continued looking out the side window, oblivious to the beautiful scenery of the world below. All that stretched before her was boundless blue sky, empty of anything but a few scattered clouds. Leah felt that her life was as empty as the sky, while not nearly as beautiful.

Unconsciously her fingers continued to toy with the wedding band, moving it up and over her knuckle, then sliding it into its rightful position over her long, tapered finger.

"Don't be so anxious to take that ring off," he snapped.

Leah froze and dragged her eyes from her hands to stare out the window again. She was utterly desolate and so very tired. The hum of the engine lulled her into a light sleep. With her head propped against the side of the plane, she felt reality slip away as she surrendered to the welcome oblivion. Even in her hazy dreams, though, tears burned the back of her eyes. One must have slipped past the shield of her thick lashes, because Cain gently brushed his finger over the curve of her cheek, waking her. Leah's throat constricted painfully at the tenderness she felt. How unbearably sad it was that she had to be half-asleep for him to demonstrate his gentle nature.

Later, much later, Leah again felt Cain's touch. Only this time it was his whole hand as he ever so carefully laid it over her stomach. A brief smile touched her mouth. She never knew how Cain felt about the baby. When he'd come to her with the pictures, after first discovering her condition, he'd been shocked and concerned. But he'd never said what his feelings were. Would Cain want a hand in their child's upbringing? Holding on to the beautiful thought of Cain with their child in his arms, Leah stirred and sat upright. Her neck ached, and she rubbed some of the soreness away, rotating her head as she massaged the tired muscles. Confident that their baby would have his love—even if she didn't—Leah spoke for the first time.

"How much farther?"

"We're almost there now."

A scan of the area revealed only dense forest below.

"Where's Reno?" Certainly she should be able to see it by now.

"A ways," he answered noncommittally.

"But shouldn't we be within sight of it?"

"No."

Cain began his descent, and Leah searched around her, looking for a place for them to land. As Cain made his sweeping approach, a large lake came into view.

Concerned now, Leah swiveled her gaze to him. "Where are we?"

"A lake."

"I can see that. What are we doing here?"

"Nothing." The plane glided effortlessly onto the smooth surface of the deep blue water. Cain's concentration was centered on controlling their landing.

"We . . . we aren't going to Reno, are we?" she whispered.

Cain turned and stared at her with eyes that looked into her soul.

"No."

Chapter 11

The Cessna coasted to a stop at the large private dock that extended from the shore. A log cabin stood back from the land, its wide porch facing the lake, a rock-hewn chimney jutting out from the shake roof. Overhead, a hawk, its wings spread wide, made a lazy circle above them. Its cry could be heard for miles. Leah sighed at the beauty of the scene. But then she remembered and she stiffened. They were supposed to be in Reno.

"I demand to know where we are." A chill raced up her spine, reminding her she was no longer in the warm desert air of San Diego, but in the mountains.

Cain didn't answer her. Instead he swung open the door of the cockpit and leaped down onto the wooden dock, that rocked with the force of his weight. "Are you coming or not?" Hands on his hips, Cain regarded her idly, giving the impression that it didn't matter to him if she sat in the plane all day.

"Tell me where we are first."

He hesitated as if debating with himself. "My home."

The curiosity to know what awaited her prompted

Leah to move. Cain gave her his hand and helped her onto the dock so that she was by his side once again.

"Why are we here? Did you need to pick up something?"

His mouth remained tightly closed as he ignored both Leah and her question. He turned aside, leaving her to follow if she chose.

Leah did. Her gaze fell on the house. This was no simple log cabin, but one of polished pine built by a master craftsman. The wide porch and open door of the two-story structure beckoned her inside.

Timidly, Leah climbed the steps to the porch and came into a huge central room. Sunlight spilled into the room from the open door, setting the interior to glowing.

Cain was kneeling in front of a huge fireplace, whittling off slivers of wood, preparing to start a fire. Briefly, Leah wondered what was wrong with igniting paper, but she didn't ask.

Her thin cotton jacket was no longer sufficient to warm her, and she rubbed her hands over her arms and closed the door. The central room led off to a quaint kitchen with all the modern conveniences.

"You might look around for something to eat," he said without turning around, intent on his task. The sound of a match being struck was followed by the first faint flickerings of the fire.

Leah's gaze wandered to the stairs at the end of the room. Four steps led to a landing and then angled to the left. Cain's photographs covered the cabin walls—if she could call this spacious home a cabin. The landing held his awards. Leah walked up the first series of stairs, and with hands in her pockets to keep her fingers warm, she paused to read the framed certificates. Her heart swelled with pride as she scanned them.

"I thought you were fixing us some lunch." Cain stood and crossed his arms over his broad chest, regarding her curiously.

"I . . . will." Her fingertips ran over one oak frame. "You never told me you won a Pulitzer."

He shrugged carelessly. "I wasn't aware it would impress you."

A lazy smile crinkled the lines about her eyes. "In other words, you'd rather eat than overwhelm me with your credits."

His returning grin was his first smile of the day. "Exactly."

The fire added a cozy warmth to the cabin in quick order. Shortly Leah served them hot tomato soup and turkey sandwiches. They both ate ravenously.

Dabbing the corner of her mouth with the paper napkin, Leah pushed her empty bowl aside. "Are you going to tell me why we're here?"

He regarded her coolly. "I could."

"Then please do. Good heavens, I don't even know where we are."

"That's the way I wanted it."

Leah forced out a light laugh. "You make it sound like you've kidnapped me."

"I have." He inclined his head toward the front door and the plane just outside. "No one knows you're here. Certainly not your precious Sidney, and I have every intention of keeping it that way."

"And just how long do you plan to hold me here?" she inquired stiffly.

"Until the baby comes."

Leah choked out a gasp. "Why, that's months . . . that's crazy." She couldn't believe what she was hearing. Had the pressures of the Kahu expedition caused Cain to lose his sanity?

"The desperate plan of a desperate man," Cain said in a clipped manner, and stood to pour himself a cup of coffee. He handed her a glass of milk. Twisting the chair around, he straddled it and regarded her as though they'd been discussing football scores.

"You're serious, aren't you?" His declaration was just beginning to sink into her bemused brain.

"Dead serious."

"But why?"

"I told you I didn't want Sidney around my child."

Leah gritted her teeth. "His name is Siggy. Why . . . why do you insist on calling him that?" Tears blurred her vision. Cain was so full of insane pride and jealous anger that he couldn't see what was right in front of his own two eyes.

Standing, Leah delivered their dirty dishes to the sink. Her arms cradled her stomach as she walked back to the table. "What if I promised not to see Siggy again? Would that convince you to let me go?"

"No."

"Why not?" she cried.

"Because if you have your freedom, you might run away from me. I couldn't take that, Leah. Not with my baby growing inside you." He caught her by the waist, bringing her close to his chair so that she had to drop her eyes to meet his gaze. "You once told me my problem was that I didn't care about anything."

A chill that had nothing to do with the room temperature raced up her spine. She recalled the conversation well. They had been planting the sonar equipment when their rubber raft was lifted from the ocean by a playful whale, threatening their lives.

"You were wrong," Cain continued. "I care. I care very deeply for our baby and for you." His hand slipped inside her sweater. He lifted it up at the waist and very gently kissed her smooth, ivory stomach.

Leah's fingers slid through his hair, holding him to her. Tears rolled unheeded down her pale face. "Are you saying—" she whispered with a harsh breath "—that you love me?"

"How can you even ask such a question? I care about you more than anything in my life," Cain breathed.

"Then why . . . why did you give me back the necklace?" Tears streaked her face and fell onto his shoulders.

Stunned, Cain lifted his head. A myriad of emotions passed over his face as he slowly stood. Taking a clean handkerchief from the back pocket of his jeans, he tenderly wiped the tears from her face.

"Why did you give me back the necklace?" she repeated, almost angry. How could he stand there with his eyes full of love when he'd practically shoved her into Siggy's arms?

"Why did you take it? I was asking you to make your choice between Harcharik and me."

"Choice?" Leah echoed in disbelief. "I . . . I thought you were telling me that . . . that what we shared was over. That the time had come to go back to our lives and that Siggy was part of my life . . . and you weren't."

"Are you crazy?" His eyes narrowed with a dark frown.

"Yes," she shouted, breaking free of his embrace. "Crazy enough to have married you and even crazier to have fallen in love with you."

Cain stiffened and raked a hand through his hair. "You love me?" he asked in a low, wondrous voice as if he couldn't believe what she'd said.

"Oh, Cain," she sobbed. "How could you have known me so intimately and not know me at all?"

He looked so stunned, so utterly taken aback, that Leah had to laugh.

"Could I have given myself to you so freely without involving my heart?" Leah asked softly.

"But . . ." he stammered.

"Do you love me?" He'd said he cared, but caring and loving were two different things.

Cain's features hardened until they were sharp and intense. "Are you crazy?"

Leah smiled. "I believe I already answered that question."

Reaching for her, Cain held her so close she could barely breathe. "I love you, Leah Talmadge Hawkins. I think I'd rather live the life of a hermit than be without you."

"How could we have been so stupid?" she asked, winding her arms around his neck. "Oh, Cain, hold me. Promise me that you'll never let me go. Not for any reason."

Swinging her into his arms, he looked adoringly into her eyes. "Are you crazy?"

Laughing, crying, Leah looped her arms around his neck and spread kisses over his face. Her lips found his jaw, his temple, his eyes and nose, lingering every place but his lips.

A low growl escaped from his throat as he paused on the landing. "I'm hoping that by the time we reach the bedroom your aim will improve, Mrs. Hawkins."

"I may require more practice," she teased, bringing her mouth a scant inch from his.

"A lifetime, my love, a lifetime."

Sometime later, Leah propped her head on her hand and basked in the lambent glow of love coming from her husband's eyes.

"I love you," he whispered, kissing the tips of her fingers. "I plan to spend the rest of my life proving it to you again and again."

"You just did." Ever so gently she pressed a kiss to his lips.

"Would you be angry if I got out my camera and took your picture? I swear I've never seen a woman more beautiful than you are at this moment."

A soft, radiant smile lit up her hazel eyes. "I think I could get to be very jealous of that camera of yours."

Surprise flickered from the depths of his dark eyes. "You needn't worry, love. Ever. Nothing will stand between us again, and certainly not my camera."

Not for a moment did Leah doubt him. At one time in his life, Cain had needed the camera because pictures revealed the emotions that he couldn't. Love had changed that.

Twisting around so that he was braced above her, he gently brushed the hair from her face. "We've never talked about the baby," he said on a sober note. "Are you unhappy?"

Her eyes widened with incandescent wonder. "I don't think I've ever been more delighted about anything in my life. I wanted to shout it from the highest mountain." She wound her arms around his neck and planted a lingering kiss on his parted lips. Averting her eyes, she tenderly brushed the hair from his temple. "What about you? How did you feel about . . . the baby?"

He chuckled. "You mean after I got over being furious that you hadn't told me?"

She nodded, still not meeting his gaze.

He paused and grew so still that Leah's heart lurched. "You want the truth, I suppose."

"Yes," she whispered.

"I got down on my knees and thanked God. I've never been more grateful for anything. I knew that if you were pregnant, then you might be willing to give our marriage a second chance. And if worse came to worst and you didn't, then I would still have a tangible part of you through our child."

"Oh, Cain, I do love you so." Now, finally, with his arms wrapped securely around her, Leah could believe that this wonderful, loving man was hers. Completely, totally, utterly hers.

White Lace and Promises

Chapter 1

Maggie Kingsbury ground the gears of her royal-blue Mercedes and pulled to a screeching halt at the red light. Impatient, she glanced at her wristwatch and muttered silently under her breath. Once again she was late. Only this time her tardiness hadn't been intentional. The afternoon had innocently slipped away while she painted, oblivious to the world.

When Janelle had asked her to be the maid of honor for the wedding, Maggie had hesitated. As a member of the wedding party, unwelcome attention would be focused on her. It wasn't until she had learned that Glenn Lambert was going to be the best man that she'd consented. Glenn had been her friend from the time she was in grade school: her buddy, her coconspirator, her white knight. With Glenn there, everything would be perfect.

But already things were going badly. Here she was due to pick him up at San Francisco International and she was ten minutes behind schedule. In the back of her mind, Maggie realized that her tardiness was another symptom of her discontent.

The light changed and she roared across the intersection, her back tires spinning. One of these days she was going to get a well-deserved speeding ticket. But not today, she prayed, please not today.

Her painting smock was smudged with a full spectrum of rainbow colors. The thick, dark strands of her chestnut hair were pinned to the back of her head, disobedient curls tumbling defiantly at her temples and across her wide brow. And she had wanted to look so good for Glenn. It had been years since she'd seen him—not since high school graduation. In the beginning they had corresponded back and forth, but soon they'd each become involved with college and had formed a new set of friends. Their texts and emails had dwindled, and as often happens their communication became a chatty note on a Christmas card. Steve and Janelle had kept her updated with what had been going on in Glenn's life, and from what she understood, he was a successful stockbroker in Charleston. It sounded like a job he would manage well.

It surprised Maggie that in all those years, Glenn hadn't married. At twenty-nine and thirty, they were the only two of their small high school graduation class who hadn't. Briefly, Maggie wondered what had kept Glenn away from the altar. As she recalled, he had always been easy on the eyes.

Her mind conjured a mental picture of a young Glenn Lambert. Tall, dark, athletic, broad-shouldered, thin—she smiled—he'd probably filled out over the years. He was the boy who lived next door, and they had been great friends and at times the worst of enemies. Once, in the sixth grade, Glenn had stolen her diary and as a joke made copies and sold them to the boys in their class. After he found her crying, he had spent weeks trying to make it up to her. Years later, his patience had gotten her a passing grade in chemistry and she had fixed him up with a date for the junior-senior prom.

Arriving at the airport, Maggie followed the freeway signs that directed her to the passenger pickup area. Almost immediately she sighted Glenn standing beside his luggage, watching the traffic for a familiar face. A slow smile blossomed across her lips until it hovered at a grin. Glenn had hardly changed, and yet he was completely different. He was taller than she remembered, with those familiar broad shoulders now covered by a heather-blue blazer instead of a faded football jersey. At thirty, he was a prime specimen of manhood. But behind his easy smile, Maggie recognized a maturity—one he'd fought hard for and painfully attained. Maggie studied him with fascination, amazed at his air of deliberate casualness. He knew about her inheritance. Of course he knew; Steve would have told him. Involuntarily, her fingers tightened around the steering wheel as a sense of regret settled over her. As much as she would have liked to, Maggie couldn't go back to being a carefree schoolgirl.

She eased to a stop at the curb in front of him and leaned across the seat to open the passenger door. "Hey, handsome, are you looking for a ride?"

Bending over, Glenn stuck his head inside the car. "Muffie, I should have known you'd be late."

As she climbed out of the vehicle, Maggie grimaced at the use of her nickname. Glenn had dubbed her Muffie in junior high, but it had always sounded to Maggie like the name of a poodle. The more she'd objected, the more the name had stuck, until her friends had picked it up. The sweet, innocent Muffie no longer existed.

"I'm sorry I'm late, I don't know where the time went. As usual, I got carried away."

Glenn chuckled and shook his head knowingly. "When haven't you gotten carried away?" He picked up his suitcase and tucked it inside the trunk Maggie had opened. Placing his hands on her shoulders, he examined her carefully and gave her a brief hug. "You look fantastic." His dark eyes were somber and sincere.

"Me?" she choked out, feeling the warmth of many years of friendship chase away her earlier concerns. "You always could lie diplomatically." Maggie had recognized early in life that she was no raving beauty. Her eyes were probably her best feature—dark brown, with small gold flecks, almond shaped and slanting upward at the corners. She was relatively tall, nearly five-foot-eight, with long, shapely legs. Actually, the years hadn't altered her outwardly. Like Glenn's, she suspected the changes were more inward. Life's lessons had left their mark on her as well.

Looking at Glenn, Maggie couldn't hide the feeling of nostalgia she experienced. "The last time I looked this bad I was dressed as a zucchini for a fifth-grade play."

He crossed his arms and studied her. "I'd say you were wearing typical Muffie attire."

"Jeans and sneakers?"

"Seeing you again is like stepping into the past."

Not exactly. She didn't stuff tissue paper in her bra these days. Momentarily, she wondered if Glenn had ever guessed that she had. "I've got strict instructions to drop you off at Steve's. The rehearsal's scheduled at the church tonight at seven." This evening he'd have the opportunity to see just how much she had changed. Of all the people

Maggie knew, Glenn would be the one to recognize the emotional differences in her. She might have been able to disguise them from others, but not from Glenn.

"With you chauffeuring me around, there's little guarantee I'll make the wedding," Glenn teased affectionately.

"You'll make it," she assured him, and climbed back into the car.

Glenn joined her and snapped the seat belt into place. Thoughtfully, he ran his hand along the top of the dashboard. "I heard about your inheritance and wondered if it'd made a difference in your life."

"Well, I now live in a fancy beach house, and don't plan to do anything with the rest of my life except paint." She checked his profile for a negative response and, finding none, she continued: "A secretary handles the mail, an estate planner deals with the finances, and there's a housekeeper and gardener as well. I do exactly as I want."

"Must be nice."

"I heard you haven't done so shabbily yourself."

"Not bad, but I don't lounge around in a beach house." He said it without censure. "I've had dealings with a lot of wealthy people the past few years. As far as I can see, having money can be a big disappointment."

The statement was open-ended, but Maggie refused to comment. Glenn's insight surprised her. He was right. All Great-aunt Margaret's money hadn't brought Maggie or her brother happiness. Oh, at first she had been filled with wonderful illusions about her inheritance. But these days she struggled to shroud her restlessness. To anyone else her lifestyle was a dream come true. Only Maggie knew differently.

"Money is supposed to make everything right. Only it

creates more problems than it solves," she mumbled, and pulled into the flow of traffic leaving the airport. Glenn didn't respond, and Maggie wasn't sure he heard her, which was just as well, because the subject was one she preferred to avoid.

"It's hard to imagine Steve and Janelle getting married after all these years." A lazy grin swept across his tanned face.

Maggie smiled, longing to keep things light. "I'd say it was about time, wouldn't you?"

"I've never known two people more right for each other. The surprising part is that everyone saw it but them."

"I'm happy for those two."

"Me, too," he added, but Maggie noted that Glenn's tone held a hint of melancholy, as if the wedding was going to be as difficult for him as it was for her. Maggie couldn't imagine why.

"Steve's divorce devastated him," Maggie continued, "and he started dating Janelle again. The next thing I knew they decided to march up the aisle." Maggie paused and gestured expressively with her right hand.

Glenn's eyes fell on Maggie's artistically long fingers. It surprised him that she had such beautiful hands. They looked capable of kneading the stiffest clay and at the same time gentle enough to soothe a crying child. She wore no rings, nor were her well-shaped nails painted, yet her hands were striking. He couldn't take his eyes from them. He had known Maggie most of her life and had never appreciated her hands.

"Are you going to invite me out to your beach house?" he asked finally.

"I thought I might. There's a basketball hoop in the gym and I figured I'd challenge you to a game."

"I'm not worried. As I recall, the only slam dunk you ever made was with a doughnut into a cup of coffee."

Hiding her laugh, Maggie answered threateningly, "I'll make you pay for that remark."

Their families had shared a wide common driveway, and Maggie had passed many an hour after school playing ball with Glenn. Hadn't seen him since his parents had moved. Janelle and Steve and the rest of the gang from the neighborhood had hung around together. Most of the childhood friendships remained in place. Admittedly, Maggie wasn't as trusting of people nowadays. Not since she had inherited the money. The creeps had come crawling out of the woodwork the minute the news of her good fortune was out. Some were obvious gold diggers and others weren't so transparent. Maggie had gleaned valuable lessons from Dirk Wagner and had nearly made the mistake of marrying a man who loved her money far more than he cared for her.

"I don't suppose you've got a pool in that mansion of yours?"

"Yup."

"Is there anything you haven't got?" Glenn asked, suddenly serious.

Maggie didn't know where to start, the list was so long. She had lost her purpose, her ambition, her drive to succeed professionally with her art. Her roster of friends was meager and consisted mainly of people she had known most of her life. "Some things," she muttered, wanting to change the subject.

"Money can't buy everything, can it?" Glenn asked so gently that Maggie felt her throat tighten.

She'd thought it would at first, but had learned the hard way that it couldn't buy the things that mattered most: love, loyalty, respect, or friendship.

"No." Her voice was barely above a whisper.

"I suppose out of respect for your millions, I should call you Margaret," Glenn suggested next. "But try as I might, you'll always be Muffie to me."

"Try Maggie. I'm not Muffie anymore." She smiled to take any sting from her voice. With his returning nod, her hand relaxed against the steering wheel.

She exited from the freeway and drove into the basement parking lot of Steve's high-rise building. "Here we are," she announced, turning off the engine. "With a good three hours to spare."

While Glenn removed his suitcase from the car trunk, Maggie dug in the bottom of her purse for the apartment key Steve had given her. "I have strict instructions to personally escort you upstairs and give you a stiff drink. You're going to need it when you hear what's scheduled."

With his suitcase in tow, Glenn followed her to the elevator. "Where's Steve?"

"Working."

"The day before his wedding?" Glenn looked astonished.

"He's been through this wedding business before," she reminded him offhandedly.

The heavy doors swished closed and Maggie leaned against the back wall and pulled the pins from her hair. It was futile to keep putting it up when it came tumbling down every time she moved her head. Stuffing the pins in her pocket, she felt Glenn's gaze studying her. Their eyes met.

"I can't believe you," he said softly.

"What?"

"You haven't changed. Time hasn't marked you in the least. You're exactly as I remember."

"You've changed." They both had.

"Don't I know it." Glenn sighed, leaned against the side of the moving elevator, and pinched the bridge of his nose. "Some days I feel a hundred years old."

Maggie was mesmerized by him. He was different. The carefree, easygoing teen had been replaced by an introspective man with intense, dark eyes that revealed a weary pain. The urge to ask him what had happened burned on her lips, but she knew that if she inquired into his life, he could ask about her own. Instead, she led the way out of the elevator to the apartment.

The key turned, and Maggie swung open the door to the high-rise apartment that gave a spectacular view of San Francisco Bay.

"Go ahead and plant your suitcase in the spare bedroom and I'll fix us a drink. What's your pleasure?"

"Juice, if there's any."

Maggie placed both hands on the top of the bar. "I'll see what I can do." Turning, she investigated the contents of the refrigerator and brought out a small can of tomato juice. "Will this do?"

"Give it to me straight," he tossed over his shoulder as he left the living room.

By the time he returned, Maggie was standing at the window, holding a martini. She watched him take the glass of juice from the bar and join her.

"Are you on the wagon?" she asked impulsively.

"Not really. It's a little too early in the afternoon for me."

Maggie nodded as a tiny smile quirked at the corners of her mouth. The first time she had ever tasted vodka had been with Glenn.

"What's so amusing?"

"Do you remember New Year's Eve the year I was sixteen?"

Glenn's brow furrowed. "No."

"Glenn!" She laughed with disbelief. "After all the trouble we got into over that, I'd think you'd never forget it."

"Was that the year we threw our own private party?"

"Remember Cindy and Earl, Janelle and Steve, you and me, and . . . who else?"

"Brenda and Bob?"

"No . . . Barb and Bob."

"Right." He chuckled. "I never could keep the twins straight."

"Who could? It surprises me he didn't marry both of them."

"Whatever happened to Bob?"

Maggie took a sip of her martini before answering. "He's living in Oregon, going bald, and has four kids."

"Bob? I don't believe it."

"You weren't here for the ten-year reunion." Maggie hadn't bothered to attend, either, but Janelle had filled in the details of what she'd missed.

"I'm sorry I missed it," Glenn said. He lifted his drink and finished it off in two enormous swallows.

Mildly surprised at the abrupt action, Maggie took

another sip of hers, moved to a deep-seated leather chair, sat, and tucked her long legs under her.

Glenn took a seat across from her. "So what's been going on in your life, Maggie? Are you happy?"

She shrugged indolently. "I suppose." From anyone else she would have resented the question, but she'd always been able to talk to Glenn. A half hour after being separated for years, and it was as if they'd never been apart. "I'm a wealthy woman, Glenn, and I've learned the hard way about human nature."

"What happened?"

"It's a long story."

"Didn't you just get done telling me that we had three hours before the rehearsal?"

For a moment, Maggie was tempted to spill her frustrations out. To tell Glenn about the desperate pleas for money she got from people who sensed her soft heart. The ones who were looking for someone to invest in a sure thing. And the users, who pretended friendship or love in the hopes of a lucrative relationship. "You must be exhausted. I'll cry on your shoulder another time."

"I'll hold you to that." He leaned forward and reached for her hand. "We had some good times, didn't we?"

"Great times."

"Ah, the good old days." Glenn relaxed with a bittersweet sigh. "Who was it that said youth was wasted on the young?"

"Mark Twain," Maggie offered.

"No, I think it was Madonna."

They both laughed and Maggie stood, reaching for her purse. "Well, I suppose I should think about heading home and changing my clothes. Steve will be here in an hour. That'll give you time to relax." She fanned her fingers through her hair in a careless gesture. "I'll see you tonight at the rehearsal."

"Thanks for meeting me," Glenn said, coming to his feet.

"I was glad to do it." Her hand was on the doorknob. "It's great to see you again."

The door made a clicking sound as it closed, and Glenn turned to wipe a hand over his tired eyes. It was good to be with Maggie again, but frankly, he was glad she'd decided to leave. He needed a few minutes to compose his thoughts before facing Steve. The first thing his friend was bound to ask him about was Angie.

Glenn stiffened as her name sent an instant flash of pain through him. She had married Simon two months earlier, and Glenn had thought that acceptance would become easier with time. It had, but it was far more difficult than he'd expected. He had loved Angie with a reverence; eventually, he had loved her enough to step aside when she wanted to marry Simon. He'd been a fool, Glenn realized. If he had acted on his instincts, he'd have had a new bride on his arm for this trip. Now he was alone, more alone than he could ever remember. The last place he wanted to be was at a wedding. Every part of it would only be a reminder of what could have been his and what he'd allowed to slip through his fingers. He didn't begrudge Steve any happiness; he just didn't want to have to stand by and smile serenely when part of him was riddled with regrets.

Maggie shifted into a higher gear as she rounded the curve in the highway at twenty miles above the speed limit. Deliberately, she slowed down, hating the urgency that forced her to rush home. The beach house had become her gilded cage. The world outside its door had taken on a steel edge that she avoided.

Although she had joked with Glenn about not being married, the tense muscles of her stomach reminded her of how much she envied Janelle. She would smile for the wedding pictures and be awed at all the right moments, but she was going to hate every minute of it. The worst part was she was genuinely happy for Janelle and Steve. Oh, Janelle had promised that they'd continue to get together as they always had. They'd been best friends since childhood, and for a time they probably would see each other regularly. But Janelle wanted to start a family right away, and once she had a baby, Maggie thought, everything would change. It had to.

Automatically, Maggie took the road that veered from the highway, and a few minutes later turned onto the long circular driveway that led to her waterfront house. The huge structure loomed before her, impressive, elegant, and imposing. Maggie had bought it for none of those reasons. She wasn't even sure she liked it. The two-story single-family dwelling on Eastwood Drive where she had grown up was far more appealing. Sometimes during the darkest hour of a sleepless night, Maggie would mull over the idea of donating her money to charity. If possible, she would gladly return to the years when she had sat blissfully at her bedroom window, her chin resting on her crossed arms as she gazed at the stars and dreamed of the future. Childhood dreams that were never meant to come true.

Shaking herself from her reverie, Maggie parked the

fancy sports car in front of the house. For this night she would put on her brightest smile. No one would ever know what she was feeling on the inside.

Janelle's mother looked as if she were preparing more for a funeral than a wedding. Flustered and worried, she waved her hands in five different directions, orchestrating the entourage gathered in the church vestibule.

"Girls, please, please pay attention. Darcy, go right, June left, and so on. Understand?"

The last time anyone had called Maggie a girl was in high school. Janelle, Maggie, the bridesmaids, the flower girl, and the ring bearer were all positioned, awaiting instructions. Maggie glanced enviously to the front of the church, where Steve and Glenn were standing. It didn't seem fair that they should get off so lightly.

"Remember to count to five slowly before following the person in front of you," Janelle's mother continued.

The strains of organ music burst through the church and the first attendant, shoulders squared, stepped onto the white runner that flowed down the center aisle.

"I can't believe this is really happening," Janelle whispered. "Tomorrow Steve and I will be married. After all the years of loving him, it's like a dream."

"I know," Maggie whispered, and squeezed her friend's forearm.

"Go left, go left." Mrs. Longmier's voice drifted to them, and Maggie dissolved into giggles.

"I can't believe your mother."

"The pastor assured her he'd handle everything, but

she insisted on doing it herself. That's what I get for being the only girl in a family of four boys."

"In another twenty years or so you may well be doing it yourself," Maggie reminded her.

"Oops." Janelle nudged her. "Your turn. And for heaven's sake, don't goof up. I'm starved and want to get out of here."

Holding a paper plate decorated with bows and ribbons from one of Janelle's five wedding showers, Maggie carefully placed one foot in front of the other in a deliberate, step-by-step march that seemed to take an eternity. The smile on her face was as brittle as old parchment.

Standing in her place at the altar, Maggie kept her head turned so she could see Janelle's approach. The happiness radiating from her friend's face produced a curious ache in Maggie's heart. If these feelings were so strong at the rehearsal, she couldn't help wondering how she'd react during the actual wedding. Maggie felt someone's eyes on her and glanced up to see Glenn's steady gaze. He smiled briefly and looked away.

The pastor moved in front of the young couple and cracked a few old jokes. Everyone laughed politely. As the organ music filled the church, the bride and groom, hands linked, began their exit.

When it came time for Maggie to meet Glenn at the head of the aisle, he stiffly tucked her hand in the crook of his elbow.

"I never thought I'd be marching down the aisle with you," she whispered under her breath.

"It has all the makings of a nightmare," Glenn countered. "However, I'll admit you're kinda cute."

"Thanks."

"But so are lion cubs."

Maggie's fingers playfully bit into the muscles of his upper arm as she struggled not to laugh.

His hand patted hers as he whispered, "You're lovely."

"Is that so?" Maggie batted her eyes at him, blatantly flirting. "And available. I have a king-size bed, too."

They were nearing the back of the church. Glenn's dark eyes bored holes into her. "Are you looking for a lover?"

The question caught Maggie by surprise. The old Glenn would have swatted her across the rump and told her to behave. The new Glenn, the man she didn't know, was dead serious. "Not this week," she returned, deliberately flippant. "But if you're interested, I'll keep you in mind."

His gaze narrowed slightly as he tilted his head to one side. "How much have you had to drink?"

Maggie wanted to laugh, and would have if not for a discouraging glare from Mrs. Longmier. "One martini."

The sound of a soft snort followed. "You've changed, Maggie." Just the way he said it indicated that he wasn't pleased with the difference.

Her spirits crashed to the floor with breakneck speed. *Good grief,* she thought angrily, it didn't matter what Glenn thought of her. He had made her feel like a teenager again, and she'd behaved like a fool. She wasn't even sure why she was flirting with him. Probably to cover up how miserable the whole event made her.

Casually, Glenn dropped her arm as they entered the vestibule and stepped aside to make room for the others who followed. Maggie used the time to gather her coat and purse. Glenn moved in the opposite direction, and her troubled gaze followed him.

A flurry of instructions followed as Steve's father gave directions to the family home, where dinner was being served to the members of the wedding party.

Maggie moved outside the church. There wasn't any need for her to stay and listen. She knew how to get to the Grants' house as well as her own. Standing at the base of the church steps, Maggie was fumbling inside her purse for her keys when Glenn joined her.

"I'm supposed to ride with you."

"Don't make it sound like a fate worse than death," she bit out, furious that she couldn't find what she needed.

"Listen, Maggie, I'm sorry. Okay?"

"You?" Amazed, Maggie lowered the purse flap and slowly raised her dark eyes to his. "It's me who should apologize. I was behaving like an idiot in there, flirting with you like that."

He lifted a silken strand of hair from her shoulder. "It's rather nice to be flirted with now and then," he said with a lazy smile.

Maggie tore her gaze from his and withdrew her car keys. "Here," she said, handing the key chain to him. "I know you'll feel a whole lot safer driving yourself."

"You're right," he retorted, his mood teasing and jovial. "I still remember the day you wiped out two garbage cans and an oak tree backing out of the driveway."

"I'd just gotten my learner's permit and the gears slipped," she returned righteously.

"Unfortunately, your skills haven't improved much."

"On second thought, I'll drive and you can do the praying."

Laughing, Glenn tossed an arm across her shoulders.

They chatted easily on the way to the Grants' home and parked behind Steve and Janelle in the driveway. The four car doors slammed simultaneously.

"Glad to see you still remember your way around town," Steve teased Glenn. The two men were nearly the same height, both with dark hair and brown eyes. Steve smiled lovingly at Janelle and brought her close to his side. "I hope everyone's hungry," he said, waiting for Glenn and Maggie to join them. "Mom hasn't stopped cooking in two days."

"Famished," Glenn admitted. "The last time I ate was on the plane."

"Poor starving baby," Maggie cooed.

Glenn was chuckling when the four entered the house. Immediately, Janelle and Maggie offered to help Steve's mother and carried the assorted salads and platters of meat to the long table for the buffet. Soon the guests were mingling and helping themselves.

Maggie loaded her plate and found an empty space beside Glenn, who was kneeling in front of the coffee table with several others. He glanced up from the conversation he was having with a bridesmaid when Maggie joined them.

"Muffie, you know Darcy, don't you?" Glenn asked.

"Muffie?" Darcy repeated incredulously. "I thought your name was Maggie."

"Muffie was the name Glenn gave me in junior high. We were next-door neighbors. In fact, we lived only a few blocks from here."

"I suppose you're one of those preppy, organized types," Darcy suggested.

Glenn nearly choked on his potato salad. "Hardly."

Maggie gave him the sharp point of her elbow in his ribs. "Glenn thought he was being cute one day and dubbed me something offensive. Muffie, however, was better than Magpie—"

"She never stopped talking," Glenn inserted.

"—or Maggie the Menace."

"For obvious reasons."

"For a while, it was Molasses." Maggie closed her eyes at the memory.

"Because she was forever late."

"As you may have guessed, we fought like cats and dogs," Maggie explained needlessly.

"The way a lot of brothers and sisters do," Glenn inserted.

"So where did the Muffie come in?"

"In junior high, things became a bit more sophisticated. We couldn't very well call her Magpie."

Darcy nodded and sliced off a bite of ham.

"So after a while," Glenn continued, "Steve, Janelle, the whole gang of us decided to call her Muffie, simply because she talked so much we wanted to muffle her. The name stuck."

"Creative people are often subjected to this form of harassment," Maggie informed her with a look of injured pride.

"Didn't you two . . . ?" Darcy hesitated. "I mean, Steve and Janelle obviously had something going even then."

"Us?" Maggie and Glenn shared a look of shock. "I did ask you to the Sadie Hawkins dance once."

Glenn nodded, a mischievous look in his eyes. "She'd already asked five other guys and been turned down."

"So I drastically lowered my standards and asked Glenn. It was a complete disaster. Remember?"

Their eyes met and they burst into fits of laughter, causing the conversational hum of the room to come to an abrupt halt.

"Hey, you two, let me in on the joke," Darcy said. "What's so funny?"

Maggie composed herself enough to begin the story. "On the way home, Glenn's beat-up car stalled. We learned later it was out of gas. Believe me, I wasn't pleased, especially since I'd sprung for new shoes and my feet were killing me."

"I don't know why you're complaining; I took you to the dance, didn't I?"

Maggie ignored him. "Since I didn't have a driver's license, Mr. Wonderful here insisted on steering while I pushed his car—uphill."

"You?" Darcy was aghast.

"Now, Maggie, to be fair, you should explain that I helped push, too."

"Some help," she grumbled. "That wasn't the worst part. It started to rain and I was in my party dress, shoving his car up the street in the dead of night."

"Maggie was complaining so loud that she woke half the neighborhood," Glenn inserted, "and someone looked out the window and thought we were stealing a car. They phoned the police, and within minutes we were surrounded by three patrol cars."

"They took us downtown and phoned Glenn's dad. It was the most embarrassing moment of my life. The Girls' Club had sponsored the dance, and I was expecting roses and kisses in the moonlight. Instead, I got stuck pushing Glenn's car in the rain and was darn near arrested."

"Believe me, Maggie made me pay for that one." Glenn's smiling eyes met hers and Maggie felt young and carefree again. It'd been so long since she had talked and laughed like this; she could almost forget. Almost. The present, however, was abruptly brought to her attention a few minutes later, when Steve's cousin approached her.

"Maggie," he asked, crowding in next to her on the floor, "I was wondering if we could have a few minutes alone? There's something I'd like to ask you."

A heavy sensation of dread moved over her. It had happened so often in the past that she knew almost before he spoke what he would say. "Sure, Sam." As of yet, she hadn't found a graceful way of excusing herself from these situations.

Rolling to her feet, she followed Sam across the room to an empty corner.

"I suppose Steve's told you about my business venture?" he began brightly, with false enthusiasm.

Maggie gritted her teeth, praying for patience. "No, I can't say that he has."

"Well, my partner and I are looking for someone with a good eye for investment potential who would be willing to lend us a hundred thousand dollars. Would you happen to know anyone who might be interested?"

Maggie noticed Glenn making his way toward them. As she struggled to come up with a polite rejection for Sam, Glenn stopped next to her.

"Sam," he interrupted, taking Maggie by the arm, "excuse us for a minute, will you?" He didn't wait for a response and led her through the cluttered living room and into the kitchen.

"Where are you taking me?" Maggie asked when he opened the sliding glass door that led to the patio.

"Outside."

"That much is obvious. But why are you taking me out here?"

Glenn paused to stand under the huge maple tree and looked toward the sky. "There's only a half-moon tonight, but it'll have to do."

"Are you going to turn into a werewolf or something?" Maggie joked, pleased to be rescued from the clutches of an awkward conversation.

"Nope." He turned her in his arms, looping his hands around her narrow waist and bringing her against the hard wall of his chest. "This is something I should have done the night of the Girls' Club dance," he murmured as he looked down at her.

"What is?"

"Kiss you in the moonlight," he whispered just before his mouth claimed hers.

Chapter 2

Maggie was too amazed to respond. Glenn Lambert, the boy who had lived next door most of her life, was kissing her. And he was kissing her as if he meant to be doing exactly that. His lips moved slowly over hers, shaping and fitting his mouth to hers with a gentleness that rocked her until she was a churning mass of conflicting emotions. This was Glenn, the same Glenn who had teased her unmercifully about "going straight" while she wore braces. The Glenn who had heartlessly beaten her playing one-on-one basketball. The same Glenn who had always been her white knight. Yet it felt so right, so good to be in his arms. Hesitantly, Maggie lifted her hands, sliding them over his chest and linking her fingers at the base of his neck, clinging to him for support. Gently parting her lips, she responded to his kiss. She savored the warm taste of him, the feel of his hands against the small of her back and the tangy scent of his aftershave. It seemed right for Glenn to be holding her. More right than anything had felt in a long time.

When he lifted his head there was a moment of stunned silence while the fact registered in Glenn's bemused mind that he had just kissed Maggie. Maggie. But the vibrant woman in his arms wasn't the same girl who'd lived next door. The woman was warm and soft and incredibly feminine, and he was hungry for a woman's gentleness. Losing Angie had left him feeling cold and alone. His only desire had been to love and protect her, but she hadn't wanted him. A stinging chill ran through his blood, forcing him into the present. His hold relaxed and he dropped his arms.

"Why'd you do that?" Maggie whispered, having difficulty finding her voice. From the moment he had taken her outside, Maggie had known his intention had been to free her from the clutches of Steve's cousin—not to kiss her. At least not like that. What had started out in fun had become serious.

"I'm not sure," he answered honestly. A vague hesitancy showed in his eyes.

"Am I supposed to grade you?"

Glenn took another step backward, broadening the space between them. "Good grief, no; you're merciless."

Mentally, Maggie congratulated him for recovering faster than she. "Not always," she murmured. At his blank look, she added, "I'm not always merciless."

"That's not the way I remember it. The last time I wanted to kiss you, I got a fist in the stomach."

Maggie's brow furrowed. She couldn't remember Glenn even trying to kiss her, and she looked at him with surprise and doubt as she sifted through her memories. "I don't remember that."

"I'm not likely to forget it," he stated, and arched one brow arrogantly. "As I recall, I was twelve and you were eleven. A couple of the guys at school had already kissed a girl and said it wasn't half bad. There wasn't anyone I wanted to kiss, but, for a girl, you weren't too bad, so I offered you five of my best baseball cards if you'd let me kiss you."

Maggie gave him a wicked grin as her memory returned. "That was the greatest insult of my life. I was saving my lips for the man I planned to marry. At the time, I think it was Billy Idol."

"As I recall, you told me that," he replied with a low chuckle. He tucked an arm around her waist, bringing her to his side. "Talking about our one and only date tonight made me remember how much I took you for granted all those years. You were great."

"I know," she said, with a complete lack of modesty.

A slow, roguish grin grew across his features. "But then there were times . . ."

"Don't go philosophical on me, Glenn Lambert." An unaccustomed, delicious heat was seeping into her bones. It was as if she'd been standing in a fierce winter storm and someone had invited her inside to sit by the cozy warmth of the fire.

"We've both done enough of that for one night," Glenn quipped, looking toward the bright lights of the house.

Maggie didn't want to go back inside. She felt warm and comfortable for the first time in what seemed like ages. If they returned to the house full of people, she'd be forced to paint on another plastic smile and listen to the likes of Steve's cousin.

"Do you ever wonder about the old neighborhood?"

Grinning, Glenn looked down on her. "Occasionally."

"Want to take a look?"

He glanced toward the house again, sensing her reluctance to return. The old Maggie would have faced the world head-on. The change surprised him. "Won't we be missed?"

"I doubt it."

Glenn tucked Maggie's hand in the crook of his arm. "For old times' sake."

"The rope swing in your backyard is still there."

"You're kidding!" He gave a laugh of disbelief.

"A whole new generation of kids are playing on that old swing."

"What about the tree house?"

"That, unfortunately, was the victim of a bad windstorm several years back."

His arm tightened around her waist, and the fragile scent of her perfume filled his senses. She was a woman now, and something strange and inexplicable was happening between them. Glenn wasn't sure it was right to encourage it.

"How do you keep up with all this?" he asked, attempting to steer his thoughts from things he shouldn't be thinking, like how soft and sweet and wonderfully warm she felt.

"Simple," Maggie explained with a half-smile. "I visit often." The happiest days of her life had been in that house in the old neighborhood. She couldn't turn back the clock, but the outward symbols of that time lived on for her to visit as often as needed. "Come on," she said brightly and took his hand. She was feeling both foolish and fanciful. "There probably won't be another chance if we don't go now."

"You'll freeze," Glenn warned, running his hands

down the lengths of her bare arms and up again to cup her shoulders.

"No," she argued, not wanting anything to disturb the moment.

"I'll collect your jacket and tell Steve what we're up to," Glenn countered.

"No," she pleaded, her voice low and husky. "Don't. I'll be fine. Really."

Glenn studied her for an instant before agreeing. Maggie was frightened. The realization stunned him. His bubbly, happy-go-lucky Maggie had been reduced to an unhappy, insecure waif. The urge to take her in his arms and protect her was nearly overwhelming.

"All right," he agreed, wrapping his arm around her shoulders to lend her his warmth. If she did get chilled, he could give her his own jacket.

With their arms around each other, they strolled down Ocean Avenue to the grade school, cut through the play yard, and came out on Marimar near Eastwood Drive.

"Everything seems the same," Glenn commented. His smile was filled with contentment.

"It is."

"How are your parents doing?" he inquired.

"They retired in Florida. I told them they ought to be more original than that, but it was something they really wanted. They can afford it, so why not? What about your folks?"

"They're in South Carolina. Dad's working for the same company. Both Eric and Dale are married and supplying them with a houseful of grandchildren."

A chill shot through Maggie, and she shivered involuntarily. She was an aunt now, too, but the circumstances weren't nearly as pleasant. Her brother, Denny, had also discovered that his inheritance wasn't a hedge against unhappiness. Slowly shaking her head, Maggie spoke: "Do you realize how old that makes me feel? Dale married—I'd never have believed it. He was only ten when you moved."

"He met his wife the first year of college. They fell in love, and against everyone's advice decided not to wait to get married. They were both nineteen, and had two kids by the time Dale graduated."

"And they're fine now?"

"They're going stronger than ever. The boys are in school, and Cherry has gone back to college for her degree." There wasn't any disguising the pride in his voice.

"What about Eric?"

"He married a flight attendant a couple of years ago. They have a baby girl." His hand rested at the nape of her neck in a protective action. "What about your brother?"

"Denny was already married by the time you moved, wasn't he? He and Linda have two little girls."

"Is he living in San Francisco?"

"Yes," she supplied quickly, and hurried to change the subject. "The night's lovely, isn't it?"

Glenn ignored the comment. "Is Denny still working for the phone company?"

"No," she returned starkly. "I can't remember when I've seen so many stars."

They were silent for a moment while Glenn digested the information. Something had happened between Denny and Maggie that she was obviously reluctant to discuss.

"Do you realize that there's never been a divorce in either of our families?" she said softly with sudden insight.

She knew what a rarity that was in this day and age. Nearly thirty percent of their high school class were on their second marriages.

"I doubt that there ever will be a divorce. Mom and Dad believe strongly in working out problems instead of running from them, and that was ingrained in all three of us boys."

"We're in the minority, then. I don't know how Janelle is going to adjust to Steve's children. It must be difficult."

"She loves him," Glenn countered somewhat defensively.

"I realize that," Maggie whispered, thinking out loud. "It's just that I remember when Steve married Ginny. Janelle cried for days afterward and went about doing her best to forget him. Every one of us knew that Ginny and Steve were terribly mismatched and it would be only a matter of time before they split."

"I wasn't that sure they couldn't make a go of it."

Maggie bristled. "I was, and anyone with half a brain saw it. Ginny was pregnant before the wedding and no one except Steve was convinced the baby was his."

"Steve was in a position to know."

Maggie opened her mouth to argue, glanced up to see Glenn's amused gaze, and pressed her lips tightly closed. "I don't recall you being this argumentative," she said after several moments.

"When it comes to the sanctity of marriage, I am."

"For your sake, I hope you marry the right woman, then."

The humor drained from his eyes and was replaced with such pain that Maggie's breath caught in her throat. "Glenn, what did I say?" she asked, concern in her voice.

"Nothing," he assured her with a half-smile that disguised none of his mental anguish. "I thought I had found her."

"Oh, Glenn, I'm so sorry. Is there anything I can do? I make a great wailing wall." From the pinched lines about his mouth and eyes, Maggie knew that the woman had been someone very special. Even when Maggie had known him best, Glenn had been a discriminating male. He had dated only a few times and, as far as she could remember, had never gone steady with one girl.

The muscles of his face tightened as he debated whether to tell Maggie about Angie. He hadn't discussed her with anyone over the past couple of months, and the need to purge her from his life burned in him. Perhaps someday, he thought, but not now and not with Maggie, who had enough problems of her own. "She married someone else. There's nothing more to say."

"You loved her very much, didn't you?" Whoever she was, the woman was a fool. Glenn was the steady, solid type most women sought. When he loved, it would be forever and with an intensity few men were capable of revealing.

Glenn didn't answer. Instead, he regarded her with his pain-filled eyes and asked, "What about you?"

"You mean why I never married?" She gave a shrug of indifference. "The right man never came along. I thought he might have once, but I was wrong. Dirk was more interested in spending my money than loving me."

"I'm sorry." His arm tightened around her as an unreasonable anger filled him over the faceless Dirk. He had hurt Maggie, and Glenn was intimately aware of how much one person could hurt another.

"Actually, I think I was lucky to discover it when I did. But thirty is looming around the corner and the biological clock is ticking like Big Ben. I'd like to get married, but I won't lower my standards."

"What kind of man are you looking for?"

He was so utterly blasé about it that Maggie's composure slipped and she nearly dissolved into laughter. "You mean in case you happen to know someone who fits the bill?"

"I might."

"Why not?" she asked with a soft giggle. "To start off, I'd like someone financially secure."

He was so serious that Maggie bit into her bottom lip to hide the trembling laughter. "In addition to being on firm financial ground, he should be magnanimous."

"With you, he'd have to be," Glenn said in a laughter-tinged voice.

Maggie ignored the gibe. "He'd have to love me enough to overlook my faults—few as they are—be loyal, loving, and want children."

She paused, expecting him to comment, but he nodded in agreement. "Go on," he encouraged.

"But more than simply wanting children, he'd have to take responsibility for helping me raise them into worthwhile adults. I want a man who's honest, but one who won't shout the truth in my face if it's going to hurt me. A special man to double my joys and divide my sorrows. Someone who will love me when my hair is gray and my ankles are thick." Realizing how serious she'd become, Maggie hesitated. "Know anyone like him?" Her words hung empty in the silence that followed.

"No," Glenn eventually said, and shook his head for

emphasis. Those were the very things he sought in a wife. "I can't say that I do."

"From my guess, Prince Charmings are few and far between these days."

They didn't speak again until they paused in front of the fifty-year-old house that had been Glenn's childhood home. Little had been altered over the years, Glenn realized. The wide front porch and large dormers that jutted out from the roof looked exactly as they had in his mind. The house had been repainted, and decorative shutters were now added to the front windows, but the same warmth and love seemed to radiate from its doors.

Maggie followed Glenn's gaze to the much-used basketball hoop positioned above the garage door. It was slightly crooked from years of slam dunks. By the look of things, the hoop was used as much now as it had been all those years ago.

"I suppose we should think of heading back. It's going to be a long day tomorrow." Maggie's gaze fell from the house to the cracked sidewalk. It hit her suddenly that in a couple of days Glenn would be flying back to Charleston. He was here for the wedding and nothing more.

"Yes," Glenn agreed in a low, gravelly voice. "Tomorrow will be a very long day."

The vestibule was empty when Maggie entered the church forty minutes before the wedding. Out of breath and five minutes late, she paused to study the huge baskets of flowers that adorned the altar, and released an unconscious sigh at the beauty of the sight. This wedding was going to be special. Hurrying into the dressing room that was located to her right, Maggie knocked once and opened the door. The woman from The Wedding Shop was helping Janelle into her flowing lace gown. Mrs. Longmier was sitting in a chair, dabbing the corner of her eye with a tissue.

"Oh, Maggie, thank goodness you're here. I had this horrible dream that you showed up late. The wedding was in progress and you ran down the aisle screaming how dare we start without you."

"I'm here, I'm here, don't worry." Stepping back, Maggie inspected her friend and could understand Mrs. Longmier's tears. Janelle was radiant. Her wedding gown was of a lavish Victorian style that was exquisitely fashioned with ruffled tiers of Chantilly lace and countless rows of tiny pearls. "Wow," she whispered in awe. "You're going to knock Steve's eyes out."

"That's the idea," Janelle said with a nervous smile.

Another woman from the store helped Maggie don her blushing-pink gown of shimmering taffeta. Following a common theme, the maid of honor's and the bridesmaids' dresses were also Victorian in style, with sheer yokes and lace stand-up collars. Lace bishop sleeves were trimmed with dainty satin bows. The bodice fit snugly to the waist and flared at the hip. While the woman fastened the tiny buttons at the back of the gown, Maggie studied her mirrored reflection. A small smile played on her mouth as she pictured Glenn's reaction when he saw her. For years she wore tight jeans and sweatshirts. She had put on a dress for the rehearsal, but this gown would amaze him. She was a woman now, and it showed.

The way her thoughts automatically flew to Glenn surprised Maggie, but she supposed it was natural after their kiss and walk in the moonlight. He had filled her dreams and she'd slept better than she had in a long while. After their visit to the old neighborhood, Maggie's attitude toward the wedding had changed. She wouldn't be standing alone at the altar with her fears. Glenn, her friend from childhood, would be there. Together, they would lend each other the necessary strength to smile their way through the ordeal. Maggie realized her thoughts were more those of a martyr than an honored friend, but she'd dreaded the wedding for weeks. Not that she begrudged Janelle any happiness. But Maggie realized that at some time during the wedding dinner or the dance scheduled to follow, someone would comment on her single status. With Glenn at her side, it wouldn't matter nearly as much.

From all the commotion going on outside the dressing room, Maggie realized the guests were beginning to arrive. Nerves attacked her stomach. This wasn't the first time she'd been in a wedding party, but it was the most elaborate wedding to date. She pressed a calming hand to her abdomen and exhaled slowly.

"Nervous?" Janelle whispered.

Maggie nodded. "What about you?"

"I'm terrified," she admitted freely. "Right now I wish Steve and I had eloped instead of going through all this." She released her breath in a slow, drawn-out sigh. "I'm convinced that halfway through the ceremony my veil's going to slip or I'll faint, or something equally disastrous."

"You won't," Maggie returned confidently. "I promise. Right now everything's overwhelming, but you won't regret a minute of this in the years to come."

"I suppose not," Janelle agreed. "This marriage is forever, and I want everything right."

"I'd want everything like this, too." Maggie spoke without thinking and realized that when and if she ever married, she wanted it to be exactly this way. She yearned for a flowing white dress with a long train and lifetime friends to stand with her.

Someone knocked on the door and, like an organized row of ducklings, the wedding party was led into the vestibule. Organ music vibrated through the church and the first bridesmaid, her hands clasping a bouquet of pink hyacinths, stepped forward with a tall usher at her side.

Maggie watched her progress and knew again that someday she wanted to stand in the back of a church and look out over the seated guests who had come to share her moment of joy. And like Janelle, Maggie longed to feel all the love that was waiting for her as she slowly walked to the man with whom she would share her life. And when she repeated her vows before God and those most important in her life she would feel, as Janelle did, that her marriage was meant to last for all time.

When it was her turn to step onto the trail of white linen that ran the length of the wide aisle, Maggie held her chin high, the adrenaline pumping through her blood. Her smile was natural, not forced. Mentally, she thanked Glenn for that, and briefly allowed her gaze to seek him out at the front of the church. What she found nearly caused her to pause in midstep. Glenn was standing with Steve at the side of the altar and looking at her with such a wondrous gaze that her heart lodged in her throat. This all-encompassing wonder was what Maggie had expected to see in Steve's eyes when he first viewed Janelle. A look so tender, it should be reserved for the bride and groom. The moment stretched out until Maggie was convinced everyone in the church had turned to see what was keeping her. By sheer force of will she continued with short steps toward the front of the church. Every resounding note of the organ brought her closer to Glenn. She felt a throb of excitement as the faces of people she'd known all her life turned to watch her progress. A heady sensation enveloped her as she imagined it was she who was the bride, she who would speak her vows, she who had found her soul mate. Until that moment, Maggie hadn't realized how much she yearned for the very things she had tried to escape in life, how much she was missing by hiding in her gilded cage, behind her money.

As they'd practiced the night before, Maggie moved to the left and waited for Janelle and Steve to meet at center front. At that point, she would join her friend and stand at Janelle's side. With the organ music pulsating in her ear, Maggie strained to catch Steve's look when he first glimpsed Janelle. She turned her head slightly and paused. Her gaze refused to move beyond Glenn, standing with Steve near the front of the altar. Even when Janelle placed her hand in Steve's, Maggie couldn't tear her eyes from Glenn. The pastor moved to the front of the church and the four gathered before him. Together, they lifted their faces to the man of God who had come to unite Steve and Janelle.

The sensations that came at Glenn were equally disturbing. The minute Maggie had started down the aisle it had taken everything within him not to step away from Steve, meet her, and take her in his arms. He had never experienced any sensation more strongly. He wanted to hold her, protect her, bring the shine back to her eyes, and teach her to trust again. When she had met him at the airport, he'd been struck by how lovely she'd become. Now he recognized her vulnerability, and she was breathtaking. He had never seen a more beautiful woman. She was everything he'd ever wanted—warm, vibrant, alive, and standing so close that all he had to do was reach out and touch her. He felt like a blind man who had miraculously and unexpectedly been gifted with sight. Maggie needed him. Charleston, with all its painful memories, lay on the other side of the world.

"Dearly beloved, we are called here today to witness the vows between Janelle and Stephen."

The rush of emotion that assaulted Maggie was unlike anything she'd ever known. She couldn't keep her eyes off Glenn, who seemed to magnetically compel her gaze to meet his. Their eyes locked and held as the pastor continued speaking. There was no exchange of smiles, no winks, nothing cute or frivolous, but a solemn mood that made that instant, that moment, the most monumental of their lives. Maggie felt a breathless urgency come over her, and an emotion so powerful, so real, that it brought brimming tears that filled her vision. In order to keep her makeup from streaking, she held one finger under each eye a hand at a time and took in several deep breaths to forestall the ready flow. The void, the emptiness in her life, wasn't entirely due to her money. What she needed was someone to love and who would love her. Desperately, Maggie realized how much she wanted to be needed. Several seconds passed before she regained her composure. The tightening lessened in her chest, and she breathed freely once again.

When the pastor asked Steve and Janelle to repeat their vows, Maggie's gaze was again drawn to Glenn's. He didn't speak, nor did Maggie, but together, in unison, each syllable, each word, was repeated in their hearts as they issued the same vows as their friends. When the pastor pronounced them man and wife, Maggie raised stricken eyes to the man of God who had uttered the words, needing the reassurance about whom he had meant. It was as if he had been speaking to Glenn and her, as well, and as if the formal pronouncement included them.

The organ burst into the traditional wedding march, and Steve and Janelle turned to face the congregation, their faces radiant with happiness. As the newly wedded couple moved down the aisle, Glenn's arm reached for Maggie's, prepared to escort her. At the touch of his hand at her elbow, Maggie felt a series of indescribable sensations race through her: wonder, surprise, joy. Their eyes met, and for the first time that day, he smiled. An incredible, dazzling smile that all but blinded her. Their march down the aisle, her arm on his elbow, added to the growing feeling that that day, that moment, was meant for them as well.

Family and friends gathered outside the church doors, spilling onto the steps, giving hearty applause as Steve turned Janelle into his arms and kissed her. A festive mood reigned as Janelle was joyously hugged and Steve's hand was pumped countless times. The photographer was busily snapping pictures, ordering the wedding party to pose one way and then another. For a brief second the fantasy faded enough to frighten Maggie. What game was Glenn playing with her? No. She'd seen the sincerity in his eyes. But pretending was dangerous, far too dangerous.

"Are you all right?" Glenn whispered in her ear.

Maggie didn't have the opportunity to answer. As it was, she wasn't sure how to respond. Under other circumstances, she would have asked him to drive her to the hospital emergency room. Her daydreams were overpowering reality. This wasn't her wedding, nor was the man at her side her husband. She had no right to feel sensations like these.

The next thing she knew, Glenn had disappeared. Maggie hardly had time to miss him when a shiny new Cadillac pulled to the curb. just married was painted on the back window. Glenn jumped out and opened both doors on the passenger side. Then, racing up the church stairs, he took Maggie by the hand and, following on the heels of Steve and Janelle, pulled her through a spray of rice and laughter as he whisked her toward the car.

Amidst hoots and more laughter, Glenn helped her gather her full-length skirt inside the automobile before closing the door and running around the front to climb in beside her.

Maggie was still breathless with laughter when he flashed her another of his dazzling smiles and started the engine. A sea of happy faces was gazing in at them. Turning her head to look out the side window, Maggie was greeted with the well-wishes of several boys and girls—children of their friends—standing on the sidewalk and waving with all their might. Glenn checked the rearview mirror and pulled into the steady flow of street traffic.

"Maggie, it was just as wonderful as you claimed it would be," Janelle said softly from the backseat.

"Did you doubt?" Steve questioned, his voice thick with emotion.

"I'll have you know, Mr. Grant, that I nearly backed out of this wedding at the very last minute. The only thing that stopped me was Maggie. Somehow she convinced me everything was going to work out. And it did."

"Janelle, I hardly said anything," Maggie countered, shocked by her friend's admission.

"You said just enough."

"I'm eternally grateful," Steve murmured, and from the sounds coming from the backseat, he was showing Janelle just how grateful he was that she was his bride.

Glenn's hand reached for Maggie's and squeezed it gently. "You look stunning." He wanted to say so much more and discovered he couldn't. For weeks he had dreaded the wedding and having to stand at the altar with his friend when it should have been his own wedding. The day had been completely unlike anything he'd expected; Maggie alone had made the difference.

"You make a striking figure yourself," she said, needing to place their conversation on an even keel.

Glenn unfastened the top button of the starched white shirt and released the tie. "I feel like a penguin."

Laughter bubbled up in Maggie. She felt happy, really happy, for the first time in a long while. When Glenn held out his arms, she scooted across the seat so that they were as close as possible within the confines of the vehicle.

The sounds of smothered giggles from the backseat assured Maggie that things were very fine indeed. They stopped at a light and Glenn's gaze wandered to her for a brief, glittering second, then back to the road. "Thank you for today," he said, just low enough for only her to hear. "You made our friends' wedding the most special day of my life."

"I . . . felt the same way about you," she whispered, wanting him to kiss her so badly she could almost taste his mouth over hers.

"Maggie," Janelle called from the backseat. "Will you check this veil? I can't walk into the dinner with it all askew. People will know exactly what kind of man I married."

"Oh, they will, will they?" Steve said teasingly, and kissed her soundly.

Maggie turned and glanced over her shoulder. "Everything looks fine. The veil's not even crooked, although from the sound of things back there it should be inside out and backward."

"Maggie," Steve said in a low and somewhat surprised tone as he studied her, "I expected Janelle's mother to cry, even my own. But I was shocked to see you were the one with tears in your eyes."

"You were shocked?" she tossed back nonchalantly. "Believe me, they were just as much of a surprise to me. Tears were the last thing I expected."

"Count your blessings, you two," Glenn said, tossing a glance over his shoulder. "Knowing Muffie, you should be grateful she didn't burst into fits of hysterical laughter." He glanced over to Maggie and leaned close and whispered: "Actually, they should thank me. It took everything in me not to break rank and reach for you." Glenn hadn't meant to tell her that, but those tears had nearly been his undoing. He had known when he'd seen her eyes bright with unshed tears that what was happening to him was affecting Maggie just as deeply. He had come so close to happiness once, and like a fool, he'd let it slip away. It wouldn't happen again; he wouldn't allow it.

Everything was happening so quickly that Maggie didn't have time to react. Glenn's breath fanned her temple and a shiver of apprehension raced up her spine. They were playing a dangerous game. All that talk in the moonlight about the sanctity of marriage had affected their brain cells and they were daydreaming—no . . . pretending—that this moment, this happiness, this love, was theirs. Only it wasn't, and Maggie had to give herself a hard mental shake to dislodge the illusion.

A long string of cars followed closely behind as the other members of the wedding party caught up with the Cadillac. Watching Glenn weave in and out of traffic, Maggie was impressed with his driving skill. However, everything about Glenn had impressed her today. Fleetingly, she allowed her mind to wander to what would happen when he left on Monday. She didn't want this weekend to be the end, but a beginning. He lived in Charleston, she in San Francisco. The whole country separated them, but they were only hours apart by plane and seconds by phone.

When he turned and caught her studying him, Maggie guiltily shifted her attention out the side window. The way her heart was hammering, one would think she was the bride. She struggled for composure.

Janelle's family had rented a huge Victorian hall for the dinner and dance. Maggie had no idea that there was such a special place in San Francisco and was assessing the wraparound porch and second-floor veranda when the remainder of the wedding party disembarked from the long row of cars that paraded behind the Cadillac. Wordlessly, Glenn took her by the elbow and led her up the front stairs.

Everything inside the huge hall was lushly decorated in antiques. Round tables with starched white tablecloths were set up to serve groups of eight. In the center of each table was a bowl of white gardenias. A winding stairway with a polished mahogany banister led to the dance floor upstairs.

Being seated at the same table as Steve and Janelle added to the continuing illusion. Somehow Maggie made it through the main course of prime rib, wild rice, and tender asparagus spears. Her appetite was nonexistent, and every bite had the taste and the feel of cotton. Although Glenn was at her side, they didn't speak, but the communication between them was louder than words. Twice she stopped herself from asking him what was happening to them, convinced he had no answers and the question would only confuse him further.

When Janelle cut the wedding cake and hand-fed the first bite to Steve, the happy applause vibrated around the room. The sound of it helped shake Maggie from her musings, and she forced down another bite of her entrée. The caterers delivered the cake to the wedding guests with astonishing speed so that all the guests were served in a matter of minutes.

Glenn's eyes darkened thoughtfully as he dipped his fork into the white cake and paused to study Maggie. He prayed she wasn't as confused as he. He didn't know what was happening, but was powerless to change anything. He wasn't even convinced he wanted anything different. It was as if they were in a protective bubble, cut off from the outside world. And although they sat in a room full of people, they were alone. Not knowing what made him do anything so crazy, Glenn lifted his fork to her mouth and offered Maggie the first sample of wedding cake. His eyes held her immobile as she opened her mouth and accepted his offering. Ever so lightly, he ran his thumb along her chin as his dark, penetrating eyes bored into hers. By the time she finished swallowing, Glenn's hand was trembling, and he lowered it.

Promptly, Maggie placed her clenched fingers in her lap. A few minutes later, she took a sip of champagne, her first that day, although she knew that enough was happening to her equilibrium without adding expensive champagne to wreak more damage.

The first muted strains of a Vienna waltz drifted from the upstairs dance floor. Maggie took another sip of champagne before standing.

Together, Steve and Janelle led their family and friends up the polished stairway to the dance floor.

When he saw the bride and groom, the orchestra leader stepped forward and announced: "Ladies and gentlemen, I give you Mr. and Mrs. Stephen Grant."

Steve took Janelle in his arms and swung his young bride around the room in wide, fanciful steps. Pausing briefly, he gestured to Glenn, who swung Maggie into his arms.

Again, the announcer stepped to the microphone and introduced them as the maid of honor and best man. All the while, the soft music continued its soothing chords, and they were joined by each bridesmaid-and-usher couple until the entire wedding party was on the dance floor.

As Glenn held Maggie in his arms, their feet made little more than tiny shuffling movements that gave the pretense of dancing. All the while, Glenn's serious, dark eyes held Maggie's. It was as though they were the only two in the room and the orchestra was playing solely for them. Try as she might, Maggie couldn't pull her gaze away.

"I've been wanting to do something from the moment I first saw you walk down the aisle."

"What?" she asked, surprised at how weak her voice sounded. She thought that if he didn't kiss her soon she was going to die.

Glenn glanced around him to the wide double doors that led to the veranda. He took her by the hand and led her through the crowd and out the curtained glass doors.

Maggie walked to the edge of the veranda and curled her fingers over the railing. Dusk had already settled over the city and lights from the bay flickered in the distance. Glenn joined her and slipped his arms around her waist, burying his face in her hair. Turning her in his arms, he closed his eyes and touched his forehead to hers. He took in several breaths before speaking.

"Are you feeling the same things I am?" he asked.

"Yes." Maggie's heart was hammering so loud, she was convinced he'd hear it.

"Is it the champagne?"

"I had two sips."

"I didn't have any," he countered. "See?" He placed the palm of her hand over his heart so she could feel its quickened beat. "From the moment I saw you in the church it's been like this."

"Me, too," she whispered. "What's happening to us?"

Slowly, he shook his head. "I wish I knew."

"It's happening to me, too." She took his hand and placed it over her heart. "Can you feel it?"

"Yes," he whispered.

"Maggie, listen, this is going to sound crazy." He dropped his hands as if he needed to put some distance between them and took several steps back.

"What is?"

Glenn jerked his hand through his hair and hesitated. "Do you want to make this real?"

Chapter 3

"Make this real?" Maggie echoed. "What do you mean?"

Glenn couldn't believe the ideas that were racing at laser speed through his mind. Maggie would burst into peals of laughter, and he wouldn't blame her. But even that wasn't enough to turn the course of his thoughts. He had this compulsion, this urgency, to speak, as if something were driving him to say the words. "Steve and Janelle are going to make this marriage a good one."

"Yes," Maggie agreed. "I believe they will."

The look she gave him was filled with questions. Surely she realized he hadn't asked her onto the veranda to discuss Steve and Janelle. After Angie, Glenn hadn't expected to feel this deep an emotion again. And so soon was another shock. Yet when he'd seen Maggie that first moment in the church, the impact had been so great it was as though someone had physically assaulted him. She was lovely, possessing a rare beauty that had escaped his notice when they were younger. No longer had he been standing witness to his best friend's wedding, but he'd participated in a ceremony with a woman who could stand at his side for a lifetime. Maggie had felt it, too; he had seen it in her eyes. The identical emotion had moved her to tears.

"Glenn, you wanted to say something?" She coaxed him gently, her mind pleading with him to explain. He couldn't possibly mean what she thought.

Remembering the look Maggie had given him when Steve and Janelle exchanged vows gave Glenn the courage to continue. "Marriage between friends is the best kind, don't you think?"

"Yes," she answered, unable to bring her voice above a husky whisper. "Friends generally know everything about each other, whether good or bad, and then still choose to remain friends."

They stood for a breathless moment, transfixed, studying each other, hesitant and unsure. "I'd always believed," Glenn murmured, his voice low and seductive, "that it would be impossible for me to share my life with anyone I didn't know extremely well."

"I agree." Maggie's mind was formulating impossible thoughts. Glenn was leading this conversation down meandering paths she'd never dreamed of traveling with him.

"We're friends," he offered next.

"Good friends," she agreed, nodding.

"I know you as well as my own brothers."

"We lived next door to each other for fifteen years," she added, her heart increasing its tempo to a slow drumroll.

"I want a home and children."

"I've always loved children." There hadn't been a time in her life when the pull was stronger toward a husband and family than it was that very moment.

"Maggie," he said, taking a step toward her, but still not touching her, "you've become an extremely beautiful woman."

Her lashes fluttered against her cheek as she lowered her gaze. Maggie didn't think of herself as beautiful. For Glen to say this to her sent her heart racing. She hardly knew how to respond and finally managed a weak "Thank you."

"Any man would be proud to have you for his wife."

The sensations that raced through her were all too welcome and exciting. "I . . . I was just thinking that a woman . . . any woman would be extremely fortunate to have you for a husband."

"Would you?"

Her heart fluttered wildly, rocketed to her throat, and then promptly plummeted to her stomach. Yet she didn't hesitate. "I'd be honored and proud."

Neither said anything for a timeless second while their minds assimilated what had just transpired, or what they thought had.

"Glenn?"

"Yes."

Her throat felt swollen and constricted, her chest suddenly tight, as if tears were brewing just beneath the surface. "Did I understand you right? Did you—just now—suggest that you and me—the two of us—get married?"

"That's exactly what I'm suggesting." Glenn didn't hesitate. He'd never been more sure of anything in his life. He had lost one woman; he wasn't going to lose Maggie. He would bind her to him and eliminate the possibility of someone else stepping in at the last moment.

This woman was his, and he was claiming her before something happened to drive her from his arms.

"When?"

"Tonight."

She blinked twice, convinced she hadn't heard him right. "But the license, and—"

"We can fly to Reno." Already his mind was working out the details. He didn't like the idea of a quickie wedding, but it would serve the purpose. After what they had shared earlier, they didn't need anything more than a document to make it legal.

Stillness surrounded them. Even the night had gone silent. No cars, no horns, no crickets, no sounds of the night—only silence.

"I want to think about it," she murmured. Glenn was crazy. They both were. Talking about marriage, running away this very night to Reno. None of it made sense, but nothing in all her life had sounded more exciting, more wonderful, more right.

"How long do you want to think this over?" A thread of doubt caused him to ask. Perhaps rushing her wasn't the best way to proceed, but waiting felt equally impossible.

A fleeting smile touched and lifted Maggie's mouth. They didn't dare tell someone they would do anything so ludicrous. She didn't need time, not really. She knew what she wanted: She wanted Glenn. "An hour," she said, hoping that within that time frame nothing would change.

The strains of another waltz drifted onto the veranda, and wordlessly he led her back to the dance floor. When he reached for her, Maggie went willingly into his arms. His hold felt as natural as breathing, and she was drawn into his warmth. The past two days with Glenn had been the happiest, most exciting in years. Who would have thought that Glenn Lambert would make her pulse pound like a jackhammer and place her head in the clouds where the air was thin and clear? Just over twenty-four hours after his arrival, and they were planning the most incredible scheme, crazy as it sounded.

"This feeling reminds me of the night we stole out of the house to smoke our first cigarette," Glenn whispered in her ear. "Are we as daring and defiant now as we were at fourteen?"

"Worse," she answered. "But I don't care, as long as you're with me."

"Oh, Maggie." He sighed her name with a wealth of emotion.

Her hands tightened around his neck as she fit her body more intimately to the contour of his. Her breasts were flattened to his broad chest; and they were melded together, thigh to thigh, hip to hip, as close as humanly possible under the guise of dancing.

Every breath produced an incredible range of new sensations. Maggie felt drugged and delirious, daring and darling, bold and extraordinarily shy. Every second in his arms brought her more strength of conviction. This night, in less than an hour, she was going to walk out of this room with Glenn Lambert. Together, they would fly to Reno and she would link her life with his. There was nothing to stop her. Not her money. Not her pride. Not her fears. Glenn Lambert was her friend. Tonight he would become her lover as well.

Unable to wait, Maggie rained a long series of kisses

over the line of his jaw. The need to experience his touch flowered deep within her.

Glenn's hold at her waist tightened, and he inhaled sharply. "Maggie, don't tease me."

"Who's teasing?" They'd known each other all these years, and in that time he had kissed her only once. But it was enough, more than enough, to know that the loving between them would be exquisite.

Without her even being aware, Glenn had maneuvered her into a darkened corner of the dance floor where the lighting was the dimmest. His eyes told her he was about to kiss her, and hers told him she was eager for him to do exactly that. Unhurriedly, Glenn lowered his mouth to hers with an agonizing slowness. His kiss was warm and tender and lingering, as if this were a moment and place out of time meant for them alone. Her soft mouth parted with only the slightest urging, and her arms tightened around his neck.

Trembling in his embrace, Maggie drew in a long, unsteady breath. Glenn's kisses had been filled with such aching tenderness, such sweet torment, that Maggie felt tears stinging for release. Tears for a happiness she had never hoped to find. At least not with Glenn. This was a wondrous surprise. A gift. A miracle so unexpected it would take a lifetime to fully appreciate.

"I want you," he whispered, his voice hoarse with desire. His breath warmed her lips.

"Yes" she returned, vaguely dazed. "I want you, too."

His arms tightened, and Maggie felt the shudder that rocked him until her ribs ached. Gradually, his hold relaxed as his gaze polarized hers. "Let's get out of here."

"Should . . . should we tell anyone?" *No,* her mind

shouted. Someone might try to talk them out of this, and she didn't want that to happen. She yearned for everything that Glenn suggested.

"Do you want to tell Steve and Janelle?" Glenn asked.

"No."

Tenderly he brushed his lips across her forehead. "Neither do I. They'll find out soon enough."

"It'll be our surprise." She smiled at him, the warm, happy smile of someone about to embark on the most exciting adventure of her life. And Maggie felt like an adventurer, daring and audacious, dauntless and intrepid, reckless and carefree. There'd be problems; she realized that. But tonight, with Glenn at her side, there wasn't anything she couldn't conquer.

Glenn raised her fingertips to his lips and kissed each one. "I'm not letting you out of my sight. We're going directly to the airport."

"Fine." She had no desire to be separated from him, either.

"I'll call a taxi."

"I'll get my purse."

The night air brought a chill to her arms, but it didn't sharpen any need to analyze what they were doing. If Glenn expected her to have second thoughts as they breezed through the streets of San Francisco, she found none. Even the busy airport, with its crowded concourses and people who stared at their unusual dress, wasn't enough to cause her to doubt.

Glenn bought their airline tickets, and she found a seat while he used his cell to make hotel reservations. When he returned, the broad smile reached his eyes. Maggie was struck anew with the wonder of what was happening.

"Well?"

"Everything's been taken care of."

"Everything?" It seemed paramount that they get married tonight. If they were forced to wait until morning, there could be second thoughts.

"The Chapel of Love is one block from city hall, and they're going to arrange for the marriage license." He glanced at his watch and hesitated. "The plane lands at ten-thirty, and the ceremony is scheduled for eleven-fifteen." He sat in the seat beside her and reached for her hand. "You're cold."

"A little." Despite her nerves, she managed to keep her voice even. She didn't doubt they were doing the right thing, and she wanted to reassure Glenn. "I'm fine. Don't worry about me."

Rising to his feet, Glenn stripped the tuxedo jacket from his arms and draped it over her shoulders. "Here. We'll be boarding in a few minutes and I'll get you a blanket from the flight attendants." His dark eyes were full of warmth, and he was smiling at her as if they'd been sitting in airports, waiting for planes to fly them to weddings, every day.

His strong fingers closed over hers, and for the first time she admired how large his hands were. The fingers were long and tapered, and looked capable of carving an empire or soothing a crying child. "Are you"—Maggie swallowed convulsively, almost afraid to ask—"are you having any second thoughts?"

"No," he answered quickly. "What about you?"

"None." She was never so positive of anything in her life.

"I'll be a good husband."

"I know." She placed her free hand over the back of his. "And I'll be a good wife."

His returning smile, filled with warmth and incredible wonder, could have melted a glacier.

"My parents are going to be ecstatic." *Shocked, too,* her mind added, but that didn't matter.

"Mine will be pleased as well," Glenn assured her. "They've always liked you."

He bent his head toward her, and Maggie shyly lifted her face and met him halfway. His kiss was filled with soft exploration, and they parted with the assurance that everything was perfect.

"After we're married, will you want me to move to Charleston?" Maggie ventured.

"No," he said on a somber note. "I'll move to San Francisco." The time had come to leave Charleston. Glenn wanted to bury the unhappiness that surrounded him there. The brief visit to San Francisco had felt like coming home. With Maggie at his side, he'd build a new life in San Francisco. Together, they'd raise their family and live in blissful happiness. No longer would he allow the memory of another woman to haunt him.

Maggie felt simultaneously relieved and confused. Her career in art made it possible for her to work anywhere. Glenn's moving to San Francisco would mean giving up his Charleston clientele and building up a new one on the West Coast. It didn't make sense. "I don't mind moving, really. It would be easier for me to make the change. You've got your career."

He slid his hand from her arm to her elbow, tightening his hold. "I'll transfer out here." Turning his wrist, he glanced at his watch, but Maggie had the feeling he wasn't looking at the time. "I'm ready for a change," he murmured after a while. "You don't mind, do you?"

Did she? No, Maggie decided; she loved California. "No, that'll be fine. You'll like the beach house."

"I don't doubt that I will."

Their flight number was announced, and Maggie returned Glenn's tuxedo jacket before they boarded the plane. The flight attendant came by a few minutes later, after they were comfortably seated, to check their seat belts. She paused and commented that they both looked as if they were on their way to a wedding. Glenn and Maggie smiled politely, but neither of them opted to inform the young woman that that was exactly where they were going. Maggie feared that if they let someone in on their plan it would somehow shatter the dream. Briefly, she wondered if Glenn shared her fears.

The flight touched down on the Reno runway precisely on schedule. With no luggage to collect, Glenn and Maggie walked straight through the airport and outside, where a taxi was parked and waiting.

"You two on your way to a wedding?" the cabdriver asked with a loud belly laugh as he held the door open for Maggie.

"Yes," Maggie answered shyly, dismissing her earlier fears.

"Ours," Glenn added, sliding into the seat next to Maggie and reaching for her hand.

The heavyset cabbie closed the door and walked around to the driver's side. He checked the rearview mirror and merged with the traffic. "Lots of people come to Reno to get married, but then a lot of folks come here to get unmarried, too."

A thundering silence echoed through the close confines of the taxi. "There won't be any divorce for us," Glenn informed him.

The driver tipped back the rim of his cap with his index finger. "Lot of folks say that, too." He paused at the first red light, placed his arm along the back of the seat, and turned to look at Glenn. "Where was it you said you wanted to go?"

"Chapel of Love," Glenn said firmly, and glanced over to Maggie. "Unless you want to change your mind?" he whispered.

"You're not backing out of your proposal, are you?" The words nearly stuck in her throat.

"No."

"Then we're getting married," she murmured, more determined than ever. "I didn't come this far in a shimmering pink gown to play the slot machines."

"Good."

"Very good," she murmured, unwilling to let anyone or anything ruin this night.

A half hour later, after arriving at the chapel, Maggie had freshened her makeup and done what she could with her hair. They stood now before the proprietor of the wedding chapel.

"Organ music is fifteen dollars extra," Glenn told her as he reached for his back pocket.

Her hand stopped him. "I don't need it," she assured him with perfect serenity. "I'm still hearing the music from the church."

The impatience drained from his eyes, and the look he gave her was so profound that it seemed the most natural thing in the world to lean forward and press her lips to his.

The justice of the peace cleared his throat. "If you're ready, we can start the ceremony."

"Are you ready?" Glenn asked with smiling eyes.

"I've been ready for this all night," she answered, linking her arm with his.

The service was shockingly short and sterile. They stood before the justice and repeated the words that had already been spoken in their hearts. The stark ceremony wasn't what Maggie would have preferred, but it didn't diminish any of her joy. This wedding was necessary for legal reasons; their real vows had already been exchanged earlier that day as they stood as witnesses for Steve and Janelle. Those few moments in the church had been so intense that from then on every moment of her life would be measured against them. Maggie yearned to explain that to Glenn, but mere words felt inadequate. He, too, had experienced it, she realized, and without analyzing it, he had understood.

Their room at the hotel was ready when they arrived. With the key jingling in Glenn's pocket, they rode the elevator to the tenth floor.

"Are you going to carry me over the threshold, Mr. Lambert?" Maggie whispered happily and nuzzled his ear. She felt a free-flowing elation unlike anything she'd ever experienced. That night and every night for the rest of her life would be spent in Glenn's arms.

"I'll see what I can manage," Glenn stated seriously as he backed her into the corner of the elevator and kissed the side of her neck.

Maggie shot him a dubious look. "I'm not that heavy, you know."

"What I suggest we do," he murmured, as he nibbled on her earlobe, "is have me lift one of your legs and you can hop over the threshold."

"Glenn," she muttered, breaking free. "That's crazy."

Chuckling, he ignored the question. "On second thought, I could probably manage to haul you piggy-back."

Deftly, her fingers opened his tie and she teased his throat with the moist tip of her tongue. If he was going to joke with her, then she'd tease him as well. "Never mind," she whispered. "I'll carry you."

The elevator came to a grinding halt and the doors swished open. Glenn glanced around him, kissed Maggie soundly, and, with a mighty heave-ho, hauled her over his shoulder, fireman-style.

"Glenn . . ." she whispered fiercely, stunned into momentary speechlessness. "Put me down this instant."

Chuckling, he slowly rubbed his hand over her prominently extended derriere. "You said you wanted me to carry you over the threshold. Only I can't very well manage you, the key, and the door all at once."

Using her arms against his shoulders for leverage, Maggie attempted to straighten. "Glenn, please," she begged, laughing until it was difficult to speak and probably just as impossible to be understood.

He shifted her weight when he fidgeted with the key. Maggie couldn't see what was happening, but the sound of the door opening assured her all was well. Her eyes studied the same door as it closed and the narrow entryway as he carried her halfway into the room. The next thing Maggie knew, she was falling through space. She gave a frightened cry until the soft cushion of the mattress broke her rapid descent.

Panting and breathless with laughter, Maggie lay sprawled across the bed. She smiled up at Glenn playfully and raised her arms to her husband of fifteen minutes. Glenn knelt beside her, his eyes alive with passion as he lowered his mouth to hers in a deep kiss that sent her world into a crazy tailspin. She clung to him, her fingers ruffling the thick, dark hair that grew at his nape. Wildly, she returned his kiss, on fire for him, luxuriating in the feel of his body over hers.

Unexpectedly, he tore his mouth from hers and lifted his head. Without a word, he brushed the soft wisps of hair from her temple and dipped his head a second time to sample her mouth. When he broke away and moved to the long dresser that dominated one side of the hotel room, Maggie felt a sudden chill and rose to a sitting position.

A bottle of champagne was resting in a bed of crushed ice. With his back to her, Glenn peeled off the foil covering and removed the cork. He ached with the need to take her physically, but feared his building passion would frighten her. Silently, Glenn cursed himself for not having approached the subject sooner. He wanted her, but did he dare take her so soon?

The dresser mirror revealed Glenn's troubled frown, and Maggie felt a brooding anxiety settle over her. For the first time she could see doubt in his eyes. The breath jammed in her lungs. No, not doubt but apprehension, even foreboding. Maggie was feeling it, too. Maybe advancing from friends to lovers in the space of a few hours wasn't right for them. Maybe they should think it through very carefully before proceeding with what was paramount on both their minds. As far as he was concerned, there wasn't any reason to wait. They were married. They knew each other better than most newlyweds. The certificate in Glenn's coat pocket granted them every right.

With her weight resting on the palm of one hand, she felt her heart throb painfully. "Glenn," she whispered brokenly, not knowing what to say or how to say it.

The sound of her voice was drowned by the cork exploding from the bottle. Fizzing champagne squirted across the dresser. Glenn deftly filled the two glasses and returned the dark bottle to its icy bed.

Handing her a goblet, Glenn joined her on the side of the mattress. "To my wife," he whispered tenderly, and touched the edge of her glass to his.

"To my husband," she murmured in return. The bubbly liquid tickled her nose, and she smiled shyly at Glenn as she took another sip. "I suppose this is when I'm supposed to suggest that I slip into something more comfortable."

"I'm for that." He quickly stood and strode across the room for the bottle, setting it on the floor next to the bed as he sat down again, avoiding her eyes the whole time.

"However, we both seemed to have forgotten something important." She bit her bottom lip in a gesture of uncertainty and laughter.

He glanced up expectantly. "What's that?"

"Clothes," she said, and giggled. They had been so afraid to leave each other for fear something would happen to change their minds that they hadn't even stopped to pack an overnight bag.

"We're not going to need them." In that instant, Glenn realized that they weren't going to wait. He wanted her. She wanted him; it was in her eyes and the provocative way she regarded him. "We have two days," he murmured, "and I can't see any need we'll be having for clothes."

He was so utterly serious that laughter rumbled in her throat. Where there had once been anxiety there was expectancy. "Maybe we could get away with that sort of thing on the Riviera, but believe me, they arrest people for walking around nude in Reno."

Smiling, he tipped back his head and emptied his glass. "You know what I mean."

Maggie set their champagne glasses aside. "No," she said breathlessly as she lightly stroked the neatly trimmed hair at his temple. "I think you'll have to show me."

Gently, Glenn laid her back on the bed and joined her so the upper portion of his body was positioned over the top of hers. His arms went around her, pressing her to his hard strength until her breasts strained against him. "I have every intention of doing exactly that."

His lips left hers to investigate her ear before tracing their way back across her cheek and reclaiming her mouth.

Maggie buried her face in the hollow of his throat, drawing in a deep, shuddering breath as his busy hands fumbled with the effort to locate the tiny buttons at the back of her dress. Every place his fingers grazed her skin, a glowing warmth spread. Again, Maggie opened her mouth to explore the strong cord of his neck, savoring his salty-tasting skin. She heard the harsh intake of his breath when she pulled his dress shirt free and stroked his muscular back.

"Oh, Glenn," she whispered when she didn't think she could stand it anymore. Her shoulders were heaving when he lifted his weight from her.

He rolled onto his back, and she heard him release a harsh breath. "Maggie." His voice was thick and husky. "Listen, are you sure about this? We can wait."

"I'm sure," she whispered, and switched positions so that now it was she who was sprawled half atop him. "Glenn, I'm so sure it hurts."

"Maggie, oh Maggie." He repeated her name again and again in a broken whisper.

She'd spent a lifetime searching for him when all along he'd been so close and she hadn't known.

His arms crushed her then, and his mouth passionately sought hers with a greedy need that seemed to want to devour her. He took; she surrendered. He gave; she received. They were starved for each other and the physical love their bodies could share. With her arms wrapped securely around him, Maggie met his hunger with her own. When he half lifted her from the mattress she was trembling.

"Glenn," she whispered brokenly. "Oh Glenn, don't ever let me go."

"Never," he promised, sitting on the edge of the bed with her cradled in his lap. "This is forever." His words were a vow. Carefully, in order not to tear her dress, his fingers released each tiny button at the back of her gown. As each one was freed, he pressed his lips to the newly exposed skin.

"Forever," she repeated, and twisted so she could work

loose the tuxedo tie and the buttons to his shirt. She pulled the shirt free of his shoulders and slid her hand down his chest to his tightening abdomen.

"Maggie," he warned hoarsely.

"Love me," she whispered. "Oh Glenn, make me your wife."

Her fingers clutched frantically at his thick, dark hair as he continued to stroke her breast.

All too soon, she was on fire for him. Consumed with desire, lost in a primitive world, aware of nothing but the desperate need he awoke within her.

Moving quickly, he laid her on the mattress and eased his body over hers.

The loving was exquisite and when they'd finished, a long moment passed before he gathered her in his arms. He rolled onto his side, taking her with him. Lying cradled in his embrace, their legs entwined, Maggie closed her eyes and released a contented sigh.

"It was beautiful," she whispered, still overcome with emotion.

Glenn kissed the top of her head. "You're beautiful."

"So are you," she added quickly. "Oh Glenn, we're going to have such a good life."

"Yes," he agreed and kissed her forehead.

Maggie snuggled closer against him and kissed the nape of his neck when he reached down to cover them with the sheet and blanket.

Glenn held her close, kissing the crown of her head until her eyes closed sleepily. Her last thought as she drifted into the welcoming comfort of slumber was of warmth and security.

Maggie woke a couple of times in the darkest part of

the night, unaccustomed to sharing her bed. Each time she experienced the unexpected thrill of finding Glenn asleep at her side. No longer was she alone. Her joy was so great that she felt like she was ten years old again, waking up on Christmas morning.

She cuddled him spoon fashion, pressing her softness to his backside. Her body fit perfectly to his. Edging her hand over his muscular ribs, she felt his strength and knew that this man was as steady as the Rock of Gibraltar. She had chosen her life mate well. Content, she drifted back to sleep.

A low, grumbling sound woke her when morning light splashed into the room from the small crack between the closed draperies. Sitting up, Maggie yawned and raised her arms high above her head. She was ravenous and pressed a hand to her stomach to prevent her rumbling from waking Glenn. A menu for room service sat by the phone, and Maggie reached for it, studying its contents with interest, wondering if it would wake him if she ordered anything.

Glenn stirred and rolled onto his back, still caught in the last dregs of sleep. Gloriously happy, Maggie watched as a lazy smile grew on his face. Pride swelled in her heart as she realized their lovemaking was responsible for his look of blessed contentment. Maybe she wasn't so hungry after all.

Her long, tangled hair fell forward as she leaned down to press her lips to his. As she drew near, he whispered something. At first Maggie couldn't understand his words, then she froze. Stunned, her hand flew to her breast at the unexpected pain that pierced her. The arctic chill extended all the way to her heart and she squeezed her eyes closed to fight back the burning tears. Choking on humiliation, she struggled to untangle herself from the sheet. Her frantic movements woke Glenn from the nether land of sleep to the world of consciousness.

He turned on his side and reached for her hand. "Good morning," he said cheerfully. At the sight of her stricken face, he paused and rose to a full sitting position. "What's wrong?"

"The name is Maggie," she whispered fiercely, shoving his hand away. "And in case you've forgotten, I'm your wife as well."

Chapter 4

Tugging the sheet loose from the mattress, Maggie climbed out of bed. Her hands were shaking so badly that she had trouble twisting the material around her.

Glenn had mistaken her for another woman. A woman he had obviously once loved and apparently still did. Holding the sheet together with one hand, she sorted through the tangled mess of clothes on the floor. The tightness in her chest was so painful she could barely breathe. The room swayed beneath her feet and she closed her eyes, struggling to maintain her balance and her aplomb. Everything had been so beautiful. So perfect. How readily she had fallen into the fantasy, believing in each minute with a childlike innocence and trust. She'd been living in a twenty-four-hour dreamworld. That fantasy had been shattered by the reality of morning and she was shamed to the very marrow of her bones.

Glenn wiped a hand over his face and struggled to a sitting position. He vaguely recalled the contented pleasure of sleeping with a warm body at his side. In his sleep he must have confused Maggie with Angie. He cursed Angie for haunting him in his marriage.

Straightening, she turned to regard him coolly before speaking. "Enough." *More than enough,* her mind shouted. Clenching the sheet in one hand, her clothes in the other, she marched across the floor, her head tilted at a stately angle. She'd never felt more like crying in her life. Her pride and dignity remained intact, but little else was as it should be.

Once inside the bathroom, she leaned against the heavy door, her shoulders sagging. Covering her face with both hands in hurt and frustration, she let the sheet slip to the floor. Equal doses of anger and misery descended on her until she was convinced she'd slump under the force of their weight. She didn't know what do, but taking a bath seemed important.

"Maggie." Glenn stood on the other side of the door, his voice low and confused. "At least talk to me."

"No," she shouted, still reeling from the shock. "I don't want to talk. I've heard enough to last me a lifetime." Forcing herself into action, she turned on the faucet and filled the tub with steaming hot water. She had been a fool to believe in yesterday's illusions. The morning had shattered the dream—only she didn't want it to end. Glenn was someone she had thought she could trust. In her heart she knew that he wouldn't be like all the rest.

"Maggie, for the love of heaven, give me a chance to explain."

Sliding into the steaming bath, Maggie bit into her bottom lip and forced herself to think. She could demand that they divorce, but she didn't want that, and Glenn didn't, either. For twelve hours she had been a happily married woman. Somehow Maggie had to find a way to stretch twelve hours into a lifetime.

In the other room, Glenn dressed slowly, his thoughts oppressive. Things couldn't be worse. From the moment Maggie had met him at the airport he had seen how reserved and untrusting her inheritance had made her. Now he had hurt her, and he silently cursed himself for doing the very thing he vowed he never would. He could still see her stricken eyes glaring down at him when he woke. He had wanted to take her in his arms and explain, but she'd jumped from the bed as if she couldn't get away fast enough. Not that he blamed her. The worst part was that he couldn't guarantee it wouldn't happen again. Angie had been an integral part of his life for nearly two years. He had cast her from his thoughts with an all-consuming effort, but he had no control over the ramblings of his mind while he slept. He stroked his fingers through his hair and heaved a disgusted sigh. Whatever it was, he wouldn't allow it to ruin this marriage. Somehow he'd find a way to make it up to Maggie.

The bathroom door opened and Glenn turned anxiously. He studied Maggie's face for evidence of tears and found none. He had forgotten what a strong woman she was and admired her all the more. He vividly recalled the time she was fifteen and broke her arm skateboarding. She'd been in intense pain. Anyone else would have been screaming like a banshee, but not Maggie. She had gritted her teeth, but hadn't shed a tear. He also remembered how the only person she had trusted to help her had been him. The guilt washed over him in dousing waves.

"Can we talk now?" he asked her gently.

"I think we should," she said, pacing, because standing in one spot seemed an impossible task. "We need to make some rules in this marriage, Glenn."

"Anything," he agreed.

"The first thing you have to do is stop loving that other woman right now. This minute." Her voice trembled, and she battled for control.

Glenn felt physically ill. Maggie was unnaturally pale, her cheeks devoid of color. Her dark, soulful eyes contained a sorrow he longed to erase, and yet he knew he couldn't. His thoughts were in turmoil. "You know I'd never lie to you."

"Yes." Glenn might be a lot of things, she knew, but a liar wasn't one of them.

"Maggie, I want this marriage to work, but what you're asking me to do is going to be hard."

A tingling sensation went through her that left her feeling numb and sick. She wouldn't share this man—not even with a memory.

"In that case," she murmured and swallowed, "I've got some thinking to do." She turned from him and started toward the door.

"Maggie." Glenn stopped her, and she turned around. Their eyes met and held. "You don't want a divorce, do you?"

The word hit Maggie with all the impact of a freight train. "No," she said, shaking her head. "I may be mad, Glenn Lambert, but I'm not stupid."

The door made an echoing sound that bounced off the walls as Maggie left the hotel room. Glenn felt his tense shoulder muscles relax. It had taken everything in him to ask her about a divorce. That was the last thing he wanted, but he felt he had to know where Maggie stood after what had happened that morning.

The curious stares that met Maggie as she stepped off

the elevator convinced her that the first thing she had to do was buy something to wear that was less ostentatious. A wrinkled pink maid-of-honor gown would cause more than a few heads to turn, and the last thing Maggie wanted was attention. In addition, she couldn't demand that her husband give up his affection for another woman and love and care for her instead, when she looked like something the cat left on the porch.

The hotel had a gift shop, where she found a summer dress of pale blue polished cotton, which she changed into after purchasing it. A walk through the lobby revealed that Glenn was nowhere to be seen. With time weighing heavily on her hands, Maggie pulled a ten-dollar bill from her purse. Already the hotel casino was buzzing with patrons eager to spend their money. Standing in front of the quarter slot machine, Maggie inserted the first coin. Pressing the button, she watched the figures spin into a blur and slowly wind down to two oranges and a cherry. Maggie stared at the fifty cents she'd won in disbelief. She didn't expect to win. Actually, it was fitting that she was in Reno. She had just made the biggest gamble of her life. The scary part was that Maggie felt like a loser and had felt like one almost from the minute she'd inherited her great-aunt Margaret's money. She felt the ridiculous urge to laugh but recognized that if she gave in to the compulsion, tears wouldn't be far behind.

Glenn found her ten minutes later, still playing the slot machine. For several moments he stood watching her, wondering how to approach this woman he had known most of his life. The woman who was now his wife. There were so many issues facing them that had to be settled before he left for Charleston. Maggie's inheritance was one thing he wouldn't allow to hang between them like a steel curtain. It was best to clear the air of that and everything else they could.

A discordant bell clanged loudly, and a barrage of celebratory characters danced across the slot machine. She looked stunned and stepped back from the machine. Without emotion, she cashed out. As she turned, their eyes clashed. Her breath caught in her throat, and she hesitated, waiting for him to speak first. Like her, he had purchased another set of clothes, and again Maggie wondered why she'd never noticed how extraordinarily good-looking Glenn was. He was a man any woman would be proud to call her husband. If he'd come to tell her he wanted out of the marriage, she didn't know what she would say. The time spent in front of the slot machine had given her the perspective to realize that Glenn was as shocked by what had happened as she was. She prayed that he hadn't come for the reason she suspected. Maggie wanted this marriage. She had been so lonely and miserable. The previous day with Glenn had been the most wonderful day of her life. Maybe she was still looking at the situation through rose-colored glasses, but the deed was done. They were married now. The other woman had no claim to him. He might murmur Angie's name in his sleep, but he was married to Maggie.

"Our plane leaves in two hours," he said, stepping forward. "Let's get something to eat."

Nodding required a monumental effort. Her body went limp with relief.

The hostess at the restaurant led them to a booth and handed them menus. She gave Glenn a soft, slightly seductive smile, but Maggie was pleased to notice that he didn't pay the woman the least bit of attention. Glenn had never been a flirt. Beyond anything else, Maggie realized, Glenn was an intensely loyal man. For him to whisper another woman's name in his sleep had been all the more devastating for just that reason.

Almost immediately a waitress arrived, poured them each a cup of coffee, and took their order.

"I want you to know that I'll do everything in my power to do what you asked," Glenn announced, his eyes holding hers. His hands cupped the coffee mug, and there was a faint pleading note shining from his eyes. "About this morning—I suppose you want to know about her."

"Yes," Maggie whispered, hating the way his eyes softened when he mentioned his lost love.

A sadness seemed to settle over him. "Her name is Angie. We were . . ." He hesitated. "Engaged. She decided to marry her childhood sweetheart. It's as simple as that."

"You obviously cared about her a great deal," Maggie said softly, hoping to take some of the sting from her earlier comments. Talking about Angie, even now, was obviously painful for him.

He held her gaze without hesitation. "I did care for her, but that's over now. I didn't marry you longing for anyone else. You aren't a substitute. This marriage wasn't made on the rebound. We're both vulnerable for different reasons. I want you for my wife. Not anyone else, only you. We've known each other most of our lives. I like you a great deal and respect you even more. We're comfortable together."

"Yes, we are," she agreed. So Glenn regarded her as an old pair of worn shoes. He could relax with her and put aside any need for pretense . . . as she could. But then she hadn't exactly come into their marriage seeking white lace and promises. Or maybe she had. Maggie didn't know anymore; she was confused.

"We're going to work this out," he said confidently, smiling for the first time that day as he reached for her hand.

"We're going to try," she suggested cautiously. "I'm not so sure we've done the right thing running off like this. We were both half crazy to think we could make a marriage work on a twenty-four-hour reacquaintance."

"I knew what we were doing every second," Glenn countered gruffly. "I wanted this, Maggie."

"I didn't know if it was right or wrong. I guess only time will tell if we did the right thing or not."

The flight back to San Francisco seemed to take a lifetime. Maggie sat by the window, staring at the miniature world far below. The landscape rolled and curved from jutting peaks to plunging valleys that reminded her of the first few hours of her marriage. Even now a brooding sense of unreality remained with her.

The days were shorter now that winter was approaching, and dusk had settled by the time the taxi pulled up in front of the beach house. While Glenn was paying the cabdriver, Maggie looked over the house where she'd voluntarily sequestered herself, wondering how Glenn would view the ostentatious showplace. Undoubtedly, he would be impressed. Her friends had praised the beach house that seemed to lack for nothing. There was a work-out gym, a sauna, a Jacuzzi, a swimming pool and a tennis court in the side yard that Maggie never used. The house held enough attractions to keep even the most discriminating prisoner entertained.

On the way from the airport they had stopped off at Steve's empty apartment and picked up Glenn's luggage. Seeing it was a vivid reminder that he was scheduled to leave in the afternoon. "What time is your flight tomorrow?" she asked, wondering how long they'd be in Charleston. They had already decided to make their home in San Francisco, but arrangements would need to be made in Charleston.

His mouth hardened. "Are you so anxious to be rid of me?"

"No." She turned astonished eyes to him, stunned at his sharp tongue. He made it sound as though she wouldn't be going with him. She should. After all, she was his wife. She could make an issue of it now, or wait until she was certain she'd read him right. They had already experienced enough conflict for one day, and Maggie opted to hold her tongue. Her fingers fumbled with the lock in an effort to get inside the house. "I have to phone my brother," she announced once the door was open.

"Denny?"

"Yes, Denny, or is that a problem, too?"

He ran his fingers through his hair and expelled an angry breath. "I didn't mean to snap at you."

Maggie lowered her gaze. "I know. We're both on edge. I didn't mean to bite your head off, either." They were nervous and unsure of each other for the first time in their lives. What had once been solid ground beneath their feet had become shifting sand. They didn't know where they stood . . . or if they'd continue to stand at all.

Glenn placed a hand at the base of her neck and gently squeezed it. "My flight's scheduled for three. We'll have some time together."

He didn't plan to have her travel with him! That was another shock. *Fine,* she thought angrily. If he didn't want her, then she wouldn't ask. "Good," she murmured sarcastically. Fine, indeed!

The house foyer was paved with expensive tiles imported from Italy, and led to a plush sunken living room decorated with several pieces of furniture upholstered in white leather. A baby grand piano dominated one corner of the room. As she hung up Glenn's coat, he wandered into the large living room, his hands in his pockets.

"Do you like it?"

"It's very nice" was all he said. He stood, legs slightly apart, while his gaze rested on an oil painting hung prominently on the wall opposite the Steinway. It was one of Maggie's earlier works and her favorite, a beachscape that displayed several scenes, depicting a summer day's outing to the ocean. Her brush had captured the images of eager children building a sand castle. Another group of bikini-clad young girls were playing a game of volleyball with muscle-bound he-men. A family was enjoying a picnic, their blanket spread out on the sand, shaded by a multicolored umbrella. Cotton-candy clouds floated in a clear blue sky while the ocean waves crested and slashed against the shore. Maggie had spent hours agonizing over the minute details of the painting. Despite its candor and realism, Maggie's beachscape wasn't an imitation of a snapshot recording, but a mosaic-like design that gave a minute hint at the wonder of life.

"This is a marvelous painting. Where did you ever find

it?" Glenn asked, without turning around. "The detail is unbelievable."

"A poor imitation of a Brueghel." A smile danced at the corners of her mouth.

"Who?"

"Pieter Brueghel, a sixteenth-century Flemish painter."

"A sixteenth-century artist didn't paint this," Glenn challenged.

"No. I did."

He turned with a look of astonished disbelief. "You're not teasing, are you?" The question was rhetorical. His eyes narrowed fractionally, as if reassessing her.

"It's one of my earliest efforts after art school. I've done better since, but this remains my favorite."

"Better than this?" His voice dipped faintly, as though he doubted her words. "I remember you scribbling figures as a kid, but I never suspected you had this much talent."

A shiver of pleasure raced up her arms at the pride that gleamed from his eyes as he glanced from the painting back to her. "I had no idea you were this talented, Maggie."

The sincerity of the compliment couldn't be questioned. Others had praised her work, but Maggie had felt a niggling doubt as to the candidness of the comments. "Thank you," she returned, feeling uncharacteristically humble.

"I'd like to see your other projects."

"Don't worry, you'll get the chance. Right now, I've got to phone Denny. He'll wonder what happened to me."

"Sure. Go ahead. I'll wait in here if you like."

Maggie's office was off the living room. She hesitated for a moment before deciding, then walked to the telephone, which was on a table next to the couch. Her back was to Glenn as she picked up the receiver and punched out the number.

"Denny, it's Maggie."

"Maggie," he cried with obvious relief. "How was the wedding? You must have been late. I tried to get hold of you all day."

It was on the tip of Maggie's tongue to tell him about her marriage, but she held back, preferring to waylay his questions and doubts. She would tell him soon enough.

Her brother's voice softened perceptibly. "I was worried."

"I'm sorry, I should have phoned." Maggie lifted a strand of hair around her ear.

"Did you get the money transferred?"

Maggie sighed inwardly, feeling guilty. Denny knew all the right buttons to push with her. "The money will be ready for you Monday morning."

"Thanks. You know Linda and I appreciate it." His voice took on a honey-coated appeal.

"I know."

"As soon as I talk to the attorney about my case, I'll let you know where we stand."

"Yes, Denny, do that." A large portion of Denny's inheritance had been lost in a bad investment, and Maggie was helping him meet expenses. She didn't begrudge him the money: How could she when she had so much? What she hated was what it was doing to him. Yet she couldn't refuse him. Denny was her brother, her only brother.

After saying her good-bye, she replaced the receiver and turned back to Glenn. "I gave the housekeeper the weekend off. But if you're hungry, I'm sure I'll be able to whip up something."

"How's Denny?" Glenn ignored her offer.

"Fine. Do you want something to eat or not?"

"Sure." His gaze rested on the phone, and Maggie realized that he'd probably picked up the gist of her conversation with Denny. More than she had intended. As a stockbroker, Glenn would know what a foolish mistake her brother had made, and she wanted to save her brother the embarrassment if possible.

Determined to avoid the subject of her brother, Maggie strolled past Glenn, through the dining room, and into the expansive kitchen that was equipped with every conceivable modern cooking device. The double-width refrigerator/freezer was well stocked with frozen meals so that all that was required of her was to insert one into the microwave, push a button, and wait.

The swinging doors opened as Glenn followed her inside. He paused to look around the U-shaped room, with its oak cabinets and marble countertops. His hands returned to his pockets as he cocked his thick brows. "A bit large, wouldn't you say? One woman couldn't possibly require this much space."

Of course the kitchen was huge, she thought, irritated. She hadn't paid an exorbitant price for this place for three drawers and a double sink. "Yes," she returned, somewhat defensively. "I like it this way."

"Do you mind if I take a look outside?" he asked, and opened the sliding glass doors that led to a balcony overlooking the ocean.

"Sure. Go ahead."

A breeze ruffled the drapes as he opened and closed the

glass French door. Maggie watched him move to the railing and look out over the beach below. If she paused and strained her ears, she could hear the ocean as the wild waves crashed on the sandy shore. A crescent moon was barely visible behind a thick layer of clouds.

Leaning a hip against the counter, Maggie studied his profile. It seemed incomprehensible that the man who was standing only a few feet from her was her husband. She felt awkward and shy, even afraid. If he did head back to Charleston without her, their marriage would become increasingly unreal. Before Glenn turned to find her studying him, Maggie took out a head of lettuce from the refrigerator and dumped it into a strainer, and then placed it under the faucet.

Rubbing the chill from his arms, Glenn returned a few minutes later.

"Go ahead and pour yourself a drink," Maggie offered, tearing the lettuce leaves into a bowl. When he hesitated, she pointed to the liquor cabinet.

"I'm more interested in coffee, if you have it."

"I'll make it."

"I'll do it."

Simultaneously, they moved, and somehow Maggie's face came sharply into contact with the solid mass of muscle and man. Amazingly, in the huge kitchen, they'd somehow managed to collide. Glenn's hand snaked out to steady Maggie at the shoulders. "You okay?"

"I think so." She moved her nose back and forth a couple of times before looking up at him. "I should have known this kitchen wasn't big enough for the two of us."

Something warm and ardent shone from his eyes as his gaze dropped to her mouth. The air in the room crackled with electricity. The hands that were gripping her shoulders moved down her upper arms and tightened. Every ticking second seemed to stretch out of proportion. Then, very slowly, he half lifted her from the floor, his mouth descending to hers a fraction of an inch at a time. Maggie's heart skipped a beat, then began to hammer wildly. He deliberately, slowly, left his mouth a hair's space above hers so that their breaths mingled and merged. Holding her close, he seemed to want her to take the initiative. But the memory of that morning remained vivid in her mind. And now it seemed he intended to leave her behind in San Francisco as well. No, there were too many questions left unanswered for her to give in to the physical attraction between them. Still, his mouth hovered over hers, his eyes holding hers. At the sound of the timer dinging, Glenn released her. Disoriented, Maggie stood completely still until she realized Glenn had moved away. Embarrassed, she turned, making busywork at the microwave.

"That smells like lasagna," Glenn commented.

"It is." Maggie's gaze widened as she set out the dishes. What an idiot she'd been. The bell she heard hadn't been her heart's song from wanting Glenn's kisses. It had been the signal from her microwave that their dinner was ready. The time had come to remove the stars from her eyes regarding their marriage.

Maggie noted that Glenn's look was thoughtful when they ate, as if something was bothering him. For that matter, she was unusually quiet herself. After the meal, Glenn silently helped her stack the dinner plates into the dishwasher. "Would you like the grand tour?" Maggie inquired, more in an effort to ease the tension than from any desire to show off her home.

"You did promise to show me some more of your work."

"My art?" Maggie hedged, suddenly unsure. "I'm more into the abstract things now." She dried her hands on a terry-cloth towel and avoided looking at him. "A couple of years ago I discovered Helen Frankenthaler. Oh, I'd seen her work, but I hadn't appreciated her genius."

"Helen who?"

"Frankenthaler." Maggie enunciated the name slowly. "She's probably the most historically important artist in the last few decades, and people with a lot more talent than me have said so."

Glenn looped an arm around her shoulders and slowly shook his head. "Maggie, you're going to have to remember your husband knows absolutely nothing about art."

"But you know what you like," she teased, leading him by the hand to the fully glassed-in upstairs studio.

"That I do," he admitted in a husky whisper.

No one else had ever seen the studio, where she spent the vast majority of her time. It hadn't been a conscious oversight. There just had never been anyone she'd wanted to show it to. Not even Denny, who, she realized, gave only lip service to her work. She led Glenn proudly into her domain. She had talent and knew it. So much of her self-esteem was centered on her work. In recent years it had become the visible outpouring of her frustrations and loneliness. Her ego, her identity, her vanity were all tied up in her work.

Glenn noted that her studio was a huge room twice the size of the kitchen. Row upon row of canvases were propped against the walls. From the shine in her eyes, Glenn realized that Maggie took her painting seriously.

She loved it. As far as he could see, it was the only thing in this world that she had for herself.

He hadn't been pleased by what he'd overheard in her telephone conversation with Denny. He had wanted to ask Maggie about it over dinner, but hesitated. He felt that it was too soon to pry into her relationship with her brother. As he recalled, Denny was a decent guy, four or five years older than Maggie. From the sounds of it, though, Denny was sponging off his sister—which was unusual, since Glenn had heard that Denny was wealthy in his own right. It was none of his affair, Glenn decided, and it was best that he keep his nose out of it.

Proudly, Maggie walked around the studio, which was used more than any other room in the house. Most of the canvases were fresh and white, waiting for the bold strokes of color that would bring them to life. Several of the others contained her early experiments in cubism and expressionism. She watched Glenn as he strolled about the room, studying several of her pictures. Pride shone in his eyes, and Maggie basked in his approval. She wanted to hug him and thank him for simply appreciating what she did.

He paused to study a large ten-foot canvas propped at an angle against the floor. Large slashes of blue paint were smeared across the center and had been left to dry, creating their own geometric pattern. Maggie was especially pleased with this piece. It was the painting she had been working on the afternoon she was late meeting Glenn at the airport.

"What's this?" Glenn asked, his voice tight. He cocked his head sideways, his brow pleated in concentration.

"Glenn," she chided, "that's my painting."

He was utterly stupefied that Maggie would waste her obvious talent on an abstract mess. The canvas looked as though paint had been carelessly splattered across the top. Glenn could see no rhyme or pattern to the design. "Your painting," he mused aloud. "It's quite a deviation from your other work, isn't it?"

Maggie shrugged off his lack of appreciation and enthusiasm. "This isn't a portrait," she explained, somewhat defensively. This particular painting was a departure from the norm, a bold experiment with a new balance of unexpected harmony of different hues of blues with tension between shapes and shades. Glenn had admitted he knew nothing about art, she thought. He wouldn't understand what she was trying to say with this piece, and she didn't try to explain.

Squatting, Glenn examined the large canvas, his fingertips testing the texture. "What is this material? It's not like a regular canvas, is it?"

"No, it's unprimed cotton duck—the same fabric that's used for making sails." This type of porous material allowed her to toss the paint across the canvas; then, point by point, she poured, dripped, and even used squeegees to spread the great veils of tone. She spent long, tedious hours contemplating each aspect of the work, striving for the effortless, spontaneous appeal she admired so much in Helen Frankenthaler's work.

"You're not into the abstract stuff, are you?" she asked with a faint smile. She tried to make it sound as if it didn't matter. The pride she'd seen in Glenn's eyes when he saw her beachscape and her other work had thrilled her. Now she could see him trying to disguise his puzzlement. "Don't feel bad—abstracts aren't for everyone."

A frown marred his smooth brow as he straightened and brushed the grit from his hands. "I'd like to see some more of the work like the painting downstairs."

"There are a couple of those over here." She pulled a painting out from behind a stack of her later efforts in cubism.

Glenn held out the painting, and his frown disappeared. "Now, this is good. The other looks like an accident."

An accident! Maggie nearly choked on her laughter. She'd like to see him try it. "I believe the time has come for me to propose another rule for this marriage."

Glenn's look was wary. "What?"

"From now on, everything I paint is beautiful and wonderful and the work of an unrecognized genius. Understand?"

"Certainly," he murmured. "Anything you say." He paused to examine the huge canvas a second time. "I don't know what you're saying with this, but this is obviously the work of an unrecognized and unappreciated genius."

Maggie smiled at him boldly. "You did that well."

Chapter 5

Glenn muttered under his breath as he followed Maggie out of her studio. Her dainty back was stiff as she walked down the stairs. She might have made light of his comments, but he wasn't fooled. Once again he had hurt her. Twice in one day. The problem was that he was trying too hard. They both were. "I apologize, Maggie. I didn't mean to offend you. You're right. I don't know a thing about art."

"I'm not offended," she lied. "I keep forgetting how opinionated you are." With deliberate calm she moved into the living room and sat at the baby grand piano, running her fingers over the ivory keys. She wanted to be angry with him but couldn't be, realizing that any irritation was a symptom of her own insecurity. She had exposed a deeply personal part of herself. It had been a measure of her trust, and Glenn hadn't known or understood. She couldn't blame him for that.

"I don't remember that you played the piano." He stood beside her, resting his hand on her shoulder.

His touch was oddly soothing. "I started taking lessons a couple years ago."

"You're good."

Maggie stopped playing; her fingers froze above the keys. Slowly, she placed her hands in her lap. "Glenn, listen, the new rule to our marriage applies only to my painting. You can be honest with my piano playing. I'm rotten. I have as much innate rhythm as lint."

Glenn recognized that in his effort to make up for one faux pas he had only dug himself in deeper. He didn't know anything about music. "I thought you played the clarinet."

"I wasn't much better at that, if you recall."

"I don't."

"Obviously," she muttered under her breath, rising to her feet. She rubbed her hands together in a nervous gesture. "It's been a long day."

Glenn's spirits sank. It had been quite a day and nothing like he'd expected. Yet he couldn't blame Maggie—he had brought everything on himself. His hand reached for hers. "Let's go to bed."

Involuntarily, Maggie tensed. Everything had been perfect for the wedding night, but now she felt unsure and equally uneasy. Glenn was her husband, and she couldn't give him the guest bedroom. But things were different from what they had been. Her eyes were opened this time, and white lace and promises weren't filling her mind with fanciful illusions.

"Is something wrong?" Glenn's question was more of a challenge.

"No," she murmured, abruptly shaking her head. "Nothing's wrong." But then, not everything was right, either. She led the way down the long hallway to the master bedroom, feeling shaky.

The room was huge, dominated by a brick fireplace, with two pale-blue chairs angled in front of it. The windows were adorned with shirred draperies of a delicate floral design that had been especially created to give a peaceful, easy-living appeal. The polished mahogany four-poster bed had a down comforter tossed over the top that was made from the same lavender floral material as the drapes. This room was Maggie's favorite. She could sit in it for hours and feel content.

If Glenn was impressed with the simple elegance or felt the warmth of her bedroom, he said nothing. Maggie would have been surprised if he had.

His suitcase rested on the thick carpet, and Glenn sighed, turning toward her. "We have a lot to do tomorrow." Frustrated anger filled Glenn at his own stupidity. Everything he had done that day had been wrong. From the moment he had opened his eyes to the time he'd mentioned going to bed. He couldn't have been more insensitive had he tried. He didn't want to argue with Maggie, and yet, it seemed, he had gone out of his way to do exactly that. There would be a lot of adjustments to make with their marriage, and he had gotten off on the wrong foot almost from the moment they'd started. Maggie was uncomfortable; Glenn could sense that. He could also feel her hesitancy. But he was her husband, and by heaven he'd sleep with her this and every night for the remainder of their lives.

The mention of the coming day served to remind Maggie that Glenn was planning on returning to Charleston alone. That rankled. Sometime during the evening, she had thought to casually bring up the return trip. But with what had happened in her studio and afterward, the timing hadn't been right. Crossing her arms over her breasts, she met his gaze.

"Oh. What are we doing tomorrow?" She couldn't think of anything they needed to do that couldn't be handled later.

"First we'll see a lawyer, then—"

"Why?" she asked, her voice unnaturally throaty. Alarm filled her. Glenn had changed his mind. He didn't want to stay married. And little wonder. She kept making up these rules, and—

"I want to make sure none of your inheritance money is ever put in my name." With all the other problems they were facing, Glenn needed to assure Maggie that he hadn't married her for her wealth. If anything, he regretted the fact she had it. Her great-aunt Margaret's money had been a curse as far as he was concerned. And judging by the insecure, frightened woman Maggie had become, she might even have realized that herself.

"I . . . I know you wouldn't cheat me." The odd huskiness of her voice was made more pronounced by a slight quiver. Of all the men she had known in her life, she trusted Glenn implicitly. He was a man of honor. He might have married her when he was in love with another woman, but he would never deliberately do anything to swindle her.

Their gazes melted into each other's. Maggie trusted him, Glenn realized. The heavy weight that had pressed against him from the moment she had turned her hurt, angry eyes on him that morning lessened. *Surely* there'd been a better way to handle that business with her paintings, he thought. She had talent, incredible talent, and it was a shame that she was wasting it by hiding it away.

"After the lawyer, we'll go to a jeweler," he added.

"A jeweler?"

"I'd like you to wear a wedding ring, Maggie."

The pulse in her neck throbbed as she beat down a rush of pure pleasure. "Okay, and you, too."

"Of course," he agreed easily. His gaze did a sweeping inspection of the room, as if he'd noticed it for the first time. It reminded him of Maggie. Her presence was stamped in every piece of furniture, every corner. Suddenly, a tiredness stole into his bones. He was exhausted, mentally and physically. "Let's get ready for bed."

Maggie nodded, and some of her earlier apprehension faded. She wasn't completely comfortable sleeping with him after what had happened. Not when there was a chance he would take her in his arms, hold her close, kiss her, even make love to her, with another woman's name on his lips. "You go ahead—I've got a few odds and ends to take care of first."

Sitting at the oak desk in her office, Maggie lifted her long hair from her face and closed her eyes as weariness flooded her bones. She was tired—Glenn was tired. She was confused—Glenn was confused. They both wanted this marriage—they were both responsible for making it work. All right, there wasn't any reason to overreact. They'd share a bed, and if he said the other woman's name in his sleep again, Maggie refused to be held responsible for her actions.

By the time Glenn returned from his shower, Maggie had gone back to the bedroom and changed into a sexless flannel pajama set that would have discouraged the most amorous male. She had slipped beneath the covers, and was sitting up reading, her back supported by thick feather pillows. Behind her book, she followed Glenn's movements when he reentered the bedroom.

He paused and allowed a tiny smile of satisfaction to touch his lips. He had half expected Maggie to linger in her office until he was asleep and was greatly pleased that she hadn't. Although she looked like a virgin intent on maintaining her chastity in that flannel outfit, he knew that this night wasn't the time to press for his husbandly rights. Things had gone badly. Tomorrow would be better, he promised himself.

Lifting back the thick quilt, Glenn slid his large frame into the king-size bed and turned off the light that rested on the mahogany nightstand on his side of the bed.

"Good night." His voice was husky and low, with only a trace of amusement. He thought she would probably sit up reading until she fell asleep with the light on.

"Good night," she answered softly, pretending to read. A few minutes later, Maggie battled to keep her lashes from drooping. Valiantly, she struggled as her mind conjured up ways of resisting Glenn. The problem was that she didn't want to resist him. He would probably wait until she was relaxed and close to falling asleep, she theorized. When she was at her weakest point, he would reach for her and kiss her. Glenn was a wonderful kisser, and she went warm at the memory of what had happened their first night together. He had held her as if he were dying of thirst and she was a cool shimmering pool in an oasis.

Gathering her resolve, Maggie clenched her teeth. By heaven, the way her thoughts were going, she'd lean over and kiss him any minute. Her hand rested on her abdomen and Maggie felt bare skin. Her pajamas might be sexless, but they also conveniently buttoned up the front, so he had easy access to her if he wanted. Again, she recalled how good their lovemaking had been and how she had thrilled to his hands and mouth on her. Her eyes drooped shut, and with a start she forced them open. Lying completely still, she listened, and after several long moments she discovered that Glenn had turned away from her and was sound asleep.

An unexpected rush of disappointment filled her. He hadn't even tried to make love to her. Without a thought, he had turned onto his side and gone to sleep! Bunching up her pillow, Maggie rolled onto her stomach, feeling such frustration that she could have cried. He didn't want her, and as unreasonable as it sounded, Maggie felt discouraged and depressed. Her last thought as she turned out her light was that if Glenn reached for her in the night she would give him what he wanted . . . what she wanted.

Sometime in the middle of the night Maggie woke. She was sleeping on her side, but had moved to the middle of the bed. Her eyes fluttered open, and she wondered what had caused her to wake when she felt so warm and comfortable. Glenn's even breathing sounded close to her ear, and she realized that he was asleep, cuddling his body to hers. Contented and secure, she closed her eyes, and a moment later a male hand slid over her ribs, just below her breasts. When he pulled her close, fitting his body to hers, Maggie's lashes fluttered open. Not for the first time, she was amazed at how perfectly their bodies fit together. Releasing a contented breath, Maggie shut her eyes and wandered back to sleep.

Glenn woke in the first light of dawn with a serenity that had escaped him for months. That morning he didn't mistake the warm body he was holding close. Maggie was responsible for his tranquility of spirit, Glenn realized. He needed Maggie. During the night, her pajama top had ridden up and the urge to move his hand and trace the soft, womanly curves was almost overpowering. Maggie was all the woman he would ever want. She was everything he had ever hoped to find in a wife—a passionate, irresistible mistress with an intriguing mind and delectable body, who surrendered herself willingly. Her passion had surprised and pleased him. She hadn't been shy, or embarrassed, abandoning herself to him with an eagerness that thrilled him every time he thought about it. She was more woman than he'd dared hope for, and he ached to take her again.

In her sleep, Maggie shifted, and her breasts sprang free of the confining top. For an eternity he lay completely still. In his mind he pictured turning her onto her back and kissing her until her lips opened eagerly to his. With inhuman patience he would look into those dark, beautiful eyes and wait until she told him how much she wanted him.

Groaning, he released her and rolled onto his back, taking deep breaths to control his frantic frustration. He had no idea how long it would be before he would have the opportunity to make love to his wife again. Two weeks, at least, maybe longer. Almost as overwhelming as the urge to make love to her was the one to cherish and protect her. She needed reassurance, and he knew she needed time. Throwing back the blankets, he marched into the bathroom and turned on the cold water.

Maggie woke at the sound of the shower running. Stirring, she turned onto her back and stared at the ceiling as the last dregs of sleep drained from her mind. She had been having the most pleasant erotic dream. One that caused her to blush from the roots of her dark hair to the ends of her toenails. Indecent dreams, maybe, but excruciatingly sensual. Perhaps it was best that Glenn was gone when she woke, she thought. If he had been beside her, she didn't know what she would have done. She could well have embarrassed them both by reaching for him and asking him to make love to her before he returned to Charleston . . . alone.

Taking advantage of the privacy, she dressed and hurriedly made the bed. By the time she had straightened the comforter across the mattress, Glenn reappeared.

"Good morning," he said as he paused just inside the bedroom, standing both alert and still as he studied her. "Did you sleep well?"

"Yes," she responded hastily, feeling like a specimen about to be analyzed, but a highly prized specimen, one that was cherished and valued. "What about you?" she asked.

The hesitation was barely noticeable, but Maggie noticed. "Like a rock."

"Good. Are you hungry?" Her eyes refused to meet his, afraid of what hers would tell him.

"Starved."

"Breakfast should be ready by the time you've finished dressing," she said as she left the room. Glenn had showered last night, she remembered; she couldn't recall him being overly fastidious. Shrugging, she moved down the long hall to the kitchen.

The bacon was sizzling in the skillet when Glenn reappeared, dressed in dark slacks and a thick pullover sweater. Maggie was reminded once again that he was devastatingly handsome and experienced, and with a burst of pride, she remembered that he was married to her. At least legally, he was hers. However, another woman owned the most vital part of him—his heart. In time, Maggie trusted, she would claim that as well.

The morning swam past in a blur; such was their pace. They began by contacting Maggie's attorney and were given an immediate appointment. Together they sat in his office, although it was Glenn who did the majority of the talking. Maggie was uncomfortable with the rewording of her will, but Glenn was adamant. He desired none of her money, and he wanted it stated legally. When and if they had children, her inheritance would be passed on to them.

After the attorney's they stopped off at a prominent San Francisco jeweler. Maggie had never been one for flashy jewels. All too often her hands were in paint solvent or mixing clay, and she didn't want to have to worry about losing expensive rings or valuable jewels. Knowing herself and her often thoughtless ways, Maggie was apt to misplace a diamond, and she couldn't bear the thought of losing any ring Glenn gave her.

"You decide," Glenn insisted, his hand at the back of her neck. "Whatever one you want is fine."

Sensing a sure sale, the young jeweler set out a tray of exquisite diamonds, far larger than any Maggie had dreamed Glenn would want to purchase. Her gaze fell on a lovely marquise and her teeth worried her bottom lip. "I . . . was thinking maybe something with a smaller stone would be fine," she murmured, realizing that she should have explained her problems about a diamond to Glenn earlier.

He pinched his mouth closed with displeasure, resenting her concern that he couldn't afford to buy her a diamond large enough to weight her hand.

"Try on that one," he insisted, pointing to the marquise solitaire with the wide polished band that she had admired earlier. The diamond was the largest and most expensive on the tray.

Maggie paled, not knowing how to explain herself. The salesman beamed, exchanging pleased glances with Glenn.

"An excellent choice," the jeweler said, lifting Maggie's limp hand. The ring fit as if it was made for her slender finger. But the diamond was so heavy it felt bulky and unnatural. In her mind, Maggie could picture the panic of looking for it once it was mislaid . . . and it would be.

"We'll take it."

"Glenn." Maggie placed her hand on his forearm. "Can I talk to you a minute? Please."

"I'll write up the sales order," the jeweler said, removing the tray of diamonds. "I'll be with the cashier when you've finished."

Maggie waited until the salesman was out of earshot before turning troubled eyes to Glenn. Her heart was in her eyes as she recognized the pride and irritation that glared back at her.

"What's the matter, Maggie?" he growled under his breath. "Are you afraid I can't afford a wedding ring for my wife? I may not own a fancy beach house, but be assured, I can afford a diamond."

Glenn's words smarted, and it was all Maggie could do to bite back a flippant reply. "It's not that," she whispered fiercely, keeping her voice low so the jeweler wouldn't hear them arguing. "If you'd given me half a chance, I'd have explained. I'm an artist, remember? If you buy me that flashy diamond, I'll be constantly removing it for one reason or another."

"So? What are you suggesting? No ring at all?"

"No . . . I'm sorry I said anything. The ring is fine." Maggie backed down, aware that anything said now would be misconstrued. Somehow she would learn to be careful with the diamond. Purchasing it had become a matter of male pride, and Maggie didn't want to cause any more problems than the ones already facing them.

"Would a plain gold band solve that?" he asked unexpectedly.

"Yes," she murmured, surprised. "Yes, it would." To her delight, Glenn also asked the jeweler to size a band for her. Maggie felt wonderful when they stepped outside. The question of the ring might have been only a minor problem, but together they had settled it without wounding each other's sensitive pride. They were making progress, and it felt good.

They ate lunch in Chinatown, feasting on hot diced chicken stir-fried with fresh, crisp vegetables. All the time they were dining, Maggie was infinitely aware of two pressing items: the heavy feel of the ring on the third finger of her left hand, and the time. Within hours Glenn would be leaving for Charleston. A kaleidoscope of regrets and questions whirled through her mind. She wanted to go with him, but didn't feel she could make the suggestion. Glenn had to want her along, yet he hadn't said a word. Silence hung heavy and dark between them like a thick curtain of rain-filled clouds. He was going back to his lost love. Dread filled Maggie with each beat of her heart.

Glenn made several attempts at light conversation during their meal, but nothing seemed to ease the strained silence that had fallen over them. A glance at his watch reminded him that within a few hours he would be on a plane for Charleston. He didn't want to leave, but in some ways felt it was for the best. Maggie seemed to assume that she wouldn't be going with him, and he was disappointed that she hadn't shown the willingness to travel with him. He might have made an issue of it if he hadn't thought a short separation would help them both become accustomed to their marriage without the issue of sleeping together. Those weeks would give Maggie the opportunity to settle things within her own mind. When he came back to her, they would take up their lives as man and wife, and perhaps she'd come to him willingly as she had that first night. That was what he wanted.

The drive back to the house and then on to the airport seemed to take a lifetime. With each mile, Maggie felt her heart grow heavier. She was apprehensive and didn't know how to deal with it. She and Glenn had been together such a short time that separating now seemed terribly wrong. Unreasonable jealousy ate at her, and Maggie had to assure herself repeatedly that Glenn probably wouldn't even be seeing the other woman. She was, after all, married to another man or so Glenn had told her. But Maggie didn't gain a whit's comfort from knowing that. For the first time in recent memory, she found herself in a situation where money wasn't part of the solution.

As they left the airport parking garage, Glenn's hand took hers. "I won't be long," he promised. "I'll need to get everything settled at the office, list the condominium with a realtor, and settle loose business ties—that kind of thing. I can't see it taking more than two weeks, three at the most."

"The weeks will fly by," she said on a falsely cheerful note. "Just about the time I clean out enough closet space for you, you'll be back."

"I wouldn't leave if it wasn't necessary," Glenn assured her as they approached the ticketing desk to check in his luggage.

"I know that." Maggie hugged her waist, feeling a sudden and unexpected chill. "I'm not worried about . . . you know." *Liar,* her mind tossed back.

Their shoes made a clicking sound as they walked together toward security.

Maggie had the horrible feeling she was about to cry, which, she knew, was utterly ridiculous. She rarely cried, yet her throat felt raw and scratchy and her chest had tightened with pent-up emotion. All the things she wanted to say stuck in her throat and she found that she couldn't say a thing.

"Take care of yourself," Glenn murmured, holding her by the shoulders.

"I will," she promised and buried her hands deep within the pockets of her raincoat. Even those few words could barely escape.

Glenn fastened the top button of her coat, and when he spoke his voice was softly gruff. "It looks like rain. Drive carefully."

"I always do. You'll note that you're here on time." She made a feeble attempt at humor.

Tiny laugh lines fanned out from his eyes. "Barely. I don't suppose you've noticed that by now my flight's probably boarding. Married two days, and I'm already picking up your bad habits."

His observation prompted a soft smile. "You'll phone?" She turned soft, round eyes to him.

"Yes," he promised in a husky murmur. "And if you need me, don't hesitate to call." He had written down both his work and home numbers in case she had to get in touch with him.

"You'll phone tonight." It became immensely important that he did. She pulled her hands from her pockets and smoothed away an imaginary piece of lint from his shoulder. Her hand lingered there. "I'll miss you." Even now if he hinted that he wanted her with him, she'd step on that plane. If necessary, she'd buy the stupid plane.

"I'll phone, but it'll be late," Glenn explained.

"I don't mind. . . . I probably won't sleep, anyway." She hadn't meant to admit that much and felt a rush of color creep up her neck and into her cheeks.

"Me, either," he murmured. His hands tightened on her upper arms and he gently brought her against his bulky sweater. With unhurried ease his mouth moved toward hers. The kiss flooded her with a swell of emotions she had tasted only briefly in his arms. She was hot, on fire, and cold as ice. Hot from his touch, cold with fear. His kiss sent a jolt rocketing through her, and she fiercely wrapped her arms around his neck. Her mind whirled and still she clung, afraid that if Glenn ever released her she'd never fully recover from the fall. Dragging in a deep breath, Maggie buried her face in his neck.

Glenn wrapped his arms around her waist and half lifted her from the floor. "I'll be back soon," he promised.

She nodded, because speaking was impossible.

When he released her, his gaze was as gentle as a caress and as tender as a child's touch. Maggie offered him a feeble smile. Glenn turned up the collar of her coat. "Stay warm."

Again she nodded. "Phone me."

Glenn claimed Maggie's lips again in a brief but surprisingly ardent kiss. "I'll call the minute I land."

With hands in her pockets for fear she'd do something silly like reach out and ask him not to go, or beg him to ask her to come, she said, "Hurry now, or you'll miss the flight."

Glenn took two steps backward. "The time will go fast."

"Yes," she said, not exactly sure what she was agreeing to.

"You're my wife, Maggie. I'm not going to forget that."

"You're my husband," she whispered and choked back the tears that filled her eyes and blurred her vision.

Then tossing a glance over his shoulder, he hurriedly handed the TSA agent his boarding pass and driver's license.

"Go on," she encouraged, not wanting him to see her cry. From all the emotion that was raging through her, one would assume that Glenn was going off to war and was unlikely to return. Her stomach was in such tight knots that she couldn't move without pain. Rooted to the spot close to security, Maggie stood as she was until Glenn turned and ran toward his gate. When she could, she stepped to the window and whispered, "New rule for this marriage . . . don't ever leave me again."

The days passed in a blur. Not since art school had Maggie worked harder or longer. Denny phoned her twice. Once to thank her for the "loan" and later to talk to her about the top-notch lawyer he had on retainer. The attorney was exactly who he had hoped would pursue his case, and his spirits were high. Maggie was pleased for Denny and prayed that this would be the end of his problems.

Without Glenn, sound sleep was impossible. She'd drift off easily enough and then jerk awake a couple of hours later, wondering why the bed seemed so intolerably large. Usually she slept in the middle of the mattress, but she soon discovered that she rested more comfortably on the side where Glenn had slept. She missed him. The worst part was the unreasonableness of the situation. Glenn had spent less than twenty-four hours in her home, yet without him the beach house felt like a silent tomb.

As he promised, Glenn had phoned the night he arrived back in Charleston and again three days later. Maggie couldn't recall any three days that seemed longer. A thousand times she was convinced her mind had conjured up both Glenn and their marriage. The marquise diamond on her ring finger was the only tangible evidence that the whole situation hadn't been a fantasy and that they really were married. Because she was working so hard and long she removed it for safekeeping, but each night she slipped it on her finger. Maggie didn't mention the wedding to her parents or any of her friends, and Denny didn't notice anything was different about her. She didn't feel comfortable telling everyone she was married, and wouldn't until Glenn had moved in with her and they were confident that their marriage was on firm ground.

Glenn phoned again on the fifth day. Their conversation was all too brief and somewhat stilted. Neither of them seemed to want it to end, but after twenty minutes, there didn't seem to be anything more to say.

Replacing the receiver, Maggie had the urge to cry. She didn't, of course, but it was several minutes before she had composed herself enough to go on with her day.

Nothing held her interest. Television, music, solitaire—everything bored her. Even the housekeeper lamented that Maggie had lost her appetite and complained about cooking meals that Maggie barely touched. Glenn filled every waking thought and invaded her dreams. Each time they spoke she had to bite her tongue to keep from suggesting she join him; her pride wouldn't allow that. The invitation must come from him, she believed. Surely he must realize that.

As for Angie, the woman in Glenn's past, the more Maggie thought about the situation, the more angry she became with herself. Glenn hadn't deceived her. They both were bearing scars from the past. If it wasn't love that cemented their marriage, then it was something equally strong. Between them there was security and understanding.

The evening of the eighth day the phone rang just as Maggie was scrounging through the desk looking for an address. She stared at the telephone. Caller ID told her it was Glenn.

"Hello," she answered, happily leaning back in the swivel chair, anticipating a long conversation.

"Hi." His voice sounded vital and warm. "How's everything?"

"Fine. I'm a little bored." Maggie was astonished that she could sound so blasé about her traumatic week. "A little bored" soft-pedaled all her frustrations. "What about you?"

Glenn hesitated, then announced, "I've run into a small snag on my end of things." *A small snag is the understatement of the century,* he thought. Things had been in chaos from the minute he had returned. The company supervisor had paid a surprise visit to him Thursday afternoon and had suggested an audit because of some irregularity in the books. The audit had gone smoothly enough, but Glenn had worked long hours and had been forced to reschedule several appointments. In addition, the realtor who listed the condominium offered little hope that it would sell quickly.

And worse, Glenn was miserable without Maggie. He wanted her with him. She was his wife, yet pride dictated that he couldn't ask her. The suggestion would have to come from her. Even a hint would be enough. He would pick up on a hint, but she had to be the one to give it.

"A small snag?" Her heart was pounding so hard and strong that she felt breathless.

"I've got several accounts here that have deals pending. I can't leave my clients in the lurch. Things aren't going as smoothly as I'd like, Maggie," he admitted.

"I see." Maggie's vocabulary suddenly decreased to words of one syllable.

"I can't let them down." He sounded as frustrated as she felt. A deafening silence grated over the telephone line, and it was on the tip of Glenn's tongue to cast his stupid pride to the wind and ask her to join him.

"Don't worry, I understand," she said in an even tone, congratulating herself for maintaining firm control of her voice. On the inside she was crumbling to pieces. She wanted to be with him. He was her husband, and her place was at his side. Closing her eyes, she mentally pleaded with him to say the words—to ask her to come to Charleston. She wouldn't ask, couldn't ask. It had to come from Glenn.

"In addition, there are several loose ends that are going to require more time than I originally planned." He sounded almost angry, an emotion that mirrored her own frustration.

"I think we were both naïve to think you could make it back in such a short time."

"I suppose we were." *Come on, Maggie,* he pleaded silently. *If you miss me, say something. At least meet me halfway in this.*

The line went silent again, but Maggie didn't want to end the conversation. She waited endless hours for his calls. They would talk for ten minutes, hang up, and immediately she'd start wondering how long it would be before he phoned again.

"The weather's been unseasonably cold. There's been some talk of freezing temperatures," Maggie said out of desperation, to keep the conversation going.

"Don't catch cold." *Damn it, Maggie, I want you here. Can't you hear it in my voice?*

"I won't," she promised. *Please,* she wanted to scream at him, *ask me to come to Charleston.* With her eyes shut, she mentally transmitted her need to have him ask her. "I've been too busy in the studio to venture outside."

"Brueghel or Frankenthaler?" Glenn questioned, his voice tinged with humor. "However, I'm sure that either one would be marvelous and wonderful." He smiled as he said it, wanting her with him all the more just to see what other crazy rules she'd come up with for their marriage.

"This one's a Margaret Kingsbury original," she said proudly. Maggie had worked hard on her latest project and felt confident that Glenn would approve.

"It can't be." Glenn stiffened and tried to disguise the irritation in his voice.

Maggie tensed, wondering what she had said wrong. He hadn't approved of her art, but surely he didn't begrudge her the time she spent on it when he was away.

"Your name's Lambert now," Glenn stated.

"I . . . forgot." *Remind me again,* she pleaded silently. *Ask me to come to Charleston.* "I haven't told anyone yet. . . . Have you?"

"No one," Glenn admitted.

"Not even your parents?" She hadn't told hers, either, but Glenn's family was in South Carolina. It only made sense that he'd say something to them before moving out west.

"That was something I thought we'd do together."

The sun burst through the heavy overcast and shed its golden rays on Maggie. He had offered her a way to Charleston and managed to salvage her pride. The tension flowed from her as her hand tightened around the receiver. "Glenn, don't you think they'll be offended if we wait much longer?"

"They might," he answered, unexpectedly agreeable. "I know it's an inconvenience, but maybe you should think about flying—"

"I'll be on a flight out tomorrow morning."

Chapter 6

Glenn was in the terminal waiting when Maggie walked off the plane the following afternoon. He was tall, rugged, and so male that it was all Maggie could do not to throw her arms around him. He looked wonderful, and she wanted to hate him for it. For nine days she had been the most miserable woman alive, and Glenn looked as if he'd relished their separation, thrived on it. Renewed doubts buzzed around her like swarming bees.

Stepping forward, Glenn took the carry-on bag from her hand and slipped an arm around her waist. "Welcome to Charleston."

Shamelessly, Maggie wanted him to take her in his arms and kiss her. She managed to disguise the yearning by lowering her gaze. "I didn't know if you'd be here."

She'd tried to call to give him her flight number, but his phone had gone directly to voicemail. She'd left a message and then later sent him a text. If he hadn't gotten her message, Maggie wouldn't have had a way of getting into Glenn's condominium.

"Of course I'm here. Where else would I be?"

"I'm so glad to see you." *Very glad,* her heart sang.

"How was the flight?"

"Just the way I like 'em," she said with a teasing smile. "Uneventful."

Glenn's features warmed, and he grinned at her answer. Captivated by the tenderness in his eyes, Maggie felt her heart throb almost painfully. His eyes were dark, yet glowing with a warm light. Although he hadn't said a word, Glenn's gaze told her he was pleased she was with him.

"Your luggage is this way," he commented, pressing a hand to the middle of her back as he directed her toward baggage claim.

"I didn't bring much." "Not much" constituted two enormous suitcases and one large carry-on. Maggie had spent half the night packing, discarding one outfit after another until her bedroom floor was littered with more clothes than a secondhand store. She wanted everything to be perfect for Glenn. She longed to be alluring and seductive, attractive without being blatant about it. She wanted his heart as well as his bed and she realized how difficult that was going to be if Glenn was still in love with the other woman.

The more Maggie thought about the other woman who had claimed his heart, the more she realized what an uphill struggle lay before her. Glenn wouldn't ever give his love lightly, and now that he had, it would take a struggle to replace her in his heart. Maggie yearned to know more of the details, but wouldn't pry. In the meantime, she planned to use every womanly wile she possessed and a few she planned to invent.

The leather strap of her purse slid off her shoulder,

and Maggie straightened it. As she did, Glenn stopped in midstride, nearly knocking her off balance.

"Where's your diamond?" he asked, taking her hand. Surprise mingled with disappointment and disbelief. "I thought you said the only time you wouldn't wear it was when you were working. You aren't painting now."

Maggie's mind whirled frantically. She had removed the diamond the morning before the phone call and placed it in safekeeping the way she always did. Then, in her excitement about flying out to be with Glenn, she had forgotten to put it back on her finger.

"Maggie?"

Her fingers curled around the strap of her purse. "Oh, Glenn . . ."

He took her hand and examined the plain gold band that he had bought her to go with the marquise.

Maggie wanted to shout with frustration. From the moment they'd ended their phone conversation she had been carefully planning this reunion. Each detail had been shaped in her mind from the instant he picked her up until they dressed for bed.

"Maggie, where is the diamond?" he repeated.

"I forgot it, but don't worry . . . I have it with me." Her voice rose with her agitation. They hadn't so much as collected her luggage and already they were headed for a fight.

"You mean to tell me you packed a seven-thousand-dollar diamond with your underwear?" His voice was a mixture of incredulity and anger.

"I didn't do it on purpose, I . . . forgot I wasn't wearing it." Somehow that seemed even worse. "And furthermore it isn't in the suitcase."

Glenn's stride increased to a quick-paced clip that left Maggie half trotting in an effort to keep up. "Glenn," she protested, refusing to run through the airport.

He threw an angry glare over his shoulder. "Forgive me for being overly concerned, but I work hard for my money."

The implication being, she thought, that she didn't work and the ring meant nothing to her. Little did he realize how much it did mean.

Maggie stopped cold as waves of anger hit her. Few words could have hurt her more. She was outraged he would say such a thing to her. For several minutes she found herself unable to speak. Nothing was going as she had planned. She'd had such wonderful images of Glenn sweeping her into his arms, holding her close and exclaiming that after the way he'd missed her, they'd never be separated again. He was supposed to tell her how miserable he'd been. Instead, he'd insulted her in a way that would hurt her the most.

Apparently, he was angry because she had forgotten to slip on the diamond ring he'd gotten her, finding her casualness with the diamond a sign of irresponsibility. She had the ring; she knew where it was.

Glenn was standing outside the baggage-handling system, waiting for it to unload the luggage from her flight, when she joined him.

"If you'd give me a second I'll—"

"Talk to me after you've gotten your ring, Maggie. At the moment, I'm worried about losing an expensive diamond."

"And you work hard for your money. Right? At least

that's what you claim. I don't doubt it. It's said that those who marry for it usually do."

Although he continued to look straight ahead, a nerve jumped convulsively in his clenched jaw, and Maggie was instantly aware of just how angry that remark had made him. "You know that isn't true. I made sure you'd never doubt my motives when I made the appointment with the attorney."

"Can I have my carry-on?"

Without a word, he handed it to her. He studied the baggage conveyor belt as if it were the center of his world. Maggie wasn't fooled. Glenn was simply too outraged to look at her.

Maggie knelt down on the floor and flipped open the lid. Her small jewelry case was inside, and the ring was tucked safely in that. With a brooding sense of unhappiness, Maggie located the marquise diamond and slipped it on her finger beside the plain gold band. Snapping the suitcase closed, she stood.

They stood side by side, silent for several moments before his hand claimed hers. Right away he noticed the diamond was on her ring finger; he arched one brow expressively. "You had it with you all the time?"

"Yes."

He groaned inwardly. He had been wanting Maggie for days, longing for her. And now things were picking up right where they'd left off, with misunderstandings and sharp words. He had wanted everything perfect for her, and once again this bad start had been his own doing.

His fingers tightened over hers. "Can I make a new rule for this marriage?" he asked her with serious eyes.

"Of course."

"I want you to wear your wedding set all the time."

"But—"

"I know that may sound unreasonable," he interrupted, "and I'm not even entirely sure why my feelings are so strong. I guess it's important to me that your wedding bands mean as much to you as our marriage."

Slowly, thoughtfully, Maggie nodded. "I'll never remove them again."

Looking into her eyes, Glenn felt the overwhelming urge to take her in his arms and apologize for having started on the wrong foot once again. But the airport wasn't the place and now wasn't the time. From here on, he promised himself, he'd be more patient with her, court her the way he should have in the beginning.

They didn't say a word until the luggage was dispensed. Maggie pointed out her suitcases.

He mumbled something unintelligible under his breath, and Maggie realized he was grumbling about the fact she claimed to have packed light for this trip. But he didn't complain strenuously.

The deafening quiet in the car was one neither seemed willing to wade into. Maggie wanted to initiate a brilliant conversation, but nothing came to mind and she almost cried with frustration. Their reunion wasn't supposed to happen this way. She sat uncomfortably next to a man she'd known most of her life and whom, she was discovering, she didn't know at all.

Glenn's condominium was situated just outside historic Charleston, with a view of Colonial Lake. Maggie knew little about the area. Her head flooded with questions about the city that Glenn had made his home for a decade, but she asked none. While he took care of her luggage, she wandered into the living room to admire the view. The scenery below revealed magnificent eighteenth-century homes, large public buildings, and meticulously kept gardens. The gentle toll of church bells sounded, and Maggie strained to hear more. Charleston was definitely a city of grace, beauty, and charm. Yet Glenn was willing to sacrifice it all—his home, his family, his job, maybe even his career—to move to San Francisco.

He must have suffered a great deal of mental anguish to be willing to leave all this, Maggie determined, experiencing an attack of doubt. Glenn had told her so little about this other woman, and Maggie had the feeling he wouldn't have told her anything if it hadn't been for the unfortunate scene the morning after their wedding. He was an intensely personal man.

The condominium was far more spacious than what Maggie had assumed. The living room led into a formal dining area, and from there to a spacious kitchen with plenty of cupboards and a pantry. A library/den was separated from the living room by open double-width doors that revealed floor-to-ceiling bookcases and a large oak desk. She hadn't seen the bedrooms yet but guessed that there were three, possibly four. The condo was much larger than what a single man would require. Her eyes rounded with an indescribable ache that came over her when she realized Glenn had purchased this home for Angie.

"Are you hungry?" he asked, halfway into the living room, standing several feet from her.

Maggie unbuttoned her coat and slipped the scarf from her neck. "No thanks, I ate on the plane, but you go ahead." The lie was a small white one. The attendant had offered her a meal, but Maggie had declined. She'd been too anxious to eat when she was only a few hours from meeting Glenn.

He hesitated, turned, then whirled back around so that he was facing her again. "I regret this whole business with the ring, Maggie."

A shiver of gladness came over her at his offhand apology. "It's forgotten."

Something close to a smile quirked his mouth. "I'm glad you're here."

"I'm glad to be here."

He leaned around the kitchen door. "Are you sure you're not hungry?"

A small smile claimed her mouth. "On second thought, maybe I am at that."

A sense of relief flooded through Glenn's tense muscles. He hadn't meant to make such an issue of the diamond. For days he'd been longing for Maggie, decrying his earlier decision to leave her in San Francisco. They had so few days together that he'd thought the separation would give her the necessary time to adjust mentally to her new life. Unfortunately, it was he who had faced the adjustment . . . to his days . . . and nights without her. Now that she was here, all he wanted was to take her in his arms and make love to her. The level of physical desire she aroused in him was a definite shock. He hadn't expected to experience this intensity. All he had thought about since he'd known she was coming was getting her into his bed. He'd dreamed of kissing her, holding her and making love to his wife. She was the woman he'd married, and he'd waited a long time for the privileges due a husband. He doubted that Maggie had any conception of how deep his anger had cut when she had suggested that he'd married her for her money. That was a problem he had anticipated early on, and it was the very reason he had insisted they see a lawyer as soon as possible.

Working together, they cooked their meal. Maggie made the salad while Glenn broiled thick steaks. Glenn didn't have a housekeeper to prepare his meals, and for that matter, Maggie surmised, he might not even have someone in to do the housework. Now that she was here, she decided, she would take over those duties. Surprisingly, Maggie discovered she looked forward to being a wife. Glenn's wife.

Later, while he placed the few dirty plates in the dishwasher, Maggie decided to unpack her bags. She located the master bedroom without a problem and gave a sigh of relief when she noticed that Glenn fully intended that she would sleep with him. It was what she wanted, what she had planned, but after their shaky beginning, Maggie hadn't known what to think. A soft smile worked its way across her face, brightening her dark eyes. Glenn longed for their marriage to work as much as she did, she thought. What they both needed to do was quit trying so hard.

When Maggie had finished unpacking, she joined Glenn in the living room. It amazed her how unsettled they were around each other still. Glenn suggested they turn on the last newscast of the evening. Readily, Maggie agreed. She supposed that this time could be thought of as their honeymoon. They were probably the only couple in America to watch television when they could be doing other . . . things.

After the news, Glenn yawned. Once again, Maggie was reminded that his daily schedule was set with the routine of his job. Staying awake until two or three in the morning, watching a late, late movie or reading would only cause problems the following morning. She would need to adjust her sleeping habits as well, although she had become a night person these past few years, often enjoying the peace and tranquility of the early-morning hours to paint. Glenn didn't live a life of leisure, and she couldn't any longer, either.

Funny, Maggie thought, the realization that she must now live according to a clock didn't depress her. She was willing to get up with him in the morning and cook his breakfast and even do the dishes. She didn't know how long this domesticated eagerness would continue, and vowed to take advantage of it while it lasted. In the morning, she would stand at the front door and send him off to the office with a juicy kiss. But from the frowning look he was giving the television, Maggie had the impression the good-bye kiss in the morning would be all the kissing she was going to get.

Glenn's thoughts were heavy. Maggie was sitting at his side and he hadn't so much as put his arm around her. He felt as though he were stretched out on a rack, every muscle strained to the limit of his endurance. It was pure torture to have her so close and not haul her into his arms and make love to her. If she could read only half of what was going through his mind, she would run back to California, he thought drily. No, he wouldn't take her that night. He'd bide his time, show her how empty his life was without her, how much he needed a woman's tenderness. Then, in time, she would come to him willingly and desire him, maybe even as keenly as he did her.

"Don't you think we should go to bed? It's after eleven." Maggie broached the subject with all the subtlety of a locomotive. Sitting next to him was torture. They had hardly said two words all night. The thick, unnatural silence made the words all the more profound.

Smoothly rolling to his feet, Glenn nodded. He hadn't noticed that the news was over. For that matter, he couldn't recall the headlines or anything that had been reported. Not even the weather forecast, which he listened for each night. "I imagine you're tired," he finally answered.

"Dead on my feet," she confirmed, walking with him toward the hallway and the master bedroom. *You're wide awake,* her mind accused. She was on Pacific time and it was barely after eight in San Francisco.

Following a leisurely scented bath, Maggie joined him, wearing a black nightshirt that buttoned up the front and hit her at midthigh with deep side slits that went halfway up to her hip. The satin top was the most feminine piece of sleepwear Maggie owned. The two top buttons were unfastened, and she stretched her hands high above her head in a fake yawn, granting him a full glimpse of her upper thighs.

Glenn was in bed, propped against thick feather pillows, reading a spy thriller. One look at her in the black satin pajama top and the book nearly tumbled from his hands. Tension knotted his stomach and he all but groaned at the sight of his wife. But witnessing her beauty and wanting her was torture he endured willingly.

The mattress dipped slightly as she lifted back the

blankets and slipped into the bed. Glenn set his novel aside and reached for the lamp switch. The room went dark, with only the shimmering rays of the distant moon dancing across the far walls.

Neither moved. Only a few inches separated them, but for all the good it did to be sleeping with her husband, Maggie could well have been in San Francisco, she decided.

"Good night, Glenn," Maggie whispered after several stifled moments. If he didn't reach for her soon, she'd clobber him over the head. Maybe she should say something to encourage him—let him know her feelings. But what? *Listen, Glenn, I've reconsidered, and although I realize that you may still be in love with another woman, I've decided it doesn't matter. We're married. I'm your wife. . . .* Disheartened, Maggie realized she couldn't do it. Not so soon, and not in a condominium he probably bought with the other woman in mind.

Glenn interrupted Maggie's dark thoughts with a deep, quiet voice. "Good night." With that, he rolled onto his side away from her.

Gallantly, she resisted the urge to smash the pillow over the top of his head, pull a blanket from the mattress, and storm into the living room to sleep. She didn't know how any man could be so unbelievably dense.

Maggie fell easily into a light, untroubled slumber. Although asleep, lying on her side, her back to him, she was ever conscious of the movements of the man who was sharing the bed. Apparently, Glenn was having more difficulty falling asleep, tossing to one side and then to another, seeking a comfortable position. Once his hand inadvertently fell onto her hip, and for a moment he went completely still. Content now, Maggie smiled inwardly and welcomed the calm. Sleeping with him was like being in a rowboat wrestling with a storm at sea.

With unhurried ease the hand that rested against her bare hip climbed upward, stopping at her ribs. Shifting his position, Glenn scooted closer and gathered her into his embrace. As if he couldn't help himself, his hand sought and found a firm breast. His touch was doing insane things to her equilibrium, and she was encompassed in a gentle, sweet warmth. Savoring the moment, Maggie bit into her bottom lip as he slowly, tantalizingly, caressed her breasts until she thought she'd moan audibly and give herself away.

Glenn was in agony. He had thought that he would wait and follow all the plans he'd made for courting his wife. But each minute grew more torturous than the one just past. He couldn't sleep; even breathing normally was impossible when she lay just within his grasp. He hadn't meant to touch her, but once his hand lightly grazed her hip he couldn't stop his mind from venturing to rounder, softer curves and the memory of the way her breast had fit perfectly into the palm of his hand. Before he could stop, his fingers sought to explore her ripe body.

Maggie remained completely still, waiting patiently for him to roll her onto her back and make love to her. When he didn't move and she suspected that he might not ease the painful longing throbbing within her, she rolled onto her back and linked her arms around his neck.

"Kiss me," she pleaded.

"Maggie." He ground out her name like a man possessed, and hungrily devoured her lips with deep, slow, hot kisses that drove him to the brink of insanity. Groaning, he buried his face in her hair and drew deep gulps of oxygen into his parched lungs. Again, he kissed her, tasting her willingness, reveling in her eagerness.

Her hands rumpled the dark thickness of his hair while she repeated his name again and again. Hungry for the taste of him, Maggie urged his mouth to hers, but his devouring kiss only increased her aching need.

"I want you," he groaned, breathing in sharply.

"Yes," she murmured, kissing the hollow of his throat and arching against him.

"Oh Glenn," Maggie groaned in a harsh whisper. "What took you so long?" The sensation was so blissfully exultant that she felt she could have died from it.

Looping her arms around his neck, Maggie strained upward and planted a long, hot kiss on his parted mouth. "How can any man be so blind?"

"Next time, hit me over the head." He arched forward then, and buried himself deep within her.

Maggie moaned. "I will. Oh Glenn, I will," she cried.

He took her quickly, unable to bear slow torture. Their bodies fused in a glorious union of heart with soul, of man with woman, of Maggie with Glenn. They strained together, giving, receiving, until their hearts beat in a paired tempo that left them breathless, giddy, and spent.

Glenn gathered her in his arms and rolled onto his side, taking her with him. Her head rested in the crook of his shoulder, their legs entwined as if reluctant to release the moment.

Maggie felt the pressure of his mouth on her hair and snuggled closer into his embrace, relishing the feel of his strong arms wrapped securely around her.

Brushing a wayward curl from her cheek, Glenn's

hand lingered to lightly stroke the side of her face. Maggie smiled gently up at him, the contented smile of a satisfied woman.

"Do you think you'll be able to sleep now?" she teased.

Glenn chuckled, his warm breath fanning her forehead. "Did my tossing and turning keep you awake?"

"Not really . . . I was only half asleep." Maggie lowered her chin and covered her mouth in an attempt to stifle a yawn. "Good night, Mr. Lambert," she whispered, dragging out the words as she swallowed back another yawn.

"Mrs. Lambert," he murmured huskily, kissing the crown of her head.

Maggie's last thought before slipping into an easy slumber was that she wasn't ever going to allow another woman's ghost to come between them again. This man was her husband and she loved him . . . yes, loved him with a ferocity she was only beginning to understand. Together they were going to make this marriage work. One hundred Angies weren't going to stand in the way of their happiness. Maggie wouldn't allow it.

Within minutes Maggie was asleep. Still awake, Glenn propped up his head with one hand and took delight in peacefully watching the woman who had become everything to him in such a shockingly short amount of time. She was his friend, his lover, his wife, and he had the feeling he had skimmed only the surface of who and what Maggie would be in his life. His finger lightly traced the line of her cheek and the hollow of her throat. As impulsive as their marriage had been, there wasn't a second when Glenn regretted having pledged his life to Maggie. She was fresh and warm, a loving, free spirit. And he adored her. She had come to him with an ardor he had only dreamed of finding in a woman. She was stubborn, impulsive, headstrong: a rare and exquisite jewel. His jewel. His woman. His wife.

The low, melodious sound of a ballad slowly woke Maggie.

"Good morning, Sleeping Beauty," Glenn said as he sat on the edge of the mattress and kissed her lightly. He finished buttoning his shirt and flipped up the collar as he straightened the silk tie around his neck.

"You're dressed," she said, struggling to a sitting position and wiping the sleep from her eyes. She had wanted to get up with him, but must have missed the alarm.

"Would you like to undress me?"

Leaning against the down pillow, Maggie crossed her arms and smiled beguilingly up at him. "What would you do if I said yes?"

Glenn's fingers quit working the silk tie. "Don't tempt me, Maggie. I'm running late already."

"I tempt you?" He'd never said anything more beautiful.

"If only you knew."

"I hope you'll show me." She wrapped her arms around her bent knees and leaned forward. "It . . . it was wonderful last night." She felt shy talking about their lovemaking, but it was imperative that he realize how much he pleased her.

"Yes, it was," he whispered, taking her hand and kissing her knuckles. "I never expected anything so good between us."

"Me neither," she murmured, and kissed his hand. "I wish you'd gotten me up earlier."

"Why?" He looked surprised.

Tossing back the covers, Maggie climbed out of bed and slipped into a matching black satin housecoat that she hadn't bothered to put on the night before—for obvious reasons. "I wanted to do the wifely thing and cook your breakfast."

"I haven't got time this morning." He paused, thinking he'd never seen any woman more beautiful. Her tousled hair fell to her shoulders, her face was free of any cosmetics, but no siren had ever been more alluring.

"Is there anything you'd like me to do while you're gone?" she offered. The day stretched before her and they hadn't made plans.

"Yes, in fact, there are several things. I'll make a list." He reached for a pad and paper on his nightstand and spent the next few minutes giving her directions and instructions. "And don't plan dinner tonight," he added. "I phoned my parents yesterday and told them I had a surprise and to expect two for dinner."

Maggie sat on the bed beside him, and unconsciously her shoulders slouched slightly. This was the very reason she'd come to Charleston, yet she was afraid. "Will they think we've gone crazy?"

"Probably," he returned with a short chuckle. "But they'll be delighted. Don't worry about it; they know you and have always liked you. Mom and Dad will be happy for us."

"I'm happy, Glenn." She wanted to reassure him that she had no regrets in this venture.

His dark eyes were serious, and his gaze held her immobile. "I am, too, for the first time since I can remember. We're going to make it, Maggie."

A grandfather clock in the den chimed the hour, and reluctantly Glenn stood. "I've got to leave."

"Glenn." Maggie stopped him, then lowered her gaze, almost afraid of what she had to say. Waiting until the last minute to tell him wasn't the smartest thing to do.

"Yes?" he prompted.

"I'm . . . Listen, I think you should probably know that I'm not using any birth control."

His index finger lifted her chin so that her uncertain gaze met his. "That's fine. I want a family."

A sigh of relief washed through her, and she beamed him a brilliant smile. "I probably should warn you, though, my mother claims the Kingsbury clan is a fertile one. We could be starting our family sooner than you expect."

"Don't worry about it; I'm not going to. When a baby comes, you can be assured of a warm welcome."

Maggie experienced an outpouring of love far too powerful to be voiced with simple words. Nodding demanded an incredible effort.

"I'll leave the car keys with you and I'll take public transportation. If you're in the neighborhood around noon, stop into the office and I'll introduce you and take you to lunch."

"Maybe tomorrow," she said, stepping onto her tiptoes to kiss him good-bye. There was barely enough time to do everything she had to and be ready for dinner with his parents that evening.

A minute later, Glenn was out the door. The condo seemed an empty shell without him. Maggie wandered into the kitchen with her list of errands, then poured a cup of coffee and carried it to the round table. She pulled out a chair and sat, drawing her legs under her. The first place she needed to stop was the bank to sign the forms that would add her name to the checking account. When she was there, Glenn had asked her to make a deposit for him.

She glanced at the front page of the paper he had left on the table and worked the crossword puzzle, then finished her coffee and dressed. The day held purpose. If she was going to see his parents, it might not be a bad idea to find someplace where she could have her hair done.

With a jaunty step, Maggie found the deposit envelope Glenn had mentioned on the top of his desk. The room emanated his essence, and she paused to drink it in. As she turned, Maggie caught a glimpse of a frame sticking above the rim of his wastepaper basket. *What an unusual thing to do to a picture,* she thought. As an artist, her sense of indignation rose until she lifted the frame from out of the basket and saw the multitude of small pictures with faces smiling back at her. Her breath came to an abrupt halt and the room crowded in on her, pressing at her with a strangling sensation. *So this was Angie.*

Chapter 7

The first thought that came to Maggie was how beautiful Angie was. With thick, coffee-dark hair and intense brown eyes that seemed to mirror her soul, Angie had the ethereal look of a woman meant to be cherished, loved, and protected. There was an inner glow, a delicate beauty to her that Maggie could never match. Angie was a woman meant to be loved and nurtured. It was little wonder that Glenn loved her. One glance at the woman who claimed his heart told Maggie that by comparison she was a poor second.

The frame contained a series of matted pictures that had obviously been taken over a period of several months. There was Angie on a sailboat, her windblown hair flying behind her as she smiled into the camera; Angie leaning over a barbecue, wearing an apron that said KISS THE COOK; Angie standing, surrounded by floral bouquets, in what looked like a flower shop, with her arms outstretched as though to signal this was hers. And more . . . so much more. Each picture revealed the rare beauty of the woman who claimed Glenn's heart.

A sickening knot tightened Maggie's stomach, and she

placed a hand on her abdomen and slowly released her breath. Although most of the photos were of Angie alone, two of them showed Glenn and Angie together. If recognizing the other woman's inner and outer beauty wasn't devastating enough, then the happiness radiating from Glenn was. Maggie had never seen him more animated. He seemed to glow with love. In all the years Maggie had known Glenn, she had never seen him look more content. He was at peace with his world, and so in love that it shone like a polished badge from every part of him. In comparison, the Glenn who had arrived in San Francisco was a sullen, doleful imitation.

Pushing the hair off her forehead, Maggie leaned against a filing cabinet and briefly closed her eyes. As early as the night before, she'd thought to banish Angie's ghost from their marriage. She had been a fool to believe it would be that easy. With a feeling of dread, she placed the frame back where she'd found it. Building a firm foundation for their marriage wasn't going to be easy, not nearly as easy as she'd thought. But then, nothing worthwhile ever was. Maggie loved her husband. Physically, he wanted her, and for now that would suffice. Someday Glenn would look at her with the same glow of happiness that Angie evoked. Someday his love for her would be there for all the world to witness. Someday . . .

Glancing at her wristwatch, Maggie hurried from the bathroom into the bedroom. In a few hours she and Glenn were having dinner with his parents, Charlotte and Mel, people she'd known and liked all her life. Family friends, former neighbors, good people. Yet Maggie had never been less sure of herself. Already she had changed outfits twice. This one would have to do, she decided. There wasn't time to change her mind again. As she put the finishing touches on her makeup, Maggie muttered disparaging remarks over the sprinkling of freckles across the bridge of her nose; wanted to know why her lashes couldn't be longer and her mouth fuller. Mentally, she had reviewed her body: Her breasts looked like cantaloupes, her hips like a barge; her legs were too short, her arms too long. Maggie could see every imperfection. Finally, she had been forced to admit that no amount of cosmetics was going to make her as lovely as Angie. She had to stop thinking of Charlotte and Mel as the mother- and father-in-law who would compare her to their son's first choice. She had to force herself to remember them instead as the friends she knew they were.

Perhaps if she'd had more time to prepare mentally for this dinner, she thought defensively. As it was, the list of errands had taken most of the day, and Maggie had been grateful to have something to occupy her time and her mind. Instead of concentrating on being bright and witty for her meeting with Glenn's parents, her thoughts had returned again and again to the discarded series of photographs. If she had found those photos, she reasoned, then there were probably other pictures around. The realization that Angie could be a silent occupant of the condominium was an intolerable conjecture.

When Glenn had walked in the door that afternoon and kissed her, Maggie had toyed with the idea of confronting him with the pictures. Sanity had returned in the nick of time. He had obviously intended to throw them away, but surely he must have realized that she would stumble upon them. Maybe it was cowardly of her, but Maggie had decided to ignore the fact that the pictures were in the other room, and pretended she hadn't seen them. For the first time since their marriage, things were going right, and she didn't want to ruin that.

"Maggie, are you ready?" Glenn sauntered into the bedroom and hesitated when he saw her. "I thought you were wearing a blue dress."

"I . . . was," she answered slowly, turning and squaring her shoulders. "Do I look all right?"

"You're lovely." He placed a hand on each of her shoulders. "Maggie, I wish you'd stop worrying. Mom and Dad are going to be thrilled for us."

"I know." Absently, she brushed her hand across the skirt of her black-and-red-print dress and slowly released her breath. "I've always been Muffie to them, and I'm . . . I'm not sure they'll be able to accept me as your wife."

Glenn's chuckle echoed through the bedroom. "Maggie, how can they not accept you? You're my wife. Mother's been after me for years to marry and settle down. She'll be grateful I finally took the plunge."

"That's encouraging," she mumbled sarcastically. "So you were desperate to placate your mother and decided I'd do nicely as a wife. Is that supposed to reassure me?"

The muscles of his face tightened and a frown marred his wide brow as he dropped his hands to his sides. "That's not true and you know it."

Ashamed, Maggie lowered her head and nodded. "I'm sorry, I didn't mean that. My stomach feels like a thousand bumblebees have set up camp. Even my hands are clammy." She held them out, palms up, for him to inspect.

"Wait until we visit my parents, then you'll know how I feel."

Slipping an arm around her waist, Glenn led her into the living room. "If you're worried, stick to my side and I'll answer all the questions."

"I had no intention of leaving your side," she returned, slightly miffed.

A faint smile touched his mouth.

The ride to Glenn's parents' did little to settle her nerves. Maggie thought she would be glad when this evening was over. When Glenn turned off the main road and into a narrow street lined with family homes, Maggie tensed. Two blocks later he slowed and turned into a concrete driveway.

Before Maggie was out of the car the front door opened and Mel and Charlotte Lambert were standing on the wide porch. Maggie was surprised by how little they'd changed. Glenn's father's hair was completely gray now and his hairline had receded, but he stood proud and broad-shouldered, just as Maggie remembered him. Glenn's mother was a little rounder, and wearing a dress. As a child, Maggie knew she was always welcome in the Lamberts' kitchen. Charlotte had claimed it was a pleasure having another woman around since she lived with a house full of men. Maggie had dropped over regularly when Dale, the youngest Lambert, was born. She had been at the age to appreciate babies and had loved to help feed and bathe him.

"Muffie!" Charlotte exclaimed, her bright eyes shining with genuine pleasure. "What a pleasant surprise. I had no idea you were in town."

Glenn joined Maggie and draped his arm around her

shoulders as he boldly met his parents' gaze. To be honest, he had been dreading this confrontation himself. His parents would be pleased for him and Maggie, and would do their best to hide their shock. But his father was bound to say something about Angie when they had a private moment. He might even suspect that Glenn had married on the rebound. He hadn't. Glenn tried not to think of Angie and ignored the nip of emotional pain associated with her name. His parents had loved her and encouraged him to marry her. Their disappointment had been keen when he told them she'd married Simon.

"Are you visiting from California?" Charlotte asked with a faint tinge of longing. "I do miss that old neighborhood. If we had a hundred years, we'd never find any better place to raise our family." Taking Maggie by the elbow, she led her into the house. "What's the matter with us, standing on the porch and talking when there're plenty of comfortable chairs inside?"

Maggie tossed a pleading glance over her shoulder to Glenn, hoping he wouldn't leave the explaining to her.

The screen door closed with a bang as they entered the house. The small living room managed to hold a recliner, a sofa, and an overstuffed chair and ottoman. In addition, a rocking chair sat in one corner. The fireplace mantel was lined with pictures of the three sons and the grandchildren.

"Mom, Dad," Glenn began, his expression sober as he met their curious faces. His arm slipped around Maggie as he stood stiffly at her side. He didn't know any better way to say it than right out. "Maggie is my wife. We've been married nearly two weeks."

"Married? Two weeks?" Charlotte echoed in a stunned whisper.

Mel Lambert recovered quickly and reached across the room to pump Glenn's hand. "Congratulations, son." Cupping Maggie's shoulders, he gently kissed her cheek. "Welcome to the family, Muffie."

"Thank you." Her voice was both weak and weary. This was worse than she'd thought. Glenn's mother stood with a hand pressed over her heart and an absurd look of shock written across her face, which she was trying desperately to disguise.

"You two . . . are married," Charlotte whispered, apparently having recovered. "This is wonderful news. Mel, you open that bottle of wine we've been saving all these years and I'll get the goblets." Within seconds, they had both disappeared.

Glenn took Maggie's hand and led her to the sofa, where they both sat. "See, I told you it wouldn't be so bad." His hand squeezed hers and his eyes smiled confidently into hers. He smoothed a strand of hair from her temple with his forefinger in a light caress.

"How can you say that?" she hissed under her breath. "Your mother nearly fainted." To further her unease, she could hear hushed whispers coming from the kitchen. The barely audible word *rebound* heightened the embarrassed flush in Maggie's red cheeks. She pretended not to hear, as did Glenn.

Glenn's handsome face broke into a scowl. It was a mistake not to have said something to his parents earlier. His better judgment had prompted him to tell them. But he had made such an issue of the necessity of Maggie and him confronting them together that he couldn't very well change plans. Informing his parents of their marriage had been what it took to get Maggie to join him in Charleston, and he would never regret that.

Mel and Charlotte reappeared simultaneously. Charlotte carried four shining crystal goblets on a silver tray, and Mel had a wine bottle and corkscrew in one hand.

"Before leaving California," Mel explained as he pulled open the corkscrew, "Charlotte and I took a drive through the Napa Valley and bought some of the finest wines available. That was thirteen years ago now, and we only open those bottles on the most special occasions."

"Let me see, the last time we opened our California wine was . . ." Charlotte paused, and a network of fine lines knitted her face as she concentrated.

Glenn tensed, and his hand squeezed Maggie's so tightly that she almost yelped at the unexpected pain. Gradually, he relaxed his punishing grip, and Maggie realized that the last special occasion in the Lambert family had been shared with Angie and Glenn.

"Wasn't it when Erica was born?" Mel inserted hastily.

"No, no," Charlotte dismissed the suggestion with an impatient wave of her hand. "It was more recent than that . . . I think it was . . ." Flustered, she swallowed and reached for a wineglass to hide her discomfort. "I do believe you're right, dear, it was when Erica was born. It just seems more recent is all."

The tension left Glenn, and even Maggie breathed easier. Mel finished opening the bottle and nimbly filled the four goblets. Handing Maggie and Glenn their wineglasses, he proposed a toast. "To many years of genuine wedded happiness."

"Many years," Charlotte echoed.

Later, Maggie helped Charlotte set the table, carrying out the serving dishes while Glenn and his father chatted companionably in the living room. At dinner, the announcement that Glenn would be moving to San Francisco was met with a strained moment of disappointment.

"We'll miss you, son" was all that was said.

Unreasonably, Maggie experienced a flood of guilt. It hadn't been her idea for him to leave Charleston. She would make her home wherever Glenn wished, but apparently he wanted out of South Carolina.

"We'll visit often," Glenn assured his parents, and, catching Maggie's eye, he winked. "Especially after the children come."

Mel and Charlotte exchanged meaningful glances, making Maggie want to jump up and assure them she wasn't pregnant . . . at least she didn't think so.

The meal was saved only because everyone felt the need to chat and cover the disconcerting silence. Maggie did her share, catching the Lamberts up on what had been happening with her parents and skimming over Denny's misfortunes, giving them only a brief outline of his life. In return, Charlotte proudly spoke of each of her three grandchildren, and while they cleared the table the older woman proudly brought out snapshots of the grandkids. Maggie examined each small smiling face, realizing for the first time that these little ones were now her nieces and nephew.

While Maggie wiped off the table, Charlotte ran sudsy water into the kitchen sink. "There was a time that I despaired of having a daughter," Charlotte began awkwardly.

"I remember," Maggie responded, recalling all the afternoons she had sat with Mrs. Lambert.

"And now I have three daughters. Each one of my sons have married well. I couldn't be more pleased with the daughters they've given me."

Maggie's hand pushed the rag with unnecessary vigor across the tabletop. "Thank you. I realize our marriage must come as a shock to you, but I want you to know, Mrs. Lambert, I love Glenn and I plan to be a good wife to him."

The dark eyes softened perceptively. "I can see that, Muffie. No woman can look at a man the way you look at Glenn and not love him." Hesitantly, she wiped her wet hands on her apron and turned toward Maggie. Her gaze drifted into the living room, and she frowned slightly. "Are you free for lunch tomorrow? I think we should talk."

"Yes, I'd enjoy that."

Maggie didn't tell Glenn of her luncheon with his mother until the following morning. She woke with him and put on the coffee while he showered. When he joined her in the kitchen, Maggie had fried bacon and eggs, which was about the limit of her breakfast skills. Learning to cook was something she planned to do soon. Rosa, her housekeeper at the beach house, would gladly teach her. Thoughts of California brought back a mental image of her brother, and Maggie sighed expressively.

"I'll need the car again today; do you mind?" Maggie asked Glenn, turning her thoughts from the unhappy subject of Denny.

Glenn glanced up from the morning paper. "Do you want to do some shopping?"

"No . . . I'm meeting your mother for lunch." With a forced air of calm, she scooted out the chair across from him. Her hands cupped the coffee mug, absorbing its warmth. She was worried about letting Glenn know she was meeting his mother. "You don't mind, do you . . . I mean, about me using the car?"

"No." He pushed his half-eaten breakfast aside, darting a concerned look toward Maggie. "I don't mind." *Great!* He thought vehemently. He could only imagine what his mother was going to tell Maggie. If Maggie was going to hear the details of his relationship with Angie, he'd prefer that they came from him, not his mother.

"Good." Despite his aloofness, Maggie had the impression that he wasn't altogether pleased. He didn't have to be—she was going, and she sensed they both knew what would be the main subject of the luncheon conversation.

"Would you like to meet me at the health club afterward?" Glenn asked, but his attention didn't waver from the newspaper. "I try to work out two, sometimes three times a week."

It pleased Maggie that he was including her. "Sure, but let me warn you I'm terrible at handball, average at tennis, and a killer on the basketball court."

"I'll reserve a tennis court," Glenn informed her, a smile curling up one side of his mouth. "And don't bother about dinner tonight. We'll eat at the club."

The morning passed quickly. Since she was meeting Glenn later, Maggie dressed casually in white linen slacks and a pink silk blouse, checking her appearance several times. All morning, Maggie avoided going near Glenn's den. She wouldn't torment herself by looking at the pictures again; stumbling upon them once had been more than enough. For all she knew, Glenn could have tossed them out with the garbage, but Maggie hadn't the courage to look, fearing that he hadn't.

Allowing herself extra time in case she got lost, Maggie left early for her luncheon date with Charlotte. She had some difficulty finding the elder Lamberts' home, and regretted not having paid closer attention to the route Glenn had taken the night before. As it turned out, when she pulled into the driveway it was precisely noon, their agreed time.

Charlotte met her at the door and briefly hugged her. "I got to thinking later that I should have met you someplace. You hardly know your way around yet."

"It wasn't any problem," Maggie fibbed, following the older woman into the kitchen. A quiche was cooling on the countertop, filling the room with the delicious smell of eggs, cheese, and spices.

"Sit down and I'll get you a cup of coffee."

Maggie did as requested, not knowing how to say that she didn't want to be thought of as company. Charlotte took the chair beside her. "The reason I asked you here today is to apologize for the way I behaved last night."

"No, please." Maggie's hand rested on her mother-in-law's forearm. "I understand. Our news must have come as a shock. Glenn and I were wrong not to have told you earlier."

"Yes, I'll admit that keeping it a secret for nearly two weeks was as much of a surprise as the deed." She lifted the delicate china cup to her mouth and took a sip. Glenn had always been close to his family; for him to have married without letting them know immediately was completely out of character. For that matter, their rushed marriage wasn't his style, either. Maggie didn't need to be reminded that Glenn was a thorough person who weighed each decision, studied each circumstance. It was one reason he was such an excellent stockbroker.

"You have to understand," Maggie said, wanting to defend him. "We were as surprised as anyone. Glenn arrived for Steve and Janelle's wedding and everything seemed so right between us that we flew to Reno that night."

"The night of the wedding?" Charlotte did a poor job of hiding her astonishment. "Why, he'd only arrived in San Francisco—"

"Less than twenty-four hours before the wedding." Maggie confirmed her mother-in-law's observation. "And we hadn't seen each other in twelve years. It sounds impulsive and foolish, doesn't it?" Maggie wouldn't minimize the circumstances surrounding their marriage.

"Not that . . . Glenn's never done anything impulsive in his life. He knew exactly what he was doing when he married you, Maggie. Don't ever doubt that."

"I don't. But I know that Glenn was engaged to someone else recently and that he loved her a great deal."

Obviously flustered, Charlotte shook her head, her face reddening. "You don't need to worry any about her."

"I have, though," Maggie confirmed, being frank and honest. "Glenn hasn't told me much."

"He will in time," Charlotte said confidently. The older woman's brow was furrowed with unasked questions, and Maggie nearly laughed aloud at how crazy the situation must sound to someone else. Glenn and Maggie had grown up fighting like brother and sister, had moved apart for more than a decade, and on the basis of a few hours they'd decided to get married.

"I think I always knew there was something special between you and Glenn. He wasn't too concerned about girls during high school. Sports and his grades took up the majority of his energy. But he was at ease with you. If there was something troubling him, it wasn't me or his father he discussed it with; instead he talked it over with you. I suppose a few people will be surprised at this sudden marriage, but don't let that bother you. The two of you are perfect together."

"I won't." Maggie swallowed, the words nervously tripping over her tongue. "Neither of us came into this marriage the way normal couples do, but we're both determined to make it work. I'd been hurt, perhaps not as deeply as Glenn, but for the past few years I've been lonely and miserable. Glenn's still . . . hurting, but I've staked our future together on the conviction that time will heal those wounds."

"I'm pleased he told you about Angie." The look of relief relaxed Charlotte's strong face.

"Only a little. He loved her very much, didn't he?" Just saying the words hurt, but she successfully disguised a grimace.

"I won't deny it. Glenn did love her," Charlotte answered, then added to qualify her statement, "more than she deserved."

Maggie had guessed as much already. When Glenn committed himself to someone or something, there would never be any doubts. He had loved her, but by his own words, he had no intention of pining away the rest of his life because she married another man. With their wedding vows, Glenn had pledged himself to Maggie. At moments like these and the one yesterday when she discovered the photos, this knowledge of his determination was the only thing that kept her from drowning in frustration.

"I think I always knew that Angie wasn't the right woman for Glenn. Something in my mother's heart told me things were wrong for them. However, it wasn't my place to intrude in his life. He seemed to love her so much."

This time Maggie was unable to hide the pain of Charlotte's words. She felt the blood drain from her face and lowered her eyes, not wanting her mother-in-law to know how tender her heart was.

"Oh dear, I've said the wrong thing again. Forgive me." Shaking her head as if silently scolding herself, Mrs. Lambert added, "That came out all wrong. He was happy, yes, but that happiness wouldn't have lasted and I suspect that even Glenn knew that." Charlotte stood and brought the quiche to the table along with two place settings.

"Please continue," Maggie urged, needing to know everything about the situation she had married into.

Seeming to understand Maggie's curiosity, Charlotte rejoined her at the kitchen table. "Glenn cared enough for Angie to wait a year for her to decide she'd marry him. I've never seen Glenn so happy as the night she agreed to be his wife. We'd met Angie, of course, several times. She has the roundest, darkest eyes I've ever seen. She's an intense girl, quiet, a little withdrawn, exceptionally loyal, and although she's hurt Glenn terribly, I'm afraid I can't be angry with her. Ultimately, she made the right decision. It would have been wrong for her to have married Glenn when she was in love with another man."

The irony of the situation was more than Maggie could stand. It was wrong for Angie to have married Glenn in those circumstances, yet he had done exactly that when he married her. Apparently, Charlotte didn't see it that way. For that matter, Maggie was convinced that had she known beforehand, she probably would have married him anyway.

"And she never did take the ring," Charlotte finished.

"The ring?"

"My mother's," the older woman explained. "She willed it to me as part of my inheritance, and when Glenn graduated from college I opted to make it his. It's a lovely thing, antique with several small diamonds, but of course you've seen it."

Maggie thrust an expectant look at her mother-in-law. "No . . . I haven't. Glenn's never mentioned any ring."

Charlotte dismissed the information with a light shrug. "I wouldn't worry about it—you'll receive it soon enough. As I recall, Glenn had it sized and cleaned when he and Angie decided—" Realizing her mistake, Charlotte lowered her gaze and fidgeted with her coffee cup. "He's probably having it resized and is keeping it as a surprise for Christmas. As it is I've probably ruined that. I apologize, Maggie."

The racket slammed against the tennis ball with a vengeance, and Maggie returned it to Glenn's side of the court with astonishing accuracy. So he had his grandmother's antique ring that was to go to his wife. She was his wife. Where exactly was the ring? *Slam*. She returned the tennis ball a second time, stretching as far as she could reach to make the volley. Not expecting her return, Glenn lost the point.

Maggie's serve. She aced the first shot, making his return impossible. Fueled by her anger, she had never played a better match. The first two games were hers, and Glenn's jaw sagged open as he went into mild shock. He rallied in the third, and their fourth and fifth games were heated contests.

"I don't recall you ever being this good," he shouted from the other side of the court.

She tossed the ball into the air and, fully extending her body, wielded the racket forward, bending her upper torso in half.

"There are a lot of things you don't know about me, Lambert," she shouted back, dashing to the far end of the court to return the volley. She felt like a pogo stick, hopping from one end of the clay surface to the other with a quickness she didn't know she possessed. At the end of the first set, Maggie was so exhausted that she was shaking. *Good grief,* she thought, she had a tennis court at the beach house that she never used. This match was a misrepresentation of her skill.

Wiping the perspiration from her face with a thick white towel, Maggie sagged onto the bench. Glenn joined her, taking a seat beside her. "You should have told me you were this good. I've never had to work this hard to win."

Her breath came in deep gasps. "That was quite a workout." She hoped he didn't suggest another one soon. A repeat performance of this magnitude was unlikely. The match had helped her vent her frustrations over the issue of his grandmother's ring—her normal game was far less aggressive.

Taking his mother's words at face value, Maggie decided the best thing she could do was patiently wait. Glenn had originally intended the ring would go to Angie, but he'd married Maggie. When he felt comfortable with the idea, he'd present her with the ring, not before. Christmas was less than seven weeks away, and Charlotte was probably right. He'd give it to her then. Maybe.

Regaining his breath, Glenn leaned forward and placed his elbows on his knees. "What did you and my mother have to talk about?" The question wasn't an idle one. His brows were drawn into a single tense line. All afternoon he had worried about that luncheon date. Maggie had a right to know everything, but he didn't want the information coming from his mother. If anyone was going to tell her, it would come best from him. He had thought to call and talk to his mother, and discreetly explain as much, but the morning had been hectic and by the time he was out of the board meeting, it had been too late.

Wickedly, Maggie fluttered her thick, dark lashes. "I imagine you'd love to know what tales she carried, but I'm not breaking any confidences."

"Did she give you her recipe for my favorite dinner?"

"What makes you think we discussed you?" Maggie tilted her flushed face to one side and grinned up at him, her smile growing broader.

"It only seems natural that the two women in my life would talk of little else." He placed his arm around her shoulder and helped her stand, carrying her tennis racket for her.

Maggie placed her arm around his waist, pleased with the way he linked her with his mother. "If your favorite meal is beef Stroganoff, then you're in luck."

"The luckiest day of my life was when you agreed to be my wife," Glenn murmured as he looked down on her with a haunting look so intense that Maggie's heart throbbed painfully. Her visit with his mother hadn't been easy for him, she realized. He had probably spent the entire day worrying about what she'd say afterward.

Her voice grew husky with emotion. "What an amazing coincidence—that's my favorite day, too."

The longing in his eyes grew all the more poignant as Glenn weighed her words. If they'd been anyplace else, Maggie was convinced he would have tossed their tennis rackets aside and pulled her into his arms.

"Come on," she chided lovingly. "If you're going to beat me when I've played the best game of my life, then the least you can do is feed me."

Laughing, Glenn kissed the top of her head and led her toward the changing room and then to the restaurant.

His good mood continued when they reached the condominium. Maggie was bushed, and although she had taken a quick shower at Glenn's club, she couldn't resist a leisurely soak in a hot tub to soothe the aching cries of unused muscles. This day had been their best yet. The tension eased from her sore muscles and her heart. The matter with the ring no longer bothered her. When Glenn decided to give it to her, she'd know that it came from his heart and she need never doubt again.

With her hair pinned up and a terry-cloth bathrobe

wrapped around her, Maggie walked into the living room, looking for her husband.

"Glenn?"

"In here." His voice came from the den.

Remembering the photographs inside, Maggie paused in the doorway. Tension shot through her, although she struggled to appear outwardly composed. With monumental effort, she kept her gaze from the wastepaper basket beside his desk.

"What are you doing?" She was exhausted, and it was late. She'd have thought that after a workout on the courts he'd be ready for bed.

"I've got a few odds and ends to finish up here. I'll only be a few minutes," he answered without looking up, scribbling across the top of a computer sheet. When he did glance up he was surprised to find Maggie standing in the doorway as if she were afraid to come into the room. "I'd appreciate a cup of coffee."

Maggie shrugged. "Sure."

"Maggie." Glenn stopped her. "Is anything wrong?"

"Wrong?" she echoed. "What could possibly be wrong?" *Just that I'm such a coward I can't bear to look and see if those snapshots are still there,* she chastised herself, turning toward the kitchen.

"I don't know." Glenn's puzzled voice followed her.

The coffee took only a minute to make. Maggie stood in the kitchen, waiting for the liquid to drain into the cup and told herself she was behaving like an idiot.

She pasted a smile on her lips as she carried the mug into his den and set it on the edge of the desk. "Here you go."

"Thanks," Glenn murmured, busily working.

Maggie straightened and took a step backward. As she did, her gaze fell to the empty receptacle. Relief washed over her. He had gotten rid of them. She wanted to dance around the room and sing.

"Glenn." She moved behind his chair and slid her arms around his neck.

"Hmm . . ."

"How late did you say you'd be?" She dipped her head and nuzzled the side of his neck, darting her tongue in and out of his ear.

Glenn could feel the hot blood stirring within him. "Not long. Why?"

"Why?" she shot back, giggling. "You need me to tell you why?"

Scooting the chair around, Glenn gripped her by the waist and pulled her onto his lap. A brilliant smile came over her as she slid her arms around his neck.

Glenn's mouth twisted wryly as he studied her. He didn't know what had gotten into Maggie today. First she had surprised him on the tennis court. Then she had behaved like a shy virgin outside his door, looking in as if his office was a den of iniquity. And now she was a bewitching temptress who came to him with eyes that were filled with passion. Not that he was complaining; he'd never get enough of this woman.

Maggie's fingers fumbled with the buttons of his shirt so that she had the freedom to run her hands over his chest. She reveled in simply touching him, and pulled the shirt free of his shoulders. His muscles rippled as she slowly slid her hands upward to either side of his neck. Unhurried, she branded him with a kiss so hot it stole his breath.

"Maggie," he whispered hoarsely, intimately sliding his hand between her legs and stroking her bare thigh. "Maybe I haven't got so much paperwork to do after all."

Smiling dreamily, Maggie directed his mouth back to hers. "Good."

Chapter 8

Two weeks passed, and Maggie grew more at ease with her marriage. She realized that a silent observer to their world would have assumed that they had been married for several years. Externally, there was nothing to show that their marriage wasn't the product of a long, satisfying courtship. It didn't seem to matter that Glenn hadn't declared his love. He respected her, enjoyed her wit, encouraged her talent. They were happy . . . and it showed.

Maggie greeted each day with enthusiasm, eager to discover what lay in store for her. She purchased several cookbooks and experimented, putting her creativity to work in the kitchen. Glenn praised her efforts and accepted her failures, often helping her laugh when it would have been easy to lose patience. In the early afternoons, if there was time, Maggie explored Charleston with Glenn's mother and came to appreciate anew what a wonderful woman Charlotte Lambert was. They never spoke of Angie again.

South Carolina was everything Maggie had known it would be, and more than she'd ever expected. She was thrilled by the eighteenth- and nineteenth-century paintings that displayed regional history in the Gibbes Museum of Art and explored the Calhoun Mansion and the Confederate Museum, examining for the first time the Civil War from the Confederate point of view. One hundred and fifty years after the last battles of the war had been waged, Maggie felt the anguish of the South and tasted its defeat.

Her fingers longed to hold a paintbrush, but she satisfied her urgings with a pencil and pad, sketching the ideas that came to her. Charlotte was amazed at her daughter-in-law's talent, and Maggie often gave Glenn's mother her pencil sketches. At Sunday dinner with his family, Maggie was embarrassed to find those careless drawings framed and hanging on the living room wall. Proudly, Glenn's eyes had met hers. They didn't often speak of her art, and Maggie basked in the warm glow of his approval.

For his part, Glenn was happy, happier than he ever imagined he'd be. In the afternoons he rushed home from the office, knowing Maggie would be there waiting for him. Maybe he hadn't married her for the right reasons, maybe what they had done was half crazy, but, he thought tenderly, he wouldn't have it any different now, and he thanked God every single day that he'd acted on the impulse. Maggie gave his life purpose. In the afternoons she would be there waiting. And the minute he walked in the door, she'd smile. Not an ordinary smile, but a soft feminine one that lit up her dark eyes and curved the edges of her mouth in a sultry way that sent hot need coursing through him. In his lifetime, Glenn never hoped to see another woman smile the way Maggie did. Often he barely made it inside the door before he knew he had to kiss her. He would have preferred to react casually to his desire for her, but discovered that was impossible. Some days he couldn't get home fast enough, using every ounce of self-control he possessed not to burst in the door, wrap his arms around her, and carry her into their bedroom. He couldn't touch, or taste, or hold her enough. Glenn felt he'd choose death rather than a life without her. Angie might have possessed his heart, but Maggie had laid claim to his soul.

He wondered sometimes if she had even an inkling of what she did to him physically. He doubted it. If she wasn't pregnant soon, he mused, it would be a miracle. The thought of Maggie heavy with his child, her breasts swollen, her stomach protruding, produced such a shocking desire within him that it was almost painful. The feeling left him weak with wonder and pride. They'd have exceptionally beautiful children.

For the first time, Glenn understood his brothers' pride in and awe of their children. At thirty, Glenn hadn't given much thought to a family. Someday, he had always thought, he'd want children, but he hadn't put faces or names to those who would fill his life. With Maggie he envisioned a tall son and a beautiful daughter. Every man wanted an heir, and now he yearned for a son until some nights he couldn't sleep thinking about the children Maggie would give him. On those evenings, late, when his world was at peace, Glenn would press his hand over her satiny smooth stomach, praying her body was nurturing his seed. A child would cement Maggie and him so firmly together that only death would ever separate them.

Their evenings were filled with contentment. Only rarely did he bring work home, lingering instead in front of the television, using that as an excuse to have Maggie at his side, to watch her. If he did need to deal with some paperwork, she sat quietly in his den, curled up in a chair reading. It was as though they couldn't be separated any longer than necessary and every moment apart was painful.

Maggie enjoyed watching Glenn in his home office more than any other place. He sat with simple authority at his desk while she pretended absorption in a novel, when actually she was studying him. Now and then he would look up and they'd exchange warm, lingering glances that left her wondering how long it would be until they could go to bed.

When they did head toward the bedroom, it was ridiculously early. The instant the light went off Glenn reached for her with such passion that she wondered if he would ever get his fill of her—then promptly prayed he wouldn't. Their nights became a celebration for all the words stored in their hearts that had yet to be spoken. Never shy nor embarrassed, Maggie came to him without reserve, holding nothing back. She was his temptress and mistress. Bewitching and bewitched. Seduced and seducer.

Maggie had assumed that the fiery storm of physical satisfaction their bodies gave each other would fade with time, not increase. But as the days passed, she was pleased that Glenn's constant need equaled her desire for him. Each time they made love, Maggie would lie in his arms thinking that their appetite for each other would surely diminish, and knew immediately that it wouldn't.

In the mornings when she woke to the clock radio, Maggie was securely wrapped in Glenn's arms. He held her close and so tight she wondered how she had managed to sleep. Some mornings Maggie felt the tension leave Glenn as he emerged from the last dregs of slumber and realized she remained with him. It was as though he feared she would be gone. Once assured she was at his side, Glenn would relax. As far as Maggie could tell, this insecurity was the only part of his relationship with Angie that continued to haunt him. One hundred times each day, in everything she did, every place she went, Maggie set out to prove she would never willingly leave him.

Life fell into a comfortable pattern, and the third full week after Maggie arrived in Charleston, the condominium sold. Maggie met Glenn at the door with the news.

"The realtor was by with an offer," she said, draping her arms around his neck and pressing her body to his.

Glenn placed his large hands on her hips as he kissed her. "As far as I can see, we should be able to make the move within a week, two at the most," he commented a few minutes later, as he curled an arm around her shoulders and deposited his briefcase in the den.

"A week?" Now that she was here, Maggie would have welcomed the opportunity to settle in South Carolina. California, Denny, the beach house seemed a million miles away, light-years from the life she shared with Glenn here.

"You sound like you don't want to move." He leaned against the edge of his desk, crossing his long legs at the ankles.

"South Carolina is lovely."

"So is California," Glenn countered. "You don't mind the change, do you?"

In some ways she did. Their time in Charleston was

like a romantic interlude—the honeymoon they'd never gotten. They were protected from the outside world. No one knew who Maggie was, or cared. For the first time in several years she was a regular person, and she loved it. In Charleston she had blossomed into a woman who boldly met a passerby's glance. She explored the art galleries without fear that someone would recognize her. No one came to her with get-rich-quick schemes, seeking naïve investors. No one rushed to wait on her or gain her attention or her gratitude. However, Maggie was wise enough to know that those things would follow in time.

"No," she told Glenn soberly. "I don't mind the move."

He turned, sorting through the stack of mail she had set on the desktop, smiling wryly. Maggie wanted to stay in Charleston for the same reasons he wanted to move to San Francisco. They were each looking for an escape to problems they would need to face sooner or later. For his part, Glenn chose the West Coast more for nostalgia than any need to escape. San Francisco felt right, and Charleston held too many painful memories.

"Will you want to live at the beach house?" Maggie's one concern was that Glenn might not like her home. Her own feelings toward the house were ambivalent. On some days, it was her sanctuary, and on others, her prison. She liked the house; she was comfortable there, but she didn't know that Glenn would be.

"Sure. Is there any reason you'd want to move?"

"No, it's just that . . ." The telephone rang and Maggie paused as Glenn lifted the receiver.

After a moment, he handed it to her. "It's for you."

"Me?" She felt her heart rate accelerate. She'd given specific instructions that she wasn't to be contacted except for her brother. And Denny would call only if he was in financial trouble.

"Hello." Her voice was wispy with apprehension.

"Who was that?"

"Denny, are you all right?"

"I asked you a question first. It's not often I call my sister and a man answers the phone. Something's going on. Who is it, Maggie?"

"I'm with Glenn Lambert."

A low chuckle followed, but Maggie couldn't tell if her brother was pleased or abashed. "So you and Glenn are together. Be careful, Maggie, I don't want to see you hurt again." He hesitated, as though he didn't want to continue. "Are you living with him?"

"Denny," Maggie had been foolish not to have told her family sooner. "Glenn and I are married."

"Married," he echoed in shock. "When did this happen?"

"Several weeks ago."

A short, stunned silence followed. "That's sudden, isn't it? Linda and I would have liked to have attended the wedding."

"We eloped."

"That's not like you."

"It wasn't like either of us. I'm happy, Denny, really happy. You know what it's been like the past few years. Now don't worry about me. I'm a big girl. I know what I'm doing."

"I just don't want to see you get hurt."

"I won't," she assured him.

"Do Mom and Dad know?"

Denny had her there. "Not yet. We're planning to tell them once we're back in San Francisco."

"And when will that be?" His words were slow, as if he was still thinking.

"A couple of weeks."

He didn't respond, and the silence seemed to pound over the great echoing canyon of the telephone wire. Denny hadn't done a good job of disguising his reservations. Once he saw how good this marriage was for her, she was sure, he'd share her happiness. Her brother had been her anchor when she broke up with Dirk. He had seen firsthand the effects of one painful relationship and sought to protect her from another. Only Glenn wasn't Dirk, and when they arrived back in San Francisco Denny would see that.

"Is there a reason you phoned, Denny?"

"Oh yeah." His voice softened. "Listen, I hate to trouble you, but there's been some minor complications and the lawyer has to charge me extra fees. Also, Linda's been sick and the kids aren't feeling that well, either—"

"How much do you need?"

"I hate having to come to my sister like a pauper. But I swear as soon as everything's straightened out I'll repay every penny."

"Denny, don't worry about it. You're my brother, I'm happy to give you whatever you need. You know that." She couldn't refuse her own brother, no matter what the reason.

"I know and appreciate it, Sis. I really do."

"You wouldn't ask if it wasn't necessary." She had hoped to make this difficult time in Denny's life smoother, but sometimes wondered if she contributed more to the problem. Yet she couldn't say no. "I'll have Shirley write you a check."

Once he had gotten what he wanted, the conversation ended quickly. Maggie replaced the receiver and forced a smile to her lips. "That was my brother," she announced, turning back to Glenn.

"Who's Shirley?" he asked starkly.

"My money manager." She lowered her gaze to the lush carpet, feeling her husband's censure. Glenn didn't understand the circumstances that had led to Denny's problems. They had both received a large inheritance. Maggie had received half of her great-aunt's fortune; her parents and Denny had split the other half. Everything had gone smoothly until Denny had invested in a business that had quickly gone defunct. Now his money—or what was left of it—was tied up in litigation.

"Does Denny need her name often?"

"Not really," she lied. "He's been having some cash-flow problems lately." *As in not having any,* her mind added. "We were talking about the move to California when the phone buzzed, weren't we?"

"You don't want to discuss Denny, is that it?"

"That's it." Glenn couldn't tell her anything she didn't already know. She was in a no-win situation with her brother. She couldn't abandon him, nor could she continue to feed his dependence on her.

"Okay, if that's the way you want it." His eyes and voice silently accused her as he turned back and sorted through the mail.

"California will be good for us," Maggie said, hoping to lighten the atmosphere.

"Yes, it will," Glenn agreed almost absently, without

looking up. "Before I forget, the office is having a farewell party for me Friday night. We don't have any plans, do we?"

Maggie had met Glenn's staff and seen for herself the respect his management had earned him. One afternoon when she had met him for lunch, Maggie had witnessed anew the quiet authority in his voice as he spoke to his associates. He was decisive and sure, calm and reassuring, and the office had thrived under his care. It went without saying that he was a popular stockbroker and would be sorely missed.

Friday night Maggie dressed carefully, choosing a flattering cream-colored creation and pale-blue designer nylons. She had never been one to enjoy parties, especially when they involved people she barely knew. This one shouldn't be so bad though, she reasoned. The focus would be on Glenn, not her.

"Am I underdressed?" she asked him, slowly rotating for his inspection. Not having attended this kind of function previously put her at a disadvantage. She didn't know how the other wives would dress and had chosen something conservative.

Glenn stood, straightening his dark blue silk tie. His warm chuckle filled their bedroom as he examined his wife. "As far as I'm concerned, you're overdressed. But I'll take care of that later myself." His eyes met hers in the mirror and filled with sweet promise.

After inserting dangly gold earrings into her earlobes, Maggie joined Glenn in the living room. He was pouring them a drink, and Maggie watched her husband with renewed respect. He was tall, athletic, and unbearably handsome. Her heart swelled with the surge of love that raced through her. She hadn't been looking forward to the party; in fact, she had been dreading it from the moment Glenn had mentioned it. Early on, she had reconciled herself to being a good stockbroker's wife, and that meant that she'd be attending plenty of functions over the years. It would be to her advantage to adapt to them now. Although he hadn't said anything, Maggie was confident Glenn knew she was determined to make the best of this evening.

They arrived precisely at eight at the home of Glenn's regional manager, Gary Weir. Already, the living room was filled with smoke, and from the look of things, the drinks had been flowing freely. As Glenn and Maggie walked in the front door, spirited cheers of welcome greeted them. Maggie painted a bright smile on her lips as they moved around the room, mingling with the guests. Everyone, it seemed, was in a good mood. Everyone, that is, except Maggie.

She didn't know how to explain her uneasiness. There wasn't anything she could put a name to, and she mentally chastised herself. Glenn's friends and associates appeared to be going out of their way to make her feel welcome. Her hostess, Pamela Weir, Gary's wife, was warm and gracious, if a bit reserved. Yet a cold persistence nagged at Maggie that something wasn't right. Glenn stayed at her side, smiling down on her now and then. Once her eyes fell upon two women whispering with their heads close together. They sat on the far side of the room and there wasn't any possibility that Maggie could hear their whispered conversation, but something inside told Maggie they were talking about her. A chill went up her spine and she gripped Glenn's elbow, feeling ridiculous and calling herself every kind of idiot. Lightly, she shook her head, hoping to toss aside those crazy insecurities.

A few minutes later, Glenn was pulled into a conversation with some of the men and Maggie was left to her own devices. Seeing Maggie alone, Pamela Weir strolled over.

"It was such a pleasant surprise when Glenn announced he had married," Pamela said.

Maggie took a sip of her wine. Glenn was involved with his friends and moved to another section of the crowded room. "Yes, I imagine it was. But we've known each other nearly all our lives."

"That was what Glenn was saying." Pamela gave her a funny look and then smiled quickly. "For a long time, Gary was worried that Glenn wanted the transfer because of a problem at the office."

Maggie forced a smile. "We decided when we married that we'd live in San Francisco," she explained to the tall, elegant woman at her side. "We were both raised there."

"Yes, Glenn explained that, too."

Maggie's throat constricted, and she made an effort to ease the strange tension she felt. "Although I've only been in Charleston a few weeks, I'm impressed with your city. It's lovely."

Pamela's eyes revealed her pride in Charleston. "We do love it."

"I know Glenn will miss it."

"We'll miss him."

Silence. Maggie could think of nothing more to comment on. "You have a lovely home," she said, and faltered slightly. "Glenn and I both appreciate the trouble you've gone to for this evening."

"It's no bother. Glenn has always been special to the firm. We're just sick to lose him." The delicate hands rotated the stem of the crystal wineglass. "I don't mind telling you that Glenn is the best manager Gary has. In fact"—she paused and gave Maggie a falsely cheerful smile—"Gary had been hoping to move Glenn higher into management. Of course, that won't be possible now."

As with his parents, Maggie was again put on the defensive. Leaving Charleston hadn't been her idea, and she didn't like being made the scapegoat. Swallowing back a retort, Maggie lowered her gaze and said, "I'm sure Glenn will do just as well in San Francisco."

"We all hope he does," Pamela said with a note of censure.

Glenn's gaze found Maggie several moments later. She stood stiff and uneasy on the other side of the room, holding her drink and talking to Pamela Weir. Even from the other side of the room, he could see that Maggie was upset and he couldn't understand why. He had known from the beginning that she hadn't been looking forward to this party. He wasn't all that fond of this sort of affair himself. But since the party had been given in his honor, he couldn't refuse the invitation. Maggie's attitude troubled him. Earlier in the evening, he'd stayed at her side, but eventually he'd been drawn away for one reason or another. Good grief, he thought, he shouldn't have to babysit her. The longer he watched her actions with Pamela, the more concerned he became. He noticed Maggie wasn't making eye contact with Pamela and when his supervisor's wife moved away, Glenn crossed the room to Maggie's side.

She lifted her gaze to his, and Glenn was shocked at the look of anger she sent him.

"What's wrong?" he asked.

She met his gaze with a determined lift to her chin. She was upset, more upset than she'd been since the first morning of their marriage. Glenn had let her walk into the party, knowing the resentment his coworkers felt toward her because he was leaving. "When we arrived tonight, I kept feeling these weird vibes that people didn't like me. Now I know why—"

"You're being ridiculous," Glenn muttered, his hand tightening around his drink. "These are my friends, and they accept you as my wife."

Glenn was on the defensive and didn't appear willing to listen to her. "You're wrong, Glenn," she murmured. "They don't like me and with good reason. We'll talk about it later."

Glenn said nothing. The sound of someone banging a teaspoon against the side of a glass interrupted their discussion.

"Attention, everyone," Gary Weir called as he came to stand beside Glenn and Maggie. With dull blue eyes that revealed several drinks too many, Gary motioned with his arms that he wanted everyone to gather around.

Maggie felt like a statue with a frozen smile curving her mouth as she watched the party crowding around them. Glenn placed an arm at her neck, but his touch felt cold and impersonal.

Ceremoniously clearing his throat, Gary continued.

"As you're all aware, tonight's party is being given in honor of Glenn and his"—he faltered momentarily, and seemed to have forgotten Maggie's name—"bride." A red blush attacked the cheeks of the supervisor, and he took a large swallow of his drink.

"As we know," he said, glancing over his shoulder to Glenn and Maggie, "Glenn has recently announced that he's transferring to California." Gary was interrupted with several low boos until he sliced the air, cutting off his associates. "Needless to say, everyone is going to miss him. Glenn has been a positive force within our company. We've all come to appreciate him, and it goes without saying that he'll be sorely missed. But being good sports, we want to wish him the best in San Francisco." A polite round of applause followed.

"In addition," Gary went on, his voice gaining volume with each word, "Glenn has taken a wife." He turned and beamed a proud smile at the two of them. "All of us felt that we couldn't send you away without a wedding gift. So we took up a collection and got you this." He turned around and lifted a gaily wrapped gift from behind a chair, holding it out to Glenn and Maggie.

Clearing his throat, Gary finished by saying, "This gift is a token of our appreciation and well-wishes. We'd all like to wish Glen and Angie many years of happiness."

Maggie's eyes widened and she swallowed hard at the unexpectedness of it. An embarrassed hush fell over the room and Maggie felt Glenn stiffen. Not realizing his mistake, Gary flashed a troubled look to his wife who was mouthing Maggie's name.

To cover the awkward moment, Maggie stepped forward and took the gift from Gary's hand. He gave her an apologetic look and fumbled, obviously flustered and embarrassed.

"Glenn and I would like to thank you, Larry."

"Gary," he corrected instantly, some color seeping back into his pale face.

A slow smile grew across Maggie's tight features. "We both seem to be having problems with names tonight, don't we?"

The party loved it, laughing spontaneously at the way she had aptly turned the tables on their superior. Laughing himself, Gary briefly hugged her and pumped Glenn's hand.

Not until they were on their way home did Glenn comment on the mishap. "Thank you," he said as they headed toward the freeway.

"For what?"

"For the way you handled that." He didn't need to explain what "that" was. Maggie knew. Rarely in his life had Glenn felt such anger. He had wanted to throw Gary against the wall and demand that he apologize to Maggie for embarrassing her that way. Of course, the slip hadn't been intentional, but it hadn't seemed to matter.

Several times in the past few weeks, Glenn had questioned whether he was making the right decision leaving Charleston. Maggie had blossomed here and seemed to genuinely love the city. Now he knew beyond a shadow of a doubt that leaving was best. Angie would haunt their marriage in Charleston. He had been a fool not to realize why Maggie had been so miserable at the party. The thought that his coworkers would confuse her with Angie hadn't crossed his mind. It seemed impossible that only a few months back he had been planning to marry someone else. These days he had trouble picturing Angie and seldom tried. Angie would always hold a special place in his heart. He wished her a long and happy life with Simon. But he had Maggie now, and thanked God for the woman beside him. He might not have courted her the way he should have, the way she deserved, but he desperately needed her in his life.

He loved her. Simply. Profoundly. Utterly. He'd tell her soon. *Not tonight, though,* he thought, or she'd think the mistake at the party had prompted the admission. Glenn wanted to choose the time carefully. For several weeks now, he had realized she loved him. Yet she hadn't said anything. He couldn't blame her. Things would straighten themselves out once they were in San Francisco. The sooner they left Charleston, the better. In California, Maggie need never worry that someone would bring up Angie's name again.

"Gary's mistake was an honest one. He didn't mean to embarrass anyone." Without a problem, Maggie excused Glenn's friend.

"I know," Glenn murmured, concentrating on his driving.

They didn't talk again until they were home, and then only in polite phrases. They undressed in silence, and when they lifted the covers and climbed into bed, Glenn gathered her close in his arms, kissing her softly. He was asleep long before she was and rolled away from her. Maggie lay staring at the ceiling, unable to shake what had happened earlier from her mind. The flickering moon shadows seemed to taunt her. All they had been doing for the past few weeks was pretending. The two of them had been so intent on making believe that there had never been another woman in Glenn's life that the incident tonight had nearly devastated them. That was the problem with fantasies—they were so easily shattered. Maggie didn't need to be told that Glenn had been equally disturbed. Angie was present in their lives; she loomed between them like an uninvited guest. With a heavy heart, Maggie rolled over and tried to sleep, but she couldn't. Not until Glenn's arms found her and he pulled her into the circle of his embrace. But he had been asleep, and for all she knew, Maggie thought bitterly, he could have been dreaming it was "her" he was holding.

Monday morning after Glenn left for work, Maggie sat lingering over a cup of coffee, working the crossword puzzle. The first thing she should do was get dressed, but she had trouble shaking off a feeling of melancholy. No matter how hard she tried, she hadn't been able to forget what had happened Friday night. They hadn't spoken about it again, choosing to ignore it. For now the puzzle filled her time. Her pen ran out of ink and after giving it several hard shakes, she tossed it into the garbage. Glenn kept a dozen or more in his desk.

Standing, Maggie headed toward his office. One thing they had decided over the weekend was that Maggie would fly ahead of Glenn to California. Like a fool, Maggie had suggested it on the pretense that she had several items that required her attention waiting for her. She had hoped that Glenn would tell her he wanted them to arrive together. But he had agreed all too readily and she'd been miserable for the remainder of the day.

Pulling open Glenn's drawer, she found what she needed and started to close the desk drawer. As she did it made a light, scraping sound. Her first inclination was to shove it closed. Instead, she carefully pulled the drawer free and discovered an envelope tucked away in the back that had been forced upward when she'd gotten the pen.

It wasn't the normal place for Glenn to keep his mail, and she examined the envelope curiously. The even, smooth flowing strokes of the handwriting attracted her artist's eye. This was a woman's handwriting—Angie's handwriting. Maggie felt the room sway as she sank onto the corner of the swivel chair, her knees giving out. The postmark revealed that the letter had been mailed a week before Steve and Janelle's wedding.

Perspiration broke out across Maggie's upper lip, and she placed a hand over her mouth. Her heart hammered so loudly she was sure it rocked the room. The letter must have meant a great deal to Glenn for him to have saved it. Although she hadn't searched through the condominium, she had felt confident that he'd destroyed everything that would remind him of the other woman. Yet the letter remained.

Half of her wanted to stuff it back inside the drawer and pretend she'd never found it. The other half knew that if she didn't know the contents of the letter, she would always wonder. Glenn had told her so little. She was his wife. She had a right to know. He should have explained the entire situation long ago, but he hadn't, choosing instead to leave her curious and wondering. If she looked, it would be his own fault, she argued with herself. He had driven her to it.

It was wrong, Maggie knew it was wrong, but she couldn't help herself. Slowly, each inch pounding in nails of guilt, she withdrew the scented paper from the envelope.

Chapter 9

Carefully, Maggie unfolded the letter and was again struck by the smoothly flowing lines of the even handwriting. Angie's soulful dark eyes flashed in Maggie's memory from the time she'd seen the other woman's photograph. The handwriting matched the woman.

Dear Glenn,

I hope that I am doing the right thing by mailing you this letter. I've hurt you so terribly, and yet I owe you so much. I'm asking that you find it in your heart to forgive me, Glenn. I realize the pain I've caused you must run deep. Knowing that I've hurt you is my only regret.

Glenn, I don't believe that I'll ever be able to adequately thank you for your love. It changed my life and gave Simon back to me. Simon and I were destined to be man and wife. I can find no other way to explain it. I love him, Glenn, and would have always loved him. You and I were foolish to believe I could have forgotten Simon.

My hope is that someday you'll find a woman who will love you as much as I love Simon. You deserve happiness. Simon and I will never forget you. We both want to thank you for the sacrifice you made for us. Be happy, dear Glenn. Be very happy.

With a heart full of gratitude,
Angie

With trembling hands, Maggie refolded the letter and placed it back inside Glenn's drawer. If she had hoped to satisfy her curiosity regarding Angie, the letter only raised more questions. Angie had mentioned a sacrifice Glenn had made on her behalf. But what? He was like that, noble and sensitive, even self-sacrificing. Angie's marrying Simon clearly had devastated him.

All day the letter troubled Maggie, until she decided that if she were to help Glenn bury the past, she had to understand it. That night, she would do the very thing she had promised she wouldn't: She would ask Glenn to tell her about Angie.

No day had ever seemed so long. She didn't leave the house, didn't comb her hair until the afternoon, and when she did, her mirrored reflection revealed troubled, weary eyes and tight, compressed lips. If Glenn could talk this out with her, their chances of happiness would be greatly increased. He had saved the letter, risked her finding it. Although he might not be willing to admit it, he was holding on to Angie, hugging the memory. The time had come to let go.

With her arms cradling her middle, Maggie paced the

living room carpet, waiting for Glenn to come home from work. The questions were outlined in her mind. She had no desire to hurt or embarrass him. She wanted him to tell her honestly and freely what had happened with Angie and why he had stepped aside for Angie to marry Simon.

Yet for all her preparedness, when Glenn walked in the door Maggie turned abruptly toward him with wide, apprehensive eyes, her brain numb.

"Hello, Glenn." She managed to greet him calmly and walked across the room to give him a perfunctory kiss. She felt comfortable, but her cheeks and hands were cold. Earlier she had decided not to mention finding the letter, not wanting Glenn to know she had stooped so low as to read it. However, if he asked, she couldn't . . . wouldn't . . . lie.

His hands found her waist and he paused to study her. "Maggie, what's wrong, you're as cold as an iceberg."

She felt ridiculously close to tears and nibbled at her lower lip before answering. This was far more difficult than she'd thought it would be. "Glenn, we need to talk."

"I can see that. Do you have another rule for our marriage?"

Absently, she rubbed the palms of her hands together. "No."

He followed her into the living room and took a seat while she poured him a glass of wine. "Do you think I'm going to need that?" He didn't know what was troubling Maggie, but he had never seen her quite like this. She looked almost as if she were afraid, which was ludicrous. There was nothing she had to fear from him. He was her husband, and she should always feel comfortable coming to him.

Maybe she was pregnant. His pulse leaped eagerly at the thought. A baby would be wonderful, exciting news. A feeling of tenderness overcame him. Maggie was carrying his child.

"Maggie," he asked gently, "are you pregnant?"

She whirled around, sloshing some of the wine over the side of the glass, her eyes wide with astonishment. "No. What makes you ask?"

Disappointed, Glenn slowly shook his head. "No reason. Won't you tell me what's troubling you?"

She handed him the drink but didn't take a seat, knowing she would never be able to sit comfortably in one position. She was too nervous. Hands poised, her body tense, she stood by the window and looked down at the street far below. "I've been waiting to talk to you all day."

He wished she'd get to the point instead of leaving him to speculate what troubled her. He had never seen her this edgy. She resembled a child who had come to her parent to admit a great fault. "If it was so important, why didn't you phone me at the office?"

"I . . . couldn't. This was something that had to be done in person, Glenn," she said, then swallowed, clenching and unclenching her fists as she ignored the impatience in his eyes. "This isn't easy." She resisted the urge to dry her clammy palms on the pockets of her navy-blue slacks.

"I can see that," he said gently. Whatever it was had clearly caused her a lot of anxiety. Rushing her would do no good, and so he forced himself to relax as much as possible. He crossed his legs and leaned back against the thick cushions of the chair.

"I thought for a long time I'd wait until you were comfortable about this . . . this subject. Now I feel like a fool, forcing it all out in the open. I wish I were a stronger person, but I'm not. I'm weak, really." Slowly she turned and hesitantly raised her eyes to his. "Glenn, I'm your wife. Getting married the way we did may have been unconventional, but I have no regrets. None. I'm happy being married to you. But as your wife, I'm asking you to tell me about Angie." Maggie watched as surprise mingled with frustration and grew across his face.

"Why now?" Angie was the last subject he had expected Maggie to force upon him. As far as he was concerned, his relationship with the other woman was over. He wouldn't deny that he had been hurt, but he had no wish to rip open the wounds of his pride. And that was what had suffered most. Even when he'd known he'd lost her, he had continued to make excuses to see and be with Angie. Something perverse within himself had forced him to go back again and again, even when he had recognized that there wasn't any possibility of her marrying him. For weeks he had refused to let go of her even though he'd known he'd lost her and she would never be his.

Now was the opportunity to explain that she'd found the letter, Maggie thought. But she couldn't admit that she'd stooped so low as to read the extremely personal letter. "I . . . wanted to know . . . It's just that—"

"Is it because of what happened the other night?"

Glenn offered her an excuse that Maggie readily accepted. "Yes."

Glenn's mouth tightened, not with impatience but

with confused frustration. Maggie should have put it out of her mind long ago. No good would come from dredging up the past. "Whatever there was between us is over. Angie has nothing to do with you and me."

"But ultimately she does," Maggie countered. "You wouldn't have married me if your engagement hadn't been broken."

"Now you're being ridiculous. We wouldn't have married if I hadn't attended Steve and Janelle's wedding, either."

"You know what I mean."

"Maggie, trust me. There's nothing to discuss." The words were sharp.

Previously, when Glenn was angry, Maggie had marveled at his control. He rarely raised his voice, and never at her. Until now. The only evidence she had ever had of his fury was a telltale leap of muscle in his jaw. He moved from his chair to the far side of the room.

"Glenn," she ventured. "I don't understand why you're so reluctant to discuss her. Is it because I've never told you about Dirk? I would have gladly, but, you see, you've never asked. If there's anything you want to know, I'll be happy to explain."

"No, I don't care to hear the sorry details of your relationship with another man, and in return I expect the same courtesy."

Her hand on the back of the sofa steadied her. All these weeks, she'd been kidding herself, living in a dreamer's world. As Glenn's wife, she would fill the void left when Angie married Simon, but now she knew she would never be anything more than a substitute. These glorious days in Charleston had been an illusion. She had thought they'd traveled so far and yet they'd been only walking in place, stirring up the roadway dust so that it clouded their vision and their perspective. Oh, she would cook his meals, keep his house and bear his children, and love him until her heart would break. But she would never be anything more than second best.

"All right, Glenn," she murmured, casting her eyes to the carpet. "I'll never mention her name again."

His eyes narrowed as if he didn't believe her. But he had asked her not to, and she wouldn't. She had swallowed her pride and come to him when he must have known how difficult it had been for her. That meant nothing to him, she realized. It didn't matter what she said or did; Glenn wasn't going to tell her anything.

Purposefully, Maggie moved into the kitchen and started to prepare their evening meal. She was hurt and disillusioned. She realized that Glenn hadn't been angry, not really. The displeasure he had shown had been a reaction to the fact that he'd been unable to deal with his feelings for Angie. But he must, and she prayed he would realize it soon. Only when he acknowledged his feelings and sorted it out in his troubled mind would he be truly free to love her.

It took Glenn several minutes to analyze his indignation. Of all the subjects in the world, the last thing he wanted to discuss was the past. He had handled it badly. Maggie was upset, and he regretted that, but it was necessary. The farewell party was responsible for this sudden curiosity; Maggie had said so herself. He should have realized earlier the repercussions.

Glenn made his way to the kitchen and pretended to read the evening paper, all the while studying Maggie as she worked, tearing lettuce leaves for a salad. Someday soon he'd make it up to her and she'd know how important she was in his life . . . how much he loved her and needed her.

In bed that night, the entire Alaskan tundra might as well have lain between them. Glenn was on his side of the bed, his eyes closed, trying to sleep. He had wanted to make love and reassure Maggie, but she had begged off. He did his best to disguise his disappointment.

Other than polite conversation, Maggie hadn't said a word to him all evening. She cooked their dinner but didn't bother to eat any of it. For his part, he could hardly stomach the fresh crab salad, although generally Maggie was a good cook and he enjoyed their meals together. Cleaning the kitchen afterward seemed to take her hours, and when she returned to the living room he had guiltily searched her face for evidence of what she was thinking.

For a full ten minutes, Glenn was tempted to wake Maggie and tell her he would answer any questions she had. Maggie was right. She did deserve to know and it was only his pride that prevented him from explaining everything. But she was asleep by then and he decided to see how things went in the morning. If Maggie was still troubled, then he'd do as she had asked. But deep down, Glenn hoped that Maggie would put the subject out of her mind so they could go on with their lives.

Maggie lay stiffly on her side of the bed, unable to sleep. She longed for the comfort of Glenn's body and the warmth of his embrace. He had hurt her, and refusing to make love had been her way of getting back. But she was the one who suffered with disappointment. She needed her husband's love more than ever. Her heart felt as if a block of concrete were weighing it down.

The more she thought about their conversation, the angrier she got. She was his wife and yet he withheld from her an important aspect of his life. Glenn was denying her his trust. Their marriage was only a thin shell of what it was meant to be. If Glenn wouldn't tell her about his relationship with Angie, then he left her no option. Maggie decided she would find Angie and ask her what had happened. From the pieces of information she'd gathered, locating the other woman wouldn't be difficult.

In the long, sleepless hours of the night, Maggie mentally debated the pros and cons of such an action. What she might discover could ruin her marriage. Yet what she didn't know was, in essence, doing the same thing. The thought of Glenn making love with the other woman caused such an intense physical pain that it felt as if something were cutting into her heart. Unable to bear it, she tried to blot the picture from her mind, but no matter how she tried, the fuzzy image stayed with her, taunting her.

By the early hours of the morning, Maggie had devised her plan. It worked with surprising ease.

Two days later, Charlotte Lambert dropped Maggie off at the airport for a flight scheduled for San Francisco. As Glenn had agreed earlier, Maggie was going to fly ahead and take care of necessary business that awaited her. From the wistful look Glenn gave her that morning when she brought out her suitcases, she realized that he regretted having consented that she return before him. Some of the tension between them had lessened in the two days before the flight. With Maggie's plan had come a release. Glenn wouldn't tell her what she wanted to know, but she'd soon learn on her own.

The Delta 747 left Charleston for San Francisco on time, but Maggie wasn't on the flight. Instead, she boarded a small commuter plane that was scheduled to land in Groves Point. The same afternoon she would take another commuter plane and connect with a flight to Atlanta. If everything went according to schedule, Maggie would arrive in California only four hours later than her original flight.

Groves Point was a charming community. The man at the rental car agency gave her directions into town, and Maggie paused at the city park and looked at the statue of the Civil War heroes. She gazed at the drawn sword of the man standing beside the cannon and knew that if Glenn ever found out what she was doing then her fate would be as sure as the South's was to the North.

The man at the corner service station, wearing greasy coveralls and a friendly smile, gave her directions to Simon Canfield's home. Maggie drove onto the highway past the truck stop, as instructed. She would have missed the turnoff from the highway if she hadn't been watching for it. The tires kicked up gravel as the car wound its way along the curved driveway, and she slowed to a crawl, studying the long, rambling house. Somehow, having Angie live in an ordinary house was incongruous with the mental image Maggie had conjured up. Angie should live in a castle with knights fighting to protect and serve her.

A sleek black dog was alert and barking from the front step, and Maggie hesitated before getting out of the car. She wasn't fond of angry dogs, but she'd come too far to be put off by a loud bark. Cautiously, she opened the car door and stepped out, pressing her back against the side of the compact vehicle as she inched forward.

"Prince. Quiet." The dark-haired woman wearing a maternity top opened the back door and stepped onto the porch.

Instantly, the dog went silent, and Maggie's gaze was riveted to the woman. Maggie stood, stunned. The photos hadn't done Angie's beauty justice. No woman had the right to look that radiant, lovely, and serene. Angie was everything Glenn's silence had implied—and more. Her face glowed with her happiness, although she wasn't smiling now, but was regarding Maggie curiously. Maggie had been prepared to feel antagonistic toward her, and was shocked to realize that disliking the woman would be impossible.

"Can I help you?" Angie called from the top step, holding the dog by the collar.

All Maggie's energy went toward moving her head in a simple nod. Angie's voice was soft and lilting, with an engaging southern drawl. She appeared to be several months pregnant.

"Bob phoned and said a woman had stopped in and asked directions to the house."

Apparently, Bob was the man at the gas station. Putting on a plastic smile, Maggie took a step forward. "I'm Maggie Lambert."

"Are you related to Glenn?"

Again, it was all Maggie could do to nod.

"I didn't know Glenn had any sisters."

Forcing herself to maintain an air of calm, Maggie met the gentle gaze of the woman whom Glenn had loved so fiercely. "He doesn't. I'm his wife."

If Angie was surprised, she did an admirable job of not showing it. "Please, won't you come inside?"

After traveling so far, devising the plan behind her husband's back, and, worse, following through with it—Maggie stood cemented to the spot. After all that, without allowing anything to dissuade her from her idea, she was suddenly amazed at the audacity of her actions. Wild uncertainty, fear, and unhappiness all collided into one another in her bemused mind until she was unable to move, struck by one thought: *It was wrong for me to have come here.*

"Maggie?" Angie moved down the steps with the dog loyally traipsing behind. "Are you all right?"

Maggie tasted regret at the gentleness in Angie's eyes. No wonder Glenn loved her so much, she thought. This wasn't a mere woman. Maggie hadn't known what to expect, but it hadn't been this. Angie was the type of woman a man yearned to love and protect. More disturbing to Maggie was the innate knowledge that Angie's inner beauty far surpassed any outer loveliness. And she was gorgeous. Not in the way the fashion models portrayed beauty, with sleek bodies and gaudy cosmetics. Angie was soft and gentle and sweet—a Madonna. All of this flashed through Maggie's mind in the brief moment it took for Angie to reach her.

"Are you feeling ill?" Angie asked, placing a hand on Maggie's shoulder.

"I . . . I don't think so."

"Here," she said softly, leading her toward the house. "Come inside and I'll give you a glass of water. You look as if you're about to faint."

Maggie felt that a strong gust of wind would have

blown her over. Mechanically, she allowed Angie to direct her through the back door and into the kitchen. Angie pulled out a chair at the table and Maggie sank into it, feeling more wretched than she had ever felt in her life. Tears were perilously close, and she shut her eyes in an effort to forestall them. Maggie could hear Angie scurrying around for a glass of water.

She brought it to the table and sat across from Maggie. "Should I call the doctor? You're so pale."

"No, I . . . I'm fine. I apologize for putting you to all this trouble." Her wavering voice gained stability as she opened her dry eyes.

A few awkward seconds passed before Angie spoke. "I'm pleased that Glenn married. He's a good man."

Maggie nodded. Everything she had wanted to say had been set in her mind, but all her well-thought-out questions had vanished.

"How long have you been married?" Angie broached the subject carefully.

"Five weeks." Holding the water glass gave Maggie something to do with her hands.

"Glenn must have told you about me?"

"No." Maggie took a sip of water. The cool liquid helped relieve the parched feeling in her throat. "He won't talk about you. He's married to me, but he's still in love with you."

A sad smile touched the expressive dark eyes as Angie straightened in the chair. "How well do you know Glenn?"

"We grew up together," Maggie said. "I . . . I thought I knew him, but I realize now that I don't."

"Do you love him?" Angie asked, then offered Maggie

a faint smile of apology. "Forgive me for even asking. You must. Otherwise you wouldn't be here."

"Yes, I love him." Words felt inadequate to express her feelings for her husband. "But that love is hurting me because I don't know how to help him forget you. He won't talk about what happened."

"Of course he wouldn't," Angie said with a sweet, melodic laugh. "His pride's at stake, and, as I recall, Glenn is a proud man."

"Very."

The dark eyes twinkled with encouragement. "First, let me assure you that Glenn isn't in love with me."

Maggie opened her mouth to contradict her, but Angie cut her off by shaking her head.

"He isn't, not really," Angie continued. "Oh, he may think he is, but I doubt that. For one thing, Glenn would never marry a woman without loving her. He holds his vows too sacred. He could have married me a hundred times after I first saw Simon again, but he wouldn't. Glenn was wise enough to recognize that if we did marry I would always wonder about Simon. Glenn's a gambler, and he gambled on my love. At the time, I don't think I realized what it must have cost him to give me the freedom to choose between the two of them."

"You mean you would have married Glenn?"

"At the drop of a hat," Angie assured her. "Glenn Lambert was the best thing to come into my life for twelve years, and I knew it. I cared deeply for him, too, but that wasn't good enough for Glenn. He wanted me to settle my past, and heal all the old wounds before we made a life together. It was Glenn who led me by the hand back to the most difficult days of my life. Glenn's love gave me back Simon, and I'll always be grateful to him for that. Both Simon and I will. We realize how dearly it cost Glenn to step aside so I could marry Simon."

Maggie grimaced at Angie's affirmation of love for Glenn and briefly closed her eyes to the pain. So this was the sacrifice Angie had mentioned in the letter.

"Knowing this, Maggie, you couldn't possibly believe that Glenn would take his vows lightly."

She made it all sound so reasonable and sure, Maggie thought uncertainly. "But . . . but if he was so strongly convinced that you should settle your past, then why is he leaving his own open like a festering wound?"

"Pride." There wasn't even a trace of hesitation in Angie's voice. "I doubt that Glenn continues to have any deep feelings for me. What happened between us is a painful time in his life he'd prefer to forget. Be patient with him."

Maggie realized that she had rammed heads with Glenn's pride when she'd asked him to tell her about Angie. His indomitable spirit had been challenged, and admitting any part of his pain to her went against the grain of his personality. Logically, knowing Glenn, it made sense.

"Glenn deserves a woman who will give him all the love he craves," Angie continued. "I could never have loved him like that. But he's found what he needs in you. Be good to him, Maggie, he needs you."

They talked nonstop for two hours, sometimes laughing, other times crying. Angie told Maggie of her own love story with Simon and their hopes and dreams for the child she carried. When it came time for Maggie to leave,

Angie followed her to the airport and hugged her before she boarded her flight.

"You're a special lady, Maggie Lambert," Angie stated with conviction. "I'm confident Glenn realizes that. If he doesn't, then he's not the same man I remember."

Impulsively, Maggie hugged Angie back. "I'll write once we've settled. Let me know when you have the baby."

"I will. Take care now, you hear?"

"Thank you, Angie, thank you so much. For everything."

Maggie's throat filled with emotion. There were so many things she wanted to say. Glenn had given Angie her Simon, and in return Maggie now had Glenn. She could leave now and there would no longer be any doubts to plague her. Angie would always be someone special in Glenn's life, and Maggie wouldn't begrudge him that. She would leave him with his memories intact, and never mention her name. Angie was no longer a threat to their happiness. Maggie understood the past and was content to leave it undisturbed.

The flight from Groves Point to Atlanta and the connection from Atlanta to San Francisco went surprisingly well. Although before Maggie would have worried that each mile took her farther from Glenn, she didn't view the trip in those terms anymore. She was in love with her husband, and the minute she touched down in San Francisco she planned to let him know her feelings.

A smile beamed from her contented face when she landed in the city of her birth. She took a taxi directly to the beach house, set her bags in the entryway, and headed for the kitchen and the phone. She had to talk to Glenn; she burned with the need to tell him of her love. In some ways she was concerned. There was a better time and place, but she couldn't wait a second more.

His phone rang, and she glanced at the clock. With the time difference between the East and the West Coast, it was well after midnight in Charleston. Discouraged, she fingered the opening of her silk blouse, wondering if she should hang it up and wait until morning.

Glenn answered on the second ring. "Maggie?" The anger in his voice was like a bucket of cold water dumped over her head, sobering her instantly. Somehow, he had found out that she'd gone to Groves Point and talked to Angie.

"Yes," she returned meekly.

"Where the hell have you been? I've been half out of my mind worrying about you. Your flight landed four hours ago. Why did you have to wait so long to call me? You must have known I was waiting to hear from you." The anger in his voice had lessened, diluted with relief from his worries.

Maggie sagged with relief onto the bar stool positioned by the phone. He didn't know. "To be honest, I wasn't sure if you wanted me to phone or not."

"Not phone?" He sounded shocked. "All I can say is that it's a good thing you did." His voice grew loud and slightly husky. "It's like a tomb around here without you."

Maggie tried to suppress the happiness that made her want to laugh. *He missed her.* He was miserable without her and she hadn't even been away twenty-four hours.

"Whose idea was it for you to leave early, anyway?"

"Mine," she admitted ruefully. "But who agreed and said I should?"

"A fool, that's who. Believe me, it won't happen again. We belong together, Maggie." He made the concession willingly.

From the moment she had left that morning, he'd been filled with regrets. He should never have let her go, he had realized. He'd tried phoning an hour after her plane touched ground in California. At first it didn't bother him that she didn't answer her cell and when he tried the house, she didn't pick up there either. He figured she'd probably gone to Denny's, Glenn assured himself earlier. Later, when he hadn't been able to get hold of her, Glenn assumed she had unplugged the phone and taken a nap. After a time his worry had grown to alarm, and from alarm to near panic. If she hadn't called him when she did—he hadn't been teasing—he would well have gone stir crazy. His feelings were unreasonable, Glenn knew that. His reaction was probably part of his lingering fear that he'd lose Maggie, he rationalized. But there was no denying it: The past few hours had been miserable.

Glenn said they belonged together with such meaning that it took a moment before Maggie could speak. "Glenn," she finally whispered, surprised at how low her voice dropped. "There's something you should know, something I should have told you long before now."

"Yes?" His voice didn't sound any more confident than her own.

"I love you, Glenn. I don't know when it happened, I can't put a time to it. But it's true. It probably embarrasses you to have me tell you like this; there are better times and places—"

"Maggie." He interrupted her with a gentle laugh. "You don't need to tell me that, I already know."

"You know?" All these weeks she'd kept her emotions bottled up inside, afraid to reveal how she felt—and he'd known!

"Maggie, it was all too obvious. You're an artist, remember? You don't do a good job of hiding your emotions."

"I see." She swallowed down the bitter disappointment. Although eager to tell him of her feelings, she had wondered how he'd react. In her mind, she had pictured a wildly romantic scene in which he'd tenderly admit his own feelings. Instead, Glenn acted as if she were discussing the weather.

"Well, listen, it's late here, too, I think I'll go to bed." She tried to make her voice light and airy, but a soft sob escaped and she bit into her lower lip to hold back another.

"Maggie, what's wrong?"

"Nothing. I'll talk to you tomorrow. Maybe. There's lots to do, and—"

"Maggie, stop. You're crying. You never cry. I want to know why. What did I say?"

The insensitive boor, she silently fumed—if he couldn't figure it out, she wasn't going to tell him. "Nothing," she choked out in reply. "It doesn't matter. Okay?"

"No, it's not all right. Tell me what's wrong."

Maggie pretended she didn't hear. "I'll phone tomorrow night."

"Maggie," he shouted. "Either you tell me what's wrong or I'm going to become violent."

"Nothing's wrong." Her heart was breaking. She'd

just told her husband she loved him for the first time, and he'd practically yawned in her face.

"Listen, we're both tired. I'll talk to you tomorrow," she finished. Before he could argue, she gently replaced the receiver. The phone rang again almost immediately, and Maggie simply unplugged it, refusing to talk to Glenn again that night. For a full five minutes she didn't move. She had left Atlanta with such high expectations, confident that she could create a wonderful life with Glenn. There was enough love in her heart to build any bridge necessary in their marriage. A half hour after landing in San Francisco, she was miserable and in tears.

Maggie slept late, waking around eleven the next morning. She felt restless and desolate. Early that afternoon, she forced herself to dress and deal with her mail. By evening her desk was cleared and she phoned Denny. She was half-tempted to paint, but realized it would be useless with her mind in turmoil. Glenn would be furious with her for disconnecting the phone, and she had yet to deal with him. He might not have appreciated her actions, but it was better than saying things she was sure to regret later.

By early evening she had worked up her courage enough to dial his number. When he didn't answer, she wasn't concerned. He was probably at the health club, she thought. An hour later she tried phoning again. By ten, Pacific Coast time, she was feeling discouraged. Where was he? She toyed with the idea of phoning his family and casually inquiring, but she didn't want to alarm them.

A noise in the front of the house alerted her to the fact

that someone was at the door. She left her office and was halfway into the living room when she discovered Glenn standing in the entryway, setting his suitcases on the floor.

He straightened just in time to see her. Time went still as he covered the short space between them and reached for her, crushing her in his arms. "You crazy fool. If you'd given me half a chance I would have told you how much I love you."

"You love me?"

"Yes," he whispered into her hair.

With a smothered moan of delight, Maggie twined her arms around his neck and was lifted off the floor as his mouth came down hungrily on hers.

Chapter 10

"Why didn't you say something earlier?" Maggie cried, and covered Glenn's face with eager kisses, locking her arms around his neck.

"Why didn't you?" She was lifted half off the ground so that their gazes were level, his arms wrapped around her waist.

Maggie could hardly believe he was with her, and she stared at him in silent wonder, still afraid it could all be part of some fanciful dream. She couldn't very well admit that it had been her conversation with Angie that had convinced her that Glenn needed to know what was in her heart. The time had come to quit playing games with each other. The shock had come when he'd already known how she felt. Well, what did she expect? She'd never been good at disguising her feelings, and something as important as love shouldn't be concealed.

"I take it you're pleased to see me?"

Happiness sparkled from her eyes as she raised her hands and lovingly traced the contours of his face. "Very."

His hold on her tightened. He hadn't slept in thirty hours. The first ten of those hours had been spent in complete frustration. He had tried countless times to get her to answer the cell until he realized she must have turned it off. The only thing that made sense was that she'd turned it off for the flight and then forgot to turn it back on, which was why he'd tried the house countless times. He needed to talk to her; to explain his reaction to her confession of loving him. It wasn't a surprise. He'd known almost from the first even if she hadn't verbalized her feelings. He'd been at a total loss to understand why she'd resorted to tears. He relived every word of their conversation and as far as he could see she was behaving like a lunatic. She announced she loved him and immediately shocked him by breaking into sobs. Maggie wasn't a crier. Several times in the first weeks of their marriage he would have expected a lot more than tears from her. He'd certainly given her enough reason. But Maggie had proudly held up her head, unwilling to relinquish a whit of her pride.

With startling clarity it had come to him in the early-morning hours. Maggie had expected him to declare his own love. What an idiot he'd been. Of course he loved her. He didn't know why she could ever question it. He had realized he felt something profound for Maggie the minute she had walked down the aisle at Steve and Janelle's wedding. She'd been vulnerable, proud, and so lovely that Glenn went weak with the memory. He had originally assumed that his friends' wedding followed the lowest point of his life, but one look at Maggie and he'd nearly been blown over. She'd lived next door to him for most of his life and he'd blithely gone on his way not recognizing what was before his own eyes.

Maggie shared his name and his devotion, and, God

willing, later she would bear his children. How could she possibly think he didn't love her? Just as amazing was the knowledge that he'd never told her. Glenn was astonished at his own stupidity. He would phone her as soon as she would talk to him, he had decided, and never again in her life would he give her reason to doubt.

In theory, Glenn felt, his plan sounded reasonable, but as the hours fled, and a rosy dawn dappled the horizon, he began to worry. In her frame of mind, Maggie might consider doing something stupid.

The first thing the following morning, Glenn decided not to jeopardize this marriage more than he had already. He would fly to Maggie on the first plane he could catch. When he tried phoning several times, and there wasn't any answer, he fretted all the more. For caring as much as he did he'd done a good job of messing things up.

Now that he was looking at her face flushed with a brilliant happiness, Glenn realized he'd done the right thing.

"Do you have to go back?"

"I probably should, but I won't." Her smile was solidly in place, he noticed. He adored that smile. "I don't deserve you, Maggie."

"I know."

Tipping back her head, she laughed, and his heart was warmed by the sound. Maggie made his heart sing. Being around her was like lying on a sunny beach on a glorious day and soaking up energy. She was all warmth and vitality, both springtime and Christmas, and he couldn't imagine his life without her. Twisting her around in his embrace, he supported her with an arm under her legs and carried her down the long hall that led to the master bedroom.

"My dear Mr. Lambert, just where are you taking me?"

"Can't you guess?"

"Oh yes," she said, and her lips brushed his, enjoying the instant reaction she felt from him when her tongue made lazy, wet circles outlining his mouth.

"Maggie," he groaned. "You're going to pay for that."

"I'm looking forward to it. Very forward."

She couldn't undress fast enough. When Maggie's fingers fumbled with the buttons of her blouse in her eagerness, Glenn stopped her, placing her hand aside. Slowly, provocatively, he unfastened each one. As the new area of her skin was exposed, Glenn's finger lovingly trailed over the perfection until he finally slipped the smooth material of her blouse from her shoulders and down her arms, letting it fall to the carpet.

Maggie felt an exhilarating sense of power at the awe reflected in her husband's eyes. Impatience played no role in their lovemaking. Glenn had taught her the importance of self-control. The excruciating wait seemed only to enhance their pleasure; the disciplined pauses heightened their eagerness. Maggie was a willing pupil.

As if he couldn't deny himself a second longer, Glenn wrapped her in his arms and in one sweeping motion buried her mouth with his.

What had begun with impatient eagerness slowed to a breathless anticipation. When they moved, it was with one accord. They broke apart and finished undressing, then lay together on the thick, soft quilt.

"I love you," she whispered, raising her arms up to bring him to herself. "Please love me," she cried, surprised to hear her own voice.

"I do," Glenn breathed. "Always."

Afterward, blissfully content, Maggie spread eager kisses over his face. Briefly, she wondered if this exhilaration, this heartfelt elation, would always stay with them. She wondered if twenty years from now she would still experience a thrill when Glenn made love to her. Somehow, Maggie doubted that this aspect of their marriage would ever change.

Glenn shifted positions so that Maggie was lovingly cradled in his arms, and his fingers lightly stroked the length of her arm. Her fingers played at his chest, curling the fine, dark hairs that were abundant there. A feeling of overpowering tenderness rocked him. He reveled in the emotion of loving and being loved, and knew what they shared would last forever. He was tired, more than tired—exhausted. He looked down and discovered Maggie asleep in his arms. Everything was going to work out, he thought sleepily. He wasn't going to lose her. . . . Slowly, his eyes drifted closed. . . . Maggie was his.

The following morning, Maggie woke and studied her husband as he slept. A trace of a smile curved his mouth and her heart thrilled with the knowledge that she had placed it there. He must have been worried, terribly worried, she thought, to have dropped everything and flown to her. Surely, he couldn't believe that she'd ever leave him. A woman didn't love as strongly as she did and surrender without doing battle.

Glenn's arrival had proved that Angie was right. . . .

Glenn took his vows far too seriously to have married her or anyone when he was in love with another woman.

Maggie didn't know what Glenn felt for the other woman anymore, but it wasn't love. Utterly content, she silently slipped from the bed and dressed, eager for the new day.

Glenn woke with a smile as Maggie's lips brushed his in a feather-light kiss. "Morning," he whispered, reaching up to wrap his arms around her waist.

"Morning," she returned brightly. "I wondered how long it'd take for you to join the living."

Glenn eased upright, using his elbow for support. "What time is it?"

"Noon."

"Noon!" he cried, rubbing the sleep from his face as he came fully upright. "Good grief, why didn't you wake me?"

Giggling, Maggie sat on the edge of the mattress and looped her arms around his strong neck. "I just did."

"You've been painting," he said, noticing that Maggie was in her smock.

"It felt good to get back to it. Charleston was wonderful, but it's great to be home and back into my regular schedule."

A light knock against the bedroom door attracted Maggie's attention. "Phone for you, Maggie," Rosa, the older Hispanic woman who was Maggie's housekeeper and cook, announced from the other side. "It's your brother."

"Tell him I'll be right there," Maggie said, and planted a tender kiss on Glenn's forehead. "Unfortunately, duty calls."

"Maggie." Glenn's hand reached for her wrist, stopping her. His eyes were questioning her as though he didn't like the idea of releasing her even to her own brother. "Never mind."

"I shouldn't be more than a few minutes. Do you want to wait for me here?"

He shook his head, already tossing aside the blankets as he climbed from the bed. "I'll be out of the shower by the time you've finished."

True to his word, Glenn leaned his hip against the kitchen counter, sipping coffee and chatting easily to Rosa when Maggie reappeared.

"I see that you two have introduced yourselves," Maggie said, sliding her arms around Glenn's waist.

"Sí," Rosa said with a nod, her dark eyes gleaming. "You marry good man. You have lots of healthy *muchachos.*"

Maggie agreed with a broad grin, turning her eyes to her husband. "Rosa is going to teach me to cook, isn't that right?"

"*Sí*. Every wife needs to know how to make her man happy," Rosa insisted as she went about cleaning the kitchen. "I teach Maggie everything."

"Not quite everything," Glenn whispered near Maggie's ear, mussing the tiny curls that grew at her temple. "In fact, you wouldn't even need to go near a kitchen to keep me happy."

"Glenn," she whispered, hiding a giggle. "Quiet, or Rosa will wonder."

"Let her." His hold tightened as the housekeeper proceeded to chatter happily in a mixture of Spanish and English, scrubbing down already spotless counters as she spoke.

The lazy November day was marvelous. They took a dip in the heated pool and splashed and dunked each other like feisty teenagers at a beach party. Later, as they dried out in the sauna, Glenn carefully broached the subject of Maggie's brother.

"What did Denny want?"

"Yes. He and Linda have invited us to Thanksgiving dinner. I didn't think you'd mind if I accepted."

"That'll be fine. How's Denny doing?"

Maggie wiped a thick layer of perspiration from her cheeks using both hands, biding her time while she formed her thoughts. "Fine. What makes you ask?"

"He seems to call often enough. Didn't you get a couple of calls from him when we were in Charleston?"

"Yes. He's been through some rough times lately."

"How rough?"

Wrapping the towel around her neck, Maggie stood and paced the small enclosure while the heavy heat pounded in around her. "As you probably know, Denny and my parents inherited a portion of Great-aunt Margaret's money. Denny made some bad investment choices."

"What happened?" As a stockbroker, Glenn felt his curiosity piqued.

"It's a long, involved story not worth repeating. Simply put, Denny invested heavily in what he felt would be a good investment, trusting friends he shouldn't have trusted and lost everything. The case is being decided in the courts now, but it looks like he'll only get a dime back on every dollar invested."

"So you're bailing him out?" The statement was loaded with censure.

Maggie had to bite her tongue to keep from lashing

out at Glenn for being so insensitive. He should know that litigation and lawyers were expensive. She was only doing what any sister would do in similar circumstances. "Listen, what's between my brother and me is private. You don't want to talk about certain things in your life, and I don't, either. We're both entitled to that."

"Don't you think you're being overly defensive?"

Maggie looked at him sharply. "So what? Denny's my brother. I'll give him money any time I please."

Glenn was taken back by her bluntness. "Fine." He wouldn't bring up the subject again . . . at least not for a while.

Thanksgiving arrived, and Maggie's parents flew out from Florida. The elder Kingsburys had reacted with the same pleased surprise as Glenn's family had when Maggie phoned to announce that she and Glenn had married. The gathering at Denny and Linda's was a spirited but happy one. Neither of Maggie's parents mentioned how brief her and Glenn's courtship had been, nor that they were shocked at the suddenness of the ceremony. The questions were in their eyes, but Maggie was so radiantly happy that no one voiced any doubts.

The traditional turkey was placed in the oven to be ready to serve at the end of the San Francisco 49ers football game. They ate until they were stuffed, played cards, ate again, and watched an old movie on television until Maggie yawned and Glenn suggested they head home. The day had been wonderful, and Maggie looked forward to Christmas for the first time since moving to the beach house.

Glenn's days were filled. He started work at Lindsey & McNaught Brokerage the Monday after his arrival in San Francisco, and continued to work long hours to build up his clientele. More often than not, it was well past seven before he arrived home. Maggie didn't mind the hours Glenn put in away from home. She understood his need to secure his position with the company branch. The competition was stiff, and as a new boy on the block, the odds were against him.

"How are things going at the office?" she asked him one evening the first week of December.

"Fine," he responded absently as he sorted through the mail. "How about a game of tennis? I need to work out some of my frustrations."

"Everything's fine at the office, but you want to use me as a whipping boy?" she joked lovingly.

Glenn raised his gaze to hers and met the teasing glimmer mingled with truth in her eyes.

"Are you sorry we're here?" she asked, on a tentative note. In Charleston, Glenn had held more than a hundred million dollars in assets for his firm, a figure that was impressive enough for him to have quickly worked his way into a managerial position. In San Francisco, he was struggling to get his name out and establish himself with new clients. Some of his previous ones had opted to stay with him but others had decided to remain with the same brokerage. From the hours he was putting in during the day and several long evenings, the task must be a formidable one.

"I'm not the least bit sorry we're living in San Francisco," he said. "Where you and I are concerned, I have no regrets. Now," he added, releasing a slow breath, "are we going to play tennis or stand here and chat?"

Just as he finished speaking, the telephone rang. "Saved by the bell," Maggie mumbled as she moved across the room to answer it. "Hello."

"Hi, Maggie," Denny said in the low, almost whiny voice she had come to know well.

"Hi. What's up?" She didn't want to encourage Denny to drag out the conversation when Glenn was in the room. Denny was a subject they avoided. She knew her husband disapproved of her handing over large sums of money to her brother, but she didn't know what else she could do—Denny needed her. The money wasn't doing her any good, and if she could help her only brother, then why not?

The argument was one Maggie had waged with herself countless times. As long as she was available to lean on, the opposing argument went, then Denny would be content to do exactly that. He hadn't accomplished anything worthwhile in months. From conversations with her sister-in-law, Linda, Maggie had learned that Denny did little except decry his misfortune and plot ways of regaining his losses. Yet Maggie could understand his circumstances well enough to realize he was in an impossible position. He didn't like it, she didn't like it, but there was nothing that either of them could do until the court case was settled.

"I just wanted you to know that I'll be meeting with the lawyers tomorrow afternoon."

"Good luck," she murmured.

A silence followed. "What's the matter? Can't you talk now?"

"That about sizes up the situation." Glenn was studying her, and Maggie realized her stalling tactics weren't fooling him. He knew exactly whom she was talking to and did nothing to make the conversation any easier by leaving the room.

"Maybe I should phone you tomorrow," Denny suggested.

"That would be better." Maggie forced a carefree note into her tone. "I'll talk to you tomorrow, then."

"Okay." Denny sounded disappointed, but there wasn't anything Maggie could do. She wanted to avoid another confrontation with Glenn regarding her brother.

Replacing the receiver, she met her husband's gaze. "You said something about tennis?" Her voice was remarkably steady for all the turmoil going on inside her.

"You're not helping him, you know," Glenn said calmly. "All you've done to this point is teach him to come to you to solve his financial problems."

It was on the tip of her tongue to tell him that she was aware of that. She had seen it all herself, but she was caught in a vicious trap where her brother was concerned. "He needs me," she countered.

"He needs a job and some self-worth."

"I thought you were a stockbroker, not a psychologist."

Maggie could tell by the tightness in his jaw that she had angered Glenn. "Look, I'm sorry, I didn't mean to snap at you. Denny's in trouble. I can't let him down when he needs me the most. If you recall, I did ask you to stay out of it."

"Have it your way," he mumbled, and handed her a tennis racket.

Their game wasn't much of a contest. Glenn overpowered her easily in straight sets, making her work harder than ever. Maggie didn't know if he was venting his frustrations from the office or if he was angry because of Denny. It didn't matter; she was exhausted. By the time he'd finished showering, she was in bed half asleep. Glenn's pulling the covers over her shoulders and gently kissing the top of her head were the last things Maggie remembered.

With the approach of the Christmas holidays, Maggie felt a renewed sense of rightness. She was in love with her husband, they were together, and her world seemed in perfect balance. Glenn worked hard, and so did she, spending hours in her studio doing what she enjoyed most—painting. With her marriage, Maggie had discovered that there was a new depth to her art. She had once told Glenn that color was mood and brushwork emotion. Now, with Glenn's love, her brush painted bold strokes that revealed a maturity in her scenes that had been missing before their wedding. She was happy, truly happy, and it showed in ways she'd never expected.

Maggie didn't mention Glenn's grandmother's antique ring, confident that he'd gift her with it on Christmas morning. And she would react with the proper amount of surprised pleasure.

She wore her wedding ring continually now, even when she worked. Glenn glanced at her hand occasionally to be sure it was there. It was an odd quirk of his, but she didn't really mind. The ring meant as much to her as their marriage vows and that was all he wanted. They had come a long way from the night she'd arrived in Charleston.

For their first Christmas, Maggie wanted to buy Glenn a special gift, something that would show the depth of her love and appreciation for the good life they shared. But what? For days she mulled over the problem. She could give him one of her paintings for his office, but he had already asked her for one. She couldn't refuse him by telling him that that was what she planned to give him for Christmas. He took one of her seascapes and she was left without an idea. And she so wanted their first Christmas together to be special.

For the first time in years Maggie went Christmas shopping in stores. Usually, she ordered through the mail or over the Internet, but she feared missing the perfect gift that would please Glenn most. Janelle joined her one day, surprised at the changes in Maggie.

"What changes?"

"You're so happy," Janelle claimed.

"I really am, you know."

"I can tell. You positively glow with it."

The remark pleased Maggie so much she repeated it for Glenn later that evening.

"So you were out Christmas shopping. Did you buy me anything?"

How she wished. Nothing seemed special enough. She had viewed a hundred jewelry display cases, visited the most elite men's stores, and even gone to obscure bookstores, seeking rare volumes of Glenn's favorite novels. A sense of panic was beginning to fill her.

"You'll have to wait until Christmas morning to find out," she told him, coyly batting her long lashes.

With so many relatives on their list, Glenn and Maggie were in and out of more department stores the following Saturday than Maggie cared to count. Soft music filled the stores and bells chimed on the street corners, reminding them to be generous to those less fortunate. The crowds were heavy, but everyone seemed to expect that and took the long waits at the cash registers in stride.

While Maggie stood in line buying a toy farm set for Glenn's nephew, Glenn wandered over to the furniture department. Lovingly, Maggie's gaze followed him as he looked over cherrywood bookcases in a rich, deep-red color. Bookcases? Glenn wanted something as simple as bookcases? Maggie couldn't believe it. After days of looking at the latest gadgets and solid-gold toys, she stared in disbelief that he could be interested in something as simple as this. When the salesman approached, Glenn asked several questions and ran his hand over the polished surface.

"Did you see something?" she asked conversationally when he returned to her side. He wanted those bookcases, but she doubted that he'd mention it to her.

"Not really," he replied, but Maggie noted the way his gaze returned and lingered over the cases.

Maggie's heartbeat raced with excitement. At the first opportunity, she'd return and buy Glenn those bookcases.

"You're looking pleased about something," Glenn commented over dinner Wednesday evening.

His comment caught her off guard, and she lightly shook her head. "Sorry, I was deep in thought. What did you say?"

"I could tell," he chided, chuckling. Standing, he carried his plate to the sink. "Do you want to talk about it, or is this some deep dark secret you're hiding from your husband?"

"Some deep dark secret."

"What did you do today?" he asked, appreciating anew how beautiful his wife had become. She was a different woman from the one who'd met him at the airport months ago. He liked to think the changes in her were due to their marriage. He was different, too, and credited Maggie with his renewed sense of happiness.

"What did I do today?" Maggie repeated, her dark eyes rounding with shock. Swallowing back her unease, she cast her gaze to her plate. "Christmas cards." The truth nearly stuck in her throat. She had written Christmas cards, but in addition she had penned a long letter to Angie, thanking her for everything the other woman had shared the day of their brief visit. In the letter, Maggie told Angie how improved her marriage was now that she'd told Glenn how much she loved him, and was confident that he loved her in return.

As impractical as it sounded, Maggie would have liked to continue the friendship with Angie. Rarely had Maggie experienced such an immediate kinship with another woman. Impractical and illogical. Of all the people in the world, Maggie would have thought she'd despise Angie Canfield. But she didn't. Now, weeks later, Maggie felt the need to write the other woman and extend her appreciation for their afternoon together and to wish her and Simon the warmest of holiday greetings. The letter had been interrupted by Glenn's homecoming, and she had safely tucked it away from the other cards she kept on top of her desk.

"I still have several things that need to be done before Christmas," she said in order to hide her discomfort.

Glenn was silent for a moment. "You look guilty about something. I bet you went out shopping today and couldn't resist buying yourself something."

"I didn't!" she declared with a cheery laugh.

Later, in the den, when Glenn was looking over some figures, Maggie joined him. She sat in the chair opposite his desk. When Maggie glanced up she found her husband regarding her lazily with a masked expression, and she wondered at his thoughts.

On the other side of the desk, Glenn studied his wife, thinking that she was more beautiful that night than he ever remembered. Her eyes shone with a translucent happiness, and a familiar sensation tugged at his heart. Something was troubling her tonight . . . no, *troubling* was too strong a word. She was hiding something from him. Which was natural, he supposed. It was Christmastime, and she had probably cooked up some scheme for his gift, yet Glenn had the feeling this had nothing to do with Christmas.

Convinced he shouldn't go looking for trouble, he shook his mind free of the brooding sensation. Whatever it was probably involved Denny, and it was just as well that he didn't know. It would only anger him.

Glenn pushed back his chair and stood. "I'll be right back. I'm going to need a cup of coffee to keep these figures straight. Do you want one?"

Maggie glanced up from the book she was reading and

shook her head. The caffeine would keep her awake. "No thanks," she said as he left the room.

The phone rang, and Glenn called out that he'd answer it. The information didn't faze Maggie until she realized that he had probably gone into her office since the phone was closer there.

He returned a minute later, strolling into the room with deceptive casualness. "It's your leeching brother," he told her.

Chapter 11

"Glenn, what a nasty thing to say." Maggie couldn't help knowing that Glenn disapproved of the way she gave Denny money, but she hadn't expected him to be so blunt or openly rude. "I hope Denny didn't hear you," she murmured, coming to her feet. "He feels terrible about the way things have turned out."

"If he honestly felt that, he wouldn't continue to come running to you at every opportunity."

Straightening her shoulders to a military stiffness, Maggie marched from the room and picked up the telephone. "Hello, Denny."

A short silence followed. "Hi. I take it I should call back another time."

"No," she contradicted firmly. She wasn't going to let Glenn intimidate her out of speaking to her own brother. "I can talk now."

"I just wanted to tell you that my lawyer didn't have anything new to tell me regarding our case. It looks like this thing could be tied up in the courts for years. I'm telling you, Maggie, this whole mess is really getting me down."

"But you don't need to worry, I'm here to help you." she offered sympathetically.

"But Glenn—"

"What I do with my money is none of his concern." In her heart, Maggie knew that Glenn was right, but Glenn was a naturally strong person, and her brother wasn't to be blamed if he was weak. They had to make allowances for Denny, help him.

"You honestly mean that about helping, don't you?" Denny murmured, relief and appreciation brightening his voice.

"You know I do."

Ten minutes later, Maggie rejoined her husband. All kinds of different emotions were coming at her. She was angry with Glenn for being so unsympathetic to her brother's troubles, infuriated with Denny because he pushed all the right buttons with her, and filled with self-derision because she gave in to Denny without so much as a thoughtful pause. Denny had only to give his now familiar whine and she handed him a signed check.

"Well?" Glenn glanced up at her.

"Well what?"

"He asked for money, didn't he?"

"Yes," she snapped.

"And you're giving it to him?"

"I don't have much choice. Denny is my brother."

"But you're not helping him, Maggie, don't you see that?"

"No," she cried, and to her horror, tears welled in her eyes. It was so unlike her to cry over something so trivial that Maggie had trouble finding her breath, which caused her to weep all the louder.

Glenn stood and gently pulled her into his arms. "Maggie, what is it?"

"You . . . Denny . . . me." She sobbed and dramatically shook her hands. "This court case might take years to decide. He needs money. You don't want me to lend him any, and I'm caught right in the middle."

"Honey, listen." Glenn stood and gently placed his arms around her. "Will you do something for me?"

"Of course," she responded on a hiccuping sob. "What?"

"Call Denny back and tell him he can't have the money—"

"I can't do that," she objected, shaking his arms free. She hugged her waist and moved into the living room, where a small blaze burned in the fireplace. The warmth of the fire chased the chill from her arms.

"Hear me out," Glenn said, following her. "Have Denny give me a call at the office in the morning. If he needs money, I'll loan it to him."

Maggie was skeptical. "But why?"

"I don't want him troubling you anymore. I don't like what he's doing to you, and, worse, what he's doing to himself." He paused, letting her take in his offer. "Agreed?"

She offered him a watery smile and nodded.

With Glenn standing at her side, Maggie phoned Denny back and gave the phone over to her husband a few minutes later. Naturally, Denny didn't seem overly pleased with the prospect of having to go through Glenn, but he had no choice. Maggie should have been relieved that Glenn was handling the difficult situation, but she wasn't.

In the morning, Maggie woke feeling slightly sick to

her stomach. She lay in bed long after Glenn had left for the office, wondering if she could be pregnant. The tears the evening before had been uncharacteristic, and she'd had a terrible craving for Chinese food lately that was driving her crazy. For three days in a row she had eaten lunch in Chinatown. None of the symptoms on their own was enough for her to make the connection until this morning.

A smile formed as Maggie placed a hand on her flat stomach and slowly closed her eyes. A baby. Glenn would be so pleased. He'd be a wonderful father. She'd watched him with Denny's girls on Thanksgiving and had been astonished at his patience and gentleness. The ironic part was all these weeks she'd been frantically searching for just the right Christmas gift for Glenn, and all along she'd been nurturing his child in her womb. They both wanted children. Oh, she'd get him the bookcases he had admired, but she'd keep the gift he'd prize most a secret until Christmas morning.

Not wanting to be overconfident without a doctor's confirmation, Maggie made an appointment for that afternoon, and her condition was confirmed in a matter of minutes. Afterward, she was bursting with excitement. Her greatest problem would be keeping it from Glenn when she wanted to sing and dance with the knowledge.

When Maggie returned to the beach house, Rosa had left a message that Denny had phoned. Maggie returned his call immediately.

"How did everything go with Glenn?" she asked him brightly. Nothing would dim the brilliance of her good news, not even Denny's sullen voice.

"Fine, I guess."

"There isn't any problem with the money, is there?" Glenn wouldn't be so cruel as to refuse to make the loan when he'd assured her he'd help her brother. Maggie was confident he wouldn't do anything like that. Glenn understood the situation.

"Yes and no."

Her hand tightened around the receiver. "How do you mean? He's giving you the money, isn't he?"

"He's lending me the money, but he's got a bunch of papers he wants me to sign, and in addition he's set up a job interview for me. He actually wants me to go to work."

By the time Denny finished with his sorry tale, Maggie was so furious she could barely speak. Lending him the money, making him sign for it, a job interview. Glenn had told her he was going to help her brother. Instead, he was stripping Denny of what little pride he had left.

By the time Glenn arrived home that evening, he found Maggie pacing the floor. Sparks of anger flashed from her dark eyes as she spun around to face him.

"What's wrong? You're looking at me like I was Jack the Ripper."

"Did you honestly tell Denny that he couldn't borrow the money unless he got a job?" she said in accusation. Her hands were placed defiantly on her hips, challenging Glenn to contradict her.

Unhurriedly, Glenn removed his raincoat one arm at a time and hung it in the hall closet. "Is there something wrong with an honest day's toil?"

"It's humiliating to Denny. He's . . . accustomed to a certain lifestyle now . . . He can't lower himself to take a job like everyone else and—"

Maggie could tell by the way Glenn's eyes narrowed that he was struggling to maintain his own irritation. "I live in a fancy beach house with you and somehow manage to suffer the humiliation."

"Glenn," she cried. "It's different with Denny."

"How's that?"

Unable to remain still, Maggie continued to stalk the tiled entryway like a circus lion confined to a cage. "Don't you understand how degrading that would be to him?"

"No," Glenn returned starkly. "I can't. Denny made a mistake. Any fool knows better than to place the majority of his funds in one investment, no matter how secure it appears. The time has come for your brother to own up to the fact he made a serious mistake, and pay the consequences of his actions. I can't and won't allow him to sponge off you any longer, Maggie."

The tears sprang readily to the surface. Oh how she hated to cry. Hopefully she wouldn't be like this the entire pregnancy. "But don't you understand?" she blubbered, her words barely intelligible. "I inherited twice the money Denny did."

"And he's made you feel guilty about that."

"No," she shouted. "He's never said a word."

"He hasn't had to. You feel guilty enough about it, but, my love, trust me, Denny will feel better about you, about himself, about life in general. You can't give him the self-worth he needs by handing him a check every time he asks for it."

"You don't understand my brother," Maggie cried. "I can't let you do this to him. I . . . I told you once that I wanted you to stay out of this."

"Maggie—"

"No, you listen to me. I'm giving Denny the money he wants. I told him that he didn't need to sign anything, and he doesn't need to get a job. He's my brother, and I'm not going to turn my back on him. Understand?"

Silence crackled in the room like the deadly calm before an electrical storm. A muscle leaped in Glenn's jaw, twisting convulsively.

"If that's the way you want it." His voice was both tight and angry.

"It is," she whispered.

What Maggie didn't want was the silent treatment that followed. Glenn barely spoke to her the remainder of the evening, and when he did, his tone was barely civil. It was clear that Glenn considered her actions a personal affront. Maybe it looked that way to him, she reasoned, but she'd explained long ago that she preferred to handle her brother herself. Glenn had interfered, and now they were both miserable.

When morning arrived to lighten the dismal winter sky, Maggie rolled onto her back and stared at the ceiling, realizing she was alone. The oppressive gray light of those early hours invaded the bedroom and a heaviness settled onto Maggie's heart. She climbed from the bed and felt sick and dizzy once again, but her symptoms were more pronounced this morning. Her mouth felt like dry, scratchy cotton.

Glenn had already left for the office, and the only evidence of his presence was an empty coffee cup in the kitchen sink. Even Rosa looked at Maggie accusingly, and for one crazy instant Maggie wondered how the housekeeper knew that she and Glenn had argued. That was the crazy part—they hadn't really fought. Maybe if they had, the air would have been cleared.

The crossword puzzle didn't help occupy her mind, and Maggie sat at the kitchen table for an hour, drinking cup after cup of watered-down apple juice while sorting through her thoughts. With a hand rubbing her throbbing temple, Maggie tried to remember how Glenn had been as a youth when he was angry with someone. She couldn't recall that he had ever held a grudge or been furious with anyone for long. That was a good sign.

Tonight she'd talk to him, she decided, try to make him understand why she had to do this for Denny. If the situation was reversed and it was either of his brothers, Glenn would do exactly the same thing. Maggie was sure of it.

Because of the Christmas holidays, the stock market was traditionally slow, and Glenn had been home before six every night for the past week. He wasn't that night. Nor was he home at seven, or eight. He must be unbelievably angry, she thought, and a part of Maggie wondered if he'd ever be able to completely understand her actions. Apparently, he found it easier to blame her than to realize that he'd forced her into the situation. Maggie spent a miserable hour watching a television program she normally disliked.

The front door clicked open, and Maggie pivoted sharply in her chair, hoping Glenn's gaze would tell her that they'd talk and clear up the air between them.

Glenn shrugged off his coat and hung it in the hall closet. Without a word, he moved into his den and closed the door, leaving Maggie standing alone and miserable.

Desolate, she sat in the darkened living room and

waited. She hadn't eaten, couldn't sleep. Leaving the house was impossible, looking and feeling the way she did. Her only companion was constant anxiety and doubt. There wasn't anything she could do until Glenn was ready to talk.

When he reappeared, Maggie slowly came to her feet. Her throat felt thick and uncooperative. Her hands were clenched so tightly together that the blood flow to her fingers was restricted. "Would you like some dinner?" The question was inane when she wanted to tell him they were both being silly. Arguing over Denny was the last thing she wanted to do.

"I'm not hungry," he answered starkly, without looking at her. His features tightened.

Undaunted, Maggie asked: "Can we at least talk about this? I don't want to fight."

He ignored her and turned toward the hallway. "You said everything I needed to hear last night."

"Come on, Glenn, be reasonable," she shouted after him. "What do you want from me? Are you so insensitive that you can't see what an intolerable situation you placed me in?"

"I asked you to trust me with Denny."

"You were stripping him of his pride."

"I was trying to give it back to him," he flared back. "And speaking of intolerable positions, do you realize that's exactly what you've done to me?"

"You . . . How?"

"You've asked me to sit by and turn a blind eye while your brother bleeds you half to death. I'm your husband. It's my duty to protect you, but I can't do that when you won't let me, when you resent, contradict, and question my intention."

"Glenn, please," she pleaded softly. "I love you. I don't want to fight. Not over Denny—not over anything. It's Christmas, a time of peace and goodwill. Can't we please put this behind us?"

Glenn looked as weary as she felt. "It's a matter of trust, too, Maggie."

"I trust you completely."

"You don't," Glenn announced, and turned away from her, which only served to fuel Maggie's anger.

Maggie slept in the guest bedroom that night, praying Glenn would insist she share his bed. She didn't know what she had thought sleeping apart would accomplish. It took everything within Maggie not to swallow her considerable pride and return to the master bedroom. A part of her was dying a slow and painful death.

Maggie couldn't understand why Glenn was behaving like he was. Only once had he even raised his voice to her in all the weeks they'd been married. But now the tension stretched between the two bedrooms was so thick Maggie could have sliced it with a dull knife. Glenn was so disillusioned with her that even talking to her was more than he could tolerate. He wasn't punishing her with the silent treatment, Maggie realized. He was protecting her. If he spoke, it would be to vent his frustration and say things he'd later regret.

Instead of dwelling on the negative, Maggie recalled the wonderful love-filled nights when they had lain side by side and been unable to stay out of each other's arms. The instant the light was out, Glenn would reach for her with the urgency of a condemned man offered a last chance at life. And when he'd kissed her and loved her, Maggie felt as though she was the most precious being in the world. Glenn's world. He was a magnificent lover. She closed her eyes to the compelling images that crowded her mind, feeling sick at heart and thoroughly miserable.

In the other room, Glenn lay on his back staring at the ceiling. The dark void of night surrounded him. The sharp edges of his anger had dulled, but the bitterness that had consumed him earlier had yet to fade. In all his life he had never been more disappointed and more hurt—yes, hurt—that his wife couldn't trust him to handle a delicate situation and protect her. He wasn't out to get Denny; he sincerely wanted to help the man.

Morning arrived, and Maggie couldn't remember sleeping, although she must have closed her eyes sometime during the long, tedious night. The alarm rang, and she heard Glenn stirring in the other room.

While he dressed, Maggie moved into the kitchen and put on coffee. Ten minutes later, he joined her in the spacious room and hesitated, his gaze falling to her wide, sad eyes. Purposely he looked away. There was no getting around it. He had missed sleeping with his wife. A hundred times he had had to stop himself from going into the bedroom and bringing her back to his bed where she belonged.

Now she stood not three feet from him in a sexy gown, and his senses were filled with her. He should be aware of the freshly brewed coffee, but he discovered the elusive perfumed scent of Maggie instead. Silently, he poured himself a cup of coffee and pulled out a kitchen chair. He tried to concentrate on something other than his wife. He reached for the newspaper and focused his attention on that. But mentally his thoughts were involved in this no-win situation between him and her bloodsucking brother. When he'd learned exactly how much money Denny had borrowed he'd been incensed. This madness had to stop and soon or he'd bleed Maggie dry.

Sensing Glenn's thoughts, Maggie moved closer, wanting to resolve the issue, yet unsure how best to approach a subject that felt like a ticking time bomb.

Propping up the newspaper against the napkin holder, Glenn hid behind the front page, not wanting to look at Maggie. Yet he struggled to keep his eyes trained on the front page headlines.

"Will you be home for dinner?" Maggie forced the question out. Leaning against the kitchen counter, her fingers bit into the marble surface as she waited for his answer.

"I've been home every night since we've been married. Why should tonight be different?"

Maggie had only been trying to make idle conversation and break down the ice shield positioned between them. "No reason," she murmured, and turned back to the stove.

A few minutes later, Glenn left for the office with little more than a casual farewell.

By noon Maggie was convinced she couldn't spend another day locked inside the confines of the beach house. Even the studio that had been her pride now became her torture chamber. One more hour dealing with this madness and she'd go stir-crazy.

Aimlessly, she wandered from room to room, seeking confirmation that she had done the right thing by Denny and finding none. She took a long, uninterrupted walk along the beach, where gusts of ocean air carelessly whipped her hair across her face and lightened her mood perceptibly. Christmas was only a week away, and there were a hundred things she should be doing. But Maggie hadn't the heart for even one.

Recently, she had been filled with such high expectations for this marriage. Now she realized how naïve she'd been. She had always thought that love conquered all. What a farce that was. She had been unhappy before marrying Glenn; now she was in love, pregnant, and utterly miserable. And why? Because she'd stood by her brother when he needed her. It hardly seemed fair.

A light drizzle began to fall, and she walked until her face felt numb with cold. She trekked up to the house, fixed herself something hot to drink, and decided to go for a drive.

The ride into the city was sluggish, due to heavy traffic. She parked on the outskirts of Fisherman's Wharf and took a stroll. A multitude of shops and touristy places had sprung up since her last visit—but that had been years ago, she realized. She dropped into a few places and shopped around, finding nothing to buy. An art gallery caught her eye, and she paused to look in the window at the painting on display. A card tucked in the ornate frame revealed the name of the painting was *The Small Woman*. The artist had used a black line to outline the painting, like lead surrounding the panes in a stained-glass window. The colors were bold, the setting elaborate. The simple woman, however, was strangely frail and pathetic, detached from the setting as though she were a sacrifice to be offered to the gods in some primitive culture.

Examining the painting, Maggie saw herself in the tired woman and didn't like the reflection.

A blast of chilling wind whipped her coat around her legs, and to escape the unexpected cold, Maggie opened the glass door and entered the gallery. The room was deceptively large, with a wide variety of oil paintings, some watercolors, small sculptures, and other artworks in opulent display.

"Can I help you?"

Maggie turned toward the voice to find a tall, slender woman dressed in a plaid wool skirt and creamy white silk blouse. She appeared to be studying Maggie closely, causing Maggie to wonder at her appearance. The wind had played havoc with her hair and . . .

"Maggie?"

Maggie blinked twice. She didn't recognize the woman. "Pardon?"

"Are you Maggie Kingsbury?"

"Yes . . . my married name is Lambert. Do I know you?"

The woman's laugh was light and sweetly musical. "I'm Jan Baker Hammersmith. Don't you remember we attended—"

The name clicked instantly. "Jan Baker." The two had been casual friends when Maggie was attending art school. "I haven't seen you in years. The last I heard, you were married."

"I'm divorced now."

Maggie dropped her gaze, desperately afraid that she would be adding that identical phrase someday when meeting old friends. "I'm sorry to hear that."

"I am, too," Jan said with a heavy sadness. "But it was

for the best. Tell me, are you still painting?" Maggie noted how Jan quickly diverted the subject away from herself.

"Occasionally. Not as much since I married."

Jan strolled around the gallery with proud comfort. "I can still remember one of your paintings—a beach scene. The detail you'd put into it was marvelous. Whatever happened to that?"

"It's hanging in our living room."

"I can understand why you'd never want to sell that." Jan's eyes were sincere. "Rarely have I seen a painting with such vivid clarity and color."

"It would sell?" Maggie was surprised. Ridiculous as it seemed, she'd never tried to sell any of her paintings. There hadn't been any reason to try. She gave them away as gifts and to charities for auctions, but she didn't have any reason to sell them. She didn't need the money, and inwardly she feared they might not sell. Her artwork was for her own pleasure. The scenes painted by her brush had been the panacea for an empty life within the gilded cage.

"It'd sell in a minute," Jan stated confidently. "Do you think you'd consider letting the gallery represent you?"

Maggie hedged, uncertain. "Let me think about it."

"Do, Maggie, and get back to me. I have a customer I know who'd be interested in a painting similar to the beachscape, if you have one. Take my card." They spoke for several minutes more and Maggie described some of her other works. Again, Jan encouraged her to bring in a few of her canvases. Maggie noted that Jan didn't make any promises, which was reasonable.

Sometime later, Maggie returned to her car. Meeting Jan had been just the uplift she'd needed. Already her mind was buzzing with possibilities. There wasn't any reason she shouldn't sell her work.

Glenn's car was in the driveway when she returned and she pulled to a stop in front of the house and parked there. A glance at her watch told her that it was later than she suspected. Her spirits were lighter than at any time during the past two days, but she didn't hurry toward the house.

"Where have you been?" Glenn asked the minute she walked in the door. Not granting her the opportunity to respond, he continued. "You made an issue of asking me if I was going to be home for dinner and then you're gone."

Carelessly, Maggie tossed her coat over an armchair. "I lost track of the time," she explained on her way into the kitchen. Glenn was only a step behind. From the grim set of his mouth, Maggie recognized that once again she'd displeased him. Everything she'd done the past few days seemed to fuel his indignation.

He didn't say another word as she worked, dishing up the meal of baked pork chops and scalloped potatoes Rosa had prepared for them. Maggie could feel his gaze on her defeated shoulders, studying her. He looked for a moment as if he wanted to say something, but apparently changed his mind.

"I was in an art gallery today," she told him conversationally.

"Oh."

"I'm thinking of taking in some of my work."

"You should, Maggie."

Silence followed. This was the first time they'd had a

decent conversation since she'd sided with her brother against him.

Their dinner was awkward, each trying to find a way to put their marriage back on track. Glenn sat across from her, cheerless and somber. Neither ate much.

"Did the mail come?" Maggie asked, setting the dinner dishes aside.

"It's in your office," Glenn answered without looking up. "Would you like me to bring it in to you?"

"Please. I'll finish up here in a minute." Well, at least they were speaking to each other, she thought. It was a start. Together they'd work things out. The situation with Denny was probably the first of many disagreements and misunderstandings they would face through the years. It might take time, she told herself, but they'd work it out. They loved each other too much to allow anything to wedge a space between them for long. They had both behaved badly over this issue with Denny, but if she'd bend a little, Glenn would, too.

When Glenn returned to the living room, he said her name with such fervor that her head came up. Unconsciously, Maggie pressed farther back into the thick cushions of her chair, utterly stunned by the look that flashed from her husband's eyes. She could think of nothing that would cause him such anger.

"Explain this," he said, and thrust her letter to Angie in front of Maggie's shocked face.

Chapter 12

Maggie's mind was in complete turmoil. She'd known it was a risk to write Angie, and later had regretted it. She hadn't mailed the card. Yet she'd left the letter on top of her desk for Glenn to find. Perhaps subconsciously she had wanted him to discover what she'd done.

Tension shot along her nerves as she struggled to appear outwardly calm. Lifting the chatty letter Glenn handed her, she examined it as if seeing it for the first time, amazed at her detachment. Whatever she wished, consciously or subconsciously, Glenn had found it and the timing couldn't be worse. They were just coming to terms with one major disagreement and were about to come to loggerheads over another. Only this issue was potentially far more dangerous to the security of their marriage. Going behind Glenn's back had never felt right. Maggie had regretted her deception a hundred times since. And yet it had been necessary. Long ago, Maggie had admitted that Glenn had forced her into the decisive action. She had asked him about Angie and he'd refused to discuss the other woman. Maggie was his wife and she loved him; she had a right to know. But all the rationalization in the world wasn't going to help now.

"How do you explain this?" His voice went deep and low, as though he couldn't believe what he'd found. Maggie hadn't trusted him to help her brother, he thought, somewhat dazed, and now he'd learned that she had betrayed his trust in another situation as well. Glenn knew he should be furious. Outraged. But he wasn't. His emotions were confused—he felt shocked, hurt, and discouraged. Guilt was penned all over Maggie's pale face as she sat looking up at him, trying to explain. There couldn't possibly be a plausible one. Not one. Feeling sick with defeat, he turned away from her.

Maggie's heartbeat quickened at the pained look in Glenn's dark eyes. "I met Angie."

"When?" he asked, still hardly able to comprehend what she was saying. He paced the area in front of her in clipped military-like steps as if standing in one place were intolerable.

Maggie had never seen any man's features more troubled. "The . . . the day I flew to San Francisco . . . I took a flight to Groves Point first and then flew from there to Atlanta before heading home."

If possible, Glenn went even more pale.

"I asked you to tell me about the two of you, but—" Maggie attempted to explain and was quickly cut off.

"How did you know where she lived?"

Admitting everything she had done made it sound all the more sordid and deceitful. She hesitated.

"How did you know where she lived?" he repeated, his rising voice cold and deliberate. Maggie was pressed as far back against the chair cushion as possible as dread settled firmly over her.

"I found her letter to you . . . and read it." She wouldn't minimize her wrongdoing. The letter had been addressed to him and she had purposely taken it from the envelope and read each word. It was wrong. She knew it was wrong, but given the opportunity, she would do exactly the same thing again.

Shocked, all Glenn seemed capable of doing was to stare back at her. She yearned to explain that she hadn't purposely searched through his drawers or snooped into his private matters. But she could see that expounding on what had happened wouldn't do any good. Reasoning with Glenn just then would be impossible. She felt wretched and sick to her stomach. The ache in her throat was complicated by the tears stinging her eyes. With everything in her, she struggled not to cry.

"What else did you try to find?" he asked. "How many drawers did you have to search through before you found the letter? Did you take delight in reading another woman's words to me? Is there anything you don't know?"

"It wasn't like that," she whispered, her gaze frozen in misery.

"I'll bet!" He moved to the other side of the living room. His anger died as quickly as it came, replaced by a resentment so keen he could barely stand to look at Maggie. She couldn't seem to let up on the subject of Angie. For months he had loved Maggie so completely that he was amazed that she could believe that he could possibly care for another woman. Worse, she had hounded the subject of Angie to death. It was a matter of trust, and she'd violated that and wounded his pride again and again.

"Are you satisfied now? Did you learn everything you were so keen to find out?" His voice was heavy with defeat. "You don't trust me or my love, do you, Maggie? You couldn't, to have done something this underhanded."

"That's not true," she cried. Glenn wanted to wound her; she understood that. She had hurt him when all she'd ever wanted to do was give him her love, bear his children, and build a good life with him. But their marriage had been clouded with the presence of another woman who stood between them as prominently as the Cascade mountain range. Or so it appeared at the time.

With a clarity of thought Glenn didn't realize he possessed, he knew he had to get out of the room . . . out of the house. He needed to sit down and do some serious thinking. Something was basically wrong in a relationship where one partner didn't trust the other. He loved Maggie and had spent the past few months trying to prove how much. Obviously, he'd failed. He crossed the living room and jerked his raincoat off the hanger.

"Where are you going?" Maggie asked in a pathetically weak voice.

He didn't even look at her. "Out."

Trapped in a nightmare, her actions made in slow motion, Maggie came to her feet. The Christmas card and letter were clenched in her hand. Glenn turned to look back at her, and his gaze fell to the brightly colored card. His mouth twisted into a scowl as he opened the door and left Maggie standing alone and heartbroken.

Maggie didn't allow the tears to escape until she was inside their bedroom with the door securely closed. Only then did she vent her misery. She wept bitter tears until she didn't think she could stop. Her throat ached and her sobs were dry; her eyes burned, and there were no more tears left to shed. She had hoped to build a firm foundation for this marriage and had ruined any chance. Glenn had every reason to be angry. She had deceived him, hurt him, invaded his privacy.

The room was dark and the night half spent when Glenn came to bed. His movements sounded heavy and vaguely out of order. The dresser drawer was jerked open, then almost immediately slammed shut. He stumbled over something and cursed impatiently under his breath as he staggered to the far side of the bedroom.

Remaining motionless, Maggie listened to his movements and was shocked to realize that he was drunk. Glenn had always been so sensible about alcohol. He rarely had more than one drink. Maggie bit into her lower lip as he jerked back the covers and fell onto the mattress. She braced herself, wondering what she'd do if he tried to make love to her. But either he was too drunk or he couldn't tolerate the thought of touching her.

She woke in the morning to the sounds of Glenn moving around the room. Her first thought was that she should pretend to be asleep until he'd left, but she couldn't bear to leave things unsettled any longer.

"Glenn," she spoke softly, rolling onto her back. At the sight of his suitcase she bolted upright. "Glenn," she said again, her voice shaking and urgent. "What are you doing?"

"Packing." His face, devoid of expression, told her nothing.

He didn't look at her. With an economy of movement,

he emptied one drawer into a suitcase and returned to the dresser for another armload.

Maggie was shocked into speechlessness.

"You're leaving me?" she finally choked out. He wouldn't . . . couldn't. Hadn't they agreed about the sanctity of marriage? Hadn't Glenn told her that he felt divorce was wrong and people should work things out no matter what their problems?

Glenn didn't answer her; apparently, his actions were enough for her to realize exactly what he was doing.

"Glenn," she said, her eyes pleading with him. "Please don't do this."

He paused midstride between the suitcase and the dresser. "Trust is vital in a relationship," he said, and laid a fresh layer of clothes on top of the open suitcase.

Maggie threw back the covers and crawled to the end of the mattress. "Will you stop talking in riddles, for heaven's sake? Of course trust is vital. This whole thing started because you didn't trust me enough to tell me about Angie."

"You knew everything you needed to know."

"I didn't," she cried. "I asked you to tell me about her and you refused."

"She had nothing to do with you and me."

"Oh, sure," Maggie shouted, her voice gaining volume with every word. "I wake up the morning after our wedding and you call me by her name. It isn't bad enough that you can't keep the two of us straight. Even . . . even your friends confuse our names. Then . . . then you leave her pictures lying around for me to find. But that was nothing. The icing on the cake comes when I inadvertently find a letter tucked safely away in a drawer to cherish and keep forever. Never mind that you've got a wife. Oh no. She's a simpleminded fool who's willing to overlook a few improprieties in married life."

Rising to her knees, Maggie waved her arms and continued. "And please note that word *inadvertently,* because I assure you I did not go searching through your things. I found her letter by accident."

Glenn was confused. His head was pounding, his mouth felt like sandpaper, and Maggie was shouting at him, waving her arms like a madwoman.

"I need to think," he murmured.

Maggie hopped off the bed and reached for her bathrobe. "Well, think, then, but don't do something totally stupid like . . . like leave me. I love you, Glenn. For two days we've behaved like fools. I'm sick of it. I trusted you enough to marry you, and obviously you felt the same way about me. The real question here is if we trust our love enough to see things through. If you want to run at the first hint of trouble, then you're not the Glenn Lambert I know." She tied the sash to her robe and continued, keeping her voice level. "I'm going to make coffee. You have ten minutes alone to 'think.'"

By the time she entered the kitchen, Maggie's knees were shaking. If she told Glenn about the baby, he wouldn't leave, but she refused to resort to that. If he wanted to stay, it would be because he loved her enough to work out their differences.

The kitchen phone rang, and Maggie stared at it accusingly. The only person who would call her this time of the morning was Denny. If he asked her for another penny, she'd scream. It used to be that he'd call once or twice a month. Now it was every other day.

On the second ring, Maggie nearly ripped the phone off the hook. "Yes," she barked.

"Maggie, is that you?" Denny asked brightly. "Listen, I'm sorry to call so early, but I wanted to tell you something."

"What?" Her indignation cooled somewhat.

"I'm going to work Monday morning. Now, don't argue, I know that you're against this. I'll admit that I was, too, when I first heard it. But I got to thinking about what Glenn said. And, Maggie, he's right. My attitude toward life, toward everything, has been rotten lately. The best thing in the world for me right now is to get back into the mainstream of life and do something worthwhile."

"But I thought—" Maggie couldn't believe what she was hearing.

"I know, I thought all the same things you did. But Linda and I had a long talk a few days ago and she helped me see that Glenn is right. I went to an interview, got the job, and I feel terrific. Better than I have in years."

Maggie was dumbfounded. She lowered her lashes and squeezed her eyes at her own stupidity. Glenn had been right all along about Denny. Her brother had been trapped in the same mire as she had been. Maggie should have recognized it before, but she'd been so defensive, wanting to shield her brother from any unpleasantness, that she had refused to acknowledge what was right in front of her eyes. Denny needed the same purpose that Glenn's love had given her life.

The urge to go back to their bedroom and ask Glenn to forgive her was strong, but she resisted. Denny was only one problem they needed to make right.

Glenn arrived in the kitchen dressed for the office. Silently, he poured himself a cup of coffee. Maggie wondered if she should remind Glenn that it was Saturday and he didn't need to go to work. No, she'd let him talk first, she decided.

He took a sip of the hot, black coffee and grimaced. His head was killing him. It felt as if someone was hammering at his temple every time his heart beat. Furthermore, he had to collect his car. He'd taken a taxi cab back to the house, far too drunk to get behind a wheel.

"Who was on the phone?" he asked. The question was not one of his most brilliant ones. Obviously, it had been Denny, but he hoped to get some conversation going. Anything.

"Denny."

Glenn cocked a brow, swallowing back the argument that sprang readily to his lips. If she was going to write WELCOME across her back and lie down for Denny to walk all over her, there wasn't anything he could do. Heaven knew he'd tried.

"He . . . he called because—"

"I know why he phoned," Glenn tossed out sarcastically.

"You do?"

"Of course. Denny only phones for one reason."

"Not this time." Her pride was much easier to swallow after hearing the excitement and enthusiasm in her brother's voice. "He's got a job."

Glenn choked on a swallow of coffee. "Denny? What happened?"

"Apparently, you and Linda got through that thick skull of his and he decided to give it a try. He feels wonderful."

"It might not last."

"I know," Maggie agreed. "But it's a start, and one he should have made a long time ago."

Her announcement was met with silence. "Are you telling me I was right?"

"Yes." It wasn't so difficult to admit, after all. Her hands hugged the milk-laced herbal tea and lent her the courage to continue. "It was wrong to take matters into my own hands and visit Angie. I can even understand why you loved her. She's a wonderful person."

"But she isn't you. She doesn't have your beauty, your artistic talent, or your special smile. Angie never made up crazy rules or beat me in a game of tennis. You're two entirely different people."

"I'll never be like her," Maggie murmured, staring into the creamy liquid she was holding.

"That's a good thing, because I'm in love with you. I married you, Maggie. I don't want anyone else but you."

Maggie's head jerked upright. "Are you saying . . . ? Do you mean that you're willing to forgive me for taking matters into my own hands? I know what I did wasn't right."

"I'm not condoning it, but I understand why you felt you had to meet her."

If he didn't take her in his arms soon, Maggie thought, she'd start crying again and then Glenn would know her Christmas secret for sure.

He set the coffee cup aside, and Maggie glanced up hopefully. But instead of reaching for her, he walked out of the kitchen and picked up the two suitcases that rested on the other side of the arched doorway.

Panic enveloped her. "Glenn," she whispered. "Are you leaving me?"

"No. I'm putting these back where they belong." He didn't know what he'd been thinking this morning. He could no more leave Maggie than he could stop breathing. After disappearing for a moment, he returned to the kitchen and stood not more than three feet from her.

Maggie's heart returned to normal again. "Are we through fighting now? I want to get to the making-up part."

"We're just about there." The familiar lopsided grin slanted his mouth.

"Maybe you need a little incentive."

"You standing there in that see-through outfit of yours is giving me all the incentive I need." He wrapped his arms around her then, and held her so close that Maggie could actually feel the sigh that shuddered through him.

She met his warm lips eagerly, twining her arms around his neck and tangling her fingers in the thick softness of his hair. Maggie luxuriated in the secure feel of his arms holding her tight. She smiled up at him dreamily. "There's an early Christmas gift I'd like to give you."

Unable to resist, Glenn brushed his lips over the top of her nose. "Don't you think I should wait?"

"Not for this gift. It's special."

"Are you going to expect to open one of yours in return?"

"No, but then, I already have a good idea of what you're getting me."

"You do?"

Maggie laughed outright at the way his eyes narrowed suspiciously. "It wasn't really fair, because your mother let the cat out of the bag."

"My mother!"

"Yes, she told me about your grandmother's ring."

His forehead wrinkled into three lines. "Maggie, I'm not giving you a ring."

He couldn't have shocked her more if he'd dumped a bucket of ice water over her head. He wasn't giving her the ring! "Oh." She disentangled herself from his arms. "I . . . guess it was presumptuous of me to think that you would." Her eyes fell to his shirt buttons as she took a step backward.

"Just so there aren't any more misunderstandings, maybe I should explain myself."

"Maybe you should," she agreed, feeling the cold seep into her bones. It never failed. Just when she was beginning to feel loved and secure with their marriage, someone would throw a curve ball at her.

"After the hassle we went through with the wedding rings—"

"I love my rings," she interrupted indignantly. "I never take them off anymore. You asked me not to and I haven't." She knew she was babbling like an idiot, but she wanted to cover how miserable and hurt she was. All those months she had put so much stock in his grandmother's ring and he wasn't even planning on giving it to her.

"Maggie, I had the ring reset into a necklace for you."

"A necklace?"

"This way you won't need to worry about putting it on or taking it off—or losing it, for that matter."

The idea was marvelous, and Maggie was so thrilled that her eyes misted with happiness. "It sounds wonderful," she murmured on a lengthy sniffle, and rubbed the tears from her face.

"What is the matter with you lately?" Glenn asked, his head cocked to one side. "I haven't seen you cry this much since you were six years old and Petie Phillips teased you and pulled your braids."

Maggie smiled blindly at him. "You mean you haven't figured it out?"

"Figured what out?"

Glenn's dark brown eyes widened as he searched her expression as if expecting to find the answer hidden on her face. His eyebrows snapped together. "Maggie," he whispered with such reverence one would assume he was in a church, "are you pregnant?"

A smile lit up her face and blossomed from ear to ear. "Yes. Our baby is due the first part of August."

"Oh, Maggie." Glenn was so excited that he longed to haul her into his arms and twirl her around the room until they were both dizzy and giddy. Instead, he pulled out a chair and sat her down. "Are you ill?"

"Only a little in the mornings," she informed him with a small laugh. "The worst thing is that I seem to cry over the tiniest incident."

"You mean like me packing my bags and leaving you."

"Yes." She giggled. "Just the minor things."

"A baby." Glenn paced the area in front of her, repeatedly brushing the hair off his forehead. "We're going to have a baby."

"Glenn, honestly, it shouldn't be such a shock. I told you in the beginning I wasn't using any birth control."

"I'm not shocked . . . exactly."

"Happy?"

"Very!" He knelt in front of her and gently leaned forward to kiss her tummy.

Maggie wrapped her arms around his head and held him to her. "Merry Christmas, my love."

Glenn heard the steady beat of Maggie's heart and closed his eyes to the wealth of emotions that flooded his being. She was a warm, vital woman who had made him complete. Wife, friend, lover . . . the list seemed endless, and he had only touched the surface.

"Merry Christmas," he whispered in return, and pulled her mouth to his.